AT THE TABLE OF WOLVES

AT THE TABLE OF

WOLVES

KAY KENYON

SAGA PRESS

LONDON SYDNEY NEW YORK TORONTO NEW DELHI

SAGA PRESS

AN IMPRINT OF SIMON & SCHUSTER, INC.

1230 AVENUE OF THE AMERICAS, NEW YORK, NEW YORK 10020

Text copyright © 2017 by Kay Kenyon

Jacket illustrations copyright © 2017 by Mike Heath

SAGA PRESS and colophon are trademarks of Simon & Schuster, Inc.

For information about special discounts for bulk purchases, please contact Simon & Schuster Special Sales at 1-866-506-1949 or business@simonandschuster.com.

The Simon & Schuster Speakers Bureau can bring authors to your live event. For more information or to book an event, contact the Simon & Schuster Speakers Bureau at 1-866-248-3049 or visit our website at www.simonspeakers.com.

Interior design by Brad Mead

The text for this book was set in Bell MT Std.

Manufactured in the United States of America

First Edition

10 9 8 7 6 5 4 3 2 1

Library of Congress Cataloging-in-Publication Data

Names: Kenyon, Kay, 1956- author. Title: At the table of wolves / Kay Kenyon. Description: First edition. | London : Saga Press, [2017] Identifiers: LCCN 2016053973 | ISBN 9781481487788 (hardcover) | ISBN 9781481487801 (eBook) Subjects: | BISAC: FICTION / Fantasy / Historical. | FICTION / Alternative History. | FICTION / War & Military. | GSAFD: Spy stories. | Occult fiction. | Science fiction. Classification: LCC PS3561.E5544 A88 2017 | DDC 813/.54—dc23 LC record available at https://lccn.loc.gov/2016053973

PART I

THE WAR OF THE TALENTS

WESERMARSCH SUB CAMP, NORTH COAST OF GERMANY

FRIDAY, MARCH 27, 1936. In the distance, across the marshland, a large black car sped under a leaden sky toward the gates of the sub camp. The road led straight across the wild plain with its sere yellow grasses. Beyond lay the immense gray wilderness of the North Sea, stretching all the way to the British Isles.

As Lieutenant Colonel Kurt Stelling stood on the parade ground, his adjutant at his side, the wind blew the scattered rain sideways, driving into his cheek like frozen needles. He clasped his gloved hands behind his back and watched as the car approached. A Mercedes-Benz 770, favored by the Nazi Party. Hitler's parade car. It bore an SD officer, Colonel von Ritter, whose purpose in coming Stelling did not know.

It was bad enough to have been holed up on this flat and frozen plain for the past ten months, much less to have to wait in the rain for a *Sicherheitsdienst* officer who must be given "every cooperation" by the sub camp's commandant. It was common knowledge that Hitler mistrusted his own army, preferring his loyal SS and their intelligence arm, the SD, to keep his secrets and discover others. Stelling had the feeling that this SD visit was to inspect *him* more than the sub camp. Despite his role in their audacious operation, they didn't like that Stelling wasn't a Party member.

He nodded at the guards, who opened the chain-link gate. The gate arms of the guardhouse rose up in a wooden salute as the car roared in, Nazi bumper flags rattling in the wind.

The car stopped, and the driver moved smartly to open the door for his passenger.

The SD officer stepped out. In plain clothes rather than in uniform, he wore a finely tailored camel-hair coat. He looked around him, observing the perimeter of the camp with its guardhouses, massive barracks compound and officers' quarters. When he had taken in his surroundings, he drew off his gloves and tucked them under his arm.

Stelling stepped forward to greet him, clicking his heels and extending a hand. They would not salute, since von Ritter was in plain clothes. "Colonel Stelling at your service, sir. Welcome." He introduced his adjutant, Lieutenant Hass.

Von Ritter made a bow and shook Stelling's hand.

He was smiling, or almost smiling. Stelling noticed how the man was completely at ease here in the work camp, as though he were in charge and not a guest. "A very great pleasure, Colonel."

The second thing he noticed was von Ritter's astonishing good looks. Somewhat over six feet tall, lanky in build, dark eyes in a patrician face, black hair combed back and hardly stirring in the wind off the sea. Stelling gestured to the camp headquarters building. "Some refreshment, sir. Please."

Stelling led the way, leaving Lieutenant Hass to escort the driver.

His adjutant had laid out food: crackers, a plate of herring, black bread and a round of Tilsit cheese with good coffee in an urn. Noting this, von Ritter smiled, as though the bread and cheese were unprofessional, leaving Stelling uncertain as to the impression he had made.

After washing up, von Ritter walked toward the outer door, putting on his gloves. "I don't mean to be abrupt, Colonel. But I have been eager to see the . . ." Here he paused, spreading his hands in apology. "The fence. You will think me foolish. But I would see the fence without delay." He gave a self-deprecating smile that left Stelling taken aback. When he smiled, the man could be called—the man *was*—beautiful.

"Of course. The fence. It is where it all began, after all. I understand."

As they turned to leave, von Ritter held up a hand and swung by the table, taking a piece of bread. "There. We will not let it go to waste!" His driver had followed them into the building, and now von Ritter waved at him to help himself.

"We will go alone, Colonel. Yes?"

Stelling followed him out, both troubled and excited. It had been a long time since he had felt such a surge of attraction. His tongue felt dry in his mouth, and his chest ached as though a stone pressed on it. The man had a charm that was not forced or manipulative, but almost playful. A man who was not afraid to enjoy himself. Despair hovered at the edges of his consciousness, reminding him that nothing could come of such longing. But to be swept away by five minutes in the man's presence . . . it was exhilarating.

They passed Barracks Unit 6. "Here are the strongest

Talents," Stelling explained. "They rank from 5.3 to 8.2 on the scale. Naturally, we take the best care of them."

Von Ritter smiled indulgently. "Naturally."

"Behind are Units 4 and 5, also assigned to the operation. Lower rankings, but still of the utmost importance." Beyond the three elite barracks were the brick prisoners' barracks. On the eastern border, the laborers were constructing the bivouacs to accommodate seventy-five army divisions for the staging phase.

"You yourself are also of the Talent—our special Talent," von Ritter said as they walked. "A 6.5. Am I correct?"

"Yes, sir. It still seems strange to me. I never guessed that I had a Talent. I was not an adolescent, after all. One forgets that those who were older when the *bloom* first began can have a Talent burst through for them, no matter the age. So, when it emerged on that day three years ago, it took me quite by surprise. The *ice* Talent. We were lucky to discover it."

"There is no such thing as luck, Colonel."

"You don't think so? You do not believe in coincidence?"

"There is only deserving." Von Ritter stopped, forcing Stelling to stop as well. He turned to him. "We cannot blame fortune for what comes our way, that is superstition. We make our destiny. That is why we will win in the coming struggle. Because we have the will and our enemies do not, England does not." His black gaze held Stelling in a disturbing, compelling lock. "Tell me that you believe this, Colonel."

"I do." He had never thought about it, but held in the man's demanding gaze, he was sure he did believe it.

"Ah, I thought so." Von Ritter clapped Stelling on the back. "Now, the fence."

They crossed a broken surface of concrete and approached a section of the perimeter fence between two guard towers. The closest guard could be seen on the tower walkway. He turned to note their approach to the fence, then swung back to survey the unrelenting flat plain, beyond which the North Sea rolled out, deeply etched with foam-tipped waves.

Stelling nodded at the fence to indicate it was the one.

"Tell me," von Ritter said.

"I stood here as we marshaled the new prisoners into a line for provisioning when they first arrived. Some of us touched the fence."

Von Ritter murmured, "And then?"

"It froze. Froze solid. It was as though a frigid current ran in a wave down the fence. Our hands tingled, then felt a shock of ice. It had frozen, holding some of us melded to the links."

"The *ice* Talent," von Ritter murmured. "Fascinating."

"We were all tested to see which of us had such a Talent. I was the only one who did."

"Such a thing had never been seen before," von Ritter said. "That the *ice* Talent could go beyond the freezing of merely small things."

"They poured cold water to release us." Stelling held up his gloved hand. "But one can still see the effects."

"Show me."

He removed his right glove. Von Ritter took Stelling's hand, turning it over, examining the scars from that day. The man's touch burned through his veins. When von Ritter broke contact, he left Stelling unable to speak.

Von Ritter stared out at the sea. "It started with you. Your Talent of the *ice*. And it will end with England under our boot." He grasped the fence with both hands. "*Sturmweg*," he mused. "Can you imagine what it will look like, Colonel? The invasion of England. They will be helpless. Stupefied. They think their island nation is protected. In *Sturmweg*, we will march to their door. More than that. To their very beds!" He turned back to Stelling. "You are a celebrity, Colonel Stelling. We have all heard this story. What a pleasure to hear it from you personally."

Stelling found himself acutely listening to the timbre of von Ritter's voice, as though drinking a shamefully expensive wine.

Von Ritter cocked his head. "What is it, Colonel?"

Stelling realized he was staring helplessly at von Ritter. He stammered, "I . . . I . . ." He felt paralyzed but longed to be set free.

Von Ritter stepped closer to him. "What, Colonel? You have something to say?"

They were very close now. "I . . . do not."

"But would like to?" Von Ritter asked quietly. "But wish that you could?"

"No."

"I think that you do."

"No, sir. What you say about England, this is true—"

"—I think it is something more personal, is it not? That you would like to say?"

"No. You mistake me."

"I do not think so, Kurt. It is Kurt, is it not?" When he got no answer, von Ritter turned away, then swung around explosively, reaching across his chest to a holster under his arm. He pressed a Luger to the side of Stelling's head.

Stelling stepped backward, but von Ritter followed, keeping the gun at his temple. "You are disgusting!" he hissed. "A corrupt thing, a mongrel." He leaned in until his face was inches from Stelling's. "Do you lie with dogs, Colonel? Tell me, are you degraded, unnatural in your manhood?"

"No," Stelling whispered. "Please." He staggered back, his head smashed against the fence. He heard the gun cock. He would die here, his brains blown through the chain link. The wind blew, carrying the smell of salt water and oblivion.

"Open your mouth," von Ritter ordered.

Stelling could not move, could not contemplate the order.

The gun muzzle prodded at his lip, chipped at his teeth. He opened his mouth, and von Ritter jammed the Luger up to the roof of his mouth, sliding the barrel savagely against his teeth. It tasted of fresh oil.

Stelling closed his eyes. It was better to die than to endure the gun in his mouth.

Then von Ritter ripped the gun out of his mouth and stood back. "Perhaps I am wrong." The gun now pointed at Stelling's legs. "Do you say I am wrong, Colonel?"

"Yes, wrong," Stelling managed to whisper. It had not been obvious how he felt, had it? No, no, it had not. But, oh God, it must have been clear in his face. Smitten, smitten. "Wrong," he repeated.

An expression of contempt crept over von Ritter's face. "You would say anything to save your life, of course." He put the gun back in its holster beneath his coat.

The wind roared in Stelling's ears, as his eyes seemed to fill with a silvery light from the low clouds. He began to realize that he was not going to die on the fence. Tears lined his eyes in a rim of ice. Sweat lay as a frozen mask on his face.

"You are a 6.5. Too valuable to lose, do you not agree, Colonel?" Von Ritter cocked his head mockingly, waiting for an answer.

"Yes," Stelling said, pushing away from the fence and finding that he was barely able to stand on his shaking legs.

Von Ritter laughed. "Say 'I am a dog but I am too valuable to kill.'"

Stelling looked into the beautiful man's eyes and thought he would rather die than obey such a command. "No."

Again, the cocked head, but now an appraising look. An almost-smile. "Very good, Colonel. You are willing to die for your honor. I admire that."

He turned and walked away.

When Stelling heard the car rumble off, he walked slowly back to the headquarters building, his senses so acute that he could hear the muted roar of the North Sea against the beach and, once inside, marvel at the remarkable smells of herring and coffee.

2

SUNDAY, APRIL 5. If Kim Tavistock blurred her eyes, the massive gray-stoned house before her could almost be called grand. A riot of ivy, bursting in spring green, cloaked the persistent gaps in the stonework. Returning from a short trip to the Midlands, Kim was pleased to find that Wrenfell looked like home. As though she had always lived there, as though she were at last thoroughly English.

Born in Yorkshire, raised mostly in America, she'd been back at Wrenfell three years now. She might not fit in completely— so many reasons for that—but the Tavistock estate held her family's history in every stone and field.

She retrieved her valise from the car as the dogs catapulted from around the back of the house. Flint, the setter, and Shadow, her border collie. She knelt to dispense rubs, noting that nothing had progressed on the repairs to the porte cochere, which was leaning heavily toward the barley field.

Walter Babbage came to carry her things. He saw her glance in the direction of the carriage porch and made himself busy gathering up her valise and camera case.

"All well here?" Kim asked, looking for a bit of welcome.

"Nowt amiss." Walter ducked his stolid head in greeting, revealing a faded cap that had once been red-and-gold plaid. "Didna expect tha' so early," he said, marching off for the house.

Flint stuck with Walter, but Shadow had become hers and raced in circles around her as she climbed the stairs. A whiff of dry rot came to her as she entered the slate-tiled foyer. They must find the slow leak, perhaps replace the entire plumbing. Her father, seldom at home, had put her in charge of the place, an assignment she relished. Managing the restoration was just the thing for a thirty-three-year-old woman with a flagging journalism career and energy to spare. But deeper than that, she felt a profound urge to restore the place that had once been home to the complete family: her American mother, her father in better days. And Robert, her beloved older brother, before he was taken from them.

In the dining hall, the mail lay strewn on the table. Sorting through it, she found a letter from Philadelphia. Her mother. Also, a note from the housekeeper, Mrs. Babbage, saying that her father had rung up to say that he was bringing Georgi Aberdare for luncheon on his way home from York on Sunday. Since that was today, she trusted that Mrs. Babbage had preparations underway. She checked her watch. Already twelve thirty.

It was odd that he was in company with Georgi—a popular and poisonous London hostess. She must have been a guest in York and offered Julian a lift home. There was no time to lose getting changed, but on her way to the entry hall, Kim pulled a chair from its spot next to the sideboard so that there were an even number of chairs on each side of the great table. Nor could she pass up the necessity of setting the candlesticks in a proper row on the mantle.

Kim ducked into the kitchen, finding that Mrs. Babbage did indeed have the meal well in hand, before hurrying up the hallway stairs to change.

She washed her face and ran her hands through her hair. The mirror showed her a bit unkempt, but a little lipstick and powder were all that could be done for now, and besides, there would be no competing with Georgi Aberdare in looks or style, even if Georgi was well over forty. Kim could not lay claim to elegance, being perhaps rather too tall at five-eight, and her hair too short, at chin length. Her strong points were said to be *good cheekbones* and *a very appealing empathy.*

As for empathy, she knew why people thought so: she was always curious about people, that was true. But it wasn't why they tended to confide in her. It was because of her Talent. The *spill.* A level 6 on a scale topping out at 10, strong enough to be disruptive but not obvious. Few people knew of her ability, and no one in her family or in the village. It was best that way. Since her adolescent years with the *spill,* she had known that it caused problems, even with—especially with—friends. People kept secrets to preserve the face they showed the world. If that facade wobbled around Kim . . . well, she had seen the discomfort she caused. Boyfriends were the worst. They resented that you knew their secrets, their anxieties. They left.

A compensation was in journalism. She couldn't deny that in interviewing, she'd often had a boost from her Talent. And a good thing too, with jobs so hard to find, and women being the last in line to get them. But her employers need never know her peculiar advantage. She got her scoops, and that was enough for them.

Many people felt the same need for secrecy, even now, so long after the *bloom* had come into the world. The onset did not have a specific date but had crept in during the last year of the Great War, starting with small outbreaks of paranormal claims and gathering power into a great upwelling of psychic gifts. These abilities visited perhaps one in a thousand after puberty, but it was hard to know the numbers, since people didn't like to say. The special abilities carried a whiff of the unsavory. Talents could, of course, be exploited. Criminals might use *mesmerizing* or *precognition* in their attempts to steal or otherwise take advantage. At the same time, the authorities in turn might use *object reading* and *trauma view* to solve a crime, so in that arena it rather balanced out.

The *bloom* might have begun at Ypres, or the Marne, or Gallipoli, when those who waited at home began to understand the unbearable losses. Scientists studying paranormal abilities thought that Talents had lain dormant for millennia, ultimately emerging from mass trauma. They theorized that, even before the *bloom*, some people had possessed Talents. And some cultures had accepted them more freely than others. The more deeply buried they had been, the more notable the outbreak. Or so they said.

A great deal was yet to be sorted out. Monkton Hall was part of that sorting, but of course she must never say anything about that.

She chose a gray wool skirt with her best sweater set and was just coming down from her room when through the foyer windows she spied a large maroon-and-black touring car enter the gate. Kim slipped quickly out the back door to cut a few flowers for the table centerpiece, but Rose, the Babbage's adult daughter, had already been put to the task, and sat among the daffodils with a shears. At nineteen, she was limited in some of her abilities, but she did very well at simple tasks.

"Oh good, Rose! Take a few branches of quince, too."

Back in the hall, she found her father and Georgi laughing over something in the bustle of removing coats. Julian Tavistock cut a fine figure at sixty-two with his solidly built frame and flawless English bearing. He nodded at Kim as he gave the coats to Walter. The Babbages were everywhere—the three of them—circulating through tasks as though there were ten of them instead of three.

Georgi produced a wide red smile for Kim. "My dear. How lovely to see you." Her acid glance took in the foyer all at once: the stripped-off paneling leading down the hall to the buttery and kitchen, and the water stain below the ceiling cornice. She looked smart in a navy blue suit trimmed in velvet. With her hair pulled back from a severe center part, she was vivacious and a little scary.

"We have quite barged in on you, I fear," Georgi said. She unpinned her hat and set it on the round hall table.

"Oh, not in the least," Kim answered. "It's very good to see you again." They had met last season at a torpid dinner at Georgi's London house with two earls and a handful of marquises, all of whom seemed to sympathize with Germany's ambitions. As did her father. Since coming home, she had had to get to know him again—there having been little communication during her American years. She didn't quite care for what he'd become.

Julian came forward and pecked Kim on the cheek. "We'll have time for a glass of sherry before luncheon." He led both women into the parlor.

"We can take our time. It's only sandwiches," Kim said. "At least, I think so. I just got back from four days in Gloucester and Shrewsbury."

Georgi accepted a sherry from Julian. "Don't worry, we shan't stay long. I have a long drive home—alone, I fear, unless I can persuade your father to come down to Summerhill for a few days."

Kim did wonder how Georgi could hope to sway her father, who had perfected a kind of inattentive passivity on which no amount of petition had the slightest effect.

A great clatter from across the foyer brought Kim to her feet and thence into the dining hall, where the daffodils lay amid shards of a vase, and Rose stood on the verge of tears. Mrs. Babbage hurried in, noting with dismay the jumble of flowers and glass. Julian and Mrs. Babbage managed to get things swept up and Rose comforted, while Kim got a few sprigs of the quince into another vase, the daffodils being a loss among the breakage.

At table, Georgi murmured that Rose did not seem *quite right*, which Julian ignored, leaving Kim with the duty to defend the girl. "Oh, she does very well, actually."

Georgi smiled pityingly. "I do hope you don't allow her around the *china*, though."

"If you had your way, Georgi," Julian said, "all our young ladies would have gone to finishing school." Mrs. Babbage served the luncheon, quarter-cut sandwiches nicely spaced on a bed of watercress.

"Oh, I hope you don't mean *equality*," Georgi said, arranging her napkin. "If you turn into a freethinker, Julian, we must ban you from the hunt."

"No danger there."

Georgi turned her attention like a gun barrel at Kim. "Julian tells me you are writing up little side tours of England."

"Yes, my magazine series. I'm seeing quite a lot of the country this spring."

"But whatever for? There is scarcely anything to tour except in London."

Kim locked glances with her. "It would make a short series, then."

"Well, if you can make something of Shrewsbury or anything in the Midlands, it's to your credit. Of course, after the *terribly unfair* matter at that American newspaper, one must do one's best."

Kim shot a glare at her father for telling Georgi about that debacle.

Georgi went on. "My own writing skills do not go beyond a nice invitation. I am useless, you see."

"Nonsense," Julian gallantly protested. "Where would the season be without you?"

"How was your trip to York?" Kim prompted, hoping to find an agreeable topic before she tipped the hollandaise sauce in Georgi's lap.

The woman sighed. "Trying, I'm afraid. Two dreary days with my cousin panting at my heels, even if he *is* an earl."

Julian coughed discreetly. Georgi stared at her plate, murmuring, "Well, that's all long over."

In turn, Kim stared at her own plate. Had Georgi just implied that she'd had a dalliance with her cousin? Kim flushed with dismay lest her father suspect what had just happened. A *spill*. Kim never knew when a confidence was coming. In fact, she knew quite well that when she *wanted* to know, all chance of a *spill* fled.

She glanced at her father. He was clueless about her Talent.

But Georgi certainly had embarrassed herself. Julian was the first to rally. "Your cousin was all for rearming and rattling swords in the face of the Hun. You took him to task, though."

Georgi managed a smile. "One does one's best."

Kim was still trying to overcome her shock at having received a *spill* from none other than Georgi Aberdare. Her cousin, panting at her heels. But *spills* did tend to be the things you most wished to hide.

Georgi accepted a helping of asparagus from Mrs. Babbage, who hadn't bothered to remove her cook's apron. "Unemployment is shrinking on the continent, that's the thing people forget. Hitler is getting Germany back on its feet. He's not popular in some quarters, but one can't argue with success."

"One might argue about his marching into the Rhineland," Kim said, trying, but not very hard, to keep an even tone.

Julian flashed a look at her. "Germany is encircled by enemies. Russia. France. Don't press them too closely, or you'll provoke Herr Hitler well and good. We don't want another war, that's the main thing."

Despite the *spill* and that it had happened in front of her father, Kim was unable to pass up their old debate. "I don't see how Germany's rearming makes peace more likely."

Georgi tapped her mouth with her napkin. "Really, Kim, you are quite behind in your thinking. Once Germany feels safe, the whole continent will be secure."

"As long as England is secure," Kim shot back.

Georgi pounced. "That's just what we've been saying! It's the way toward peace."

Looking from Georgi to her father, Kim felt like an outsider at her own table. Not that it was exactly her table; it was her father's, of course. She was grateful to be taken in, as she could not yet afford to live on her own.

Her exposé on animal vivisection in the *Philadelphia Inquirer* had ruined her career. Medical researchers protested the attack, and readers objected to the sensational content in an uproar that went well beyond Philadelphia. No one wished to read about the torture of animals over their morning bacon and eggs. When Kim had quit in protest at being put on the obituaries, she found herself blackballed. Thus, she must make something of the English countryside, which quite frankly, she felt lucky to be able to do.

Mrs. Babbage brought in a tray of sherbets as conversation turned to whether Julian would come down to Summerhill in the fall for the grouse. Hunting was another topic about which Kim had best remain silent. She had sometimes been accused of liking animals better than people, which was patently untrue. Except that animals were innocents. And as the *spill* constantly reminded her, people were not.

At last, Julian stood. "Let me show you the village, Georgi." A sly smile: "You haven't seen Yorkshire until you've seen Uxley."

"Oh, does this country tour never end?" Georgi wailed in good humor. But they were soon off, with Georgi no doubt enduring a trip to the village in order to please Julian, whom she seemed keen on charming.

Kim watched them driven away by the chauffeur, down the long driveway. Kicking off her shoes, she splayed her toes against the cool flagstones of the hall.

It was then that she noticed a puddle of water by the floor trim. *The pipes really must be replaced*, she thought with dismay, but when she looked closely, she saw that Rose's plaid coat was the cause, dripping wet.

In the kitchen, Rose sat on a stool, rolling out biscuit dough under her mother's supervision.

"Rose," Kim asked as she ducked in, "why is your coat soaking wet? Did you fall in Abbey Pond?"

Rose grinned at this. "The snow melted! Little storms goin' on!"

The weather was on and off again, but Kim hadn't seen snow since mid-March. Perhaps Uxley had shared in the bad weather that had visited the Midlands.

She wandered into the parlor and gazed out the window, down the driveway where the maroon-and-black car had disappeared. She had been looking forward to being home after being on the road a few days with her assignment, but the argument about Germany had disconcerted her.

She picked up the LNER booklet from the coffee table and settled onto the couch to peruse the little orange tract. The London and North Eastern Railway timetable fell open to the weekday schedule with its rows of precise departure times from nearby York. The 2:18, the 2:42. York to London or Edinburgh. She relaxed into it, feeling the assurance of British regularity and accuracy. Here you had a 4:41 arrival in Leeds and a 5:10 in Doncaster. It was like the clockwork underpinning of the world, a mirror of the orderly universe. She had seen how easily the world could spin out of control. The LNER timetable was a great comfort.

Another comfort was Monkton Hall. All those who participated in its program were subject to the strictures of the Official Secrets Act, so it was necessary to pretend that her trips to the North York Moors were for a writing assignment rather than top-secret research into Talents. Her case worker at Monkton Hall said that the next war—and war was coming, he assured her—would be won by Talents. Decrypts of German army communications showed that they strongly believed in potential military uses of Talents.

Ominously, they had almost a decade's head start.

TUESDAY, APRIL 7. Over one of the awkward luncheons she typically had with her father, Kim asked, "Have you spoken to Walter about the porte cochere?"

Julian scooped up Mrs. Babbage's excellent pea soup. "I haven't yet." He and Walter Babbage always had schemes for the estate; she was learning they usually came to nothing.

"You've been home two days."

"Mm."

"Well?" The soup had his entire attention. "So then, when will you speak to him?"

He nodded absently. "Today."

"The workmen have gone off to start a new project in Coomsby. We always seem to be on the bottom of their list."

"It's not as though we ever use the carriage porch," her father said.

"No, but if we don't care about it, we should remove it, or someday it will collapse on the vicar or Georgi Aberdare."

He made eye contact at last. His very deep blue eyes reminded her of Robert. "You don't like her, I suppose."

"I don't, but I wouldn't like to see her buried beneath our porte cochere."

"Faint praise, my dear," he said.

Discussions like this were duels to the death. He would never be pinned down. It turned her combative. "She doesn't see—none of you see—what thugs the Nazis are." There might be no point in discussing it, but still, she could not shake the urge to persuade her father to a more liberal position.

"The reaction to Nazism might be overblown," he said. "People returning from Germany say most of this talk is hysteria. If you want to fit in, you mustn't come off as a warmonger."

"A warmonger." How quickly words became ammunition. She put down her spoon, her appetite gone at the mention of this dark and vast subject. They didn't have to hate Germany for Robert's sake. He had died at Ypres, one of the nineteen thousand killed, one of the eight thousand British. But she didn't think she hated Germany for that. It wasn't about hate. It was about love. How she had loved her older brother, who seemed perfect to her, in his knowledge, grace, and in all things.

Somewhere between father and daughter, there was a place of peace on this subject. They had not found it yet.

He glanced at the letter sitting by her plate. "From your mother?" At her nod, he went on. "All well with her?"

At fifty-nine, her mother had married again, and it seemed to be lasting, four years in. "Yes. She seems happy with Frank."

"Mm." He put his spoon down, addressing the tension in the

room. "Kim, we don't need to talk politics at the table, do we? As we do not seem to agree . . ."

"You're right. Let's not." A fleeting smile passed between them, perhaps not heartfelt but good enough for now.

As he went back to his soup, she reread her mother's letter, formulating an answer to yet another query as to whether she had "met" anyone yet. She had, of course, met a few men over the past three years, but none of them quite took, not seriously. *I'm sure I shall, Mum* was what she would say.

"I'll just duck into the village," she said, receiving an agreeable nod from Julian. She excused herself, taking her plate into the kitchen with compliments to Mrs. Babbage.

On her way into town, she caught a glint of morning light off Abbey Pond. It was hard to see from the road but never far from her mind. At the next curve was the petrol station. Every time she passed it, the same memories came, sometimes touching her lightly, and at other times striking rather deep. It was the old site of the animal shelter, where as a child Kim had broken in one December night and chased the animals into the snow. Otherwise, they would have been euthanized, which in Kim's eleven-year-old view was tantamount to a war crime. A few in the village thought that what happened to the animals that night was her fault and served her right. But Robert had been dead only a few weeks, and most people believed she had been distraught and couldn't be held to account. Her mother had already had a breakdown and soon took refuge with her daughter in America.

Kim made her small purchases at the chemist's and the butcher's shops, enjoying her stroll up the cobbled high street and past the eighteenth-century parish church, All Saints. The village of Uxley was just large enough, at 3,047 people, to have a charming village square complete with the Barley and Mow pub and the old coaching inn, the Three Swans.

Across the square from the inn was the Dropped Stitch, owned by her friend Alice Ward. On the way in, Kim passed Vicar Hathaway with a parcel tucked under his arm.

He nodded at her. "Another project for Mum," he said, gesturing to the package by way of explaining that he had not taken up knitting. James Hathaway was just youthful-looking enough in middle age to be considered eligible, with a round face and a sharp nose that always reminded Kim of a penguin. That, and his habit of ducking his head to emphasize a point.

Kim nodded cheerfully. "The world needs more sweaters!"

"Yes, with this weather. You don't know if it's winter or summer. Someplace in between, I expect."

Just as he was turning away, she thought to ask, "Has there been snow, actually?"

"Snow? Not a bit of it. It *is* April." He ducked his respects. "Good day, then. Sign up for the raffle?"

All Saints was fundraising for restoration of its bells, which hadn't rung for a decade. "I already have!" Kim called out to his retreating back. He waved that he'd heard her.

Alice hailed Kim from the back of the store, where she was unpacking boxes. Kim pitched in to help put the new yarns in their pigeonholes. Alice was making a rather slapdash affair of it.

"Perhaps we could put them in order," Kim said. "You know, the blues next to the greens. Like a color spectrum."

Her back turned, working the cubbyholes, Alice's frizzy red hair looked like another variant of yarn. "Give it up." She took a few skeins from Kim and mashed them into a slot. "Once you start wanting yarn to be tidy, you go mad. You can end up at Prestwich Home." The mental hospital up north.

"I saw James on his way out. Did he stay for a chat?"

"No, he was in a proper hurry." Alice pushed her hair out of her face, searching for more room in the overstuffed rack. "He bought a nice angora."

"I think his mother doesn't knit at all." She handed Alice a green worsted. "He buys yarn as an excuse to see you."

Alice smirked. "Even so. Why does he need an excuse? He's known me for ten years." Moving behind the counter, she produced a bottle of Dodd's gin. She poured out a generous dollop into two teacups, sliding one toward Kim.

Kim raised her cup in a halfhearted toast. "If he only knew he was driving you to drink."

"Yes, perhaps he'd take pity." She raised her cup and tossed off half of it. "Where've you been? How's the repairs?"

"Shrewsbury. Stopped dead."

"Sounds like a telegram."

"It's just so frustrating. I mean, the trip was a success, but as to the remodel, Walter is no help at all, nor Father either. He brought a lady friend by for lunch the other day, one of those society hostesses everyone is mad about."

"*Someone* around here should have a love life."

James Hathaway liked to squire Alice Ward around. It looked well for him to be accompanied, so she was the default companion. More sisterly than wifely, to Alice's long-suffering dismay.

"I'm always afraid he'll find out I'm one of *those people*." Alice sipped at her gin.

Alice had confided in her last year about her secret Talent. "But he's not the suspicious sort, is he?" Kim asked.

"Then why does he bring it up so often around me? Every time he does, I think I'm done for. But I suppose he'd never come

by if he thought that. So, I'm safe from telling my future husband the most important thing about me."

"It's not the most important thing about you."

Alice lowered her voice. "I have *trauma view*. I'm a freak."

"You've always managed to keep it to yourself, why would—"

"—Well, I told *you*."

Kim stopped short. Alice didn't have any idea why she had
revealed something she was determined to hide. A pang of
shame gripped her. Alice had become a good friend, and it was
rather late now to reveal that she'd hidden her own Talent. And
Kim didn't even know if Alice's reveal about her Talent *had* been
forced or been prompted by a growing trust between them. A
trust that she was putting in jeopardy. Oh, she truly did not wish
to know things that were too dear. Or too dark. It had always felt
like peeking through a window.

At that moment, she almost told Alice: *Watch out for me. I'm
sorry, but I have the* spill.

The moment passed. Changing the subject, Kim said,
"Maybe James isn't such a great match for you."

"Great? I'm thirty-five. I'm not waiting for great. I know
what he is and how he lives his life, and I think he's fine and
caring. You look at some of the husbands around here . . ."

She poured another splash in both their cups. "There's some
as knock their wives around a bit. The wives come into the shop,
and maybe one has a little bruise, and then, right on the spot, I see
what happened: how he slapped her and she staggered back and
fell against the creamware hutch, and plates broke, and how he hit
her again for that. I don't *want* to see it, but it comes." She shook
her head. "Too bad I don't see the good things that happen."

"I'll bet the degree of emotion makes it so much more present in people's minds."

Alice shrugged. "Well, it is called *trauma view*, not *cheery view*."

"I'm betting that James doesn't have any inkling. It's your right to keep it private." In some circles, to claim you had a Talent was to invite social annihilation. You might as well announce that you were a Bolshevist, exotic dancer, lesbian—or all three.

"I probably oughtn't to have told *you*."

"Alice. You know that I would never tell." It was Kim's promise to herself, never to abuse her Talent.

"Do you fancy catching the matinee tomorrow? I can close the shop early."

"Oh, drat. I'm afraid I have to go up to Monkton Hall, sorry. Another freelance job, you remember." Kim's cover assignment was writing a history of the archives. This made her project a history of the archival history, which never failed to crush any polite interest that might arise.

"Oh, right," Alice said. "The book. How's it coming?"

Inwardly, Kim cringed at the lie. Alice had shared her secret of the *trauma view* Talent, but Kim was hiding her own Talent. Not good for a friendship, perhaps, but for this piece of her life, she felt she had no choice.

"Making progress," she answered, hoping there would be no more questions.

Alice put the gin away along with the unwashed cups. "James thinks Talents go against the church. He says it sets one person against the other, with some having powers and some not. There's nothing in scripture about it."

"Parable of the Talents?" When Alice didn't smile, Kim said, "Maybe he could forgive it. Isn't that in scripture?"

"Of course he could forgive it. He just wouldn't marry it." She walked with Kim to the door. "Want some company up to . . . where was it?"

"Monkton Hall, on the moors. But the archives aren't set up for viewing. It's all being organized, so they limit visitors. Let's see a film this weekend over in Coomsby. I'll ring you up."

"Righty-ho," Alice said, oblivious.

Out in the fine April sunshine, Kim considered Alice's Talent and the intense discomfort she must experience when it kicked in. As though one's own pain were not enough, and now one had to experience others' as well.

Some things we aren't meant to know, Kim thought. But since the *bloom,* sometimes one *did* know anyway.

4

THE ROAD TO THE
NORTH YORK MOORS

WEDNESDAY, APRIL 8. Kim's appointment at Monkton Hall took her on a scenic forty-minute drive through the rolling hills called the Wolds and through the broad Vale of Pickering. Crossing the main highway, she went up a gently rising gravel road. Soon, she was in a wilder country of dense oak forests, bog lands, isolated cottages and idyllic valleys: the moors.

A dirt road led into Blackvern Wood, and in its shadows the April day grew chill. At the curve in the road, she came into view of Monkton Hall.

The place was a sprawling redbrick Elizabethan mansion, with bay windows of leaded glass and a peaked tiled roof sporting brick chimneys with decorative chimney pots. The whole gave the impression of a dowdy Elizabethan matron with a fanciful hat.

It was there that, eleven months before, Kim had been assigned to a rigorous Talent testing program. Though her part of Monkton Hall's work was small, it felt constructive and useful, given that she was virtually in a foreign country, intermittently employed, and living with a father who had become something of a Nazi.

Officially, Monkton Hall was called the Historical Archives and Records Centre (HARC), the cover name for a top-secret research arm of government investigating military uses of Talents. Monkton Hall's atmosphere of secrecy was defined by its cardinal rule: "Say nothing here. Say nothing there."

Kim pulled into the car park and, collecting her sack lunch and thermos of tea, set out for the iron gates that lay open in a false appearance of welcome. To one side of the generous paved courtyard was a smaller brick building that had once been a stable and had been converted into a canteen.

As Kim made for the main entrance, she found herself on an intersecting path with the thin, fiftyish office manager, Miss Drummond, crossing the yard from the canteen with her tiny spaniel on a leash.

"Good day, Miss Drummond," Kim called, falling into step beside her, as it appeared that both were headed toward the front door.

"Oh no, not here," Miss Drummond said with a look of consternation as the dog lifted a leg to relieve itself.

At that moment, the women saw Monkton Hall's director, Fitzroy Blum, an impressively large man, heading toward them from the main porch. "Worse luck," Miss Drummond hissed. "He doesn't approve of Pip as it is."

Kim thought it might be the end of Pip, to be caught urinating in the courtyard. Before she had quite formulated a plan, she unscrewed the thermos and dropped it, spilling its contents to mix with Pip's little mistake.

Now upon them, Blum nodded a greeting, glancing at the leaking thermos. As Kim stooped to retrieve it, he scrutinized her rather closely, as though on the alert for traitorous behavior. But then he boomed a "good morning," smiling brilliantly, like FDR, Kim thought, but somehow rather fake.

Miss Drummond fluttered a smile at him, which fell away the moment his back was turned. "I hope it isn't broken," she said as Kim retrieved the flask.

"No, I'm sure not. Clumsy of me."

"Quick thinking, I should say." Miss Drummond turned to watch Fitz enter the south wing. "He's not all he seems, that one."

"He smiles a lot for one who doesn't like dogs. I've never found the two quite go together, have you?"

This was an intimacy too great for Miss Drummond, who sniffed, "I couldn't say." Grasping Pip's leash, she hurried him toward the safety of his basket beside her desk in the foyer. Kim followed in her wake. She settled herself onto the bench in the foyer, and consulted her Helbros wristwatch. 11:17. Thirteen minutes to wait.

Kim admired the interior, with its grand staircase to the gallery where Fitzroy Blum's office was and the old and rather elaborate carvings on the paneling and ceiling. It was just the sort of place where one could believe the rumor that there was a Catholic chapel buried behind the wall of the great room.

Pip was already asleep in his basket, twitching in what might be a dream chase after a squirrel or a dog-hating director.

Looking around, Kim felt glad of Monkton Hall's quiet authority, its mission to plumb the depths of the *bloom* phenomenon. Slowly, knowledge of this extraordinary change was building. But how far they had come! When she'd first suspected that she was one of the exceptional few with a Talent, it had all been mysterious and more than a little confusing.

Age twelve was very young to have the rules change, the rules for how life was, how one dealt with others. In those early days, meta-abilities seemed more superstition than fact. Erratic claims had begun to mount, but few concluded that a transformation had come upon the world. Kim had assumed that receiving deep confidences was a common experience. Then, in grade school, her friend Emma had guessed that Kim had the *spill*—Emma herself having a Talent, *hyperempathy*. It was then that Kim had first realized she was different from most other people.

Monkton Hall valued her difference. She could not yet say that *she* did, but this place was still a comfort.

At precisely eleven thirty, Miss Drummond sent her through to the Hyperpersonal Talents section and the office of her caseworker, Owen Cherwell.

On her way down the corridor, she passed the closed doors of the other divisions: Mentation, the arena of advanced deduction and perception, and Psychokinesis, studying abilities affecting objects and the environment, Talents regularly tested out on the moors.

Next door to Owen Cherwell's section Kim occasionally saw Stanley Yarrow, the bald and rotund director of Psychokinesis. Owen frequently complained of the crashing noises erupting from Yarrow's precincts, evidence of *transport* and *damaging* Talents, abilities that fortunately manifested over very short ranges and with limited explosive force. Still, Yarrow dismissed the other Monkton Hall divisions as less important, a posture of some annoyance to Owen. He had much preferred Yarrow's predecessor, Sam Reuben, who had shared his hearty dislike of Fitzroy Blum.

Owen was waiting for her beside his crowded desk. "Saw the whole thing from the window," he chuckled. "And Fitz will never know if you meant to do it."

"Of course I meant to." She was certainly not going to stand by and let that bear of a man terrorize a small dog.

"Yes, but he can't be sure. Uncertainty drives Fitz barmy." A deep smile creased his face. Owen Cherwell had charmed her from the beginning, with his quirky manner and kindly face haloed by thin but flyaway hair, rather like a dandelion gone to seed. In his late forties, he wore round glasses and a lab coat that made him look the typical professor, as indeed he had been at Cambridge's Experimental Psychology Department.

He led her to the brainwave machine, the dynograph. The apparatus could chart what parts of her brain were activated during *spills* and how that related to other brain functions. Owen sometimes shared the printouts with their lovely data points and correlations. It made order out of chaos, and that was something Kim very much approved of, along with train timetables, to-do lists and indexes in books.

"Fitz may be high and mighty," Owen said as he adjusted the electrode cap, bristling with leads and wires, snugly onto Kim's head, "but Miss Drummond is well-connected herself. Her family has been in service to the Duke of Bedford for a hundred and fifty years. So he can't properly evict the dog, even if Fitz *is* in the King's circle."

He stood back, examining the electrode cap fit. "I'd love to do some defensive tests to calibrate how you'd do *against* a *spill* Talent. But we haven't had any other *spill* Talents for quite a while."

A resounding crash came from down the hall, causing Kim to jump.

"Steady on," Owen said, not even looking up from the graph paper. "It's just Stan Yarrow testing a lady with a *sounding* Talent."

"Poor woman. I hope that Talent is one that can be controlled?"

"Oh yes, no end of trouble if it just came on without warning."

Kim felt a bit of envy. If only she had such control. She continued their conversation, keeping it going, since talk was the realm where *spills* occurred.

"So then, how *would* I do against another *spill* Talent? More susceptible, or less, because I'm familiar with it?" Kim had no idea if she'd ever been around someone with her Talent.

"We don't know yet. And you probably don't know if you've ever *spilled* to someone, do you?"

"I think I could tell. That is, if I was shocked that I told something private, I might guess that's what happened. But I wonder if I could be successful in thwarting someone with the *spill*. That is, if I knew they had it."

"The best way to limit your susceptibility is to stay away from such people," Owen said airily, reminding her of her difficulty in maintaining friendships. "Some people, of course, are immune to the *spill*. Immune to Talents in general." The ink writer attached to the dynograph slid up and down, making zigs and zags. "Fitz is a very strong *natural defender*. That's why he got the job and I didn't. It helps if our chief isn't susceptible to spying. Ah. There's a spike!"

"I got a *spill* out of you?"

"Well, I dare say you did! Fascinating. The dynograph detects it, but the *spill* Talent herself doesn't, of course." He grinned, and circled the spike with a red pen.

"So, Fitz Blum is immune." Kim left alone the news that Owen had wanted the chief's job.

"For the most part. No one is immune to the Psychokinesis Talents. Moving objects, spreading a shadow across a swath of ground, that sort of thing."

He fiddled with knobs on the machine. "But your *spill* Talent, I've been meaning to ask you. Have you ever had a friend—here in England—disclose a Talent to you? If you have, you might just let me know."

"But you get people through the Talent Registration Office." It had taken her some time to decide to register, as she considered the risk to her privacy. But it had been one of her best judgments.

"Well, many don't register."

Even the existence of the Registration Office was not generally known. It wasn't advertised; one at a time, people were encouraged to come in, having been vetted in some way. Her accidental vetting had been with a nice-looking captain in the Royal Navy. After three or four dates, he had given up enough secrets that he asked her outright if she had the *spill*. He was a former Monkton Hall subject himself, for *hypercognition*. She apologized for prying, confessing the truth of her ability. He then explained how to register. She was not greatly surprised that he never called again.

Owen went on. "You'd be surprised how many subjects we get on to from volunteers like you. Now and then, you must meet other people with special abilities?"

Kim shook her head. "I'm sorry, but I'm afraid I can't recruit for you, if that's what you mean."

"You don't have to decide right now. Think about it."

"I can't do it, Owen. If friends *spill*, it's bad enough knowing what I shouldn't. Telling someone *else* . . . no."

"You wouldn't make much of a spy, then," he said lightheartedly.

She smirked. "So, does that happen here? The recruitment of spies?"

"Certainly not." He watched the ink writer arm slide up and down. "Besides, a spy can't have *scruples*, God knows."

After her session, Kim made her way out to the main foyer. As so often, she heard Fitzroy Blum's rather penetrating laugh from his office up the curved staircase. It seemed more of a territorial bark than a true laugh.

UXLEY, EAST YORKSHIRE

Rose looked greedily at the used books spread out on the table in the vestibule. She already had two Nancy Drews under her arm. She planned to use up the rest of her day off reading in the hammock in her favorite Wrenfell place: the kitchen garden.

With the church door wide open, the warm spring air wafted in, but still Rose grabbed her sweater more closely around her. Her mum was always saying how she wore too many coats and sweaters, and no need, now the weather was so fine.

She picked up the Mary Poppins one, liking the picture of the woman in the hat with little flowers sticking out of it.

Vicar Hathaway had ducked out of the chapel to see who'd come in. "No need to pay," he said. "Just take them, Rose."

She thanked the vicar and tucked the books into her canvas bag. Rose left her bicycle where it rested against the churchyard wall and walked in the direction of the sweet shop. It was right hot in all the sweaters, but a body might need them, she knew.

The sun was very mean, pressing down on her, and her skin itched something fierce.

It was still another block to the square. Walking made the heat worse, and her breath came in gasps. She felt like she was burning up inside her sweaters. In the middle of the square, she put down her bag, unable to move another step.

Before she even decided what to do, she furiously undid the buttons on her top sweater, letting it drop from her shoulders onto the cobbles. Then, the next sweater, the one she had to pull over her head, that one came off, and down in the heap. Then came her shirt and underthings. It felt so good, the breeze on her skin, the cool, velvety air. She could breathe again, just a little. She shuffled off her skirt and panties.

Someone shouted at her. People were milling about. Rushing up to her was Mr. Marcus looking angry and then Frank Hobbes and Polly from the doctor's office, and here came the sweet store owner, Mr. Mayfield, running out of the shop. Everyone talking at once, and a policeman's whistle from up high street.

Some schoolboys were dancing around her, yelling *naked* and *boobies*. But why was she standing in the square with no clothes on? She grabbed at her sweaters but couldn't decide whether to first put on her bottoms or her tops. One of the boys hollered, "Underpants, underpants," grinning, but not like a joke.

Then Miss Alice came out of the yarn shop, rushing over. She was yelling something, and people stood aside, letting her in.

"Rose, dear," she said. Stepping in front of her, she turned to the crowd. "Get along now, you're doing no good here. You boys! Leave off—shame on you!"

She grabbed a sweater and helped Rose into it, fastening the front quick-like. "There, Rose, we'll just put some clothes on.

Step into your skirt, that's right." Then, picking up the great pile of sweaters and the book bag, she took Rose's elbow and led her across the square, through a crowd of people who were looking ever so cross, as though they didn't know how hot she'd been and maybe could die if the sun kept at her.

Once in the yarn shop, Miss Alice closed the door and locked it.

It was lovely cool and dark in the shop, and all the pretty yarn, sleeping like kittens in their boxes.

Miss Alice looked to be in a state. "Rose, what is it, what happened?"

She began to realize that she had taken off her clothes out in front of everyone. The tears came rushing out as Miss Alice put her arms around her. "I were so 'ot," Rose sobbed.

Alice got her to sit down and drink a glass of water, as some older boys came up to the store window and beat on the glass, making faces.

Miss Alice raced over to the window. "I know your mum and dad, Eugene, Rudy! Get along with you!" Off they ran, screaming and laughing.

With the second glass of water, a worse thing happened. Constable Benny came knocking. When Miss Alice went to the door, they had a row.

"No, you *can't* come in, Constable. She's had a horrible fright."

"So 'ave we all, Miss Ward."

"What utter nonsense! She's the one that's frightened, the rest of you got your eyes full and did *nothing* to help."

There was more, but Rose couldn't hear until Miss Alice started yelling, "I've known you since you were in nappies, Benny, and if you don't trust me to get her settled at Wrenfell, you'll just have to put me in jail with her!"

She slammed the door. While they'd been going at it, Rose had managed with the rest of her clothes.

"Never you mind Benny," Miss Alice said. She went to the window, frowning as Constable Benny walked away. "Bloody hell," she muttered.

In surprise, Rose covered her mouth. Her mum would never allow her to say *bloody* or *hell*.

THURSDAY, APRIL 9. The police van arrived at half past nine in the morning. Kim had been briefed on the disrobing incident the night before, on her return from Monkton Hall. The entire household was on edge, expecting the authorities to turn up, and now they had. An anxious Mrs. Babbage announced that Constable Simkins and another official had come to the door.

Wishing her father were there, Kim rose to greet them as they were shown into the parlor.

Simkins introduced a Superintendent Oates from the constabulary in Coomsby. Short and burly, the man had his investigative face on. Her heart sank. They were hell-bent to make something more of this than was needed.

Mrs. Babbage lingered, her face a map of concern. Kim tried to take command. "I would have thought this a local matter, Superintendent." She cut a disapproving glance at Simkins, who had the grace to look stricken.

"We've come for Rose Babbage," Oates said, "so we can process the matter of her disrobing in the square. There are decency statutes. It can't be just swept under the carpet, you see, even if the girl is backward."

Mrs. Babbage came forward. "But yer honor, the way of it is tha' our Rose, she likes 'er sweaters, and just got 'ot, is all. See, she got caught in a blow, it was in the early fall, so I remember. We were pickin' blackberries, an' poor thing, she was down the road a ways and got the worst o' it. An' ever since then, she's afraid, you see. Of gettin' cold. Nowt any more to it."

"That's as may be," Oates said, "but the girl's never been quite right, and we need to assure it doesn't happen again, not in front of schoolchildren, to say the least."

Kim snapped, "And how do you propose to assure that, throw her in jail?"

"No, no, nothing of the sort. We're having Dr. Dunn come down from Prestwich Home." Mrs. Babbage shook her head in consternation. "He'll do an evaluation, talk to the girl, assess where we stand as to her mental—"

"—Prestwich Home? The asylum up on the moors?" They couldn't be serious. "She's not crazy, Superintendent, nor is she mentally sick in the way you've latched onto."

A brief knock, and Walter Babbage opened the parlor door. He glared at the policemen. "Tha's a car pulled up, miss. Ye better coom."

"Yes, Walter. In a moment." She nodded at Mrs. Babbage to leave them for a moment.

With the door closed, she said, "Can this doctor talk with Rose here?"

"I'm afraid the doctor must have her in hospital for the mental evaluation."

"This is all very wrong, Superintendent. You are causing terrible distress for the parents and for myself. And Rose will be baffled and frightened. She'll . . ."

Shouts came from the yard. Kim hurried into the foyer, where through the open front door she could see Walter Babbage arguing with a stranger standing by a van.

Kim strode outside to confront the man whom she presumed was from Prestwich Home. She put on her best lady-of-the-manor air. "How do you do? I presume you are Dr. Dunn? From the asylum?"

Dunn forced a smile. "We call it a mental hospital. But yes." Slim and bald, he had a small mustache, as diminutive men often did. He wore a gray suit and sweater vest along with a reddish bow tie, entirely too jaunty for his unpleasant mission.

"I'm Kim Tavistock. I'm afraid there's been a bit of a misunderstanding about my maid. Rose won't be able to go with you. It's out of the question."

Superintendent Oates interjected, "Then I'm prepared to charge her and bring her into Coomsby."

Mrs. Babbage had come out on the porch, parking herself in front of the door like a lorry.

Kim turned to Oates. "Haven't we gone a bit faster than is quite needed? My father will be very distressed to hear that she's being institutionalized without a proper proceeding."

"Your father can speak to the magistrate, if he likes. But I must ask you to have Rose come out. She can pack a few things. . . ."

Walter shouted. "Why, ya right arsehole!"

Superintendent Oates stiffened. "I'm going to pretend I did not hear you taunting a police officer. Who are you?"

"Ah'm 'er bloody father, you 'orse's arse!"

"That will *do*, Walter." Kim stepped in front of him and shooed him with her hands, trying gamely to make him go inside.

Dr. Dunn stepped forward. "You needn't worry about Rose, Mr. Babbage. She'll have her own room, the best care—"

Walter exploded. He lunged at Dunn, knocking him against the car. "By Gawd, ye'll not be takin' 'er t' a madhouse!"

Simkins and Oates managed to pull him away as Dunn straightened his coat. He shook his head at Oates. "I'm fine. Tempers flare in these situations."

Despite his calm demeanor, Dunn grated on Kim. He put on a concerned, well-meaning attitude, but at the moment, she concurred with Walter that the doctor was a right arsehole.

In the end, Dr. Dunn had his way. Constable Oates could not be swayed, and the Babbages faced giving their daughter either to the police or the doctor. So as not to unduly alarm Rose, Kim kept her demeanor calm, but she felt the shock of them taking away a member of her household.

The four of them—Kim, Walter, Constable Simkins and Superintendent Oates—waited in the yard in rigid silence as Mrs. Babbage helped Rose to pack. Kim cast about for a last-ditch measure to prevent what was happening, but she could think of nothing. If her father had been there, he would never have allowed this. No matter their differences, she knew that he would have protected Rose.

When Rose emerged on the porch with her valise, no one said a word. Walter's face was a frozen scowl. Constable Simkins could not bring himself to meet Kim's eyes. But shame wasn't enough. People had to *do* something, not just stand by. Yet here she was, silent, helpless.

As Rose came down the steps, Dunn sprang into action to open the door of the van.

Rose looked directly at Kim. "Mum said you might coom wi' me." Her quiet trust pierced Kim to the core.

Kim looked at Dr. Dunn, who slowly shook his head. "I can't, Rose. But Mr. Tavistock and I will come for you soon."

Rose nodded uncertainly, then carried her valise to the car without a backward look. It was terribly brave, Kim thought.

Mrs. Babbage leaned against the doorframe, trying to make a confident smile for Rose and failing dreadfully.

Just when they thought that the worst was over, and as the car trundled away, Rose pressed her face against the back window with a look of confusion and dismay.

THURSDAY, APRIL 9. Julian Tavistock sat in a chair across the wide mahogany desk from his boss. The man everyone referred to as E was merely a silhouette against the bright panes of his windows overlooking Broadway, a fit image for the head of the Secret Intelligence Service, forever in the shadows. SIS, referred to by those in the organization as the Office, occupied the third and fourth floors of a large office block just off of Parliament Square.

Because E and Julian had been friends since Eton, E had his chief spy reporting directly to him, despite grumblings from the assistant director.

"I'm afraid I have to go home for a day or two," Julian said. "It's a family matter." Kim had called him this morning, telling him about Rose. It hadn't gone over well that he couldn't come home on the next train.

E nodded at the statement. He had family issues of his own,

including a wife with a severe eating disorder whose skeletal thinness kept her housebound. "Take the time you need, of course."

Julian had heard the urgency in Kim's voice, and he hated not being able to rush home immediately. He would go up on Sunday, the soonest he could manage.

E turned to business. "I see you're keeping tabs on this von Ritter fellow. What's he doing in London? What do you make of him?"

Julian was building up the dossier. "His name is Erich von Ritter. *Sicherheitsdienst*, SD." The Nazi intelligence service. As a secret organization, SD often wore plain clothes and used cover stories to justify their travels. "He's nominally a part of South Munich Pharmaceuticals. An aristocrat, family money, and good connections in Berlin. Very much undercover. And we've learned he's a friend of Georgi Aberdare."

"Damn poor timing, I should say, this Nazi poking around, just when the PM is jockeying for some room. I'll wager he hasn't come to sell headache powders at Temperance Hospital." E turned his chair and gazed out the side window, bringing his high forehead and strong jaw into view. He still had the look of a soldier. A survivor of the Marne and, for a decade and a half, Whitehall politics.

Julian said, "We've got him under surveillance, chief."

"Keep on him, then. You're the best we've got, Julian. You can handle him."

"It's awkward, though. Wallis Simpson is at Newmarket Saturday for the Guineas Stakes. Von Ritter is an acquaintance of Sir Lionel Bowes and will be there with him. If von Ritter's looking for an introduction to the King's mistress, that could be his chance. I'll be there too, of course."

"I dare say he'll get a cordial hearing from the woman. And there's not much we can do about it."

"No, there's not. If he gets a chance to talk to Mrs. Simpson, I'm sure von Ritter will mention his acquaintance with Georgi Aberdare. If Mrs. Simpson likes him, that's one degree of separation from the King." Given her relationship with Edward VIII, Wallis Simpson couldn't outright support Germany, but the Office thought she leaned strongly in that direction.

E nodded unhappily. "The bloody fools. Mrs. Simpson believes in Hitler and the new Germany, making apologies for them, the same as the Aberdare woman."

Another of Julian's assignments, to position himself in Georgi's circle. He would much prefer to be in the thick of the action, but he seemed to have a knack for infiltrating the drawing-room set.

"Julian, I have another matter to discuss with you." E leaned over the von Ritter file and clasped his hands on top of it. "We have a situation brewing." He glanced at the door as though assuring himself that it was closed. "A mole. At the highest levels." He let that statement sink in before going on. "Our decrypts suggest that the Germans have a source. I've authorized an investigation, as demoralizing as that may be." He paused. "And I'll be questioned. I thought you should know."

"Good Lord." Julian's mood plummeted at this news. There had been rumors of a mole for months, but it was unprecedented for E to be questioned. His old friend had given his life to the SIS, entering the service right after the war and bringing Julian in ten years later. Now this. Who could the mole be? Not E, of that Julian was sure. But you could never prove loyalty, so once questions were asked, it had a chilling effect on morale.

"This is a blow," Julian said. "I'm damn sorry to hear it."

"Well, it can't be avoided. I hope you'll try not to get

involved in the paranoia. Our work is too important to let this affect performance."

Julian nodded, his thoughts roaming into the forest of suspicion that could so easily infest the service. Who was it? And how highly were they placed?

E pulled out another file and opened it. "Then there's Norden on the German north coast. Our German agent in Saxony reports a buildup of armored vehicles and supplies in some outlying depots around the port. They've got convoys running up there at night into a minor labor camp in the Wesermarsch."

This was news. "That's peculiar, isn't it? If they've got their sights on Denmark, Norden is a bit off the supply line. Are there any reports of naval activity there?"

"Not yet. Our signal intelligence has picked up a code phrase, *Sturmweg*, that we'll be tracking."

"Storm way," Julian mused.

"Let's keep after Aberdare's circle on both counts. We need to find our mole, and whoever it is may be involved in this *Sturmweg*, too. Given all this, it doesn't help matters to have your daughter involved at HARC." The Historical Archive and Records Centre up at Monkton Hall. "For one thing, we can't send you up there."

"Something about Monkton Hall, chief?"

"No. But in case of need, Fitzroy Blum has his finger on the pulse of things, the Talents, whatnot. This is just the way that covers get blown. Unexpected meetings. It's cleaner if your daughter isn't involved in a military research facility."

Kim was undoubtedly curious about her Talent, but the testing should be over by now. "She did catch me by surprise." Not that he had reason to expect her to confide in him. At great cost, he maintained his right-leaning views so that he had credibility with Nazi supporters here. That included keeping up the front with Kim, and he feared she had grown to dislike him for it. Not much to like in him, then, when he was scarcely present for her. In his job, he did best to avoid *spill* Talents. Even his own daughter.

E made a small smile of commiseration. "See about moving her along to another hobby." Tapping the HARC file, he went on. "Churchill and his circle set great store by the place. The man has his madcap ideas, so I don't wonder he's big on military use of Talents. A waste of time, if you ask me. We won't be stopping the Germans by *mesmerizing* a company of soldiers in a hayfield."

"Perhaps, but Monkton Hall is making progress on abilities that produce real damage." Julian always pushed at E on this topic, though the two of them had never agreed about the role of Talents in war.

E waved this away. "Yes, these so-called psychokinesis Talents. Well, so far your *damaging* Talents and what have you are only good for mischief. Bring me a scale-10 for one of these, then we'll see."

There was only one 10 so far tested at Monkton Hall, and that was the First Lord of the Admiralty, Winston Churchill. He was a *conceptor*, giving him enormous powers of influence in rousing people. Interesting that another powerful *conceptor* was on the world stage at the same time: Adolf Hitler. These were the most famous examples of those who came into their Talents as adults, since they were far past puberty when the bloom occurred.

E went on. "No, we won't have your war of the Talents, Julian. Wars will always be fought with steel." Glancing at the mantel clock, E rose, signaling the meeting was at an end. E walked him to the side door, the one that led to the stairs down to the secretarial pool in the Veterans' Benefits Division.

He paused at the door. "This Georgi Aberdare. Is she working for them, do you think, or just a dupe?"

"I can't see what use she'd be to the Germans, but she does attract a nasty crew."

E nodded, and closed the door behind Julian as he descended the stairs.

Julian was troubled by the revelation that the mole rumors had now escalated into an investigation. There were always traitors who would fall for the German narrative of denial, lies and reassurance. And money, he didn't doubt. Lots of it.

Apparently, now they had a taker in the ranks of service.

NEWMARKET, SUFFOLK

SATURDAY, APRIL 11. At the Guineas Stakes, Erich von Ritter didn't stay for the running of the horses. He emerged from an exclusive hospitality pavilion, escorted by Sir Lionel Bowes, and headed for his car. Julian, in disguise with homburg and mustache and carrying an ebony-handled umbrella, had observed him closely in the tent. He had drunk his champagne in a corner, where he witnessed the unfortunate but expected introduction of the German agent to Mrs. Simpson. She looked very smart in cream and blue, but it wasn't Simpson who stole the show this time; it was von Ritter. People seemed eager to meet the handsome industrialist, and the man was smooth among the fawning crowd.

Julian followed when von Ritter left the pavilion in the company of Sir Lionel. His target passed Rory, one of Julian's men, who studied his racing program and then strolled in pursuit. In the thick crowd, Julian tailed behind.

Once in the car park, Sir Lionel and von Ritter made their goodbyes. Julian's car was parked just outside the entrance, where Rory now made his way. With Julian's eyes on the target, his man would have the car ready to go when Julian caught up.

The first race had not yet started. Most people began making their way to the reviewing stands, but von Ritter, his mission accomplished, would not be staying. He got in his car, and the vehicle moved slowly through the throng toward the exit gate. Julian moved past the vehicle on foot, noting as he approached his own car that Rory was not behind the wheel.

Rory was standing, staring at the front passenger tire. A puncture. They were common enough, but Julian had never believed in coincidence.

Rory kicked at the tire. "Bollocks!"

Julian watched von Ritter's car speed off down the motorway. He turned to signal to their second car, waiting on a side lane some hundred meters down the road, that he was off the surveillance.

At that, a diminutive elderly lady in wire-rimmed glasses and a cloche hat pulled out of the lane in a Morris Eight and followed the Mercedes-Benz. Elsa was very good at vehicular pursuit, but Julian hated to be left behind.

SUNDAY, APRIL 12. "You might have come home right away,"
Kim said as she and her father drove up to Prestwich Home.

"Nothing to be done about it," Julian said. "I had a meeting
with our supplier from Glasgow. He made a special trip."

"So now Rose has spent three nights in a lunatic asylum, and
all for the whisky trade."

Julian, as usual, didn't rise to the bait.

"Even Constable Simkins went along with it. Nobody stood
up for her except Alice and Walter Babbage. Shutting her away
is wrong. It isn't . . . English."

They turned onto a deserted road nosing up into the
westernmost edge of the moors. Julian's silence said, *Don't over-
dramatize. Wait and see.* One had to play both parts to have a
conversation with him.

They passed through Prestwich Home's park gate flanked

with tall, rough-cut granite. Once parked, they saw the full expanse of the long Palladian-style manor made of gray stone. Devoid of charm or any attempt at decoration, it was less a manor than a fortified castle. Kim's heart sank.

A nurse came out of the front door, a large woman who waited for them to approach, frowning at them the closer they got.

"You'll be the Tavistocks, then," she said without enthusiasm.

They followed her into a dark foyer. High windows splashed light onto the recesses of a beamed ceiling, allowing little illumination to spill to the floor.

"Dr. Dunn expected you this mornin'," she said, leading them farther into the place, where the smell of cooked cabbage hung heavily. At shortly past noon, the drive had taken longer than they expected.

The nurse led them to the intersection of two long corridors, one that came in from the entryway and a second that ran perpendicular, like the nave of a church.

The nurse rapped twice on the door at the crossroads, then opened it, announcing them.

Angus Dunn sat at a dark carved desk. He looked quite the country gentlemen in gray flannels and, under a tweed jacket, a gray-and-white argyle sweater vest. At his throat, a maroon bow tie. He rose to shake hands with them as Kim introduced him to her father.

"Rose is settling in very well," Dunn began.

Annoyingly, Julian said, "Good, glad to hear it." He looked around. "I've always meant to see the place, but up here on the moors . . ." He shrugged. "Prestwich was the architect, I believe?"

"Yes, Roland Prestwich built it in 1725 for the Earl of Thirsk. The Earl wanted it to hold back the Lancs, who felt they had rights to the grazing lands. It's never fallen."

Julian steepled his hands in front of him. "An excellent place, Doctor. With a fine reputation."

Dunn nodded his appreciation. "I know you're eager to learn how we're getting on with Rose."

"Actually," Kim said, "we've come to take her home."

"You must be terribly concerned about her," Dunn said with a condescension that Kim found difficult to bear. "That's only to be expected. I'm concerned as well, I must say."

Julian said, "Oh? We were rather expecting that you had had time to assure yourself of Rose's competence."

"I wish I could report that to be the case." Dunn smoothed his short mustache, opening a file that lay before him. "We've completed a preliminary evaluation. It indicates that she understands that what she did was wrong. But her nature is to be agreeable, and thus it's been difficult to access her issues around self-exposure."

"Assuming that there are any issues," Kim said.

Dunn looked startled to be addressed by her. "Oh, there are issues."

"Just let us take her home, and she'll be fine, Doctor. Being naked is not a crime, and it is *not* a symptom of madness."

He shook his head. "We don't use that term. The gradations of mental conditions are more subtle, and many people who have trouble functioning in one area can do very well in another. Often, the good can mask the bad."

Julian said, "What are the results of your evaluation, Doctor? We still haven't heard specifics."

"Our preliminary evaluation is that, at age nineteen, Rose Babbage is a mental defective with an arrested emotional development at an approximate age of ten or eleven. Mind you, with proper therapeutic—"

"She is not a mental defective," Kim snapped. "Nor is she ten years old!"

"On the contrary, Miss Tavistock. Using the Binet and Simon classification tests, we can place her firmly in the category of moron, which, granted, is a step up from idiot or imbecile. It is based on reliable science. Now, with proper therapeutic treatment, she may be able to live a productive life. But she is likely to require the most up-to-date care. Especially with her latest incident."

Julian frowned. "Incident?"

"Yes. Rose exposed herself to a Prestwich medical worker."

Kim and her father stared at this pronouncement.

"Mind you, I had concerns even before, but now . . ." Dunn spread his hands. "I think a case can be made that she needs close supervision. At least for a few weeks."

"How did this come about?" Julian asked.

"Well, a nurse had helped her dress for bed—"

"She doesn't need help putting a nightgown on!" Kim exclaimed.

Her father spoke sharply. "Kim." He nodded at Dunn. "Please go on."

"The nurse stepped out into the hallway for a moment, and when she turned back, Rose stood naked at the door of her room."

"She wouldn't have done that," Kim said, "unless she was wearing her coats and sweaters and was too hot."

Dunn's forehead crumpled in concern. "I know that this is distressing to hear."

She was quite done with hearing his false notes of concern. "Really, Doctor, who are these witnesses, anyway?"

"Nurse Conway, whom you met." He paused. "And myself."

It seemed very unlikely, despite the fact that Rose had indeed disrobed in public once. But the day had been hot, and Prestwich was decidedly cold. She had taken a dislike to Dunn and was not prepared to give him much credence. She hoped Julian did not.

Dunn watched the two of them absorb his statement, and then slipped the knife in deeper: "There are those who feel mental defectives such as your maid should be sterilized. There are voices being raised."

Julian put his hand on Kim's arm to stop her from leaping up from her chair. "What *voices*?" he asked.

"The Order of Decency, for one." Dunn nodded. "There are others."

Kim lashed back. "So, now we are allowing any sort of fanatics to demand roundups of people they happen to be afraid of! That makes us no better than the Nazis." Why did Dunn care so much about treating Rose? He must have larger concerns as head of a mental hospital, even if he ascribed to some twisted view of genetic purity.

Dunn kept his voice low and calm. "Fanatics didn't decide to bring her here. I did. And I shall decide when to release her."

Julian turned to her. "Kim, please wait outside. I need to talk to Dr. Dunn without constant interruption."

She locked gazes with him, not trusting that he would properly defend Rose but realizing that she was losing the battle with Dunn. She pushed her chair back and left the room.

Out in the hallway, the cold of the place settled upon her flushed face. From inside the office, she heard her father's voice, steady and agreeable.

Far down the hall, an orderly pushed a food caddy. She noticed that he first unlocked the doors before going in. So, Rose was under lock and key. How had things come to this?

Undoubtedly, they would not wish for her to look around, but in her present mood, she felt inspired to do so. Keeping an eye out for the big nurse, she turned down the cavernous hall, away from the slowly progressing food cart.

Her heeled shoes clicked briskly against the flagstone floor, echoing and giving the impression that she walked through a cave. Her old investigatory instincts kicked in at once as she became acutely alert, looking for evidence of what Prestwich Home might be hiding. For it was exactly the kind of place that would have secrets. It was a pity that these stone hallways could not talk.

This wing of Prestwich gave onto several large rooms framed with arched doorways, through which she spied massive fireplaces gone cold and furniture stacked in warehouse fashion. Silence commanded the place, perhaps not ominously but with a soulless efficiency which made it somehow worse.

At the end of the hall were a broad staircase going up and a smaller version leading to the floor below. From above, she heard people talking on the stairs and coming nearer. She ducked down the stairway and was quickly out of sight, hoping that whoever it was would not be headed in her direction. At the bottom, Kim found herself in the service and utility precincts of the place. Institutional wall sconces led down a musty corridor, with doors designated as LINENS, CLEANING and ELECTRICAL.

On one side of the hallway were shelves stacked with blankets and what looked like folded coats for winter weather. This display gave Kim the impression that the inmates—she thought of them that way—would be expected to take the fresh air on a regular basis, even in winter.

Her impression that the basement was only for storage was soon dispelled by the sight of a nurse pushing a quite large woman in a wheelchair. The nurse saw Kim and, leaving her charge, walked briskly in her direction.

"'Ere, now, what's this?" the nurse said, frowning.

"Oh, sorry, I appear to have gotten lost. I was just meeting with Dr. Dunn. . . ."

At that moment, she spied an old man being escorted by an orderly down the hall in her direction. He was so thin, he looked skeletal, and his six-foot height was crowned with a green plaid tam. He pointed to her quite rudely, but the orderly took no notice and steered the old man into what might have been the privy.

"Ye'll be wantin' to get on," the nurse said. "There's no walkin' about, you know."

At that point, Dunn rounded the stairs, spying them. The tour was over.

"Miss Tavistock. You are wandering, I see." He came down the stairs with her father close behind him. "We've just been up to see Rose."

"You have? Oh, *I* wanted to see her!"

Dunn didn't answer but rudely walked away to confer with the nurse. Her father gestured for her to come along, and she allowed him to take her by the elbow. He leaned in, saying, "Rose is quite all right, you'll be glad to hear."

"Well, I don't—"

"And she's coming back with us."

This surprising statement instantly lifted Kim's spirits.

When they reached the main floor, Dunn had not caught up with them yet, and Julian continued. "He's releasing her into our care on strict conditions of supervision." He cut a glance at her. "I had to put some pressure on him, so I'm quite sure we have made an enemy of the man."

"Did you threaten to open the gates to a Lancashire regiment?"

"I mentioned a Whitehall contact. He got rather high-handed

and mentioned his own. I was able to trump him. Dunn's face became quite the color of his bow tie."

Kim looked at him with a burst of admiration. "You must have been persuasive."

"I believe I was, my dear." He gave her a brief smile, lovely to see.

Dunn caught up to them. "This is a temporary arrangement, you may be sure." He kept his face neutral except his eyes, which were hooded and resentful. "I mean to have her back for tests, sir."

Julian turned his own bland look on the doctor. "I trust that won't be necessary."

"We shall see." The doctor turned to see Nurse Conway leading Rose down the hall toward them, carrying her valise.

Dunn said, "You are to keep her under strict supervision. You understand."

"Yes," Julian smiled, "we do understand. Thank you, Doctor."

Rose approached, looking wide-eyed. She pulled away from the nurse's guiding hand and Kim went to her, putting her arm around her. Julian took the valise.

Just as they were walking down the front steps, the old man she had seen earlier, the tall one in the green tam, came rushing around from the side of the mansion, his bathrobe flapping, exposing pajamas six inches too short for his frame. He was followed by an orderly who only caught up with him some thirty yards from the car.

"Th' road to hell!" he cried. The orderly had hold of him, but the old man was stronger than he looked and shook his fist. "I tell you, th' road to hell!"

"Good God," Julian said. "It's old Harry Parslow."

The nurses helped the orderly to bring the old man under

control, walking him back the way he'd come toward a door that Kim hadn't noticed before.

Dunn said, "Yes, Mr. Parslow. He does tend to shout on occasion. Don't be alarmed."

Before his attendants could get him back inside, Parslow shouted back, "Paved in ice! You'll see, damn you!" The door thunked behind the group, and the Prestwich yard fell silent again.

"Eighty-four years old," Dunn said. "Quite gone, I'm afraid."

As Rose took her seat in the back of the roadster, Dunn leaned in to her through the open window and patted her shoulder. "We'll see you soon, Rose."

Rose glared at him. "You bloody won't!"

Julian was now at pains to leave before they could be prevented and, suggesting that Kim get in back with Rose, bid Dunn farewell and quickly got them underway. They sped through the granite gates and out onto the moors.

"Who is Harry Parslow?" Kim asked her father.

"Used to own the chemist's shop. That was in your grandfather's time. I thought he'd passed."

Despite the rather startling and sad appearance of Harry Parslow, Kim felt renewed. England wasn't Germany. Not only that, but her father had fought the enemy. And won. Apparently, he was in a good mood as well, because he turned on the radio and they had swing bands all the way through the Wolds.

WESERMARSCH SUB CAMP,
NORTH COAST OF GERMANY

SUNDAY, APRIL 12. It had begun. All through the night, the motorized columns snaked across the salt flats, bringing supplies and light armored units to the depot at Wesermarsch. Lieutenant Colonel Stelling drank another cup of cold coffee and watched from his office window as the trucks came in, headlights tunneling out of the darkness.

It was the first night of many to come, with the delivery of equipment, food, fuel and ammunitions. Following these, the *panzers*. This show of military might, always a source of pride, now felt like a profound threat. He fingered the small item in his pocket, the reminder of the disaster he faced, his suddenly changed prospects.

Lieutenant Hass came in with dispatches. Stelling nodded for him to leave them on the desk, and turned back to the window. Was it just his imagination that Hass waited a moment, staring at him before he left the room?

Now through the camp gates came the half-tracks, churning mud as they rumbled past the headquarters building. If the British noted any unusual activity, they might think it was in support of a planned offensive based at Norden three miles away and aimed at Denmark. Decrypts and other intelligence assured the High Command that England was blind to Germany's intentions. England and France were still trying to absorb the shock of Germany's liberation of the Rhineland. They could not imagine there was more to come.

Dawn bloomed as a pale threat to the east. Soon, the empty supply trucks would be leaving through the gate. Stelling wished that he were on one of them. How much time did he have?

In his pocket, he fingered the dread arm patch. He had found it on his desk one morning last week. On that morning, he knew that he was a dead man. The patch was only the beginning of the psychological game they would play with him, to punish him for what he was. Once he had fully absorbed the hazard he faced, he had begun his plans for escape.

Wrenching his attention back to the window overlooking the yard, he noted the arrival of the trucks with the first division of troops, part of the *Panzerwaffe*. The soldiers would be quartered by the eastern gate, taking their exercise out of sight in the warehouses.

Sturmweg would come soon. He was not privy to the date. Not even Field Marshal von Rundstedt knew, since it depended on the weather. There must be a major storm for it all to work as planned. April was a fine month for storms.

Stelling noted the van from Luckenwalde had come up last, following the truck convoy. He had been told to expect four people, one rated as a 7.4. They were Poles and Belgians but would be treated very well. They must be kept calm.

Focused ice events swirled now and then around Barracks 4 and 5, but if any spies kept watch on the camp, it would seem typical north-coast weather. The subterfuge needed only a few weeks more. The sub camp was secure. But the other side of things, the English side, this was most delicate. The *Sturmweg* landing point had been chosen, but the work to support that site must be carefully planned.

Nestled among England's moribund aristocracy was an individual who could leverage Talents in an up-to-now unimaginable manner. The rumor was that he—or she—was English. Ironically, the British equivalent of Luckenwalde, Monkton Hall, had found this person. The intelligence was soon in German hands, and the individual *in unserer Tasche*. In our pocket.

He fingered the patch. It gave him a jolt every time he touched it. For seven days, he had kept the insignia on his person, handling it, using it to set his resolve. Undoubtedly, von Ritter had quietly told one of Stelling's own officers to be aware of his commander's failings and make an example of him. Hound him.

And kill him when *Sturmweg* was over.

The Luckenwalde van passed out of the gates. Dawn seeped over the flats, painting the mudflats grayish gold.

Turning at last from the window, he took the patch from his pocket. It was a pink triangle, the insignia that homosexual laborers were forced to wear in the camp. The patch spoke to him, saying, *We know what you are.* He would be less than a Pole or a Jew, inferiors who at least did not presume to be German army officers. He was useful for a time. But after *Sturmweg?* The terrible hour with Erich von Ritter haunted him.

As Stelling watched, the van wound its way down the long road. Yes, let it go. His plan to escape must be both subtler and more audacious. There was only one way the camp's commandant could leave, now that he was watched. He wished he knew which one of his officers was charged with undermining him. A far more useful Talent than his *ice* ability would be *object reading*, the power to know who had owned the triangle patch left on his desk. Was it his deputy, the slow-witted one? Or his adjutant, the smart one? He had formed his plan with great care. To fool his adjutant.

If he failed, he would be shot, 6.5 Talent or not. But if he succeeded, where could he go? England? Hardly.

It would soon be occupied by Germany.

WRENFELL HOUSE,

EAST YORKSHIRE

MONDAY, APRIL 13. "Now then, Blaze," Rose told the gray hen, "dinna push!"

Behind the piggery and the henhouse, Rose scattered feed from her can of pumpkin seeds, making sure even the smaller chickens had some. Blaze was the biggest hen, blue-gray with her tail feathers standing up high and her red comb all jagged on top. She pushed her way to the front, clucking and bobbing.

The feeding done, Rose took out her shears from the empty feed can and went into the meadow full of tall grasses and flowering bluebells. The day was fine, with just a few puffy clouds getting in front of the sun. She let her top sweater flap open, catching a breeze. Blaze followed, begging. She'd saved a few seeds in her sweater pocket and let them fall, though the hen would have to scratch hard to get them. "Tha's a proper hen, now!"

Something was not right. The day was fine, but it hid a wintry feeling, one that Rose remembered too well. She looked up, and there in the sky was a gray hole. You had to look hard, but it was there, like an old gray moon. It began to fall.

A ribbon of frigid wind sliced at her, curling over her head and neck, then whipping around and circling back to her. The wind was starting to go round and round. Oh, it was coming, the cold. The bitter cold. The gray came down, smudging the world away. Snow began swirling around her.

The little storm was back.

Behind the veil of snow, Blaze had disappeared. Rose watched in dismay as the snow circled around her in a slow funnel, bending the grasses low. She began to run toward the yard. She always ran, though it did no good. Pulling her sweater closer around her with one wet, cold hand, she clutched the bluebells to her chest. But then she paused in confusion. Where were the henhouse and the piggery?

The sides of the storm became thick and heavy. She knew there was no escape from it. The small room full of winter. Rose knew a little storm never lasted long, but still, what if some day it didn't go away?

Snow settled on her arms like sheep's wool. "Blaze!" she called, just to hear her own voice. "Blaze!"

She sank to the ground, pulling her top sweater over her head. How she hated to be cold! It was something terrible to shiver and feel your blood go slow and icy.

"Blaze, 'ow you doin', old Blaze!" she whispered to herself for comfort. She wrapped her arms close to her sides. "Dinna be afraid. We'll get to the 'enhouse and we'll be right warm." Inside her big sweater pulled over her head, it was safe. Soon, she'd be home and dry. Outside the winter walls, it was a fine day, and warm, wasn't it? You couldn't see it, but you knew it was there. The right world, with Mum and Da and the great house.

Rose waited, humming to herself to push away the sound of the wind. But the winter room lost its moaning wind. The day became still and quiet.

When she peeked out of her sweater, she saw a lovely sight: Blaze standing big and fat, with her red comb shining in the sun. She cocked her head to the side to see if Rose was there in her big sweater. Blaze shivered her feathers, sending the snowmelt flying.

Some flicked onto Rose's face. She laughed. "Aye, Blaze! How ya doin'!"

Picking up her dropped bouquet of flowers, Rose trudged back across the yard. She would lay her sweaters out to dry on the big table in the piggery. It did no good to tell Mum or Miss Tavistock that there was a gray room that came down from the sky. They never believed it, and her mum looked worried when Rose tried to explain.

No one knew about the little storms. Just her and Blaze.

HALLWORTH CASTLE RUINS, NORTH YORK MOORS

WEDNESDAY, APRIL 15. The wind blew steadily from the east as Kim made her way up the path overgrown with bracken and shaggy heather. She wished she'd worn her walking shoes, but she hadn't expected to be meeting Owen Cherwell on the moors.

He'd run out after her at the car park at Monkton, just as she was setting out for home. He had her thermos, which she believed she had misplaced, but of course he'd taken it while she wasn't looking during her session. This was the excuse to see her outside and ask her to meet him a short ride away at the Hallworth ruins.

Kim reached the top of the hill, where the moors fell away into a shallow glen brushed with lavender and bright eruptions of daffodils. Hallworth Castle lay nested amid this, a twelfth-century ruin, reclining in glory.

She was very curious to know what was so important it

could not be said at Monkton. As she descended the path toward the ruins, she found herself refreshed by the expansive view to the west, over miles of undulating basins and hills, helping to fortify her against her worries over Rose.

Her father's defense of Rose was gratifying, but now the Order of Decency from Coomsby was stirring up fears over naked women. Everyone in Uxley had been quick to agree this could not be tolerated.

Over the past week since the Prestwich visit, Kim had determined that Rose must have more suitable duties, ones that could prove her maturity. She had begun to train Rose to the duties of household maid, which Rose undertook with the greatest industry.

Owen had said to meet him at the barbican, at the entrance. She had no idea what a barbican was, but the castle entrance could not be missed. It was a square tower with crumbling battlements, a four-story survivor of the former grand castle. Making her way through the ruined gate, she walked into a field of half-buried building stones. The wind subsided in the lee of the tower, making the day almost warm.

Here, the footprint of the old castle reared up in piecemeal evidence of its former layout, corralling waving grasses and flowering currants. From this high point, she looked out on the vast expanse of the moors stretching north and west. No prospect could be more forbidding in winter or more beautiful in spring than this undulating land, with shadows and sunshine flitting over the far hills and near swells of heather. This, surely, was England as it had been for thousands of years. She did love it. She knew why Robert had loved it, not only for its beauty, but because it was wild and free.

Kim heard the click of a bicycle chain and saw Owen coming

around from the far side of the ruins. She walked down to the front gate to meet him.

"There you are!" He leaned the bicycle against a stone wall, his face flushed from his uphill ride. "You seemed a bit distracted today, Kim."

"Did I? The moors clear one's head, though."

"I rather thought the moors held things in. Let's hope they do, anyway."

Kim asked, "So, what's a barbican?"

"You're in it." He pointed to the walled passage jutting out from the castle gate that created an enclosure on three sides. "Castle defenders had an enemy confined in a nice deathtrap here." He smiled. "Thanks for meeting me. Sorry to make a mystery of it." He looked around, as though watching for Scots creeping through the gooseberries. They passed the gateway, into the rubble field.

He turned to her. "I'm going to break silence. I hope you know I'd only do this if I trusted you."

He was going to break the Monkton Hall vow? She thought that very ill-advised. But it wasn't going to be a *spill*, thank goodness—nothing that she was bringing on. Owen, probably knowing she would worry about that, was being careful to let her know it was his intention to share a secret.

"We need your help," he said. Now that he had begun, he seemed aware of the gravity of what he was about to do. He ran his hand through his hair, pushing it away from a sweat-stained forehead.

Kim nodded to encourage him. "Sometimes you have to say something." She hadn't known it was a conviction until just now.

"Right, then. Here it is: you know what the *hypercognition* Talent is?"

"It's figuring things out faster than you have the facts."

"Close. It's the ability to make lightning-fast deductions based on any slight awareness or buried set of observations. To put things together that would normally slip from consciousness. I have a subject with this Talent, in fact a 9 on the scale. She's only seventeen, but I don't think she's making it up."

"Making up that she has *hypercognition*?"

"No, making up that she knows a spy." He walked on, circling around the ruined footprint of a hall. "You mentioned once that you know Georgiana Aberdare."

Kim nodded, her curiosity peaking at the conjunction of the two subjects, *Georgi* and *spy*.

"My young subject was a guest of Georgiana Aberdare for a few weeks during Christmas. She became convinced that Aberdare was involved with the Germans. Or knew someone who was."

Kim absorbed this quite surprising revelation. "On what evidence?"

"She doesn't even know. That's the way of this Talent. You can't bring the reasons to consciousness, you just . . . go there. To the conclusion. I tend to believe her, because Georgiana Aberdare used to be Fitz's lover. And Fitz, of course, is playing for the other side."

"Fitzroy Blum?" It took her breath away. "But he's . . ."

"I know. But there's a possibility he's working for the Germans. Monkton Hall knows it has a leak. From signal intelligence, we know that Monkton Hall's cover is blown. It could be a leak at any level, but I think it's internal. There are little things that implicate Fitz, things I've told him alone. And now the Germans have it. But it's still not proof."

Kim traced back in her mind to all the times she'd seen

Blum. And then to Miss Drummond's comment, *He's not all he seems, that one.*

"Mind you, I'd report him, but I need hard evidence."

"But he might be a spy!"

"Yes, yes. But you see, he beat me out for the job he holds, and anyone would assume it's sour grapes on my part. I watch him like a hawk. But so far, no proof."

Kim sat down on a low wall, staring south, toward Monkton, hidden from view by a copse of oaks. "You want me to get next to Fitz. So he'll *spill.*"

Owen looked startled. "Next to Fitz? Don't be daft. That's much too dangerous. And he's a *natural defender.* Your Talent would have no effect on him."

"Then . . ." She stopped. "You want me to get to Georgi Aberdare."

"Exactly. She may be working for the Germans or know of Fitz's activities. Fitz dumped Aberdare a year and a half ago. She despises him and may not be on guard about his secrets."

Already, Kim had a list of objections. She lined them up: Georgi had nothing in common with Kim and was hardly going to invite her for a London shopping expedition or tea at Summerhill. Kim didn't know what to listen for, what might be a damning clue. And she knew from experience that if you wanted to know something, it was the last thing you were likely to hear.

Owen regarded her closely. "Am I losing you?"

"Why would Georgi tell me anything about Fitz? If they're both on the same side?"

"Because she hates him. She's slept with half the mink-and-manure set of northern England, and it's always Aberdare who does the dumping. It went poorly with her to have it go the other way around. Besides, if she knows Fitz is a traitor, that's a very big secret and makes it all the more likely she'll *spill* it." He paused. "And I wouldn't say they're on the same side. She might have fallen for Hitler's lies, but that doesn't make her a traitor."

Owen watched her closely, as though he could see her brain at work, the dynograph clicking away at pros and cons.

Kim gazed at the northward-stretching moors. The scent of heather and warm mosses came to her in a high wave. It surprised her how the land made you love it. It was seductive, to be asked to fight for England, like a bestowal of an unlooked-for honor.

Owen's agitation increased. "Look here, Kim. I know you don't like using your Talent."

She put up her hand to stop him. She knew what he was going to say, that sometimes one had to do a difficult thing, the larger good, et cetera, et cetera. How many years she had held her ground, never using ill-gotten information, and now . . .

Owen went on. "You know that Germany's rearming. The bloodletting will begin again, and it will be soon."

The thought was never far from her mind. But right now she was thinking of Rose. If Hitler's ideas spread, what would become of her? How close were even the good folk of Uxley, some of them, from committing her to an asylum? A few steps. And from there?

Owen took a conciliatory tone. "I know that it's not easy to spy on people, but—"

"I'll do it."

"You will?"

"Maybe I wouldn't get anywhere with Georgi. But I could try." How could she not at least do this much?

Owen beamed. "I knew I had you pegged. From the moment you covered for Pip, I knew you had it in you."

"And you don't have anyone else you can turn to? I'm it?"

"Well, it's not as though you're the last resort."

"But am I?"

He scrunched his mouth into a rather-not-say grimace. "The thing is, you have the *spill*, the Aberdare contact and the perfect cover story."

"Cover story?"

"Some writing assignment or other. 'Country hostesses of Northamptonshire,' let's say."

Owen had hit upon the very thing. A professional assignment would make a visit plausible, since she couldn't just ring Georgi up and suggest the cinema.

He cocked his head. "You do have to be committed, you know. It has to be worth the risks."

"Risks?"

"If Fitz is a spy, if she's covering for him, you could be in danger."

That rather settled it. "I don't care."

"You must care. But not shirk from what must be done."

She almost hoped there would be danger. Something more than navigating social conversation with Georgi Aberdare.

"I'll go see her. My writing an article on country manors is something that would make sense to her. And she's after my father, so she'll want to be nice to me."

Owen put a hand on her arm. "Thank you. And I don't expect you to continue in this endeavor. I'd just like to see if a *spill* could give me some evidence to bring to the authorities. You'll go to Summerhill, see what transpires, with nothing lost if it doesn't work out."

As they walked back through the barbican, she asked, "What shall I do if I find out something?"

"We can't talk at Monkton. We'll work out a dead drop, a place where we can leave messages."

"How will we know when there's a message?"

"We'll leave two chalk marks on a wall or lamppost somewhere. Then, nearby, but not too near, a hiding place for a message. We'll find one." He picked up his bicycle from its resting place. "I wouldn't put it past Fitz to have Monkton Hall bugged. Say nothing, Kim."

Just before he shoved off, she said, "What will you do if we learn something? It's not likely to be proof, is it?"

"No, I suppose it will be hard slogging, no matter what we discover. The man's in the King's circle, you know." He paused as he kicked the bike pedal into position. "And the thing is, they don't *want* to know. The prime minister, the leadership. They want to believe Germany, the lot of them. Churchill is the only one who says Hitler's going to take over Europe. And nobody's going to listen to *him*, certainly."

They took their separate paths away from the ruins. She walked to her car, acutely aware that she had just breached one of her fundamental principles: that she must never exploit her Talent to pry into lives, to discover hidden things.

As she drove away, she felt a weight of apprehension press down on her. And at the same time, an unexpected, strange joy.

PART II

WALKING ON ICE

SUMMERHILL ESTATE, NORTHAMPTONSHIRE

FRIDAY, APRIL 17. Under threatening skies, Kim paused in her four-seater Austin 10 to savor a particularly fine view of the Aberdare country home. The grand edifice, framed by the curving arm of a river, nestled amid acres of tended grass.

Summerhill, like all the great country houses of England, was built to impress. The focal point of the mansion was the graceful dome in the center of the enormous facade. She would capture this view with her Leica for her supposed magazine piece, but the real picture she wanted was of Georgi Aberdare's heart.

After an initial expression of surprise, Georgi had seemed pleased to hear from Kim.

"Would your father be joining us?" she had asked.

"He has meetings in London, I'm afraid."

"Oh, meetings! He is entirely too serious. Really, Kim, why

did you come all this way from Pittsburgh—or Pennsylvania, was it?—if you weren't to civilize him?"

"Philadelphia."

"All those Ps. But never mind, just come on Friday."

And so it was settled. She would go down to Summerhill, take pictures, write up a nice piece and sell it somewhere. All of this, false pretenses, and now that it was truly underway, a bit unnerving. Her mother would certainly be astonished. There had been moments when Kim was as well, but it was not as though she were planning to steal the family jewels. The theft, if it came, would only be secrets.

Her father would not be pleased to discover that she'd gone on a three-day trip so soon after Dr. Dunn discharged Rose from Prestwich Home. He had gone out on a limb for Rose's release, and they were responsible for anything that might happen. But Alice had volunteered to stay at the house to keep an eye on Rose, so he couldn't mind terribly much.

She drove on, crossing an arched stone bridge. To one side she saw a charming gazebo built on an elbow of land jutting into the river, and several canoes tied to a little dock. At the mansion's front entrance, she was met by a footman who hurried out to open the car door. A thickset butler was stepping down from the porch to greet her when someone hallooed from one side of the home.

A fit-looking man in a tennis sweater and pleated slacks waved at her with his racket and mopped at his face as he approached her.

"Kim Tavistock, isn't it?" he said. "I'm Hugh Aberdare. Welcome to Summerhill. Thought you'd get caught in the rain, but it's holding off."

"Lord Daventry, so good to meet you. You needn't have

broken off your game." She extended her gloved hand, and he shook it as a maid came down the steps to join the butler.

"Call me Hugh, please. And I'm glad to give up the game, Edgar is skunking me. Do you play?"

"A little. You'd skunk me, I'm sure."

He smiled, a boyish, fresh grin. "We're gentlemen except on the court, so watch out. Georgi doesn't play, of course."

He presented the butler, Griffith, who introduced the maid, a slim blond girl named Charlotte who would look after her.

Hugh led her into the grand foyer, with its marble floor and massive oil paintings lining the wall up the grand staircase. "Georgi's out back," Hugh said, waving at the deeper recesses of the house. "Holding court. Come as soon as you're settled."

The maid led her toward the staircase where the footman had already disappeared with her portmanteau. When she was halfway up the stairs, Georgi emerged below.

"There you are!" she called out. "So you arrived safely." She wore a stunning pink-and-black taffeta day dress with an A-line hem. "Good! But you still couldn't persuade Julian to come?"

Leaning into the railing, Kim said, "He had commitments in London, I'm afraid."

Georgi put her hand on her chest. "I'm heartbroken! Everyone wanted to meet him. And you, of course. Don't rush, we're watching the tennis match, and if we can get old Hugh back, we can witness his usual drubbing."

Hugh produced a jaunty smile and escorted his sister back down the hall, his arm around her shoulder, chatting amiably.

Kim had missed luncheon and was pleased to see a tray of cold cuts and a wedge of goose pie waiting for her in her room. But after a few bites, she pushed the tray aside.

She'd had the long drive down from Uxley to prepare for her subterfuge with Georgi, and though she felt she should be committed—the stakes were that Monkton Hall might have a German spy, after all—she felt unsettled. Here she was, exploiting her Talent for the first time, something she thought she'd never do.

One had to learn to live with the *spill*. And she thought she *had* learned. You don't use what you've been told. *Spills* stay locked away, as people had a right to keep them. But the world had changed. The need for her *spill* had changed. So she told herself.

There was a knock at the door.

Charlotte ducked her head in to ask if anything was needed. At that moment, the door flew back against the wall and two small white Scottie dogs barreled into the room, chasing each other. "Loxley!" Charlotte cried, "Parker!" She charged after them, which the two dogs made into a game, evading her with ease.

"Don't worry," Kim cried, "they're adorable!" Little more than puppies, their broad backs and long-haired muzzles were classic Scottie, as was their refusal to be subdued by scolding. Kim knelt down and was soon the center of a roundabout chase. "Who do they belong to?"

"Lady Georgiana, miss. The pups don't have proper manners, beggin' your pardon." She managed to hook their collars with a leash and led, or rather hauled, the dogs away.

"Who shall I be meeting today, Charlotte?" Kim asked, brushing off her skirt.

Straining against the puppies pulling in the other direction, the maid answered, "There'll be Sir Edgar Thackeray and Lady Beatrice, and a new gentleman, miss. His name was foreign-soundin', so I heard."

"Will my outfit suit, do you think, Charlotte? Or should I wear the cream satin blouse with the cowl neck?"

"Miss, I think the satin would do better, if I may say so."

Kim checked her watch. 2:33. So it was to be fancy downstairs, even if it was midafternoon. Kim quickly changed, threw on a single rope of pearls, and made her way to the grand staircase.

As she descended, she admired the center-table floral display, a huge vase filled to overflowing with peonies and lilies. Kim leaned into them to catch their fragrance.

"They are very large, these roses," came a voice from behind her.

Kim turned to find a man standing in the hall leading to the salon. He approached her. Impeccably dressed, he wore a London-cut midnight blue suit. Perhaps in his late thirties, his hair was very dark, worn slicked back from a quite handsome, if narrow, face.

"They are roses, yes?" His accent was decidedly German.

"Oh, peonies, I think. They're different."

"As you see, I do not know my flowers. At least not English ones." He bowed. "If I may introduce myself: Erich von Ritter, mademoiselle. Lately of Munich."

"How do you do? I'm Kim Tavistock." She paused. "Of, um, Uxley."

He seemed charmed by this, as he bowed and flashed a quick smile. There was something playful about him, but not far beneath that was a deep formality. She thought he had to strain not to click his heels.

"Allow me to escort you to the drawing room. We are waiting for you, you see."

She took his arm. "So they sent you after me."

"Not at all. I took it upon myself. I hope you do not mind."

When they entered the dining room, Georgi looked up to

see the two of them framed in the doorway. "Our lost guest
from Yorkshire," she declared. Hugh stood by Georgi, cradling
a drink.

"Well, I *hope* I'm not lost," Kim said, moving forward for
introductions. She met Sir Edgar and his wife Lady Beatrice, who
insisted she be called Bea. Sir Edgar, still florid from the tennis
match, was a large man with small, shrewd eyes. He extended a
meaty hand, seeming to take her measure. Bea was blessed with
a generous figure and that pale English skin untouched by the
sun. "The writer!" she pronounced. "And published, we understand. So glad you've come!"

Kim thanked her and turned to Georgi. "I hope I may wander
where I must—to get the essence of Summerhill?"

Georgi waved a hand. "You have free rein, my dear. If you get
lost, just pull on a bell cord, and we'll have you back in a trice."
Her stunning outfit made her the undoubted center of attention in the huge parlor, with its hand-painted Chinese wallpaper,
Amritsar rug and white ornamental plaster ceiling. "What will
you write up first?"

"I should very much like to see the famous down-valley view
of Summerhill and take a photo. Would you like to accompany
me? This is a good time of day for the shot."

Georgi made an incredulous face. "Climb the hill? Oh, not I!"

Erich von Ritter said, "Allow me to accompany you."

"Erich, really," Georgi said, "you just got here and have
no idea what view she's talking about. Hugh will take her, of
course." Von Ritter bowed his acquiescence. It occurred to her
then that Georgi and von Ritter might be lovers. The way she
looked at him was quite possessive.

Sir Edgar said, "Mind you, there's to be a storm. The big hill
is no place for you if we get a dousing."

Bea waved the comment off. "Oh, she mustn't miss the view, though. This is *journalism*, Edgar. She has deadlines. Best to go now, I should think."

With that nod of good-natured encouragement, Kim excused herself to change once more, this time into slacks and sturdy shoes. Hugh was not the companion she had planned on, but she could hardly demur now.

With her Leica hanging by its strap over one shoulder, she and Hugh left the house by the dining room's French doors. Outside, they crossed an extensive terrace anchored by urns full of ornamental grasses.

The sky had turned to purple smoke in the east, looming evidence for the dousing Sir Edgar had predicted.

"We'll just make it," Hugh said.

As they climbed the hill, Kim wanted to ask about von Ritter but thought she shouldn't show that kind of interest. Over the weekend, she would no doubt be able to find out how the Aberdares knew him, and perhaps discover if he was quite what he seemed, or if he might even be a German spy. Of course there was no reason why every German in England must be a foreign agent.

They came into a clearer view of the manor's beautiful mansard roof and its noble array of chimney stacks. On their way to the top, Hugh explained Summerhill's history, from its inception in 1790 as a palace for a duke and its succession of wealthy owners. He finished, "And now Summerhill's mine, I suppose."

"How fine to be part of that tradition," Kim said as a few splats of rain came in on a freshening wind.

"Yes, of course. It's a great weight of responsibility as well. I have to live up to it, and quite frankly, Georgi would have been better at it."

"I'm sure not. You look like this is your element!" And he did. She knew him to be thirty-four, a good ten years younger than his sister, and a stalwart of the East Midlands social set. He fell short of handsome but made up for it with his air of artless enthusiasm.

He smiled. "It's good to have someone new here. Someone who isn't Georgi's."

"Is Herr von Ritter Georgi's?"

"In her thrall, of course."

But this interesting line of conversation trailed off as they made the top of the hill. There, they could see the great house set against the rolling hills to the north, its graceful dome in splendid view, with the river a silver necklace at its throat. Summerhill was indeed a palace, but there was little time to admire the prospect. The blue-black storm front advanced.

Kim unsnapped the camera case, pulling out her Leica II, the camera she'd used since her *Inquirer* days. She quickly adjusted the rangefinder, hoping that the last of the sun would hit the dome just so. It did. She used the separate optic to frame the picture, holding the camera steady, and clicked off several shots.

"Lord Daventry, can we have you in the photo?"

He shrugged, and stood where she directed. "It feels wrong without my sister."

"Well, she had her chance," Kim said merrily.

He struck an aristocratic pose for the camera as she set a slower shutter speed and took the shot.

Thunder boomed, making clear they were not to be spared a dousing. Rain pattered down as Kim hastily put the camera in its case.

As they descended the hill, the rain began falling in earnest.

Hugh covered Kim's head with his jacket, circling his arm around her waist to steady her on the path. They raced across the lawn, laughing because they were kicking up as much water from below as they got from above.

They dashed through the French doors, stomping the water off their shoes and laughing at each other's state of soaking. Charlotte was just hurrying up with fresh towels, the Scotties at her heels.

"Not a very gracious welcome to Summerhill," Hugh apologized as his valet appeared to assist him.

"On the contrary, it was an adventure! In fact, I loved it."

Hugh produced a boyish smile. "I dare say I did too."

Heavy rains threw a dark curtain over the estate grounds, pounding on the flagstone walks and obscuring the view out the parlor windows so that she could no longer see the bridge over the river.

Tea was a subdued affair interrupted by rolls of thunder. Hugh poured a shot of bourbon in his tea on the sly, but Kim supposed the lord of the manor could do as he wished. Erich von Ritter paid court to Georgi, so that Kim had little chance of a private chat with either of them. Still, how extraordinary it was to be in this patrician home, ferreting out possible traitors to the realm. She wasn't sure what she could accomplish, but she loved that she had dared to come. The idea that she could be useful, and bravely so, stirred her.

She didn't want to diminish her purpose. But it was actually all rather fun.

At dinner, the storm showed no sign of weakening, but the occasion was a glittering one, with lit tapers and sparkling crystal. Kim sat between Sir Edgar and Bea, with Hugh at the head of the table, and next to von Ritter, Georgi in an emerald green backless dress.

Georgi paused over the consommé. "Kim, Julian tells me that you're managing a renovation of Wrenfell at Uxley. I'm sure I wouldn't know where to begin if I were you."

"Perhaps a dome?" quipped Sir Edgar.

Georgi laughed.

"Well, I've been thinking of converting the piggery into a guest cottage," Kim said. "Extra buildings are so useful that way." It was naive-sounding to mention such a humble thing at this table, but naive was exactly how she wished to sound, to put Georgi at ease.

"What on earth is a piggery?" Georgi said.

Thunder cracked overhead, shaking the French doors, as the rain fell down in sheets on the terrace.

Von Ritter laughed. "Georgiana, it is a shelter for pigs, of course. That is excellent, Miss Tavistock! Make use of everything." He raised his wineglass to her. "She is practical, like our German women."

The server offered the sole as von Ritter went on. "Your father is Julian Tavistock, in the whisky trade, Georgi tells me. We would have things in common, both of us in commerce. Do you think so?"

"Oh, I'm quite sure you would," Kim said. They might indeed get on, she thought.

"Kim is on the left, I'm afraid," Georgi said. "Worlds apart from her father. Yorkshire is full of Communists, I've heard." The way she said *Communists*, it did seem she was just being outrageous.

Von Ritter smiled, shaking his head. "Do not accuse her, Georgiana. She is without a champion at the table."

"I'm sure I will take up her cause," Bea huffed, "if no gentleman will. I think Yorkshire is known for its sheep, not its Communists!"

Kim said, "I'm afraid the biggest political controversy in Uxley is how to raise money for the new bells at All Saints." That was not entirely true, of course. It was women disrobing in public, but she hoped no one had heard of that in Northamptonshire, three hours away.

"Just as long as the anti-vivisectionists aren't successful in recruiting you," Georgi said with a wicked smile.

That was hitting a bit hard, Kim thought. She was about to reply when Sir Edgar jumped in. "Anti-vivisectionists? I dare say they're troublemakers! Why would they come after you?"

Georgi said, "Julian told me something about that affair, but I'm afraid I didn't get the details. Do tell, my dear."

Hugh helped himself to the platter of roast beef held by a servant. "I don't think she wants to, Georgi."

From somewhere, a draught flickered the candles, as though a servant had opened one of the many doors of the house. "Oh, I don't mind," Kim said, recovering. "I'm a hopeless animal lover, and I got in trouble with an article I wrote back in the States. It pointed out the terrible practices of researchers and their animal subjects."

"Perhaps science must take precedence?" von Ritter suggested.

"Oh, it did. They fired me."

Bea objected, "But they must have approved it if they published it!"

Kim was starting to warm to the woman. "Yes, but it was easier to let me go than face the hue and cry."

"So unfair," Georgi murmured, turning her attention to von Ritter.

When the women gathered alone in the drawing room and

Bea had excused herself to the powder room, Kim sat next to Georgi. Her own ankle-length chiffon with its flounce on the hem seemed hopelessly out of date. The slim silhouette was all the rage.

Kim opened by saying, "I think I got the last of the sun when I took my down-valley picture of Summerhill."

Georgi nodded, looking toward the windows, where rain fell steadily. "Just in time, then. It will be muddy for a week. It's why paved streets are so superior."

"I know what you mean. Sometimes I miss Philadelphia."

"Yes, you are quite the orphan, aren't you? Mother on one continent, father on another. And a father who's never home, is he?"

"He likes London, as you do. People are open-minded, willing to embrace new ideas, I suppose."

"Exactly. But at least *I* was here, and I did so hope your father and I were friends. Really, I am quite put out with him. So, my dear, what does he say about me?" She made a conspiratorial expression, as though it would be their little secret.

"Well, he said I should have been nicer to you. And I feel awful if I wasn't!"

"Nonsense, you were utterly charming, in your own way. Your father speaks so highly of you and how you are taking Wrenfell on as a project. My brother, on the other hand, is hopeless when it comes to practical affairs, and I get dragged into Summerhill business. It's why I'm here now. Quite trying, actually."

"It doesn't seem fair. Naturally, you have your own interests."

"Well, at last, someone who understands me!"

Bea was just returning. "Really, Georgiana. As though we don't all fawn upon you. And Hugh is your biggest supporter, of course."

Georgi shrugged. "Good old Hughy." She shook her head. "The way he's mismanaged things. He's bled his fortune dry, you know."

The comment fell flat as Bea and Kim shuffled in their seats. Georgi had lost her poise, parting her lips to speak and then thinking better of it.

As a server approached with a tray of sherry, Bea took one, saying brightly, "Well, here are the men, joining us early."

Hugh, Sir Edgar and von Ritter had come in, trailing the smell of expensive cigars. Kim had a moment to consider that Georgi had blurted something she must regret. Something that, if true, she would not have told Kim, and perhaps not even Bea.

Before long, Georgi was playing hostess with the larger group, where they were engaged in a discussion of the political divide in Spain. Sir Edgar held forth against Communist agitators, who obviously incited violence in the cities, with Bea insisting that secularism was a great destabilizer and one must really sympathize with the plight of the Catholics. No one spoke up for the Republicans. They were all certain of the virtue of their right-leaning views. Her gaze traveled over the group. She could well imagine any one of them working for the Nazis. But did any of them—did Georgi—know if Fitzroy Blum was a spy?

She drifted to the fireplace, where a lovely fire had gone to embers.

Von Ritter separated himself from the conversation and brought her an aperitif in a striking color of green. "In honor of Lady Georgiana's dress," he said.

"Oh, it looks like cough syrup!"

"Take it, Miss Tavistock. It will do you good." He sat next to her on the divan.

"Am I in need?" she asked, taking a sip.

"Georgiana can be vicious. And it is her . . . how do you say . . . her lawn?"

"Her turf. Yes, it certainly is her turf! But I think she's just high-spirited, don't you?"

He smiled as though she had said something terribly witty. "Would this be the Yorkshire part of you or the Philadelphia?"

Kim smiled in return. "Both, probably!" She sipped her cordial. "I take it you mean to warn me about Georgi. But surely you wouldn't have come to Summerhill if you didn't expect to enjoy her company."

"Oh, I do enjoy her. And now you are here. It is delightful."

As he sat at her side, he kept watch as Georgi snaked her way among the guests.

"Thank you. But I don't hope to compete with our hostess."

He turned to her. He had very dark eyes, almost unnaturally deep. "Perhaps you do not give yourself enough credit."

She blushed. He did fluster her. He was really quite unfairly handsome.

From across the room, Georgi beckoned to him. Von Ritter stood and turned to Kim. "Offer me your hand."

She did so and he bowed, taking her hand and kissing it. "She will hate that," he said.

Kim watched as he went back to Georgi's side. An attractive man. Playful. A little dangerous, she thought.

The evening deepened, and rounds of conversation continued in the group at large rather than in more exploitable, intimate ones. It was 11:24 by Kim's watch when Georgi signaled that they might retire.

She lay in bed a long time before sleep came. Whatever secrets the Summerhill crowd held, they were still locked away. Methodically, she began to order the few pieces she did have. Von

Ritter was smooth, his sociability tinged with blatant flirtation. He seemed just the sort who could be a German agent. Hugh and Georgi had a complicated relationship, a mixture of affection and resentment. Most interesting so far, Georgi's startling comment about her brother being ruined. Was it possible that a man with so grand an estate could be in financial trouble? A *spill*, it had to be. But wouldn't treason be her foremost secret, if in fact she harbored such thoughts?

Despite having little to show for her efforts so far, she found herself surprisingly at ease with her clandestine role, even using her *spill* ability. She had to admit that her Talent had begun to feel like a more welcome part of herself. At least in service to a worthwhile thing.

10

SUMMERHILL ESTATE, NORTHAMPTONSHIRE

SATURDAY, APRIL 18. "How is Rose doing?" Kim asked, using the telephone in the foyer.

Alice's voice sounded reedy as the storm played havoc with the telephone lines. "Well, we've got the curtsy down, that's sure. But she's on edge with the storm. She's worse than the dogs for shying away at the thunder."

"Oh, is it bad up there?" There had been a steady downpour at Summerhill all night, but it seemed to be tapering off.

"You never heard such a clamor! And the river is up too, so they're worried about it breaching the banks down at Coomsby. So, how's Summerhill? Is it grand?"

"Yes, it's a regular castle. Adjectives fail me."

"Hear that? This thunder is—" The end of her sentence was lost.

Kim brought the mouthpiece closer. "Hello, Alice? Alice,

can you hear me?" But the connection was gone. "Drat." She replaced the receiver.

Hugh came down the staircase, looking a bit worse for wear. He had missed breakfast, but there would be plenty of eggs, kidneys, bacon and haddock left on the sideboard.

"Join me for breakfast?" he asked. "It's too dismal to eat alone."

"Of course. Perhaps afterward, you can show me your car collection. I'd love to get a picture of the Bentley."

"We'll need a canoe to the get to the garage."

"Let's take a look outside. I think it's all very dramatic. A storm at the castle!"

"You can't mean to head out into this bloody mess."

"Just a peek. It's my reporter instinct." She went to the front door and opened it, Hugh following. Rain slanted across the front lawn on the wind.

Hugh peered out. "I say, it's—"

"Loxley! Parker!" shrieked a woman's voice from behind them.

Down the stairs raced the Scotties, trailing their leashes, with Charlotte in pursuit.

Hugh cursed as the dogs converged on him, yapping, leashes wrapping around his ankles. As Hugh shook himself loose, the puppies raced out the door. Kim lunged for a leash, but it was already snaking out of reach as the Scotties each tore off in different directions.

Charlotte burst out onto the porch, calling them. When she turned back, she said, "Oh no, what will Lady Georgiana say? Oh, your Lordship, I'm sorry, I didn't know how to stop them. They got loose and—"

"Don't worry, Charlotte! Send Frank and Peter after them. We'll soon get them rounded up."

Kim made for the staircase, rushing up.

Hugh called after her, "Where the deuce are you going?"

"I'm going to find them!"

He hurried after her, catching up with her at the head of the stairs.

"It's my fault, I opened the doors," she explained.

He looked at her as though she had lost her mind. "You do things your own way, don't you?" He rushed down the hall, calling back to her, "I'm coming with you."

When Kim emerged from her room clad in sturdy boots and a man's rain slicker that she'd found in the armoire, Hugh was nowhere to be seen. She hurried to the front door just as she heard voices approaching from the parlor. She slipped out.

In the yard, she couldn't she see very far in the steady rain, but the dogs' white coats should be a help. She'd seen the direction that one of them took, down the slope of the lawn toward the boathouse. She hurried in that direction. As she drew closer to the swollen river, she saw that it was moving very fast.

"Loxley!" she called. "Here, boy! Parker, come!"

The current tore past the boathouse, nearly engulfing the dock. Under the boathouse eaves, no Scotties took refuge. She walked along the bank of the river, calling to the pups.

Ahead was the gazebo on its promontory in the river. Beyond lay a copse of trees marching into a vale, reminding her how unlikely it was that one could find an animal that didn't wish to be found. She began to feel a pang of fear for the dogs. Animals racing out from imprisonment was an indelible memory, that of deep snows and a frozen pond. And the thing that waited for the animals. Her fault. All of it so close upon Robert's death that events had conflated in her eleven-year old mind: senseless death, and the innocents who were made to face it.

When she came up to the neck of land that led to the gazebo, she saw that water was starting to lap onto the spit. Charging across, she gained the gazebo just as she noted someone hurrying toward her across the lawn. Hugh must have caught up to her.

She had just kneeled down to look under the benches that formed a collar around the five-sided structure when Erich von Ritter tramped in.

"You are determined to be the heroine," he said. He wore a belted double-breasted trench coat but no hat. He had rushed out to find her, perhaps.

She got to her feet. "They're not here."

"The staff will find them. Let me escort you back before the river rises."

"If they came down here, they might have been swept away." She looked down river, watchful for white spots in the churn.

Von Ritter took her arm. "Shall we go back?" He guided her to the gazebo opening, but they paused there, seeing that the water had already flooded over the spit.

"We can wade," Kim said.

"No, the river is too fast. It is rising even as we speak." The spit was a torrent, a second arm of the river.

A crash to her left caused her to jump. The two canoes tied to moorings on the spit had just broken free and were racing with the river toward the bridge.

"I suggest we wait it out," von Ritter said. "The river was to crest this morning. Give it an hour." He reached into the pocket of his suit and retrieved a cigarette case. Snapping it open, he offered her one. She'd given up smoking two years earlier, but if one could not smoke while stranded in a raging river, when could one?

Using his lighter, he lit her cigarette, then his own. "I am afraid Georgiana is forming up a firing squad. Your maid is done for."

She inhaled the smoke with a rush of pleasure. "But the puppies will come home full of mud, having had an adventure."

"All the worse, if they had fun," he said, smiling.

"I suppose you're right." Clotted fog rolled down the river, enclosing them in whiteness. "It's freezing out here."

"Take my coat." He unbelted his trench coat and instructed her to take off the slicker so she could wear the coat under it.

"You'll be cold," she protested but, cigarette dangling from her lips, she shrugged into the trench coat, tying the belt snuggly. They sat on the bench. Von Ritter draped the slicker over both of them, and with his arm around her shoulders, warmth returned. She was acutely aware of their shoulders touching, the intimacy of the shared garment.

They smoked, listening to the river rushing by. Von Ritter seemed content to enjoy his cigarette. But silence was against her purpose.

"How do you happen to know Georgi?" Kim asked.

"We met in Bonn when she was on holiday, and by chance we were both on the same train down the Rhine Gorge. She was with people, and she added me on as she does."

"So you're one of Georgi's people."

He glanced up. "No, I think that rather she is one of mine." That did seem rather pointed, as though he were keeping score. "Are you warm enough? Here, come closer, or we will never make it to luncheon."

"I thought you said one hour," she chided, but sidled in to him. Heat radiated beneath the raincoat, but whether it came from him or was a flush of her own, she could not tell.

He went on. "Georgi has the German viewpoint. Very forward-thinking, unlike some of your countrymen."

"I can't pretend to agree."

"No, I should not like you to pretend." They watched as branches swept by in the swollen water, all racing under the arched bridge some fifty yards downstream.

"Is the water rising?" she asked, trying to see the spit through the gazebo door.

"I cannot tell from here. I would have to get up from our snug nest to see," he said good-naturedly.

"Never mind." From far in the distance, someone called for Loxley. The pups had perhaps gotten to Northampton by now.

As they sat in silence, Kim decided she could get by with an artless stab at her topic. "There may be a war," she ventured. "Your country and mine."

"It need not come to that." He adjusted his arm around her shoulder. "Lean into me. For warmth. It does no harm until we are enemies."

It was only sharing a rain slicker in a storm, and even if he might be a Nazi, he could hardly be motivated to throw her in the river.

"We do not need a war of arms. It is rather a war of ideas," he said. "We are on the eve of a great change, Miss Tavistock. You know what it is I am referring to?" She wasn't sure, and remained silent. He went on. "The *bloom*. It has changed everything—how we regard the world—our powers of accomplishment. It is a new regime, hovering so close, we do not think to look up to see it envelop us."

She did not like it that he had brought up the topic. It threw her off. She would use the *bloom* against him and preferred not to have the subject in play.

The rain crackled on the gazebo roof, streaming off the eaves. "A lot of people would prefer not to think about it," she said. "We don't know what it will really mean for any of us."

"It means that great men will rise."

"Does it?"

"It means that great leaders will become prophets of change. We have such a man in Germany." He glanced sideways at her. "Whatever you may think of us." He flicked his cigarette into the river. "In this country, you have no great men. Churchill is a nineteenth-century throwback, still yearning for empire. The *bloom* has brought us to a new level. Men of high Talent who direct destinies. Choristers, if you will."

"Choristers?"

He paused as a gust of wind brought a torrent of staccato pattering on the roof. "A figure of speech."

"Such an interesting word."

"Is it?"

"Yes, as though we're all singing the same song." She added, trying for an ironic tone, *"Deutschland Über Alles."* From the national anthem of Germany.

"Perhaps. But a chorister will bring you down."

She had not heard the word before and thought that perhaps he had used the wrong English word. "Do you mean Hitler? He is a chorister?"

"No. One of your own," he said.

"But who?"

He stared at the river. "I did not think you were so interested in politics, Miss Tavistock."

"Well, I'm interested in most things."

"Ah, the reporter. Saving animals. It is all very noble." He separated from their embrace to turn to look her at her. "You would have made a good German."

She met his dark gaze, wanting to appear friendly, but not in a way that would arouse suspicion. "I think not."

"Of course, you are loyal with reason. Georgiana told me that you lost a brother in the Great War. I am sorry."

He had no right to raise that particular subject. Georgi had no right to have shared it. "I think we should go back." She made to get up, but he put his hand on her knee, restraining her.

"You do not talk about your brother?"

"I . . . I don't."

"How was he killed?"

The mist thinned. Lights from the house pierced the tattered wool of the fog. She gazed in the direction of the invisible manor.

"In Belgium. At Ypres."

"Ah, Ypres," he said softly.

"He charged into the fray on his horse. It was his favorite black, one he had at Wrenfell."

"But Ypres was not a battle for the horses."

"It . . . it was not. Not that day." The day, as she had imagined it for so many years, came to her vividly. "Robert was an expert horseman. But that day, that afternoon, his captain was killed, and though he was only an acting sublieutenant, it fell to Robert to lead the attack. They were retaking the village. It had been raining for weeks and he came over the hill. Just beyond was a crater that appeared to be a slight gully. As he galloped through, the sides . . ."

Von Ritter's face reflected that he knew what came next.

She stammered, "It . . . it—"

"—collapsed, did it not? There was no escape."

"Several riders were caught. The mud lay thick at the bottom, trapping the horses' legs. The men dismounted, trying to help their mounts, trying to escape, but it was so deep, they couldn't move. With the attack rushing forward over the nearby ground, the sides gave way, sliding down into the crater. They all drowned, with their horses." Tears streamed down her face.

Von Ritter's hand went to her knee again, pressing it. "He died a hero."

They sat in stillness for a time. She let the cold breeze clear her eyes. They had drowned. In their innocence, in their nobility. When her mother learned this, the manner of Robert's death, she had run mad with grief. The household descended into further sorrow and horror. Many families lost sons. But this was Robert, the only son, the only brother. The memory pierced her anew.

The neck of land leading from the gazebo was now just a few inches deep in water. A servant had come down from the house with a flashlight. *Torch* they call it, she reminded herself. A dull chill had overtaken her. As the servant led the way, she and von Ritter splashed across the spit, walking slowly up to the house. Summerhill must have lost power, because the windows were dark.

She was numb. How, *how* had she revealed this old, private wound to a person she hardly knew? And to a German?

Then she knew. She had *spilled* to him. She had never *spilled* to anyone before, but in this instance, she was quite sure. He had turned the tables on her.

Von Ritter had a Talent, a very strong one. It could have been worse. She could have told him about her work at Monkton Hall, that she was a *spill*, what she was really doing at Summerhill. But at the moment, all she felt was disgust.

As Kim and von Ritter entered the candlelit foyer, Hugh and Georgi were arguing.

Hugh refused to dismiss Charlotte, and Georgi was laying down a withering fire against his position. Kim explained how the puppies' escape had been her fault, but Hugh and his sister barely heard the pronouncement. Strangers could have no role in the family war.

As Kim made her way up the staircase to her room, von Ritter was the only one who noticed. He was watching her with a dark intensity she had not seen in him before.

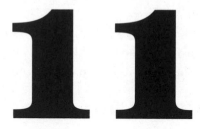

11

WHITE'S, A GENTLEMAN'S CLUB, LONDON

SATURDAY, APRIL 18. Sir Simon Harwell was one of Julian's favorite lunch companions. Ruddy-complexioned, both sly and humorous, he had a knack for gossip, unwittingly providing the occasional tidbit of information for SIS consumption. The two men enjoyed a lamb cutlet and smoked trout luncheon at White's, the exclusive gentlemen's club to which E—and the Duke of Cambridge—also belonged. It was said that the staff at White's was so exceptionally discreet that E had his most sensitive post delivered to White's rather than his office.

Harwell noted the arrival of a trim man in impeccable dress who was seated alone, across the room. "That fellow in the corner, Tavistock. Do you know him?"

Glancing over, Julian replied, "Civil service, isn't he? Something to do with the War Office, if I'm not mistaken."

Thin and alert, the man sat alone at the table, with perfect posture, squinting at his sole in cream through wire spectacles.

"Heath Millington. Alistair Drake's right hand man."

"Ah, that's up there, isn't it? The Joint Intelligence Committee, then." Julian was at pains to appear clueless about politics. Simon Harwell had striven to rectify this over ten years of lunches without making significant headway.

"No, old boy, he's with the CID, Committee for Imperial Defence. The PM chairs it, but nothing's on the docket unless Heath Millington has run the numbers." He leaned in. "The blighter has the sharpest tongue at CID and even the PM is afraid of him."

"The devil he is." Julian cut another glance at the man.

"The trouble with you, Tavistock, is that you judge everyone by the cut of his jib. Learn to look beneath. There's no end of entertainment!"

Over pears à la Condé, Julian saw E enter the dining room to be shown a table by the window.

"Now there's a toff for you," Harwell said. "His wife's money. Has all the best connections in Whitehall."

"Does he, now. I was at Eton with him."

"In the intelligence service is the rumor, rather high up."

"Do you mean to say he's a spymaster?" Julian let a bit of incredulity into his voice.

Harwell shrugged. "The stories he could tell, eh?"

"I dare say. Well, his secret's good with me."

Soon after, Julian left the club for the short walk to his flat. His umbrella tossed about in the wind as he walked down St. James's Street. As was his custom, he stopped for the paper at a certain newsstand where a field agent might also happen to browse.

The newsagent was tucked under the eaves of the stand, out

of the wind. He nodded at Julian, a frequent customer. Julian recognized the man standing nearby perusing a magazine, but they didn't take note of each other. Rory left when he was sure Julian had seen him, and turned up the street to duck into a crowded tearoom. Tucking a newly purchased paper under his arm, Julian followed, gaining the entryway packed with patrons with their umbrellas. He looked around as though sizing up the competition for tables. As he did so, Rory worked his way next to him and informed him that "the Chemist" had turned up at the country home of "Sunflower." Receiving a nod that he'd been heard, the agent left. Julian waited a couple of minutes and, muttering about the wait, ducked back out onto the street.

Von Ritter was at Summerhill. It would have been better to have known this the moment the man left London, but he had given them the slip. Now their contact at Summerhill had managed to get word to London. It seemed Julian would be spending a weekend with Georgi after all. Last week she had invited him once again, but with von Ritter in London, he had turned her down.

At his flat, he made quick work of packing for a country weekend as he framed an excuse for having changed his mind. He tried to call ahead, but the operator couldn't make the connection due to telephone lines being down.

It was the devil getting a taxi in the rain, but eventually, he commandeered one. On the way to King's Cross Station, he thought about von Ritter being at Summerhill and wondered who he was there to see, or whether he was just polishing his image among the aristocratic set with their valuable connections to the royal family or Whitehall.

He took his seat on the 2:07, soon joined by an elderly woman who wrestled a portmanteau and herself into the seat opposite. He hadn't expected to see Elsa.

As the train pulled out of the station, she retrieved her knitting from a little cloth bag on wooden legs. Amid the knits and purls of her flying needles, she managed to impart the names of the others in residence that weekend at Sunflower's house. They were, besides von Ritter, Hugh Aberdare, Sir Edgar and Beatrice Thackeray. And Kim Tavistock.

Julian let this information settle in, watching Elsa knit, listening to the rhythmic beat of the wheels on rails. The clacking of the train created a calm suspension of the world, as though one might pass through it without needing to enter the fray. But sooner or later, the train would stop. Kim at Summerhill. How extraordinary.

Talking casually as she knitted, Elsa said that Kim, whom she referred to with a code name, "Sparrow," was writing up a story on Summerhill and had taken photographs of the home.

Very bad timing, Kim. She had always had bad timing.

The train chuffed on into Herefordshire with its enclosed fields, and in the near distance, the Chiltern Hills, its woodlands black in the rain. How singular that Kim would be writing an article about Georgi's country house—much less spending a whole weekend there—when she disliked the woman. Unfortunate that she had chosen to do so when Erich von Ritter was there, but if one were going to see Georgi Aberdare, one would likely find her in the company of some of her German friends.

Always before, his job and his personal life had remained separate. It was highly unlikely that the two would overlap, especially as he had only his daughter to consider. Damned nuisance, E had said about her involvement with Monkton Hall. Now this. But of course, it wasn't just this Summerhill business. His intelligence cover might be secure, but his relationship with his daughter . . . he admitted, it suffered. She had the *spill*. He had secrets. A bad combination, one he was at pains to thwart by a remote stance with his daughter. There were times when he wondered what he had given up, if he had in some way lost both his children and, this time out, it was his fault.

Coming around a curve, the train slowed. They were deep into Bramingham Wood. The train rolled to a sudden halt, with luggage shifting in the rack above and people leaning to the windows to see why the train was stopping.

Word soon swept through the carriages. A mudslide on the tracks.

He and Elsa exchanged glances. "Oh, dear," she said in a convincing tremulous voice. "Now what?"

PARISER PLATZ, BERLIN

SATURDAY, APRIL 18. In Pariser Platz, not far from the Brandenburg Gate, the rain fell in silver sheets. Kurt Stelling stood in a doorway, watching number five. He could see activity in the mansion and hoped that the tenant was at home and might leave for lunch or on some other errand of state. He would wait and watch.

He was hiding in the very heartland of his enemies. *Enemies.* It was strange to think that the country he loved had become his foe. Strange also to think how suddenly he had come to ruin. His intense attraction to the handsome Erich von Ritter had unmasked him. And the man had been so outraged, he would not let it go.

Soon, they would be hunting him. But not yet, he hoped. When they discovered his escape, they would watch all the embassies. He must find refuge that afternoon.

His plan had worked perfectly so far. His first step had been to replace his usual driver with one who had a similar build to himself. That had been last week, when he had found fault with Corporal Breck and assigned Sergeant Dressler to drive when he toured the camp.

The previous evening, he had checked his Luger by breaking it down and reassembling it. There would be little point in trying to shoot his way out of any trouble, but it must work flawlessly should he need to turn it on himself.

At 10:34 that morning, just close enough to lunch for ideal timing of the second leg of his plan, he called his adjutant into his office. The lieutenant came to attention and saluted.

Colonel Stelling returned the salute, stiffening his demeanor, but not too much, not wishing to overplay it.

"Lieutenant Hass, I have matters to take care of and will be gone for a few days."

"Yes, Colonel."

He could see Hass's surprise, though the man tried to hide it. Hass might think that his commanding officer was up to something, especially if it had been Hass who put the triangle on his desk. But Stelling had planned for that, orchestrating these few minutes carefully, to strike a certain tone of confusion and concern.

He glanced away as though he were viewing some awful scene, one that had been playing through his mind and now stalked him minute by minute. "I am called to Berlin."

Hass waited for his orders.

"I expect to be gone for three days. Four at the most. You will take command in my absence."

Hass nodded his understanding. "Yes, sir."

Again, Stelling looked to the side, letting Hass wait, adding to the image of a distracted man, but not a panicked one.

Hass finally said, "When will you leave, Colonel?"

"Immediately. Tell my driver to be ready in twenty minutes. And to pack a bag for a three-day trip. I will not need him once in Berlin, but he must be ready to return with me on Tuesday."

"Yes, Colonel. Right away."

Stelling did not dismiss him but turned to the window and clasped his hands behind his back. He left the lieutenant standing for a few moments. When he turned back, he said, "You know all that must be done with our elite inmates. See that no mistakes are made." He hoped that would place a suggestion with the lieutenant that he thought he was being called to Berlin because of something with *Sturmweg* that he had bungled. "I trust you will handle your new duties with the utmost care. Everything by strict procedures. You understand?"

"Yes, Colonel! It will be done."

"That will be all, Lieutenant." When Hass left the office, Stelling waited a few minutes, then walked to his room across the yard in the officers' quarters to pack. Liverwurst sandwiches waited on his table, as he had ordered. He opened one and laced it with a small amount of a pesticide used to control vermin. Opening the other sandwich, he transferred the mustard to the poisoned sandwich to help cover the taste. He hoped it was a suitable dose to sicken the man without the obvious need for a doctor.

He left twenty-five minutes later with Dressler at the wheel. After lunch on the road in Dallgow-Döberitz when his driver became ill and vomited, Stelling insisted that he could not drive and left him to rest at a farmhouse, saying that he must rush to Berlin without him and would see that he was picked up on the way back. While the husband and wife took in the driver, Stelling drove off with Dressler's kit as though he had been in such a rush that he had forgotten to leave it at the farmhouse.

Now he had a very useful shirt, sweater, pants and shoes that Dressler had planned to use when off duty.

That was what Stelling wore when he walked into a clothier on the outskirts of Berlin and bought a suit. His driver's clothes did not fit him perfectly and might draw attention to him.

Those hours had been perilous, but this surveillance of Pariser Platz was the most desperate. If the ambassador, André François-Poncet, did not take him in, he had no other diplomatic contacts. He would have to attempt communication at one embassy after the next, all within blocks of the Reichstag.

He and François-Poncet had met two years earlier at a dinner in Berlin. If the man remembered him, he might at least hear him out. The deep flaw of this plan was the chance that François-Poncet no longer held his post or was not in residence today. The British embassy might be his next try, but he thought extraction to Paris infinitely safer than to London.

There was only one reason why François-Poncet or his successor would risk getting him out of Germany. But Stelling was in no way sure they would realize his value. He had little choice. If he was to succeed, it must be in the next few hours before his ruse of being called to Berlin was discovered. He stared hard at the blue front door of the embassy and the beautifully framed windows of its ground floor.

In the distance, a pounding noise. If he hadn't been paying such strict attention to the embassy, he would have been aware earlier of the sounds of discordant music. And marching feet. To the right, on the far side of the plaza, a formation of Brownshirts marched up Wilhelmstrasse to the intersection of the Unter den Linden and turned away, Nazi flags heavy with rainwater. The boots of the SA pounded in admirable unison as they followed the flag bearers. Stelling would have given the Nazi salute—it was dangerous not to—but the storm troopers were a block away and took no notice of a man huddled in a closed office building doorway on the plaza.

At 2:45, a Rolls-Royce came around from the back of the embassy gate and drove under the porte cochere. Stelling hurried across the street. When he saw someone emerge from the house, he called out, *"Monsieur François-Poncet, un moment. Je suis un ami!"* He called himself a friend. An exaggeration.

The man turned to look at him. Yes. It was he. One of his attendants moved to the gate to investigate.

The ambassador moved to the edge of the porch. *"Qui êtes-vous?"*

"Colonel Kurt Stelling. Nous sommes rencontrés deux ans auparavant à la réception de l'Ambassadeur de Pologne." A wave of relief washed over him as François-Poncet walked down the driveway toward him.

When he was a few paces from the wrought iron fence, the ambassador said in German, "What is this, Colonel Stelling?"

"Sturmweg," Stelling whispered. He leaned into the gap in the fence. "It is *Sturmweg*, monsieur. I am at your mercy. And so is England."

A few seconds passed as the rain splattered on the ambassador's impeccably tailored coat and hat. The Brownshirt band grew louder as it turned back on its route to the Reichstag.

Stelling held on to the gate until he felt it begin to open.

13

SATURDAY, APRIL 18. Kim woke from a dead sleep late in the afternoon. She had intended to lie down for only twenty minutes after luncheon to collect herself. The morning had shaken her, with her search for the dogs and finding herself sharing a coat—and more—with von Ritter.

The house lay in deep quiet. With an hour until tea, Kim decided to preserve her cover by exploring the house and taking notes. Notebook in hand and camera slung over her shoulder on its strap, she made her way in the direction of the solarium. The power was still out, darkening the hallways and stealing the color from rooms she passed—a billiard room, den and library— all cloaked in gray.

After wandering into a few dead ends, she found the long gallery she had been told to expect. An array of windows splashed a sodden light on a long wall of paintings. The windows gave onto a courtyard, and in a parallel wing across the way, another hall flanked by windows. There she saw two people talking. Sir Edgar and Erich von Ritter. No reason why they shouldn't be there, but it was not close to either the parlor or the guest rooms.

She backed away so that she could observe them without being seen. Sir Edgar, to her mind, was not bright enough to be engaged in anything subversive. His wife, however, had an intelligence cloaked by drawing-room cheeriness. It could all be harmless. And yet, since any spies would be at pains to hide their purposes, how could she know? She supposed that, in this line of work, one must cultivate suspicion in everyone.

She began to examine the paintings in the gallery. As she looked at one of them, a scene of snarling hounds cornering a fox, she heard the sound, very faint, of barking. The Scotties!

As she moved down the gallery, the yapping grew louder until she found herself facing a door from which the sound was coming. Turning the doorknob, she found a stairway down. Louder barking assailed her. It was more than one dog, and they were close by. Halfway down the stairs, she found herself in dark gloom, with only a splash of light coming from upstairs.

"Here, Parker!" she called. "Here, Loxley!" A furious cascade of puppy yaps greeted her, but muffled.

"Here, Parker, come!" she called as she descended.

A sound from behind startled her. She whirled around, heart racing. A figure stood on the stairs, a dark silhouette lit from behind.

"Miss Tavistock?"

"Oh, yes? Who's there?"

"Beggin' your pardon, miss. It's Peter, the footman. I din't mean to frighten you! I saw the door open. . . ."

"Oh, that's all right, but the Scotties are here! Can you hear them?"

He had a flashlight and approached her, keeping the beam on the floor. "You're right, miss, I hear 'em!" He aimed the light at the door across the narrow hall. "In there. They must have come in to the old cellar for shelter. One o' those mole holes, like as not." He went to the door. "Could you call to them when I open the door? They're not keen on me, and they might hide back in storage."

"Of course. And they probably still have their leashes on, so they'll be easy to catch!"

Peter opened the door, but no coaxing was necessary. The Scotties rushed at them, yapping with excitement. Redolent with mud, they nearly bowled Kim over, but she managed to maintain her balance as Peter grabbed the leashes.

"Found you!" Kim cried in relief.

As they started up the stairs, Peter said, "You might not want to stray so far, miss. The house, as big as it is, and so few of us here."

"Well, I can hardly get lost inside Summerhill."

"No, miss. But there's parts of the house not used. If you took a fall, and with no one around . . ."

"Thank you, Peter. I'll remember that."

Kim made a grand entrance into the sitting room. The puppies were caked in filth, and Parker—or was it Loxley—took that moment to shake himself vigorously, flinging out dried mud.

Georgi rose, gasping, "Thank God!"

Hugh strode forward to greet her, grinning. "Well done, well *done*! Where on earth did you find them?"

And now Bea and Sir Edgar chimed in and Kim was made to recount how it had all come about, as Peter was sent off with orders for puppy baths.

"They were in the basement the whole time," Kim announced, trying to make a point for Charlotte's sake. "So, no harm was done!"

Erich von Ritter approached her with a glass of sherry, bending into her and murmuring. "You are a Valkyrie. My congratulations."

To her chagrin, she found herself heavily blushing under his admiration. But why was he so attentive? Perhaps it was his game to bring most women to heel. For a moment, she thought he might have the Talent of *attraction*, so strong was his appeal. But of course, after the gazebo, she knew what his gift was.

Dinner had been cold cuts on the sideboard lit with candles. Everyone was in a fine mood with the rescue of the dogs, and Kim received her compliments in a self-deprecating manner. She didn't want to be known for her sleuthing.

Coffee—which the servants had managed using a fireplace in the kitchen—was served before a splendid and more decorative fire in the parlor. Rain, blown by a freshening wind, pattered against the windows. It seemed the storm was hovering right over Summerhill, reluctant to relinquish its command of the mansion.

Von Ritter sat next to Kim on the divan, and as Sir Edgar related a longish story about a lost collie, the German pursued a quiet side discussion with her. He wore an expensive camel-hair suit that set off his black hair and eyes, a contrast to Hugh who, slouching against the mantel, looked rather rumpled.

Kim did not wish to incur Georgi's jealousy, if she and von Ritter were lovers, but she had begun to feel that von Ritter was a dangerous man, one her skills might unmask. It was as though she was wandering through a maze, unsure of the next turn but forced to choose a path by guesswork. This German business-man was not the focus of her mission as prescribed by Owen. Yet she found herself captivated by a journalistic penchant. The pursuit of a story—or, in this case, the thrill of the chase.

Watching Sir Edgar, von Ritter said in an undertone, "You *would* march on to save the little dogs. I have confidence in you, now that you accomplish what others could not."

"It was just luck."

"But mademoiselle, there is no such thing as good or bad luck. Only merit or lack of it."

"Whose fault, the dogs, then?"

"Charlotte's, of course." He sipped his port.

"But I opened the door!"

He turned to her. "Miss Tavistock. I do not think you believe this. I think you like to seem gracious."

"Oh, and I am not really gracious?" she said, teasing him.

"You are not a girl of a Yorkshire farm." She waited, trying not to let her smile wobble. It wasn't easy to meet his gaze, because for some reason, he seemed more direct than before.

"No," he went on, "not so much a Yorkshire girl. More a woman of the world."

"I take that as a compliment," she said breezily.

He turned more toward her, draping his arm along the back of the divan. "Of course, you are not completely from Yorkshire. But from the United States of late. True?"

"Georgiana, again?" she said teasingly. He shrugged as though Georgi were the last thing on his mind. "Well, I've been back three years. This feels like home now."

"Does it?" He looked more closely at her as though he could tell by her expression whether she truly meant this. "I wonder if these people accept one outside their own class so easily."

"Well, perhaps not easily. But Uxley does." It sounded a bit prim. She had an urge not to be prim around him. And how very strange. Surely she could not be attracted to someone whose ideology was Nazism.

He didn't seem to be listening to her, as he allowed his gaze to trail over her face, her hair, in a quite personal manner. She noted that her sweating hands left a stain on her silk skirt.

"You are a warrior maiden," he murmured, with the ghost of a smile. "This is what I think. Am I wrong?"

"You are thinking of opera. Wagner?"

His smile deepened, as though she were being very clever, and now he looked at her quite pointedly. "I am thinking of *you*. And you keep me . . . let me see, the expression is . . . *at bay*?"

"But we're just getting to know each other, Herr von Ritter."

"We know each other." He seemed very certain—of something. She felt pinned by his dark gaze.

Georgi was watching them, obviously bored with Sir Edgar.

"The storm," Kim murmured. He meant that they had shared deeply. More than mere strangers. "The gazebo."

His gaze traveled over her like a new owner surveying his property.

And why *his* property? Because he liked knowing something highly personal about her. If she wasn't wrong, he was enjoying the aftermath of the *spill*, having taken pleasure in subduing her natural reticence. He did seem intent on an emotional conquest, for what else could be his motive? Unless he knew she was a valuable *spill*, and hoped to woo her to his cause. But how indeed could he know that, when he could not have expected her to be at the weekend gathering, and therefore could not have checked on her at the compromised Monkton Hall?

To continue their conversations, she must pretend to be moved by him.

But Georgi was making an announcement.

"It's been a long day. Perhaps we should make an early evening of it. I'm completely worn out." She glanced at von Ritter, who gave the smallest smile, as though it were an agreement between them.

Hugh snorted. He pushed away from the fireplace, lurching a bit. "I thought we might have cards, but if you're moving the game upstairs . . ." He looked between his sister and von Ritter.

"Don't be revolting," Georgi snapped. "I'm going to check on Parker."

"Well then, goodnight. Kiss the dogs for me."

Georgi gave him a pitying glance and, rising, bid goodnight to her guests.

Von Ritter stood as well. "May I accompany you? I have a great affection for dogs."

She smirked her acquiescence, and von Ritter made a curt bow to the ladies, nodding to Hugh and Sir Edgar. And just like that, he had released Kim, as though he had suddenly concluded she could not entertain him. As the two of them left the parlor, in the fireplace the flames blazed higher under a downdraft.

Bea leaned in to her husband, patting his knee. "Enjoy your evening. Wake me if the river laps at the door." By Kim's watch, it was 10:23. Early for bed, by Summerhill standards. But with Bea's pronouncement, the ladies were retiring. She could not be the only who remained.

As Kim and Bea climbed the stairs, Bea murmured, "I hope that Georgi will not take Herr von Ritter too seriously. He is enchanting, but . . ."

"But?"

"Well. I do not think he is quite our sort."

Instantly attentive, Kim managed to make a polite, inquiring face.

Bea glanced at the empty hall down which Georgi and von Ritter had passed. "I don't trust him, my dear."

"Trust him?"

Bea paused as they reached Kim's bedroom door. "He's not English," she said with a frank stare.

"Well, German, of course."

"Precisely my point. He's entirely too clever to be just a businessman." But she did not intend to go further with the thought. She patted Kim's arm. "Goodnight, my dear. You don't seem the sort to thrive on gossip. But we do. Not always our best side." With that, she was off to her own room.

Kim watched her go. Not the sort to thrive on gossip? If only Bea knew, she was exactly the sort.

14

ALL SAINTS CHURCH, UXLEY

SUNDAY, APRIL 19. Organ music spilled into the churchyard as Alice Ward stood at her father's grave, clutching her umbrella against a rain-laden wind. With Mrs. Babbage and Rose nearby, she knelt to place a sprig of bluebells at his headstone.

The resting place of Regimental Sergeant Major Stanley Ward at All Saints looked upon the river at a place where the ground sloped gently toward the water. On nice Sunday mornings, the long shadow of the bell tower blanketed it.

VERDUN, 1916, the headstone noted.

Most of the dead from the war lay buried in France and Flanders either where they fell or in nearby military graveyards. But Alice's father had died of infection from his wounds in hospital in Dorset, and she'd been able to bury him at Uxley.

Visiting the grave made a nice way-stop before entering the church and gave Walter time to park the old Bedford truck down the street so that when they joined the congregation, Walter's solid presence might be an inducement to civility. Already people coming up the path to church were noting Rose and murmuring.

Walter came up the walk, and together the four of them went up the stairs to the open doors.

Alice and the Babbages became the center of attention. They chose seats in the back of the nave. Marcus Willoughby gave a decent nod to Alice, as well he might, being next door to the knittery with his dry goods. Across the aisle, Florence Hobbes gave them a cross look, muttering to her husband, who looked at Rose in some suspicion as though fearing she might disrobe in church.

Alice settled herself next to Rose, who wore her best flower-print dress with, thankfully, only one bulky sweater. Just when Alice thought they might get on just fine, Violet Layton and her husband turned to stare at them from two pews in front, setting off a few giggles from their boys Eugene and Rudy. Alice knew more about Violet and her husband than she wished she did. Under the woman's purple straw hat might be a purple bruise, she knew.

Now entering the church was Benny Simkins, not in uniform today, and old Howard Knightly, and here was Polly Fitzsimmons, and a dozen other people that Alice had known since childhood. She noted a couple people whom she did not know, perhaps guests of locals or tourists stranded by the weather.

"It's too warm," Rose said, rather too loud.

Quickly, Mrs. Babbage slipped her arm around her daughter, pulling her cardigan off her shoulders so that it slumped down on the pew back. "There you go now, Rose. We'll keep it 'andy, right i' back." Rose frowned, but as Alice took hold of her hand, she relaxed, settling back.

It was when everyone stood at James Hathaway's entrance

from the vicary, that Alice had her vision, her unwelcome *trauma view*. It was:

People standing in a long line.

James crossed the chancel to take a chair beside the pulpit, as Dorset Withers came to the lectern to read the scripture. But Alice hardly noticed this. What she was noticing was all in her head but also played out before her:

A white sky over a barren ground, a gully, defining the path that a long line of people must pass through.

Dorset's reading, normally in a voice that carried so well down the nave, turned murky, as though heard through a wool blanket. "Then shall the King say unto them on his right hand, Come, ye blessed of my Father, inherit the kingdom prepared for you from the foundation of the world."

They were featureless people, strangers to her. Some were dressed in fine suits, and some in laborers' garb, women and men. But they weren't walking; they were standing still, holding a long rope that joined them all.

"For I was an hungred, and ye gave me meat: I was thirsty, and ye gave me drink: I was a stranger and ye took me in: Naked, and ye clothed me: I was sick and ye visited me: I was in prison, and ye came unto me."

The white sky descended, covering the people in hoarfrost. No. The frost came not from above but below, like a miasma from a cold swamp.

Dorset's voice went to static and mumbles, but Alice knew the words by heart.

"Then shall the righteous answer him, saying, Lord, when saw we thee an hungred, and fed thee? or thirsty, and gave thee to drink? When saw we thee a stranger, and took thee in? or naked, and clothed thee? Or when saw we thee sick, or in prison, and came unto thee?"

It was not a rope they were holding but a long length of metal links. A chain, frozen and dripping with green icicles. Their hands were stuck to the chain, melded with it.

"And the King shall answer them and say unto them, Verily, I say unto you, Inasmuch as ye have done it unto one of the least of these my brethren, ye have done it unto me."

One person stood to the side. Man or woman, it was not clear, except that the person wasn't holding the chain, but standing with arms raised, as though exhorting them to hold fast.

Dorset closed the Bible. "Matthew 25: 34–40." Alice put a hand to her forehead, as though she might rub away the dismaying vision.

"Are you all right, then, Alice?" murmured Mrs. Babbage across Rose.

Who were the strangers in the congregation today? Who could have brought such a terrible vision? It was in someone's memory. Like Violet's beating from her husband, it came with someone being near. It could be Benny Simkins. Didn't he see all manner of terrible things in his work? Or was some stranger among them who brought this vision of hell, one who controlled people and forced them together, as if with a chain?

"Alice?" Mrs. Babbage was staring at her, and now Rose, looking worried.

"Oh, yes. I'm quite all right," Alice whispered.

James was at the pulpit now, and began. "Verily, I say unto you, Inasmuch as ye have done it unto one of the least of these my brethren, ye have done it unto me."

People were very quiet and still all through the sanctuary.

James was repeating another line from the reading: "I was a stranger and ye took me in: Naked, and ye clothed me: I was sick and ye visited me."

As Alice calmed herself, she noted that James's sermon was about compassion for the less fortunate and Christian charity. James Hathaway, the most timid of the villagers, was taking a stand: he was admonishing people for Rose's sake. That's why people sat so still. They were ashamed to meet anyone's eyes.

Oh, James, Alice thought. *My great, fine knight. Give them their medicine.*

But with another part of her mind, she was still thinking about the bizarre *trauma view.* She noted the strangers and where they were sitting. But she didn't put it past the town to have a villain in it.

She'd seen too much of the underbelly of things to believe that people were as they seemed.

15

SUMMERHILL ESTATE,
NORTHAMPTONSHIRE

SUNDAY, APRIL 19. By morning, the storm had passed.
Clouds scudded across the rolling grounds of the estate, occluding the sun at intervals, but it was merely a remnant of the
great Saturday storm. Over a cold breakfast, they heard about
the damage throughout Northamptonshire, with the east and
north taking especially hard hits. Washouts had closed many
roads, and walls of mud left trains stranded on their tracks. Von
Ritter did not show up for breakfast, but Georgi was in high
good humor, claiming that they were all roughing it and doing
splendidly. On the battery-operated radio that had been brought
into service, the news soon passed from the devastation to the
upcoming Olympic games in Berlin. With the phones still out,
Kim could not check on Wrenfell, but she felt it must be all on
the mend.

Later, standing on the front porch with her Leica, Kim snapped off a couple of shots of the cleanup effort. Most of the able-bodied men were shoveling mud around the stables and the garage, and even von Ritter's driver and Hugh's footman joined in.

At last the garage driveway was clear, and Hugh raced the engine on a large silver convertible. He tore out of the garage, mud splattering as he came, screeching to a halt at the front steps. "Miss Tavistock! You must come for a ride."

"But I'm working!" She raised her camera as proof.

"Oh, come on," he said, grinning. "It's time for some fun after all this."

Bea had come out onto the porch. "You must go. Have a little fun, Kim." It seemed that Bea was the sort who looked after people, and she would much rather Kim got on with Hugh than with a German.

"I'll just get my coat." Kim hurried up to her room to grab her things, then made her way back to the porch, where the car rumbled and Hugh leaned over to throw open the door. Before she had quite settled into her seat, Hugh spun gravel and the motorcar charged out of the yard and down the driveway.

They careered over the bridge and raced down the road. Hugh laughed with pleasure as he drove. "The Bentley is a raging animal and needs letting out now and then," he said, loud enough for the onrushing wind not to carry his words away.

Slowing down at a crossroad, he then gunned the engine, roaring down a road that ran parallel to the river. He yanked the wheel around a curve in the road, driving down the middle of the road as though he owned it, which of course he did.

He looked over at her, grinning. "It's splendid, don't you think? To be on the brink of death! And yet live!" The car's rear end drifted to the side on the next curve, causing Kim to gasp, but Hugh straightened the wheels out and barreled on.

Cresting a hill, they sped downward, gaining now on the woods that lay in the vale. Clouds had drifted over the sun, making Kim glad of her coat. They passed through the treeline, where it grew dark, and Hugh flipped on the headlights. With a patch of fog dispersing the beams, the road was hard to see, but they flew on. Then Hugh stepped hard on the brake, fishtailing the car into a parking area, where they sat, car idling. A sizable pond lay before them.

"Sorry," Hugh said. "I hope I didn't frighten you."

She smiled. "Well, the drive had its moments."

He turned off the engine. "You're a good sport, Kim. You've made the best of an awful weekend." He looked in the direction of the house, hidden behind the screen of trees.

"I'm so glad you stood up for Charlotte," she said. "It's a bad time to lose a job."

"If Charlotte goes, Georgi goes, I promise you!"

"What? You'd send your sister packing?"

He fished out a cigarette and lit it, blowing a stream of smoke. "I just might."

"Well, she isn't really at home in the country, is she." Kim's hands had grown very cold, and she shoved them into her coat pockets. The air smelled of snow, so deep were they into the woods.

He'd been gazing at the pond, and now turned to her. "She loves Summerhill, but she takes care not to show it. The same way she pretends she doesn't get on with me. Those rows we have, it's how she shows love." He smirked at Kim's skeptical glance. "It's the Aberdare way."

It wasn't Kim's imagination that she smelled snow. A dusting fell on the lake's glassy surface. As the temperature plummeted, she pulled her coat tighter.

"Oh, terribly sorry," he said. "Would you like a smoke?" He offered her the pack, tapping one out. She shook her head.

"It's good of you to listen. I feel I can talk to you."

"Of course you can, Hugh." *Of course.*

He went on, "I noticed you're rather taken with Erich von Ritter. But I'd watch out, if I were you. Georgi grabbed him during her trip to Germany last year. As you might imagine, she doesn't share."

"He seems to be flirting with me. It's odd, but I can't tell, exactly."

Hugh inhaled deeply, brow furrowed. "He isn't good enough for Georgi." He cut a sly glance at her. "Or you."

Across the lake, gusts bent the tree branches. "The weather's changed," she said. "Maybe the storm is coming back." The wind hit them then, a strong blast laden with shards of ice.

Hugh seemed deep in thought, not noticing that headlights were approaching them from down the road.

A long black car pulled in beside them. Georgi rolled down the passenger-side window. In response, Hugh did the same. "At least you didn't crash the Bentley," she said.

Beside her at the wheel was von Ritter. He nodded at Kim, his face gray in the forest gloom, the deepening fog.

"Join us, my dear," Georgi said to Kim. "Hughy's a frightful driver."

"Oh, that's all right," Kim said. She turned to Hugh. "We'll make our way back, won't we?"

"Right-o." He leaned over to catch von Ritter's eye. "Race you back!"

He turned on the engine and backed up fast, an expert turn. They sped off, and as Hugh drove out of the trees, he put his hand on Kim's knee, grinning as though they had beaten back the enemy.

Georgi and von Ritter followed them. At the top of the hill, they passed out of the little storm that had come through and sunlight flooded over the land.

Hugh wound up the gramophone, looking eager for the dancing Georgi had proposed. Candles flickered from the two mantels and on end tables as Georgi blew the lint off the record and put it on the turntable. "Anything Goes" filled the salon, and Sir Edgar gave his arm to the lady of the house.

Von Ritter paired with Bea, and Hugh saw a clear path to Kim. She wore her flounced chiffon again and, watching Georgi sparkle in jeweled satin, felt very much the country girl.

Hugh came over to her. "Dance?"

"I don't think I shall, after you broke your promise." She kept her tone light, but she had been shocked to find that Charlotte had been sent away after all.

"What promise?"

"That you would keep Charlotte on. 'If Charlotte goes, Georgi goes,' I believe you said."

He crumpled his lips and glanced at his sister. "She wouldn't have it. I'm sorry. But we gave her a good letter. And, after all, the dogs could have drowned."

She was thoroughly disappointed in him, but she must let it lie.

Hugh smelled of tobacco and whisky, but he was a smooth dancer. Tonight, he was rather turned out, in an exquisitely tailored suit, but like so much about the Earl of Daventry, however, his tie was a bit askew.

"I'm glad you decided to write us up," he said as they danced. "Will you sign a copy for me when it's published?"

"Of course. If you'll sign the picture I took of you on the hill."

He smiled. "You drive a hard bargain, but done."

"You and Georgi have a complicated relationship," she said. "Do you share her politics?"

"Georgi doesn't *share*, remember?"

"Well, she'd make an exception there, I should think."

"I have German friends as well as English. And now American, so I hope I shan't have to choose." He spun her out, and adroitly enough, she ended back in his arms. "Let's not ruin Cole Porter with politics."

She acquiesced. She must still pretend to enjoy all of them, even the lord of the manor, who could not dispense justice for his own staff.

Champagne flowed, mixing with Gershwin and Tommy Dorsey. She sat out a foxtrot and wondered if von Ritter had had enough of her or would be friendly. He certainly seemed to have changed his tune with her, but it was not long before he caught her eye and, grabbing a champagne bottle, approached.

Standing before her, he filled her flute to the brim. "I haven't meant to ignore you this evening."

"Were you?"

"Ah. I am not missed when I am absent." He sat with her on the divan, watching Georgi dance with her brother. "They are perfect together, yes?"

"In a way."

He made a half-smile. "Yes, one develops a sense about people, how they fit in, what their strengths are."

"If you can discern that, perhaps you are one of those great men you spoke of, Herr von Ritter." She meant to recapture the mood they had established on the river. Perhaps she could learn whether von Ritter was on assignment or *running* Georgi Aberdare, if that was the term.

"I am not in that order of being," he said. "But we serve where we can."

"What can one person do? Events are too big to sway." She meant to give him an opening to say *something*. But it was likely too late to catch him in carelessness or a *spill*. It was Sunday night, and the group would disperse tomorrow.

"You could serve." He saw how she was about to demur. "Yes, my Yorkshire girl. She who would save the puppies."

So he *did* hope to recruit her, then. She sipped her champagne. "You make too much of that."

"But we are not talking about puppies." He looked at her rather more sharply. It was very difficult to play this game of falsehood and implication, and she feared von Ritter was much better at it than she.

"You could be among those who work to keep your country from war. Rally the peace, might one say? I think peace is what you want." He paused, murmuring: "After Ypres."

He draped his arm along the back of divan, leaning in. "You are concerned that the maid not lose her job, because she will fall into poverty. It is a nice sentiment, but sentiment does not save us. Work is freeing, but more work will not save us. It is by working *together* that the world will find peace."

"Working together. But however shall we manage to do that?"

"When a great man rises up among us. One whose power of persuasion crosses all boundaries."

"Making us neither German nor British nor French. . . ."

He nodded with satisfaction. "You understand."

"Does this togetherness happen because of the *bloom*? Is that what you're saying? Talents have been among us for quite a while, but we're none the better for it."

"Germany is better."

"Because of Hitler, you think. And England, because of . . ." She now recollected the odd word he had used. "Because of a chorister?"

Von Ritter regarded her silently for a few moments. Then, ignoring her question, he said, "You have a horror of war. You wish to do something, but you cannot see your way."

She so wished she had not told him about Robert. But she was able to say with feeling, "If war comes, I can't think how we will bear it a second time."

"Then let us not fight."

"Let us not," she whispered.

"Show me your true self, Kim. Before we must go our separate paths."

Georgi was headed toward them. He leaned close to her. "Leave your door open tonight."

She was so surprised, she was caught without a reply.

"It does no harm, until we are enemies." His comment at the gazebo about sharing a rain slicker. His gaze stirred her, as it became clear that this was a proposition.

"Herr von Ritter . . ."

"You must call me Erich. Under the circumstances?" He stood. "It was not happenstance or luck that brought us together on the river. There is only *merit.* I saw it in you. And you see it in me. Am I wrong?"

"Wrong about what?" Georgi said, sidling up to von Ritter and taking his arm.

He flashed an ironic smile at Kim. "About great men."

Georgi waved her champagne glass in dismissal. "How you do go on about that. Kim is a *Communist,* as I keep telling you." Kim managed a weak smile.

"Then she must be chastened," he said playfully.

There was no way Kim could answer him with Georgi standing there. When the two of them went off to enjoy a waltz, Kim slipped out of the room.

In the hall, she put a hand to her burning cheeks, thankful to have escaped the candlelit salon. The next step with von Ritter was not going to be just talk.

As she approached the stairs, she saw the footman, Peter, down the corridor, with the Scotties on their leashes. He noticed her and gave a nod before disappearing around a corner.

Once in her room, she paced, trying to calm down. Von Ritter wished to convert her with persuasion, charm, and sex. He seemed to believe she would follow him. Because of Robert, because of the peace that might come if they all pulled together. Well, she would not be von Ritter's Yorkshire trophy. If he was a spy and had an important secret, the price of discovery was higher than she was willing to pay. Owen didn't expect her to sleep with her targets, she felt sure.

Too agitated to sleep, she sat in a chair with the LNER timetable, and had got as far as the holiday schedule when she heard a sound in the hallway. She watched as the door handle turned. The latch encountered the lock and the handle slowly released.

I'm not joining hands, Herr von Ritter. Or anything else, either.

She was very glad to be leaving this place in the morning.

16

ON THE ROAD FROM SUMMERHILL

MONDAY, APRIL 20. It was a relief to be on her way. The Austin purred along, slewing mud from the tires but gamely handling the quick-drying roads. Kim had a suitcase full of muddy clothes, memories of a chaotic weekend, and a few last photos of Lord Daventry (at the great fireplace) and Lady Georgiana (commanding the staircase). Von Ritter managed to be absent from the photo session.

The goodbyes were rather disorganized, with everyone leaving at once, and she had a charming bow from von Ritter across the foyer, but minus his signature smile.

She had not made a success out of her spying assignment, but she had tried her best. In retrospect, she felt that she and Owen had been naive to think she could extract a specific secret from someone. Georgi Aberdare did seem merely a superficial drawing-room aristocrat, worrying about her brother and having boudoir adventures with houseguests. But if Georgi was traitorous, Kim had failed to penetrate to the truth. She had deep suspicions about Erich von Ritter, of course. But he had skated free and was likely too clever a target for the likes of her.

Thinking of von Ritter, she still hated having confided in him about Robert. She should have realized that her adversaries would have Talents. As soon as Kim had met von Ritter, she should have been on guard. But at least the only thing she'd given up was entirely personal. She would tell Owen how von Ritter had tried to recruit her to his cause, but in truth, he might merely be a supporter of the German regime. Not all ideologues were spies.

The road climbed steeply into a hilly and wooded area. There the hillside slumped in places, with trees tipping precariously out of plumb in the unstable mud.

At least one other car had preceded her on the road, leaving deep tire tracks, so she had proof that the road was passable. She looked forward to finding a public phone box in working order at one of the towns along the way, where she would call ahead to find out how Wrenfell and Uxley had fared in the storm.

With these thoughts keeping her company, she failed to see that a car had come up behind her, showing impatience by hugging her bumper. The side of the road held little extra room for her to pull over, so they would have to wait until she had passed the upcoming curve in the road, sweeping sharply to the right.

She could just make out that at the curve, the prospect gave out to the valley below, wide and deep.

In her rearview mirror she saw that the car was swerving in toward the cliff face and trying to push past her. It would not do, because there was no room for two cars abreast unless she moved perilously close to the cliff edge.

With this driver trying to pass, her instinct was to slow

down, but now she feared hitting the brakes too forcefully, lest she lose control on the curve.

As she approached the curve, the car behind swerved even closer, forcing her to the very edge of the road. She slammed onto the brakes and came to a skidding stop. The engine stalled while the other car sped past.

Kim's heart drummed sharply. Over the hood of the car was a terrifying blue-sky view of the valley. She was well forward of the shoulder and staring out at a dizzying height.

In the next moment, the front of the car crunched down as the shoulder slumped a few inches. Through the windshield she surveyed the prospect of a three-hundred-foot drop into the valley. Panic numbed her mind. She must get out but feared to open the door lest the movement tip the car over the bank.

The front wheels sank a few more inches. The sensation was of a slowly gathering mudslide of which she and her car would soon form a part.

She looked to the side to see if there was anything to grab onto if she threw open the door and flung herself out, but there were no shrubs or trees.

Carefully opening the door, she pushed it gently as wide as she could. There was no impediment, but she saw at once that she had only air to step into unless she launched herself at an angle, pushing back toward the shoulder, where a small slurry of mud formed a narrow shoulder. There was no choice. She must escape the car.

Kicking wildly at the floorboards, she dove out, reaching for the solid earth. She landed, sprawling on her face in the mud. Behind her, the car groaned in protest, and the front end sank further, now leaving the car at a twenty-degree angle, dangling over the chasm.

She lay hugging the ground for a few minutes before she could absolutely confirm that she was not going to fall. Behind her, the car creaked and groaned, settling a few inches further into the soft edge of the cliff. Would it go over?

A terror seized her that if the car plunged down, it might take the shoulder with it. She crawled away from the embankment, finding a tree well back from the edge. She rested against it, catching her breath, eyeing the car's precarious tilt but deciding it might hold fast.

The car that had recklessly tried to pass had disappeared, the driver unaware of the havoc he had caused. And she had failed to get his license plate number. No, she had actually looked as he came up on her tail. There had been no license plate.

She looked at her car, immediately abandoning the idea of retrieving her luggage, her camera. Let it all go over the cliff. Just as long as she was not inside with it.

Covered with mud, she began walking down the road toward Summerhill, trusting she would find a ride from some good Samaritan so that she would not have to hike all the way back to the manor.

It was a great surprise when the next person driving up the road was her father.

Julian sat on a rock by the stream as Kim washed off the worst of the mud on her face and arms.

He handed her a greasy towel from the boot of the Ford he had rented back in Dunstable. "It's all I have."

She accepted it with wry smile, still quiet, perhaps more embarrassed by now than in shock. The thought of the danger she'd been in on that cliff wedged in his mind like a black stone.

When he had first seen her walking down the road, he had

thought it was a wandering victim of a landslip. Seeing that it was Kim gave him a most profound shock. How much more so when he saw her car half-hanging over the cliff edge.

Someone had done this on purpose. Von Ritter, he thought. But why? Julian couldn't imagine why the SD would try to kill his daughter, unless. . . unless she had stumbled into a *spill* situation where the man had revealed an operation to her. And she had imagined a harmless weekend pursuing a freelance article on grand English manors.

When he'd driven up to Summerhill, he'd had little hope of finding the group still assembled, but as it was on his way, he made the stop. By eleven that morning, everyone had left except Sir Edgar and his wife, so his chance for a close-up view of von Ritter had passed. At the news that Kim had left earlier, he begged off a luncheon invitation from a very put-out Georgi and had set out to find his daughter.

"And the car that passed you had gone around the next curve, so they didn't know you had almost gone over?"

She was still using the wet cloth on her skirt, to little effect. "I think so. But they were speeding, so perhaps they didn't wish to know the consequences." Her responses all had that flat affect of one who was stunned by events—or using that to cover up something.

"We could go back to Summerhill." He hadn't much experience being solicitous of her, but now was the time if ever there was. "I'm sure Georgi would put us up."

She answered with alacrity. "No, let's go home." As she slid into the passenger side of the car and he took the wheel, she added with a small smile, "But thank you."

As they set out, he made a try at a fatherly statement. "If I had made it up for Georgi's weekend, this might have been avoided."

"Because you're the better driver?" She was watching the scenery pass by—including washed out driveways and the occasional downed telephone pole.

Of course he was a better driver. His training included obstacle motor courses and every conceivable type of skill useful in intelligence work. "No, not at all, Kim. It could happen to anyone, of course."

As they drove north into East Riding, he tried to come to grips with what Kim was involved in. Was it possible that she was pursuing some amateur prying into what she might think was a nest of Nazis? He couldn't see her as that reckless. But what did he really know of her? He'd spent the last three years trying to keep his distance lest he let drop something in a *spill*. A level 6 was dangerous. E didn't like the household situation, but he could hardly order Julian to send his daughter packing for America.

And had it anything to do with Monkton Hall? Someone she'd met, something she'd learned? *Damn it all to bloody hell.* At the same time, if she had stumbled across something important from Georgi or von Ritter, he would have liked to know what it was.

"How did you land the writing job involving Summerhill?"

"I didn't. It was a freelance job, and what with knowing Georgi . . ."

"Whom you dislike."

She looked at him. "We can't always do what we like. I'm trying to make a go of it. Make something of myself, do you see? I mean, you are hardly home to know what I do, and I'm not sure you see the position I'm in. Living with a parent. At loose ends at thirty-three." She broke off and stared out the window again, finally adding, "But I am sorry I made a mess of it."

He thought she might be on the verge of tears. Why had he started to question her like a suspect? What a damn fool he was.

"I should be home more often." There was a father buried somewhere inside of him and sometimes he spoke the truth.

His relationship with Kim had gone off the tracks somewhere in the past. Whether he had been too absent during her American years or had overplayed his German sympathies, he didn't know. Did she really believe that he didn't honor Robert's memory? Even his stance as a German sympathizer all these years later did not imply such a thing.

They were pulling into Wrenfell. He wanted to tell her that he had loved Robert as much as she and would have given anything to have died in his place. That not a day went by when he didn't think of Robert and miss him more than he could bear. That he didn't want to lose her, too.

But what he said was, "Don't worry about the car. We'll get it back in one piece."

She looked at him and it seemed she wanted to say something, too, but all that came out was, "I just hope no one takes the Leica."

17

MONDAY, APRIL 20. André Marchand took out a crumpled pack of Gauloises, tapped one out, offering it to Philippe, who shook his head. Marchand lit his cigarette, inhaling deeply.

Philippe offered, "He's bluffing. He needs to get out of Germany for some reason."

Marchand blew the smoke out in an impatient stream. Colonel Stelling sat across the warehouse floor, eating a sandwich, hunched over, as exhausted as the rest of them.

If this was the real thing, Marchand had to have a breakthrough and soon. "I don't think he's bluffing."

"Because of *Sturmweg?* You believe it means an invasion?"

"If I believed him, we'd give him reason to divulge details more quickly."

They'd been questioning him all night. Now, as dawn crept in, Marchand was no closer to knowing how important Stelling was. Commandant of the Wesermarsch labor camp near Norden. Claimed to know of an invasion of England launched from Norden. A landing on the coast. Where on the coast? Stelling didn't know. When? Soon. But when? He didn't know. Before he would talk, he demanded extraction to France. Stelling was a man very afraid of capture. Well. He had abandoned his post, gone over to the French CE. Naturally, he was anxious to leave.

If he was lying, it was a very good lie. One likely to get him to Paris, if Marchand gave the word.

It was galling. They had given him their word that he would be gotten out of Germany, but he must see that they had to be sure his information was worth the very dangerous extraction.

Marchand looked at his watch. 5:25 AM. He had to decide. If they were to smuggle him out, it would have to be today, before the Germans discovered him gone. Perhaps they already knew, but Marchand thought Stelling's feigned recall to Berlin had a reasonable chance of giving him a couple days' head start. There was no unusual security activity yet; no roadblocks or control checks at train stations. That could change.

He stubbed out his cigarette and walked over to Colonel Stelling.

Stelling saw that it was beginning again with this Captain Marchand: the same questions, patiently repeated, asked a little differently. He would have to give up something more, something convincing, but he must withhold key pieces so that he maintained his value to smuggle across the French border.

He would not tell them of the *ice* Talent. That was the most important piece. Yes, he knew how the invasion would happen. *But, with regret, not for you to hear, Capitaine Marchand.*

Hearing that, Marchand had lit a cigarette. Stelling knew

that the man had to decide whether to apply force. That would be a mistake and the French knew it. Once torture began, his information would grow increasingly unreliable. Fear and horror could produce as many lies as truths.

"Colonel Stelling," Marchand said in German. He stood before him, not taking a seat this time.

Stelling looked up at him. Ah. He had decided.

"Colonel Stelling. A car is coming for you. Are you prepared?"

Stelling glanced at the trickle of light through papered-over windows. "It will be in daylight?"

"The first part. We must get you out of Berlin without delay, if we are going. So it must be now. You will ride in the trunk for part of the way. You agree?"

"Yes."

"My superiors will decide whether you stay in France to receive British debriefing there or go to England. You understand I have done all I can."

"Yes, Captain. Thank you." He had told them he did not want to go to England. That would shortly belong to the Third Reich, even with the advance intelligence he would give. How could Britain stop what was coming? Not even he knew where the landing would take place.

"You will change cars along the way. Do not be alarmed. You will have expert help. If you are stopped, this is your passport." Marchand handed it over. Stelling opened it. His picture that they had taken last night. "Your name is Otto Werner, from Leipzig."

Marchand stepped back and saluted. "*Bonne chance.*"

Stelling returned the salute. "*Merci, mon capitaine.*"

They gave him a change of clothes. While he was dressing, daylight flooded into the murky warehouse for a few seconds as they drove a Simca inside. He met Gunter, business dress, a bland face, just the type to be invisible when looked at. He opened the trunk, motioning Stelling in.

Not more than a half hour later, the car stopped. Gunter opened the trunk. A small garage, smelling of iron and oil. "Quick, we are changing cars. We may have been followed." Stelling heard the name of his new driver, Helmut, florid and rotund, who nodded a sober greeting. Then he was in the trunk again. Outside, a burst of conversation that he couldn't quite make out. Agitated. They got under way again.

It was misery riding this way, swaying with every turn, unable to see, knees crunched up to his chest. Before long, the motor turned off. Gruff voices outside. A roadblock. Why hadn't he taken a seat up front sooner? If they found him in the trunk, it was over. In the hot confines, he had sweated through his shirt and jacket. His hand rested on his pistol, lying on the floor next to him.

Then the car started up again. They were through. But now he knew there were roadblocks. Very bad for their long drive to the French border.

Another hour in which Stelling had time to imagine what Lieutenant Hass might have done when he left. Check on him with High Command? Or the driver, left sick at the farmhouse. Would he have taken a turn for the worse, needed a doctor, all leading to the unraveling of Stelling's story? *He went on without you, without calling for another driver? The colonel took your kit with him?*

The trunk came open in a blast of sun and fresh, pine-scented air. They were in a stand of trees next to a wide field.

Helmut watched the field as Stelling relieved himself.

"Where are we?" Stelling asked when he rejoined him.

"Nowhere." Helmut lit a cigarette and coughed a laugh. "Poland, if you want a name."

Stelling's heart sank. It was as bad as Germany. The Poles might not harbor him; why should they, and risk so much?

"We had to turn east. Roadblocks, control checks everywhere. We got unlucky. They are looking for you."

Now he understood why they had turned east. They would never have made it safely in a six-hour drive to the French border.

Helmut looked to the sky. "They're sending a plane."

"A plane. To go where?"

"Denmark. Then England."

This was not the plan. It was much more dangerous. They would be watching for planes, especially this close to Berlin. "Whose plane?"

"The RAF. England wants you, Herr Werner. They are risking their pilot to get you there."

They waited on the packed dirt road, barely more than a cow path, looking out over a flat valley, narrow enough for secrecy but leaving little room for pilot mistakes.

In a half hour, they heard the plane approaching from the north. Helmut stepped out of the trees and aimed his flashlight, giving a Morse code signal for a T, a code saying *Safe. We are here.*

The plane, a Hawker, responded with its landing lights, Morse code for G. *Acknowledging. We are who you expect.*

The biplane touched down at the last possible moment, bouncing heavily, wheels hitting ruts and brush.

The pilot pushed himself out of the open-air cockpit, yanking the leather flying cap off his head, waving it. Curly hair, tall and thin, looking cocky and British, as Stelling imagined.

Helmut urged Stelling to hurry. He ran across the field to

the plane. But as he did so, figures appeared out of the woods on the other side of the field. Polish police.

Not Poles. German SS, firing as they came. Stelling had his pistol out. He rushed forward, skidding to a halt by the fuselage, using it as cover. They were three against maybe six SS. *A chance.* But Helmut was in the woods, sinking back into its deep cover.

Stelling picked off one of the SS, the one in the lead. But in another moment, the pilot went down, fallen half out of the cockpit.

So, then, it was over.

Kurt Stelling heard the men shouting, coming closer. *Quickly now.* He raised the pistol to his head and made sure of his aim. He had known it might come to this, was surprised he had gotten so far. The glimpse of a black SS uniform. He pulled the trigger.

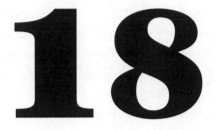

18

MONDAY, APRIL 20. "You look a fright," Alice said as Kim escorted her to the car. They walked past the spring bulbs, now flattened near the walkway. Mud lay four inches thick in the car park.

"All I can think about is a bath," Kim said. That was not precisely truc. She was eager to leave Owen a message at the dead drop, but she'd have to figure out how to do that discreetly. It wouldn't happen today, with long shadows stretching across the yard, and any evening excursion sure to draw Julian's notice.

"It wasn't serious, was it?" Alice scrutinized her. "How did you get so covered in mud?"

"The car went in the ditch. It was a total mess getting out with all the mud from the rains. Honestly, I'm embarrassed that it happened at all." She explained how Julian had arranged for a garage to pick the car up. "And you? How did it go with Rose?"

"She was a little rattled by the storms, but she took very well to her maid duties. Except for barging into things. And . . ." She rolled her eyes "We had a visit from one of those Order of Decency people. A very unpleasant man demanded that Rose not be allowed into town. Before Walter chased him off the property, the man said that the Germans had the right idea: lock up the *degenerates*. Can you imagine?"

Kim shook her head in disgust. Nazism was creeping in, even to Uxley. They weren't going to get their hands on Rose, she vowed.

Alice looked at her with a worried expression.

"Something?"

"No. It's been a long weekend." Alice dug in her pocket for her car keys.

Kim's thoughts hardly stretched beyond the urgent need for a bath. "Well, it was really awfully good of you. . . ." She stopped at the expression on Alice's face. "What? There is something, isn't there."

"It was a *trauma view*. Another one."

"Oh, but here? At the house?" Kim hugged herself, as the evening chill set in.

"It was at church. This one was a bit different."

"How do you mean, *different?*" She waited, but when Alice remained silent, she said, "Do you want to talk about it?"

Alice smiled. "No, you must get cleaned up. Come by tomorrow, when we'll have more time. Get on with you, now."

When Alice left, Kim looked up to find Mrs. Babbage at the door, announcing tea. Perhaps tea would allow her and Julian to have a proper conversation. As they had driven home, she'd had a strong urge to tell her father what really had happened. He had seemed, for a moment, to want to know. Or to know *her.* Perhaps he'd been shaken by the sight of the car perched on the cliff edge, and actually had been concerned for her. But fortunately, she'd overcome the impulse for family intimacy. She did love her father. But her work at Monkton was under the Official Secrets Act. And, as another layer, she owed Owen her silence.

After midnight, when Kim was asleep, Julian took his pipe out on the back stoop and had his smoke, gazing up at the sky, heavy with stars before the moon rose. Assuring himself that all was quiet, he made his way to the barn.

He didn't light the lamp but made his way to Briar's stall in the cool dark. He gave the horse some strokes when she nosed at him. "There's a lass," he murmured. Here in the Wrenfell barn, it seemed unlikely there was another world beyond this humble place, smelling of horseflesh and hay. The clatter of London and its outrageous concerns couldn't be reconciled with this world. What did London smell like, feel like to the touch? It had no substance, not like Wrenfell. But it was in charge. He could have pretended otherwise. *Life must be lived. War may come, but one goes on. Conquerors come and then they go, with nothing much changed in the end.* But he'd made his choices.

Briar expected more and soon got a handful of oats, snuffled and gone, just as a shadow appeared at the back door. Walter, coming in from the pasture side.

He shut the door, making his way in the dark without misstep to stand beside Julian.

"All well, then, Walter?" Julian asked, lighting his pipe again.

"Nobut th' usual. Excep' this." Walter put a folded piece of paper into Julian's hand.

"From Badger?" he asked, using the code name of a field agent.

"Aye. Th' other day, i' town."

Julian held the paper, feeling London stretching out an arm. He lit a match to read the note. Burning it with the same match, he stomped it out on the stone floor. A German commander at Wesermarsch prison camp had attempted to defect. The operation was bungled by CE, the French intelligence service. He would have to go back to London, just when he felt uneasy about leaving Kim alone.

He looked at Walter. "Do you still have your pistol?"

"Right good 'un, too."

"Kim will want looking after. You understand."

"Someone aboot 'ere?"

"I'm not sure. But keep an eye on any strangers. Watch, as you do, but trust no one. Egret will come up to keep an eye out." He used Elsa's code name.

"Aye, then."

Briar was impatient with this line of conversation, the dark, the skimping of oats. She nickered, and Walter got her a feed bag while Julian thought about the news of a major defection gone wrong.

"I'll be leaving tomorrow, Walter." It was London's hand on his arm, pulling him back. He wouldn't say *dragging*. He was interested, which was the truth of it, that he wanted it.

"Tha's wha' ah thought, sir." Walter wouldn't have read the note, but he'd been Julian's asset since the beginning at SIS and knew how these things went.

From her bedroom window, Kim watched Julian leave the barn. It was very dark outside, but the kitchen light threw just enough illumination that she could see that he had gone into the barn for about ten minutes and then out again, without a flashlight or a lamp. It was a bit peculiar. She considered going out to see what he was up to, but one thought held her back: Did he want to hide what he was doing?

She heard him come up the stairs and go into his room. Curiosity overcame her, and after a few minutes, she carefully made her way down the stairs and into the yard. She risked a flashlight, because her father's room did not give onto the back of the house.

When she entered the barn, she smelled a wisp of smoke in the air. Very faint but unmistakable. Her flashlight found a blackened area of the floor with bits of straw singed at the edges. She stirred the remnants of a burned paper.

Sitting on her heels, staring at the burned spot, she brooded. Why would he burn something here? Why would he be in the barn so late at all, and in the dark? He had something he needed to get rid of secretly. She stared at the floor. There was a perfectly logical explanation for this, but it eluded her. Her thoughts lately had been too much with Germans and spies, but in truth, there was a clandestine war going on, and some people had chosen the wrong side, no matter how well-meaning they might be, how patriotic. . . . She stood up and went to Briar for the comfort of rubbing her head.

Was Julian working for them? Had he gone over to the wolves? She couldn't credit it. But it would explain what he did in his long absences. He might not be the indolent country gentleman that he appeared.

It was only because it was late at night that she could even imagine this about her father. Surely, this act of burning something in the barn under cover of dark was innocent.

But she had entered a world of paranoia and subterfuge. It influenced her perceptions. Stained them, perhaps.

Leaving the barn, she looked toward the back of the house. All dark and silent. Knowing things. Keeping them.

19

SIS HEADQUARTERS, LONDON

TUESDAY, APRIL 21. "The bloody French." E stood at the window, looking out on the street below. It was 10:30 PM. Everyone at SIS had worked late today, and some weren't done yet.

Julian sat on the hard sofa in the corner of the office, having waited most of the evening for this meeting, which kept getting postponed as E was summoned to meetings with the Committee of Imperial Defence. The Kurt Stelling debacle was keeping Whitehall awake tonight.

England was on high alert for an attack on the coast. But they had just lost the man who could have told them where and how. The report from the French CE agent in charge of Stelling couldn't have been worse news; the agent had escaped ambush in Poland, reporting that the SS had closed in on the rescue plane before it could take off and that Stelling had shot himself rather than be captured.

Julian longed for his pipe, but E had never approved of

tobacco. Fortunately, he approved of scotch, and poured out a tot for each of them.

E took a comfortable chair opposite Julian. In the outer office, Miss Hennessey was just locking up. She peeked in, an attractive fortyish woman possessed of an unnerving calm. She wore her hair swept onto her head in a roll like an ocean wave. SIS said if the wave ever crashed, the service would fall. Most of the agents and intelligence officers in SIS were former military men, notoriously superstitious about minor things that, as fate would have it, might tip things in the wrong direction. "Anything else, sir?"

"No thank you, Olivia. It'll be another long day tomorrow. Get some rest." She had very high security clearance and E trusted her with his files, his appointment book and the lives of his agents.

She nodded at Julian and closed the door quietly.

E swirled his scotch. Dark shadows under his eyes betrayed his weariness from the last twenty-four hours. "We told CE to get him out right away. But they insisted on interrogation. Six hours lost, and that gave the High Command time to discover he'd run. Why did the man go to the French? If he'd come to our embassy, he'd be ours."

It was maddening to have come so close to netting a major defector. "If he was extracted here, and the invasion succeeded, he'd be in German hands."

E shared a dark look with Julian. England occupied by German forces. It was the ultimate nightmare. They knew it might come to aerial bombings. But invasion?

Baldwin didn't believe it. The Prime Minister and his cronies thought it could be a concoction of the Germans to hide their true expansion plans, or even a ruse by the French to assure British rearmament in case of war, a rearmament that wasn't happening because of a crippled economy and the British public's fatigue with war. Baldwin didn't *want* to believe it. It colored what he was willing to hear, and it meant that the British public would not be told.

E's contempt for this position was barely disguised. Maybe they couldn't confirm Stelling's claims in detail, but British agents in Germany had been reporting massive troop movements into Norden and Wesermarsch. *Sturmweg*, which SIS had been tracking for some weeks by wireless, was a named operation of interest. It might be related to this putative invasion by sea.

The War Office wanted to know the insertion point. Stelling had claimed he didn't know. That might have changed had they gotten him to a safe house in London.

E set his glass down. "I want a questionnaire gotten out to Woodbird." Their mole in the *Abwehr*. "We must have confirmation of the operation code word. Strengths of the troops. Whole order of battle. Highest priority is the insertion point. Also Colonel Stelling's background, politics, personal situation, who he reports to."

He glared at the window in the direction of the War Office. "Dammit, we need backup evidence. CID is treating Stelling's claims as unreliable. Alistair Drake considers Stelling an opportunist who needed to get out of Germany. CID wants confirmation if he was on the take or was running from other troubles."

"It's what the French thought too."

"Yes, but they jolly well lost us a pilot by running Stelling over the border."

"Which we told them to do. . . ."

E scowled and picked up his glass, staring into it. "We played the hand we were dealt. In another hour, we could have had him." He brooded over his drink. "Drake's bad enough, but his undersecretary is worse. Heath Millington's a toady. Tells Drake what he wants to hear, and writes his CID reports in the most understated way possible. The PM led the discussion tonight, and within forty-five minutes, we were adjourned. Forty-five minutes!"

Alistair Drake was the man who had authorized an investigation into E as the potential source of the suspected leak in security. The two had hated each other since an old scandal during the war.

Julian said, "We needed Stelling. Once again, the French badly bungled it. I hear Churchill's steamed."

"And how *he's* heard anything is another thing Drake doesn't like."

"Churchill's always had his own sources," Julian said.

"Quite. Perhaps we ought to ask *him* what the bloody hell is going on with *Sturmweg.*" E tossed off the last of his whisky. "Get on this tonight, Julian."

Julian nodded.

E remained seated. "We'll hit them hard as soon as they sail," he mused. "We'll have plenty of warning."

"Unless they sail by night," Julian said. The damn truth of it was, the RAF was hardly a robust threat. Naval guns would be waiting for British planes. No, a beach landing was not impossible. Daring and risky, yes. Possible to ignore, no.

"Why now?" E asked. "That's one thing nagging at me."

"Perhaps they want to take us out of the equation early. Then they can have Czechoslovakia, France and Belgium without out a fight. Maybe they've got a weapon they're confident in. Something new."

E sighed. "Your war of the Talents." His tone of voice said everything.

"A storm. The Germans like to have operational names that mean something."

"While we're at the guessing game, what kind of Talent would they have found?" E asked, challenging his chief spy to make sense of it.

Julian shrugged. "Maybe it has to do with weather."

"Weather. I shouldn't think they'd expect to bring down the British Empire with a typhoon." E shook his head. "The known German agents in England, most of them are ours. And they know nothing."

It was true, many German agents in England had been turned. But while SIS was delivering chicken feed—useless information—to the Germans, the double agents had not exactly been able to deliver much to their British handlers, either.

E put his empty glass on the coffee table. "Inform me of any developments. No delays." He stood up, the meeting over. "Give me something, Julian. I need ammunition, or I'm completely outgunned at Imperial Defence. Baldwin isn't going to raise an alert for the whole coast. But if we had a specific site—Dover, let's say . . ." He clapped Julian on the shoulder as he walked him to the back stair door. "Give me a landing site, you can have my job."

"Thank you, chief, but I'm afraid I wouldn't put up two minutes with Heath Millington."

"By Christ," E lamented. "I can't *give* the bloody job away."

On the way past Olivia's desk, Julian had a passing thought. Actually the same thought he'd had for a long time now. "Fancy a drink?"

She looked up at him with total poise. "Work to do."

"Ah, right." He gave her his best smile. "Well, carry on then." He gave her an approving nod as though he too was keen on working late.

He took the lift down to the basement canteen—the infamous watering hole of the intelligence services, and no place to bring a lady. He had his drink and one more for good measure.

20

TUESDAY, APRIL 21. A crash came from the parlor. Rose was dusting.

In the hall, Kim met Mrs. Babbage drying her hands on a dish towel and looking worried. Kim nodded to her. "I'll look in on her."

As Kim entered the parlor, she saw Rose just replacing a candlestick on the refectory table. "How are you getting on, Rose?"

Rose swiveled around. She had a heavy sweater over her dress and the apron with ruffles her mother had made for her. "Oh, miss! Only the candle broke, not the candlestick!" She curtsied, and as she swiped out the side of her apron, she knocked against the end table, nearly toppling a Chinese vase.

"Well, that's fine, then," Kim said. She heard a car door slam out in the yard.

Rose looked sharply toward the windows and went to look,

pulling back the curtains to peer out. Her forehead rumpled in concern. "Those people coom again," she said. Shadow and Flint had set up furious barking in the yard.

At the window, Kim looked out to see Walter Babbage leaning into the window of a car and gesturing. It was that brown Talbot the folks from the Order of Decency drove, back again. *Decency*. The very word was preposterous.

"We may not need any more dusting today, Rose."

Rose shoved the curtain back into place and Kim suggested a cup of tea in the kitchen, where they took refuge from unwanted visitors.

Kim waited until after luncheon, then took the truck into town, the Austin being still in a garage in Northamptonshire, getting a thorough cleaning after its recovery from the embankment. Walter was already down at the river, helping to stow the sandbags that had prevented flooding in town. A few downed trees, but all in all, Uxley had fared better than some towns, especially farther south.

Julian had gone to London yesterday, and she was glad not to have to keep up a pretense in his company. She tried not to feel so cold toward him. But what was he up to, hobnobbing with Georgi's fascist crowd and sneaking into the barn late at night to burn things? And gone, supposedly to London, with a frequency that suggested it was not merely social engagements and a dabbling in a whisky business that he hardly seemed to care about. Then, if she was tallying up the evidence—which she had to admit she *was*—Julian had maintained an emotional distance from her from the moment she had arrived on his doorstep. It was possible that her views were not merely opposite his own, but abhorrent. These were the damning things. On the other hand, this was her father, steady, kind, said to be reasonable even by her mother. . . .

She drove down the steep lane behind the Three Swans to the staging area where tents had been erected to serve hot drinks, and the sandbag removal was underway on the banks. She'd serve drinks for a while, then run up to the dead drop. *Meet me in Uxley, Abbey Pond, tomorrow at dusk.* The dead drop was in a village a few minutes south of Monkton Hall, where Owen could easily check for the chalk marks that signaled the dead drop was loaded. She hoped he'd check today. It would only take her an hour, there and back.

Standing by the truck, she watched the efficient removal operation, with many hands heaving the sandbags into flatbeds for hauling up the lane to the armory. Until next time. Seeing her, Frank Hobbes touched his cap, looking happy to be out with the rest of the town to set things to rights. Dorset Withers waved at her. There was a sense of celebration that the storm was past and they'd kept the river in its place.

Alice hailed her from behind a table in the refreshment tent. "Where's your apron?"

Kim joined her. "I thought I should wear my Wellingtons for the mud."

Alice smirked. "So far, there's more eating than working. We've gone through all the scones and it's only ten."

James Hathaway came around from the side, dressed in hip waders and a moth-eaten sweater.

"Vicar," Kim said. "Come to supervise?"

"Oh no, we'll all work today!" he said, mouth full of scone. "I say, are you going to write up our little clash with the big storm? Could make a nice piece, community coming together to fight the raging river."

She hadn't given a moment's thought lately to real work, and the *Uxley Courier* didn't use stringers, but she smiled at James. "We'd need to get a proper photo of the vicar chipping in to help."

"Well," he said, "not eating a scone!" Finishing, he wiped his hands on his trousers and looked at the sandbag crew for his proper spot.

"I'm afraid there's a hole in your sweater," Kim said to tease him.

"I have a fix for that," Alice said gaily.

"Never throw out one of Mum's!" He waved as he made off toward the river.

There were thermoses of coffee and tea, and knowing her place, Kim took over the coffee side of the table.

"Now that he's off," Alice said, "I'll tell you my little event." She looked around, to make sure no one was within hearing. "The Babbages and I went to church on Sunday. Rose was with us." She snorted. "We had the row all to ourselves. People stared. You'd think she'd pilfered the collection tray!"

"But that's not the event you referred to."

"No. It was one of my *trauma views*, and it came on me, a proper vision. Right as I sat in the congregation." She stared out at the river, mouth flat, as though seeing it all again. "I saw people holding a long, icy chain. All in a line they were, holding on, people of all sorts, but no one I knew. And they were, it looked like, glued to it."

"What, glued?"

"No, it was more like frozen. I had the impression the ice was so thick, or they'd been holding it so long. And then someone directing the thing, hands raised up like a symphony conductor or something."

A beat. "Like a what?"

Alice stopped when a worker came by. She poured tea into his thermos top, and he walked to the side to enjoy it.

She whispered. "Like the person was in charge. Directing things."

"But what did you say it reminded you of?"

Alice frowned at Kim's intensity. "Like a symphony conductor?"

"Yes, that's it. Like a symphony conductor," Kim murmured. Like a chorister.

"What, though? What do you make of what I saw, then?"

"I'm not sure, Alice. Maybe that someone's up to no good. That they're forcing people."

Alice frowned, considering. "But what do you suppose the *chain* meant?"

"Who was in the congregation that day? Anyone in church you didn't know? A stranger?"

"There were some that I took for weekenders. Maybe two people." Alice poured more tea for a longer line of men, now.

Kim was thinking about that word, chorister. And how it might have actually meant something important. Might have been a *spill*. Is that why the car forced her off the road? Von Ritter *spilled* and then tried to kill her?

Alice glanced at Kim, uneasy with her silence. "You think I'm daft? That this thing, whatever it is I've got, that it's getting out of hand?"

"No, Alice, no. Don't think like that. It's a gift."

She snorted. "A gift?"

"What if there's a crime, and you're the only one who can see it? Wouldn't it be worth it to know, to stop it?"

"Holding an icy chain doesn't sound like a crime." She narrowed her eyes at Kim. "Does it?"

ABBEY POND, UXLEY

WEDNESDAY, APRIL 22. Kim stood on the edge of Abbey Pond, staring at the water. They called it Abbey Pond, though the village abbey had been gone three hundred years, fallen into ruin and its stones carted away. Just a deer path was left of what had once been the road to the abbey, but people used it enough and it had a sign, so Owen shouldn't miss it.

Here in the woods, dusk hung heavily. The pond mirrored a faded sky, colorless, making the water look icy. It was always the icy pond she saw when she came there, no matter the time of year. At the pond, it was always December 1914. One of the coldest winters in memory.

When the animals died on the ice, she had blamed herself. It was her fault, of course, even if it was the wolves that got them.

She'd let the animals loose from the shelter, and as they sought their escape route, they ran down the hill, cats and beagles and the big old Newfoundland nobody had wanted. That year, she'd been eleven years old. Robert had just died in Belgium, and she had felt it her duty to protect the animals that, she'd heard, were going to be euthanized before the shelter had to close for lack of funds. *Euthanized.* She'd learned what the word meant. It meant *killed.* She'd had enough of death.

The animals ran down the embankment onto the ice. The wolves were waiting. Once thought extinct in Britain, they'd come down from the hills, ranging far in search of food. They'd found a perfect table. A smorgasbord.

When her father brought her here the next day to see what happened—she had confessed everything to him that morning—the splotches of red on the ice didn't seem like they could be dogs. But they were. The cats had been smarter or less able to plow through the snow. The surface was dotted with bodies frozen in their own sheen of blood.

Ever afterwards, it was how she thought of death. Like blood and ice.

She'd always believed that her Talent started to come upon her then. Beginning with the trauma of Robert's death, and then the horror of *those* deaths, the ones she had caused. And maybe it was also when she had turned away from her father. They had stood there, staring at the bodies that looked like they had been mowed down by machine guns. He had wanted her to learn something. But what?

She and her mother had left within the month. If she had said goodbye to her father, she couldn't remember. It didn't matter now.

Footsteps behind. She turned.

Owen sat on a fallen tree trunk as he came to grips with Kim's report. "I send you out for three days on your own, and here you've stirred up a hornet's nest."

"I've bungled it, I suppose." Kim had crossed one leg over her knee and scraped mud off her boot with a stick, making little progress.

He smiled. "Hardly. You've broken it open. But damn near got yourself shoved off a mountain."

"Someone was trying to kill me, you think?"

He didn't answer, but his look said *yes.*

"Why didn't they stay to finish the job, then?"

"Maybe they wanted it to look like an accident. To avoid a suspicious death."

The scene at the curve in the road came back to her, tinged with dread. When Owen had said there was risk, this is what he had meant. She might die.

"But why?"

"This von Ritter fellow, the one that might be a German spy, lost control and gave you a *spill*. The chorister. Maybe that was something he was at pains to hide. He tried an approach with you, to turn you. When that failed . . ." His voice trailed off.

She stared at the muddy stick in her hand, finally flicking it away. "He told me a chorister will bring us down. He meant bring England down. And that it would be 'one of our own.'" There was obviously something much larger there than she and Owen had guessed. "Will they try to come after me again?" She looked around the woods, afraid for the first time.

"I don't know. I think if they were going to kill you outright, they would have driven back down that muddy road and made sure you went over."

Owen stood up, brushing off the seat of his pants, and walked down to the water's edge. He looked around. "This isn't the best place for a meeting. Too many places to hide."

She joined him on the pond's edge. In the quiet forest, a breeze rumpled the water.

"This is getting serious," he said.

"Don't say we're quitting. We're not quitting."

"Perhaps we shouldn't delay any longer but let someone know what we've got," he said.

"They won't believe us! All we have is my claim that von Ritter referred to a chorister, which might or might not relate to a vision a friend of mine had who won't be tested and has zero credibility. It's nothing. They'd laugh you out the door."

He ran his hand over his scalp, through his already-wild hair.

"I'm not giving up." She stared out at the placid lake losing color by the moment, turning dark. You had to fight them, or the wolves would come out from the woods and feast.

Owen lowered his voice. "Here's the thing. Your friend's *trauma view*. It means something to me."

"The chain?"

"No. The ice. Remember that I told you that Stanley Yarrow wasn't the first to be involved with the Psychokinesis unit?"

She nodded as he went on. "It used to be run by Sam Reuben, but he left last year to take care of his son. The boy—fifteen years old—was beaten in broad daylight by young toughs who painted swastikas on him and left him paralyzed. It was right in the middle of Pickering, to everyone's dismay. The thing is, Sam was working on a project having to do with temperature decreases. *Cold cell*, it was called. We were told it couldn't be substantiated and that there were other priorities. We dropped it when Sam left."

Kim pounced on the idea. "It's a Talent. And the Germans don't want us to have it."

"Maybe Sam was making progress, after all."

"My God, do you think they attacked his son?"

"It's possible. The incident left him in need of constant care. A good pension and Sam was out the door."

"It ties nicely in with Fitz," she said. "He was the director, the one who stopped the cold cell research, wasn't he?"

"Yes. It might just be Nazi thugs who beat up the boy. But to follow up the *cold cell* idea, I can pay Sam a visit. He's right up there in Pickering, still."

"He won't talk about Monkton Hall, will he? The Official Secrets Act."

"We'll have to see. But you'll come along for the *spill*."

Kim grinned. They wouldn't be quitting. You had to fight them, with whatever you had. She knew that now. "Yes, sir."

The light was seeping out of the woods. They turned up the

path. Owen muttered, "And as to your friend, it would be terribly helpful if he or she *would* be tested."

"Then they'd know I'm a subject at Monkton, too."

"You know about *them*. It's hardly a fair exchange."

He didn't understand. Having the *spill* meant that no one would trust you again. They'd always feel like you were prying. A great way to kill a friendship.

But so was lying.

21

THURSDAY, APRIL 23. The next day, Kim and Owen sat in their parked car across the street from the building where Sam Reuben had a flat. The cobblestone street and row houses lay under a blanket of brownish fog. They waited, hoping he'd come home. He had moved from Pickering, Owen had discovered. Now, on the outskirts of Liverpool, his fortunes seemed to have declined.

"If they pensioned him off, it wasn't a very good pension," Kim said, noting the cramped look of the street, with its joyless, shuttered windows. Coal smoke was thick enough to scrape at her throat.

"Any pension is a good one, these times." Owen consulted his pocket watch. It had been a two-hour wait, and they'd already drawn attention for parking on a street devoid of parked cars. A few young men walked by, dressed shabbily, out of work. They looked at Kim and Owen, marking them as outsiders. Nice clothes, a posh car.

"Maybe he stopped for a pint."

"With his son needing him at home? That wouldn't be like Sam."

They waited. It was a risk to talk to Reuben. He might report them for breaking with secrecy. It would be his duty to do so, but Owen thought he might not, given their old relationship.

"Here he is." A man had come around the curve in the cobblestone street, heading toward the flat. Owen held up a hand for Kim to stay in the car. Without knowing Reuben's telephone number, they hadn't been able to call ahead. Now there was no telling what his reaction might be. Owen got out of the car and hurried across the street to meet Reuben as he approached the steps to his flat. After a few minutes, they looked over at Kim and began walking in her direction.

Owen opened the door for Kim to get out. Reuben stood next to the car, fixing her with an unhappy look. Sam Reuben was small of build with a high forehead and a few strands of hair arranged for maximum effect. He wore a heavy jacket that hung loose on his thin frame.

"Let's take a walk," Reuben said, in a cultured voice at odds with the neighborhood.

Owen exchanged a look with Kim. *This won't be easy. He doesn't want us here.*

They turned down an alley smelling of rotting garbage. Coal smoke gathered more thickly here, trapped between the tenements.

"A woman at Oxford, eh?" Reuben said.

"I'm in the graduate program. Was," Kim said, using their planned story. "Before I came to the records centre." They wouldn't call it HARC, much less Monkton Hall.

Reuben stopped and turned to them. "I'm not sure I know what you mean, *records centre*." He glanced toward the street, fidgeting.

"No," Owen said. "We don't need to use names." He paused, clearly at a loss now that they were talking in an alley surrounded by corners and windows above, where anyone might hear.

"It has to do with Fitz," Owen finally said.

"Fitz?"

"I think he's unreliable." He let that sit for a moment, trying to gauge Reuben's reaction.

"Unreliable," Reuben repeated. He looked down the alley, as though he might see the man himself. "Don't be daft."

"But Sam, signal intel has picked up things the other side oughtn't know. Not unless Fitz is handing over things."

"Oh? Well *someone* might be. It might not be him."

"I can put it to the test. If you help, Sam."

Reuben nodded, getting the picture clearly enough. "I haven't heard from you in a long time, Owen."

"I know. You moved away. When?"

"Six months. Since Michael died."

"I didn't know. I'm very sorry."

So that was the man's son, Kim figured.

"It was an embolism. The clot was lying within him, waiting to come loose. Then it did."

A gust of wind sent papers flapping down the alley. Kim was there to see if he'd *spill* something, but it didn't feel right. This man had suffered enough, and now they wanted to pull information out of him, even if it put him in jeopardy. How far she had sunk. It had started nobly enough, and now, this alley.

"Sam," Owen said, "you were working on a *cold cell* Talent. I need to know what you learned. Please. It could be important."

"Learned? We learned to leave it alone, that's what. You're not starting it up again?"

"No. But it was Fitz who canceled the research, isn't that right?"

"Of course it was Fitz. He told me personally."

"Well I have a suspicion that Fitz canceled it because the Germans told him to."

Reuben paced away, running his hands through his thinning hair. Then he turned back, looking at them, accusing. "I'm not listening to this. I'm not listening to you. I don't see you for a year, and all of a sudden you want me to . . . break with my pledge. For all I know, *you're* working for them." His face hardened. "Leave me alone."

Owen said, "I think Fitz could have had Michael beaten."

Reuben looked like he'd been struck.

It was ruthless to put Sam Reuben through this, especially as they had only circumstantial evidence to go on. It felt like bloody hell.

"I can't prove it," Owen went on. "But the *cold cell* work was important, and Fitz put an end to the research. Maybe he had to silence you."

Reuben was just a black silhouette against the marginally brighter street outside the alley. "He could have just killed me, then."

"It would have attracted attention. Maybe he wanted you gone. To care for Michael."

Reuben put his hand to his forehead.

Kim spoke for the first time. "Sam. We're trying to save lives."

"Lives." Reuben looked around him, as though the alley were full of people whose lives had been snatched away. He was a shadow in the alley, a man who'd had a career at Oxford and, for a short time, at Monkton Hall. Now a ghost.

Reuben whispered, "Fitz told me that the research was a threat. It was dangerous." His face was sweating, and he wiped his hand over it, leaving a smudge. "Weather, agriculture. It could alter food production if a Talent was at the high end of the scale. We had one person under study who could have been disruptive. We didn't dare tinker with it." He sneered. "I guess you know about that."

Owen shook his head. "I don't know anything."

Kim's mind was racing. They did know something. The chorister, according to von Ritter, was English. Was this the person Reuben had had under study? She tried not to think about it, so as not to chase the *spill* away, if *spill* it was. Maybe just the honest truth.

Reuben spoke in a fierce whisper. "But you come here with a story that Fitz lied. That he gave up the *cold cell* Talent to the Germans. You know enough to get us all thrown in prison, or worse." He shook his head. "They killed Michael. And they'll come after me next." He started backing away. "Get out of here. Leave me in peace." When Owen and Kim made no move, he spat, "Get out, get out!" He waved a hand as though fending off a blow. "If you come back, I'll report you. So help me God, I will."

"I'll keep your secret," Owen said.

"No one keeps secrets. HARC is full of holes. And you're one, too. A hole. Think of that."

He turned and stalked away, leaving them alone in the alley.

They gave him a few minutes before going back to the car. Kim's throat tasted bitterly of coal smoke as Owen took her by the arm, steering her quickly toward his car.

They settled into the car as Reuben let himself into his row apartment.

"A disruptive person," Owen said. "I'd very much like to know who that was."

"He's not going to say. He's terrified," Kim said.

Owen started the engine. "Drummond's log. We need to see it."

"Fitz wouldn't have left a record."

"Not a record. But something to go on. There might be a Talent rating, a name, something. But we have to see it." He pulled out into the street, speeding back in the direction of the main highway.

The log. Kim couldn't imagine how they would get the log away from Miss Drummond. Unless . . . "Drummond's one of yours?"

"No. We'll have to find a way."

They had a two-and-a-half-hour drive to figure it out, but she'd be driving alone. Owen pulled into the car park at the Huyton branch library where they'd left Kim's truck.

"Did you bring things for an overnight?" Owen asked.

"No, I didn't expect I'd need to."

"Stop and buy what you'll need." He leaned into the car window as Kim got behind the wheel. "Are you still game?"

Kim braced her hands on the wheel of the car to stop them from shaking. "Of course."

"Not *of course*," Owen said, narrowing his eyes. "If it's a major Talent, enough to be disruptive, as Sam said, we could be into military uses. *Now* it's dangerous. You understand that."

"Yes." She did understand. She had understood from the moment that she'd been forced off the road in the mud. She was no heroine, no Valkyrie. But she wasn't a coward, either.

Kim took a deep breath. "See you at the records centre."

By five o'clock, she'd checked into a small sixteenth-century coaching inn in the village not far from Monkton Hall. Using a few sheets from her notebook, she dashed off a breezy letter to her mother and stuffed it in a hotel envelope for posting. A stab of guilt pricked her to be so late in answering, but then she realized it had only been one week since her mother's letter had arrived. One week. In that time, it seemed that she had entered a different life, one that was oddly beginning to feel normal.

She sat for a few moments, letting the reality sink in. Here she was, determined to use her *spill* for a good cause—but one week!—how quickly she was moving deeper into the territory. The territory of prying and pursuit. For a good cause, she reminded herself.

And now the next lie.

Walter Babbage answered the phone when she called home saying she had worked late on the archives project and, since she was still not finished with some particulars, would spend the night in Pickering.

"Where are tha stayin', then?"

"The Queen's Head Inn."

"Sounds propah fancy," he muttered.

"Well, the hot water comes out of the cold tap, and the cold from the hot," Kim said. "But it will do for a night."

She hung up, wondering why Walter wanted to know her hotel. And how she and Owen were going to get past Miss Drummond in the morning. Not to mention Fitz Blum.

22

MONKTON HALL, NORTH YORK MOORS

FRIDAY, APRIL 24. Kim had an eleven o'clock appointment with Owen, a session devoted to careful dynograph calibrations. They were both too nervous to pretend to talk, so the session was quiet, with Owen setting things up at the window so that Kim could keep an eye on the yard.

At eleven forty, as was her habit, Miss Drummond came down the main porch steps and crossed the courtyard with Pip.

Kim turned to Owen. "I'm terribly sorry, but could we take a break? I didn't have breakfast in my hurry to make this appointment. Just a quick lunch? I promise to concentrate better then."

A few minutes later, she entered the east building of the Monkton Hall complex, the canteen with staff quarters above. About thirty other people were scattered at tables, many alone, others in twos and threes. A few women from the secretarial pool sat at a table by the door and sized her up as she went in.

Kim stood behind Drummond and several others as they lined up for their portion of beef brisket and green beans. She hoped that the woman wouldn't sit with anyone else, but as Owen had predicted, she took a seat alone at a table near the bowed window.

"May I join you?" Kim said, holding her tray and managing to look eager but not presumptuously friendly.

Miss Drummond stared up at her. With her dark hair pulled back in a bun, she looked every bit of her fifty years. They did not seem to have been happy years. "Pip is too nervous for company, I'm afraid. So nice of you to ask."

That had been a no, Kim realized after a beat. "Oh, but Pip and I are friends, I thought. After we both had a little accident together on the flagstones out there. A bond?" She looked at Pip for some kind of confirmation, but he cocked his head as if waiting for her to make a cogent point.

"Please, Miss Drummond."

Drummond frowned and glanced at the seat opposite her, giving permission for her to sit. "It's not encouraged," she said, sniffing. "Fraternizing."

"Well, I'm not the enemy," Kim tried to joke.

Drummond looked at her as though she had just barked out a state secret.

Kim sat down, her heart beating fast. This was the first time she would expose her clandestine role, and of course, Drummond might report her immediately to Fitz. If so, she had a cover story of wanting to check if her father had ever been tested for a Talent. It would come to a bad end but might deflect them from suspecting her true motives, and at least prevent them from tracing her back to Owen Cherwell.

The window was trimmed out in ruffled chintz, and the walls

had little rows of flowers corralled by vertical lines. It all seemed very ordinary and country-cottage, jarringly at odds with the place's real purpose. Paranormal research. Military applications.

She picked at the beef brisket until finally Miss Drummond said, "I presume you want something from me, something which I will feel obliged to deny. We have no openings for young ladies seeking employment. If you're thinking about that post in the indexing section, it was filled last week."

Kim coughed, having tried to breathe as she was swallowing. "Indexing?" She took a sip of water. "No, it's a different sort of favor, Miss Drummond."

The woman stared at her. At his mistress's feet, Pip put his muzzle down on his paws but managed to watch Kim nevertheless.

Here, in the midst of this awkward approach, Kim knew it was no use. It wasn't going to work, saying her father had been acting so strangely, and she felt certain it had to do with a Talent suppressed, one that he denied and she would like to confirm. It was a weak story, and even were it believable, Drummond would remain totally unmoved by personal problems. Owen thought otherwise, but Kim guessed that Drummond was concealing a deep dislike of Fitz, a dislike that might have started with Pip's coming to work but which extended to darker regions. And Kim had had experience with people who loved their pets. They would always wish you ill if you were mean to their dog.

"I need to see the logbook," Kim said, keeping her voice barely audible.

Miss Drummond chewed her mouthful, looking as though she had bit into a hunk of tar. She raised an eyebrow at Kim, maintaining a truly frightening silence.

"There is a spy at Monkton Hall," Kim said.

"And it is you."

"In a manner of speaking."

"There is only one *manner*."

Kim was in for it now. She had to go on before Miss Drummond lurched from the table and called the guards.

"You said that Fitzroy Blum is not what he seems."

"Neither, it would appear, are you, Miss Tavistock."

"But I think he's got entirely the wrong friends. Very dangerous ones. I'm trying to prove it." She had to get it all out, without delay. "Three minutes alone with the log. Leave it open on your desk today at closing. If I'm caught, you were careless, and I'm the only one who suffers."

Pip moved closer to Miss Drummond, picking up the tension at the table. He rubbed against her leg.

Kim stumbled on. "He's passing secrets. Everything you do here is going straight to . . . them."

Miss Drummond put down her knife and fork. She pulled her lunch tray closer, placing her unfinished lunch on it. Then she raised her eyes to Kim's, regarding her with a formidable scowl that made Kim want to slink away or apologize profusely, though it was far too late for either.

At last, Miss Drummond stood, taking Pip's leash in hand. "I will see you in the loo in ten minutes. Enjoy your lunch." With that, she departed the canteen.

Kim had completely lost her appetite. She pretended to eat, fighting with an impulse to check in with Owen. It wouldn't help. Everything rested with Drummond now.

At the requisite time, she made her way to the main building and the women's lavatory. As she crossed the foyer past Drummond's empty desk, she glanced up to the mezzanine to see that Fitz Blum was chatting with someone near the railing.

He glanced down at her, confident, completely at ease with his position and his handy *natural defender* Talent that assured he would not be susceptible to *spills.*

He might have observed Drummond going in first. But she made for the lavatory door.

The woman was waiting for her. She turned on the tap, letting it run, and faced Kim. "My dear, you are a terrible spy."

"Oh," was all Kim could muster.

"There are now thirty-five people who saw us sit together at lunch." She paused, letting this fact sink in, a fact she was obviously not pleased with.

"I'm sorry. I didn't know how else to talk to you."

She glanced at the door. "If someone comes in, go into a stall immediately. Do you understand?" Kim nodded. "Now, then. I don't know who you work for, but you are far too naive and feckless to be working for the other side. I can either turn you in or trust you. One of these actions may assure that I spend the next few years in jail."

Jail? Though Kim had thought of death and torture, she had not yet considered jail. It seemed a tawdry end.

Drummond had been regarding her with a withering stare. It demanded a response.

"I think . . . that is, I have some evidence that our director is working against us. And I happen to believe that just because someone is a friend of the King, he should not be immune from the consequences of being a traitor. You can believe me or not. But *I* am no traitor. My brother died in the Great War and I owe him something. I don't know what, but it's not to stand by and *do nothing.*"

Drummond summoned a deep breath, letting it out slowly. She glanced behind her and pointed to the last stall. "At precisely two o'clock, come into the loo. You will see that the stall has an OUT OF ORDER sign."

With a thudding heart, Kim realized that Drummond was going to help.

"If no one is here, enter the stall. The log will be in a sack on the floor, as though it had been left behind. You will have ten minutes to peruse it. When you are finished, replace the log in the sack and leave it on the floor. Wait until no one else is in the loo, and leave." She stared at Kim in some exasperation. "You do have a watch?"

"What? Oh. Yes. Two o'clock exactly." She licked her lips with a tongue that was utterly dry. "Thank you. Thank you for helping."

"You might well thank me. But I shall not be drawn into your schemes any further, so kindly do not ask." She turned off the water and went to the door.

Miss Drummond glanced back. "Catch the bastard," she murmured, and walked out of the restroom.

THE MOORS

Kim had an hour and a half to wait. She had no plausible reason to be at Monkton Hall and didn't want to slip into Owen's office, which Miss Drummond would be sure to note was not an appointment listed in the schedule.

She took a short drive into the moors. After the meeting with Drummond, she felt the need to be out outside in the crisp air, and she knew just the place: Hallworth Castle.

As she got out of the truck at the car park, she buttoned her coat. A stiff breeze had come up, and though the day was bright, a few raindrops slanted in from a flat-bottomed thundercloud in the north. She made her way up the trail to the ruins. It was here that she had first become Owen's accomplice, and she wanted to recapture the certainty she'd felt that day, of England and her part of it. She and Owen were following clues that might amount to nothing. She was exploiting knowledge gained from her friendship with Alice Ward, without revealing herself to her friend. Now she had urged Miss Drummond to break with the Official Secrets Act, with what consequences, she did not know. Worst of all, she had come to distrust her own father. Was she in fact embarked upon an enterprise that could mean Julian's ruin? Unable to sleep last night, she found herself wishing that she hadn't seen him enter the barn, where he had burned something that she took to be incriminating. Was it better to know or not know? That had always been her dilemma.

The barbican loomed ahead. It seemed very confining to walk down that aisle of stone where one would be invisible to the outside world, where anything might happen. But to reach the viewpoint, it was the closest way. Passing through, she came into the center of the ruins. Before her stretched the rolling vales and hills, splendid and wild. The towering rain cloud bore down upon the ruins, cutting out the sun, stamping the color from the moors, but even so, it was a thrilling view.

Movement to her left drew Kim's attention. About a hundred yards away, a woman sat on an upright stone, having a sandwich. White-haired and petite, she wore a cloche hat and a nice tweed coat, seemingly oblivious to the threatened rain.

Noticing Kim, she waggled her fingers and held up her sandwich as though to say *lunchtime*. Kim waved back.

It was fine to have just one other person at the ruins, but with a little old lady in a tweed coat sitting nearby with her picnic lunch, it was no longer quite the wild scene she had so favored before.

She strolled for a while longer to use up the time. The prim lady was still seated at her viewing post when Kim left the ruins. It was 1:38, time to leave for her appointment in the loo.

MONKTON HALL

As she approached the main entrance of Monkton Hall, she caught a glimpse of Owen at the window of his office. He must be bursting with curiosity, but he would have to wait a little longer. They had arranged a debriefing in the only place at Monkton where they could be sure of privacy: the ancient bricked-in chapel. There was an entrance—not secret, but seldom remembered or used.

But now she was headed to the loo. Once inside, she found a couple of women chatting by the sink and, noting the sign on the stall next to the restroom wall, she went into another stall and sat on the toilet. By her Helbros, it was 2:02. Once the women left, she knelt on the floor to make sure she saw no other feet under the stall doors. Then she exited her stall and went into the one with a makeshift sign on it, OUT OF ORDER.

A bulky sack rested against the wall. She sat on the toilet stool and opened the bag, drawing out the log.

She carefully opened the covers of the thick book. As Owen had explained to her, each research subject's name was entered by date of first appointment. She carefully opened the book at the place where the ribbon marked the final entry. It was two weeks before, April 4, 1936. Reginald Oldstrum, 23, TV, 3. That would mean one Reginald Oldstrum, twenty-three years old, *trauma view* Talent, ranking of 3. Miss Drummond's finely leaded pencil notations were crisp, interspersed occasionally with different handwriting from when she had been absent.

Kim's hand shook as she traced down the column of Talents. She was looking for CC, *cold cell*, a Talent with very few subjects. Here was Theodore Vaughn, CC, 2; and Grace Hull, CC, 4.

As she swept down the page, she heard someone come into the restroom. Carefully, she lifted her feet off the floor lest they see someone in the stall marked out of order. But still she scanned the page, using every moment. She was half through the book, sweating profusely, careful to miss nothing. It was 2:06. Four minutes left.

Working backward in time, here was her own name. July 18, 1935. Kim Tavistock, thirty-two (as she had been when she started at Monkton Hall), S (*spill*), rank of 6.

The toilet flushed, the sink faucet came on, the door clicked shut. She read on as swiftly as she could.

Her finger stopped on the page, her heart crimping. She knew this name. Hugh Aberdare. November 30, 1934. CC, 1. How extraordinary. Georgi's brother had a Talent.

She went on, coming up to the first entry in the book. In her search, she'd found no one with a *cold cell* rank of over 4. She had failed to memorize the name of the person with that rank and was about to return to the entry when she turned back to the page with Hugh Aberdare's name. She looked very closely. The *1* was scrunched to the left. It was not in a strict line with the rankings above and below it. She frowned. Perhaps the second digit had been erased. She looked more closely, but the only evidence was the *1* being out of alignment.

She stared at the stall door, her mind churning. At Summerhill, she and Hugh had sat together in his Mercedes in the woods, and in the sudden bitter cold, snow had fallen around them.

Owen's young subject with the Talent of *hypercognition* had said Georgi Aberdare was hiding something about a German plot. Maybe what she was hiding was that she knew what her brother was up to. She might be in on it, or had discovered it. Georgi knew something, and Owen's *hypercognition* young lady had sensed it.

Hugh Aberdare . . . She scrutinized his entry in the logbook. He was, she felt sure, categorized as a 10.

Kim stepped into the old buttery of the mansion. It lay in the back of Monkton Hall, easily accessed from the rear garden. When the canteen and kitchen had relocated to the adjacent building, HARC used the buttery for equipment storage.

By the fading light that fell from the casement windows of the storage room, Kim found the entrance Owen had described, an ancient planked door. The handle of the door was missing, but she could lift the latch that protruded.

The chapel was in pitch darkness. She left the door open for the meager light.

The sweat on her face turned icy in this buried room, and she held her arms around herself for warmth. It was very hard to contain her excitement. Hugh Aberdare had found a way to outdo his sister. Strange that at Summerhill he had not seemed interested in politics. He could have been dissembling, of course. Not that being a 10 for a *cold cell* Talent signified that he was a traitor. Or a chorister.

A figure appeared in silhouette in the doorway. "Kim?"

"Here," she whispered.

Owen rummaged near the wall for a few moments, then lit a candle in an iron candleholder and shut the door.

The chapel was smaller than Kim had expected. To her

disappointment, the walls were gouged where materials had been removed. All that was left of the altar was a raised platform with a bricked-in window framed by a pointed gothic arch. Though the various owners had done violence to the place, one feature remained still lovely. A vaulted ceiling with delicate pilasters flew above them, too inaccessible for easy pillaging.

Owen held the candle high. "They bricked in the sanctuary during the reign of Elizabeth I. It wasn't a good time to be a papist." With his flickering candle and flyaway hair, he looked like a Victorian gentleman lighting his way to bed. "You met with Miss Drummond."

"Owen, I saw the log." She recited her actions of the last three hours, and her accomplice listened without interruption until he heard about Hugh Aberdare.

"A 10?" Owen was skeptical. "In any case, Hugh Aberdare's Talent was strong enough that Fitz risked shutting down the entire research and getting rid of Sam Reuben."

Kim nodded. "So that the Germans could exploit *cold cell* Talents, not us."

"And perhaps they have found its use," Owen said. "To bring England down."

"But how? Destroy our crops? Ice up our planes?"

"They might mean to destroy our shipping, our navy, in the Channel. With floating ice."

"What, with icebergs?"

He caught her incredulous tone. "Well. Churchill had a scheme to freeze pontoons of hay and float them in the English Channel to sink enemy convoys. It could be done."

Owen went over to the altar and sat down. He placed the candle beside him and Kim joined him. They stared into the denuded room.

"Reuben said the project was shut down as being too disruptive," Kim said. "And that there was one disruptive person. No one else in the log can possibly fill the bill." She was aware that they were sitting on a Catholic altar with a lit candle. If she had been religious, she might have hoped for divine inspiration. But they so far were left with just their conjectures. Incomplete. Tantalizing.

Kim went on. "Von Ritter said one of our own will bring us down. We might know who that is! And we have a *trauma view* of a frozen chain, tying this to *cold cell* Talents, in a way."

"Right. And when your friend of the *trauma view* said that the people held a chain, he or she was seeing how they were *linked*. So that they could work in concert."

"Sing together," Kim said.

"Yes. Sing. Conducted by one person with a very specific Talent."

"The *chorister*," Kim said in wonder. The word echoed in the vaulted chapel.

"That means there's a chorus," Owen said. "Many people, all with the *cold cell* Talent. Working together."

"Not here!"

"Maybe here, maybe in Germany."

"Or both sides." She sighed, realizing a missed opportunity. "I should have written down the other *cold cell* Talents listed in the log." She'd never get the log from Drummond again.

"Well. All in all, intriguing, but nothing definitive," Owen said. "We don't know what the *cold cell* weapon is. And if Hugh Aberdare is merely a 1 after all, then we've still got nothing."

"Why didn't your *hypercognition* subject—that teenager who spent Christmas at Georgi's—why didn't she read Hugh Aberdare instead of Georgi? They may both be involved, but it seems Hugh is the main one."

"Right, but Lord Daventry wasn't there, according to the girl. This was at Georgiana's London house."

She was beginning to see a course of action and wished, dearly wished, there were an alternative. "Perhaps I should confront Georgi."

"Determined to go over the cliff, are you?"

"I could lay the evidence before her and give her a chance to clear herself. To tell what she knows."

"And she goes straight to Fitz and reports you?"

"No." She was working this out as she went along. "I tell her I'm from the authorities. Working undercover. And that her head will be on the block."

He shook his head in exasperation. "You'll blow your cover. You'll be no use ever again."

And no use ever again if they killed her. She tossed it off with, "Someday you'll find a 9 or an 10 for the *spill*. You won't need me anymore."

"But you're perfect. In some way, you just don't *seem* like a spy." He stood up. "I have to get back."

Kim held her ground. "But what are we to *do*?"

"I have to think. We're stuck for the moment. Give me a few days to work something out."

They walked to the door. Owen said, "You're not to contact Georgi. It's madness to walk in there and tell what we know."

She felt horribly let down. They had come so far, but now they were at a dead end.

"You will not confront Georgi Aberdare, Kim."

"No." It was the only possible thing for her to say. They couldn't argue here, and Owen had to get back to his post.

"I'll contact you in a few days," he said, blowing out the candle. They slipped through the door to the storage room.

"Wait ten minutes, then leave." He put a hand on her shoulder. "Good work, Kim. You've accomplished a jolly miracle, you know that."

"Thank you," she said, not at all satisfied.

He left through the door to the south garden.

She stood there, wishing that she had urged him to hurry. To decide tonight. To come up with a plan *now*, not in a few days. But she had the distinct impression that she had just been relieved of her mission. *Jolly good work. Well done, old girl.* He had let her do the legwork, but when it came to strategy, he was keeping it to himself.

Kim could imagine herself disobeying. Going to Georgi despite Owen's injunction. Because in good conscience, he was never going to let her risk her life.

But if she did this, what were the chances that Georgi would implicate her own brother? She thought back to all she had seen between brother and sister, and all at once, she put together what had been going on at Summerhill. In this brother-sister relationship, the love was one-way. Hugh loved his sister. Wanted her approval, no matter how she abused him. But Georgi didn't love *him*. In fact, she despised Hugh. It came out in every interaction she had with him. It was Hugh who wanted her regard. He might love Georgi. But it would never be mutual.

If Kim played a role with Georgi as a covert investigator with the police, her charade would be ruined only if Georgi divulged it. And she would be no worse off then than she was now, with no way forward. She supposed it was dangerous. But if the authorities were on to you, killing one police officer would not help you. She thought Georgi would cooperate to save her own skin.

She couldn't be sure. Was it worth it, was it even sensible, to try?

A conviction was growing in her that in the realm of espionage, there were no certainties. If you waited until you were safe, if you delayed until you knew the absolute truth, you would never take action. You would play it safe, sit on the sidelines. You'd listen to judicious people like Owen. You'd let evil happen, all with the excuse that it might get you ostracized, ruined, or killed. The good folk of Uxley had not rallied for Rose. People in this country were doing nothing, and doing it left and right.

No, Georgi wasn't a sure thing, but she was the next step.

PART III

PEOPLE OF THE FOG

23

THE PARK, UXLEY

MONDAY, APRIL 27. Kim had her train ticket to London in her handbag. Over the past two days, she had methodically organized her approach to Georgi. She was ready.

Now, killing time an hour before her train, she was in the city park next to the station. Alice was with her, having volunteered to drive her down from Wrenfell.

They stood in front of the war memorial, a tall marble slab with a metal plaque attached, listing the names of the Uxley men who had lost their lives in the Great War.

"Twenty-eight names," Alice said, sighing. "I think I have them all memorized."

Twenty-eight seemed a small number, and it was, compared to the tally of the country's fallen. But for Uxley, a catastrophic loss.

Robert's name was the third down, as they were listed in the order of their deaths. It was a comfort to have his name inscribed here, as they had not been able to have him home for burial. He was interred in Belgium.

After Ypres, the family had had a few things returned to them: the coins from his pocket that day, his sword, his horse's bridle. There were his personal effects from his bivouac, now in a chest in a bedroom on the third floor at Wrenfell. No one could bear to give them to the relief effort. Baron's bridle hung on a nail in the barn, the old dried mud still clinging to it; it spoke of Robert more than his uniform or his sword, though it was a piece of tack like many others. At times, Kim had seen her father touch that bridle absently if they were talking in the barn, as though he might have done so every time he was in there. As indeed he might. She did.

"He was, what," Alice said, "twenty-three?" Strands of her hair, escaping from under her hat, lit up a fiery red in the sun.

"Twenty. It's so odd to think I'm older than he was. I always think of myself as the younger sister." She looked down to the river, with its load of sun-infused water, endlessly running. She murmured, "I should never have gone past him."

"Yes, you should. He gave his life so that we all could go on." Alice took Kim's arm and they walked slowly back toward the station. As they passed the bandstand, they saw a few words chalked onto the back wall that they hadn't noticed before: GET RID OF IMBECILES.

Alice snorted, and shook her head. "I'll tell the constable. We'll soon have it gone."

Seeing the scrawled words darkened Kim's thoughts. It was a poison. A slow drip of a concoction—part hate, part fear—and one that could sicken Uxley. And the enmity could spread. It *was* spreading, she feared. Words on a bandstand in a park. She worried what it could become.

When they got to the train platform, they sat on a bench to wait. "We all wonder why it is that we should be alive and not they," Alice said, still thinking about Robert. "You know there's no answer to that."

"But there's an obligation."

"Yes. To live well. Fully."

"No," Kim said. "To stand against them." She met Alice's gaze. "When the wolves come."

"They're after Rose, you mean."

Yes, Kim thought. *Among others.*

THE DORCHESTER HOTEL, LONDON

Georgi was sitting at a lovely round table under a potted palm in a corner of the Dorchester. She wore an elegant black suit with a little spray of a hat perched on her upswept coiffure. Kim stopped for a moment at the entrance, gathering her resolve.

When she'd learned that Georgi was in London, she'd determined that it was best to meet where she could be sure there were no listening devices. She'd have to think of these things now that she was on her own.

The maître d' escorted her to Lady Georgiana's table, where Kim managed to smile and sit and thank Georgi for meeting her.

"Oh, I could not miss this! Julian Tavistock's daughter is in need of a private conversation. I cannot imagine." Georgi accepted an opened menu from the waiter. "Champagne," Georgi told him.

"I don't think . . ." Kim began.

Georgi flashed an irritated look at her and said, "The Veuve Clicquot."

"How are Loxley and Parker?" Kim asked, scanning the menu, wishing her French were up to the challenge.

"Oh, back to being such scamps. They miss you. You must come and stay again sometime soon."

And bring my father, Kim thought.

"And bring Julian. He is ignoring me, which is dreadful of him. However do you stand him?"

"I'm stuck with him, I'm afraid."

When the waiter arrived with their champagne, he poured for them and took their orders of sole for Kim and glazed duck for Georgi.

Kim was ready with a planned speech, but it wouldn't do to discuss business during the meal. The English simply didn't, so she must endure banter and participate somehow, although she and Georgi had nothing in common except her father. And the Summerhill weekend.

"It was very good of you to have me down for the weekend. And so lovely to meet Sir Edgar and Bea Thackeray."

"It was a disaster, my dear. We're still shoveling mud. And you ran your car a bit off the road and were rescued by Julian! I can't imagine a less successful weekend, but you are very good to say otherwise."

The waiter appeared and filled her glass, which she had emptied much too quickly.

"I notice that you didn't mention the charming Herr von Ritter." Georgi gave that frightening red smile for which she was justly famous.

"No. I can't say I found him charming. Not exactly."

"Really? Then you must be immune. Do you prefer women?"

Kim managed not to sputter her champagne.

Georgi rounded her eyes innocently. "Some do, you know."

"I should not like to criticize a man who was a guest at your home."

"Well, it isn't *my* home, it's Hugh's, so feel perfectly free."

"He flirted with me. Rather too hard. I didn't find him sincere."

Georgi raised a glance at the waiter, who appeared instantly to pour. "Sincerity. Is that valued, then, in Pickering?"

"Uxley."

"Oh, Uxley. But if one must be *sincere*, one can hardly flourish in the right circles."

The luncheon proceeded in agonizing short stabs of conversation. Kim thought about giving Georgi some warning of what was to come, but there was no ramping up to the subject of one's brother being a traitor. She wondered when Hugh had first been visited by his extraordinary Talent, and how he had kept it secret. People who were beyond adolescence when the bloom began could come into their Talent at any time. He must have gone to Monkton Hall for answers. And, if he was a 10, he could have been picked off by Fitzroy Blum and recruited to the German cause.

When at last the meal was over, Kim began, "It's about Hugh."

Georgi raised an eyebrow. "You came all the way to London to discuss *Hugh?*"

Kim put her napkin on the table, grateful to be done with food. "He's gotten himself in a bit of trouble. I was hoping you could help."

"Well, Hugh is nothing but trouble. What is it this time?"

Time for the plunge. The dining room with its linen tablecloths and gold velvet chairs practically shouted for her to behave, to remain on the topics of idle pursuits, but it was not to be.

"I think you know that Hugh is working for Erich von Ritter." At Georgi's incredulous look, Kim pushed on. "We know quite a bit about them. Enough that Hugh could be brought up on charges. I want to ask for your help. So that you can make clear where you stand."

"We? What do you mean, *we?*" Georgi had closed down, sitting back in her chair and looking at Kim like she had admitted to being a Bolshevik.

"I can't disclose who I work for. I'm coming to you because I'm terribly afraid Hugh is dealing with some very bad people."

"Are you with the police? Is that what this is about? His debts?" She reached for her champagne, her hand shaking. After taking a sip, she said, "Did you come to Summerhill to write it up? Or to catch my brother borrowing money from the wrong people?" Her eyes were dark slashes, her fingernails lacquered and ready for battle.

She steadied herself to tell the next part. The piece that, if Georgi was a traitor, might put Kim in the sights of Nazi conspirators. "Hugh has been tested by the government. For Talents. Did you know?"

"Certainly not. Talents?"

"He's rated very high in one Talent. The Talent relates to ice and cold, and can be used in warfare, in fact."

Georgi looked around the room as though expecting Kim's associates to raid the Dorchester. When she looked back to Kim, she murmured wonderingly, "I really think you believe all this."

"It doesn't matter what I believe. But if we don't stop your brother, he's going to help Germany get onto a war footing with us. Germany has been developing the use of Talents as weapons for years. And Hugh is helping them."

Georgi shook her head slowly. "Our little Yorkshire girl is a government agent. I dare say you played the rube very well, Kim. But I am terribly disappointed. I liked you better when you were *sincere.*"

It smarted, but Kim was not going to allow Georgi the upper hand. "If you know anything, it will go better for you if you give him up. I don't think you're such a fan of Germany that you would help them with a weapon."

"What kind of weapon is snow? Or the cold, did you say? Really, you are seeing conspiracies everywhere, even in the weather!" Georgi glared as a waiter approached, and he faded back. She leaned forward, lowering her voice to a whisper. "You are trying to ruin us. Trump up some wild ideas of weapons and Talents. . . . Why are you doing this?"

"It's Hugh who is doing it. I think von Ritter is involved, but on that score, I'm less sure. I can only tell you that there's evidence against Hugh already." She saw the fight going out of Georgi and softened her tone. "I believe you're hoping there won't be a war. But if you thought one was coming, you'd be loyal to your country."

Georgi had grown very quiet. The venom had risen into her fangs, but she hadn't struck. She was considering her options.

"I don't know what Hugh has gotten into. I'm not involved with this, whatever it is." She turned a sly look on Kim. "If you had any proof, you wouldn't be having lunch with me, you'd have arrested him."

"There's no proof yet. There might not be proof until it's too late. Georgi, do you want to give England to Hitler?"

Georgi rolled her eyes. "How you do dramatize." She toyed with her champagne flute, turning it round and round. "It's his gambling debts," she finally whispered. "It all came to a crisis last summer, when he began taking steps to sell Summerhill. By September, he was solvent again. Rolling in cash."

"German cash," Kim murmured. Georgi had just given Hugh a motive. The need to sell Summerhill.

Georgi snorted. "I did wonder what he'd done to earn it."

Oh, it was a *spill*, she guessed, a lovely *spill*. Kim held her breath lest she ruin the moment with too much delight.

Georgi stared at her champagne. "He really is an utterly pathetic creature."

"And von Ritter is his handler."

"To think that Erich would go behind my back." She was lost in her thoughts, in the misery of having been taken of advantage of by someone whom she hoped to take advantage of herself.

The check came, and Georgi signed for it, waving the waiter away when he tried to offer dessert. So, they were not going to sit for another fifteen minutes while Georgi went into headlong *spill* mode. *Mustn't be greedy*, Kim thought.

"Georgi. You can't tell anyone of our conversation. My work is protected by the Official Secrets Act. You understand." Once you started lying, it was dreadfully easy, even essential, to keep doing it.

Georgi nodded.

"There's nothing more you can help us with?"

"No. I've told you, I don't know anything. Except this: Hugh told me the day before yesterday that I should stay close to home for a while."

Kim went on alert. "Oh? Why?"

"He wouldn't say. But he made me promise not to travel for a while. He was rather anxious, as he gets now and then."

"For how long? Did he say?"

"No. I haven't any travel plans for the foreseeable future, so

I promised, just to get him off the topic. Is it an attack, is that what you think?" She waved her jeweled hands, smirking. "A giant snowstorm that will halt the trains and bring us to our knees?"

Bring us down, Kim thought in increasing dread. One of our own will bring us down. "You're sure he didn't mention a date?"

"He did not. I can see you're trying to make something out of this, but Hughy is often over-solicitous for me, as though *I* were the one needing help." She collected her handbag and fixed Kim with an appraising look. "I also have the deposit certificates for his bank accounts. I suppose you could trace the money. Would that prove to you people that I'm an innocent and cooperative family member?"

"It would be a good start."

"Excellent, then." Georgi stood. "Good day, Kim. It's been a brutal lunch but endlessly fascinating. Now that I know you better, with your quick wits and ruthless pursuit of the weak, I think you could have made a lovely addition to my circle. Too bad you have to work for a living."

As Georgi turned away, Kim called her name.

She turned back.

"It would also be helpful to know, helpful for our investigation, if you had any information on whether my father is involved in any of this."

Georgi's lip curled. "Poor little farmhouse spy. You'll never be able to trust anyone, will you? Not even your own father." With that, she swept out of the room.

24

MONDAY, APRIL 27. The afternoon had turned steely gray, with the sun passing unnoticed through a sky thick with smoke and threatened rain. The park's drab greens framed the walkways, speckled with visitors strolling, pushing prams, sitting on benches.

Kim had to keep moving, to walk off her agitation. Hugh Aberdare had warned his sister not to travel *for a while*. Alarmingly, one could draw the conclusion that even traveling right now was not a good idea. If a strike was planned against England, Hugh's entreaty suggested it might come soon, very soon. Along with this chilling insinuation, Georgi had revealed a motive for Hugh to help Germany: money.

But it was all still conjecture.

What could they bring to Whitehall, after all? A *spill* in a gazebo, a friend with visions, a logbook that showed Hugh as a 1 for *cold cell* abilities. Then there was Fitz, who had discontinued a minor arm of research, research that a former employee was terrified to discuss. Sam Reuben was their best lead. But would the authorities question him on such slim evidence and risk starting an investigation against Fitzroy Blum, a confidant of King Edward?

She sat next to the lake, head in hands. She was operating behind Owen's back, in effect betraying the man who trusted her. Was this, then, the life of a spy, to lie, suspect and betray? Georgi's words came back to her. *You'll never be able to trust anyone, not even your father.*

And as for Georgi, she had seemed genuinely surprised by Kim's suggestions about Hugh. There were any number of times during the luncheon when she might have wobbled or exposed herself as a liar. Instead, she came off as an estranged sister who thought Hugh was in trouble. But not as a traitor. How desperately Georgi must have wished to remain unaware of Hugh's activities! But one took note of details that fit well with one's wider views, and Georgi saw her brother as incompetent, foolish. A *pathetic creature.* She likely would not have even imagined that he would be taken seriously by German intelligence. She must have assumed that von Ritter was in Summerhill to enjoy her in the drawing room and the boudoir. It was an interpretation of events that was very Georgi Aberdare. If she was pretending, it was a bravura performance. And the thing was, Kim didn't think Georgi was an actress. She was merely superficial, self-centered, and clueless, through and through.

A flock of ducks came skimming over the water, landing in formation and, after a few moments, swept into the air again as though practicing for a larger operation.

Kim sat for a while, letting her thoughts fall into place. There was a step she did not want to take, one that she had been unwilling to seriously consider until now. It was a desperate step but one that might glean the proof she needed. Compared to that, even a visit with her father seemed reasonable. Julian might be her last chance.

Her last chance to keep from walking into the enemy camp.

ALBEMARLE STREET, LONDON

It was dusk. Kim stood in front of a building that she was sure was famous. It was noble, with fourteen tall columns on the frontage. Her father had told her the name of the building, but she could not remember it.

She walked past this imposing front, having taken a cab to the vicinity of her father's flat, which she had visited once or twice. She might go to him tonight and tell him everything. But she had not yet decided to confide in him. She would walk past 27 Albemarle Street. No harm in that.

Intermittent rain spat down on her, reminding her that she would have to take cover eventually. She was glad of her green plaid wool coat that kept her snug against the unseasonably cold London spring. Her brown hat came very far down across her forehead, and she felt sure that if she saw her father, she could turn away in time and not have to meet him.

She had never felt more solitary. At this busy corner of London, people crossed in every direction on their way to supper appointments and errands and to meet friends. She had no London friends other than her cousin Theodora and her husband. In three years, they had only met twice. Then there was her father's brother, William, but he and Julian had fallen out, so the family was not close. She was alone. It was difficult not to feel the stranger. Everyone thought of her as American, even, at times, her father. It was true that she had adapted to being alone. She had been eleven when her mother had taken her to the States. In that year of 1914, Kim wouldn't have cared if they had moved to the South Pole or to China. She had carried her world inside her, full of memories and imaginings. The outside world was dangerous and too full of turmoil to be trusted. There was war, death, divorce. She had been carried along like a piece of bark on a river, but inside, she had been sufficient unto herself.

Now, though, she looked up at number 27 Albemarle and wondered if she had needlessly separated herself from an ally. And if her father was involved in something dark, she thought it time that he came clean about everything. But if, as she hoped, he could convince her that he was not involved in anything disloyal, his judgment about what she had discovered could be valuable. Since he had the usual Eton contacts of a man in his social position, he might be able to identify someone to whom she and Owen could go once they felt able to make a case. Of course, it would mean telling him about her activities.

She felt frozen at the choice point, standing on the sidewalk, watching the building. A light was on in the window of his unit.

Pulling the belt of her coat tighter in the cold spring air, she tried to discern what sort of man lived behind those windows or lived there sometimes. The summary came to her unsparingly: He had let her mother take his daughter to America; he had turned against Robert. She knew it wasn't fair to think so, especially about Robert, but her mind went there, to an emotional truth that might have no daylight logic, but which was no less persuasive for that.

No, she wasn't going to do it. She could not go to that apartment and tell Julian everything, not yet. She didn't have enough to persuade him of a conspiracy. And trust in her father was, if not dead, at least a reach too far.

So, then, Erich von Ritter.

A cold resolve overtook her. Her next move would be to play cat and mouse with the man from Munich.

But who was the cat, who the mouse?

A SECURE FLAT, LONDON

Julian sat in the chair of honor, the only one with arms. The windows were shuttered and curtained, and a pole lamp threw a circle of yellow light on the map before him. His team sat around him on straight-backed chairs, a pot of tea and food wrappers littering the table before them.

Elsa leaned against the hutch, eager to get back to her job, watching Kim Tavistock. She had begun her surveillance of Kim on Friday. Thanks to a report from Walter Babbage that Kim was spending the night at an inn near Monkton Hall, Elsa had been waiting for her when she left the Queen's Head Inn that morning. But what had started as a protection detail for Kim against a possible von Ritter threat had just turned more complicated.

Fin sat holding a burning cigarette that he didn't smoke and which had an ash an inch long. Rory smoothed out the map on the table, staring at it as though at any moment, it would arrange itself in a more pleasing configuration.

"He's a bloody magician," Fin muttered. "We had 'im at Mayfair, then *pfft*, gone."

Julian was tired of the words *we lost him* when it came to Erich von Ritter. When they found him again, he was going to disappear well and good, into the maws of the service. Once he vanished, the Germans would realize he was compromised, but it might not matter to them, depending on how big their plans were.

Fin, who had taken a special dislike to von Ritter at Summerhill—where Fin's cover was "Peter," part-time footman to Hugh Aberdare—was convinced that von Ritter had tried to kill Kim. And he'd been mightily sick of the Scotties by the end of the latest weekend at the Aberdare estate. He was ready for some action.

"Right, then," Julian said, having heard the reports. "Von Ritter last seen at Sir Lionel Bowes's in Mayfair. House under surveillance, phone tapped." He looked up ironically at Fin. "This time, you've got the back door watched?"

Fin snorted in appreciation and lit a cigarette from the nub of the last one.

Julian went on, nodding at Rory. "Your team is on Georgi Aberdare's house and telephone. She met with my daughter today at the Dorchester."

And why had Georgi and his daughter met yet again? No one in the room was saying that she was one of them. They were still willing to talk as though Kim needed protection, having come into harm's way by virtue of a high-stakes *spill* that had come to her in some chance encounter. He wondered which team members actually believed that, or if anyone had doubts about her loyalty. As for himself, he believed that she had gotten next to someone in the hopes of a *spill*. And succeeded. Someone at Summerhill, likely von Ritter, who then had his driver try running her off a cliff. It must have been one hell of a *spill*.

Kim's rating as a 6 was a significant ability, if just short of a major talent. She had lived for a long time with the experience of people confessing to her. He wondered what that had been like for her. Disconcerting, embarrassing, unnerving . . . or fascinating? Maybe she was doing investigative reporting into something she learned at Monkton Hall. If so, she had been in trouble from the moment she decided to exploit HARC's secrets. The little fool.

He shifted his gaze to Elsa, who had continued the tail to London and the restaurant. He summarized: "Kim left the luncheon and walked through Hyde Park for an hour and a half, meeting no one. Then she went to my apartment building, watched it for ten minutes, and left. Now at the Strand Palace in the West End."

Elsa nodded.

"Does she think she's being followed?"

"Not a bit. She looks like she just broke up with her boyfriend. Watching the ducks. I fancy she was thinking of throwing herself into the lake."

Hyde Park at dusk and Kim didn't worry about wandering around or who might be following her. Even after the cliff incident, she was unwary. But troubled, Elsa reported. Troubled about what? They couldn't actually afford to have people on Kim, not with all the leads they were following. E would put a stop to it at some point. For now, Julian judged her at risk.

Fin flicked his ash, considered whether he needed a fresh cigarette, and let the old one burn. "He's in London. Gone to ground, but he's got to come up for air sometime."

Rory rustled through the fish and chips wrappers, looking for scraps. "Put a tail on Hugh Aberdare, then? He knows von Ritter, too. Maybe knows him better than we think."

"We don't even know if he's still at Summerhill," Fin muttered.

"Let's keep Georgi's house the main focus. I want a list of

her visitors. Photos, names, addresses. Meanwhile, police have a description of von Ritter."

Von Ritter wasn't their only lead. They had Woodbird listening at the *Abwehr*—or they did unless he was playing a double game and feeding them useless information—and then Harp probing his contacts on the edges of Luckenwalde, hoping to land a disaffected German or two to work for him. Questionnaires had gone out by wireless to both of them, listing areas urgently needing intel.

Elsa buttoned her coat and pushed off from the hutch. "Who we really needed was Commandant Stelling." She glanced at Julian. "We should have sent you after him, boss. Show the frogs how an extraction's done."

Fin nodded happily, remembering. "That bloke you got out of the Turkish prison. Full daylight it was, too."

"Cousin of a duke," Julian said. "I'd have been shot had I failed."

Rory looked thoughtful: "Maybe Stelling was a plant, to throw us off a bigger plan."

"But it was the SS that prevented him from leaving," Julian pointed out.

Fin shrugged. "They screwed up?"

Elsa said, "Make what he *did* reveal seem credible?"

Rory offered, "Knew he wouldn't last through interrogation? Left him saying just enough to have us watching the coast while they invade Poland?"

Elsa shook her head. "We're not going to help Poland, anyway." She grimaced. "Or Czechoslovakia."

Julian muttered, "Any takers for France?"

Elsa smirked and left the room. Out in the hallway, she donned a preoccupied-old-lady expression and clutched her black straw bag with its snub-nosed Colt revolver. Old women were wonderfully invisible, she thought.

Kim spoke into the receiver. "May I speak with Owen?"

Mrs. Cherwell said, "Who shall I say is calling?"

"Tell him his ten o'clock appointment. If that's all right."

"Yes, it's all right. Hold the line."

Kim wondered what Mrs. Cherwell looked like. Dowdy and dependable? Thin and a worrier? All she knew was that, while they had no children, they doted upon nieces and nephews. She imagined Monkton Hall formed a rather large chunk of Owen's life.

"Hello?" Owen's voice.

"It's me. Find another phone and call me. It's important." She gave him the number and hung up.

"So, you're working without me," he summarized. She had relayed Georgi's comment about staying close to home and Hugh's financial reversal.

"I'm sorry. But yes."

He was silent for a few beats, while she wrestled between abject guilt and defensiveness.

"Kim. If they have a big operation going, and you're nosing around, they will pick you up. They will force you to tell everything. It would be extremely ugly. You have no idea."

She did have some idea, but was trying very hard not to think about it. "You have no right to decide what I can and can't sacrifice. It's gone too far to stop now."

"Don't be silly. It's not gone too far. You can still go back to Uxley, and you ought to."

She wasn't going to argue. Silence stretched between them.

"What are you going to do now? Aren't you out of options?"

"I don't know. I might be."

There was a long pause, big enough to drive a truck through. "Might?"

"Owen, I don't know. It's late."

"You *do* know."

She paused, and after a few moments, it was too late to lie. "I'm going to offer to work for von Ritter." How else to get next to him for a *spill*, or even to earn his trust outright? Von Ritter had wanted to recruit her. Well then, she would say yes.

She didn't know where he was, but she thought Georgi might be able to contact him.

"Christ God," he whispered. "He'll never believe you."

"He will. Because he wants me. He believes we met at the gazebo for a reason. He believes in destiny."

"You are not Erich von Ritter's destiny, and he knows that as surely as he can spell *Nazi*."

"Right. But he believes he's *my* destiny. He collects people for his cause. He already approached me at Summerhill."

"And then tried to *kill* you."

"Because I said no. All I have to do is say yes."

"You're daft! He'll find you out. And he will kill you this time. Kim, please listen to me. Don't throw your life away."

Kim stared out at the crowded West End evening scene. A river of fog rolled down the street, lit up by car headlights. "Owen, I was going to go home. Until she revealed Hugh's plea not to travel for a while. Now I don't think I can. Whatever is going to happen, it might be soon. Even in the next few days."

"Then I'll go to Whitehall and give them what we have. Let me try."

She had to get off the telephone. Her resolve was shaky

enough without Owen lobbing reasons—even foolish ones—
that seemed to give her an out.

"You can try, Owen. But I can't wait, don't you see? I don't
believe they'll listen or, if they do, that they'll take action. This
is Lord Daventry we're talking about. They won't want to
believe it."

He groaned. Then his voice came to her thin and defeated.
"If you discover something, how will you communicate it to
me . . . Or am I out of the picture now?"

"Owen?"

"Yes?"

"The dead drop. Every day. The dead drop."

She hung up. Outside the phone booth, the rain spattered
down in golden drops infused by the light from street lamps. She
gazed at the wash of light, the oncoming cars, the people bent
against their umbrellas. It all looked so beautiful, so surprising,
as though she had never before seen a cityscape or the rain at
night.

It took her less than a minute to hail a cab. In the rain, she
took that for a sign, or as much of one as she was likely to get.

TUESDAY, APRIL 28. Julian was waiting for E at 7:15 AM when he arrived at his office. After an all-nighter with Fin at the wireless listening post, Julian had gathered his notes and gone directly to 54 Broadway. There he had alerted Olivia Hennessey, who was always at her desk at seven, that he must see E at once.

Fin ran two agents in Germany, and had sent each of them a questionnaire related to four subjects: Colonel Stelling, Norden, the Wesermarsch sub camp and the villa in Luckenwalde, the latter being the German equivalent of Monkton Hall. What they got back was stunning: The existence of a German asset with a newly discovered Talent rated at the highest level.

E stood at his window, keeping an eye on the pavement below, watching for his next appointment.

"So, our *Abwehr* mole came through, did he?"

"Yes, rather a jackpot. A highly rated—top of the scale—Talent in the hyperpersonal group. Called *chorister*, apparently.

It comes with Woodbird's judgment of a moderate degree of certainty."

"Any confirmation of this new Talent from Harp?"

"No. He isn't inside Luckenwalde yet; he has a likely person to approach, but he wants our approval to try it."

"That anti-Nazi contact of his. I don't like the sound of it."

"A risk, but it's time to give Harp his rein."

E pursed his lips. "This new Talent. *Chorister*, did you say?"

"Yes. An odd term, but Woodbird says the *Abwehr* believes in it. It's most likely being fed to them from Luckenwalde. He says it's an ability to aggregate Talents for a larger combined effect. And this person, whoever he is, is a 10 on the scale. We may be facing a major German weapon capability."

"By God." E cut a look at Julian. "Your war of the Talents." He shook his head. "Maybe something to it after all."

"I need direction on how to proceed on the Luckenwalde agent."

E grimaced and let the window curtain slip back into place. "Here comes our man." E moved his paperweight, the one with the rock embedded in heavy glass, to the forward edge of his desk. It was a memento of the war, but E had never explained it beyond that. "I want you listening in. Let's see if Millington can be brought around."

"So we don't have Foreign Office support?"

E smirked. "The matter is already under consideration at the CID, so the Foreign Office is letting it play out. Besides, now that I'm under investigation, I've got as much credibility as Mata Hari."

The canker in the service, whoever it really was, was doing irreparable harm. True, Julian had started looking at his colleagues a bit differently these days, but the idea that E was implicated, that was beyond the pale.

E waved him out. "Let's see what Millie has to say. He speaks for Alistair Drake, you can be sure."

Julian went through to the front office, where Olivia escorted him to the "pen," the room off the reception area where the piped-in conversations of E's office could be heard and a visitor remain unaware.

Olivia Hennessey was tall, a few inches shy of Julian's height. She was an attractive woman, but romance and the Office didn't mix. E's firm rule, even if it was a relic of a past era.

She removed the charm bracelet from her wrist. One of the pendants dangling from it was a key, which she used to unlock the door. She ushered Julian into the windowless room. Heavy green baize covered the walls.

"Wear your headphones," she said. "If you turn up the volume loud enough for me to hear, the service will have to shoot me."

"Only if they found out," he said, taking his seat at the room's small table.

She looked at him in amusement. "Keeping secrets, here?"

"Gallantry has its standards," he said, hoping for a laugh.

He got one, and her updo shook slightly.

Don't come down now, Julian prayed. This wasn't the week to tempt fate.

"Enjoy," she said, and slipped from the room.

Within ten minutes, Julian was ready to use his revolver in service to his country. By murdering Heath Millington.

"You're putting too much store by this German colonel." Millington's voice was smooth and soft, more suitable to a banker than the undersecretary to one of the most powerful committees of the cabinet. "What was his game is what I'd like to know."

Julian took his pipe out of his coat pocket, forgetting that he wasn't to smoke it in E's realm. He chewed on the stem and turned up the volume on the headphones.

"There doesn't appear to be a game." E's voice. "We've got our people on Stelling's background. Lived within his means. Didn't appear to be skimming funds or trading in counterfeit pounds with that bad lot in the *Abwehr*. No debts to speak of, good future at age forty-one. Never married."

"There you are, then, a homosexual. Steps into an indiscreet relationship, and the High Command decides it's time for another purity sweep. Once Stelling gets word he's going to jail, he makes a run for it. Needs a ripping good story to get out of Germany, and the French fell for it."

"Yes, could be." A pause, just long enough. "*Sturmweg*, though. At Wesermarsch, he was in the right place to know of an invasionary force out of Norden." E was adopting his careful, pragmatic tone. Don't escalate the tension with a man five inches shorter than you, or he bares his teeth like a terrier. It wouldn't do to make an outright enemy of Millington, even if he tended to constantly snap at the heels of SIS.

"Well, then," Millington said. "*Sturmweg*. What do we have, really? It's all wireless intercept, a complete phantom operation."

With disgust, Julian saw how the meeting would go. Millington sided with Drake, who sided with the PM. Stanley Baldwin went in the direction that the British people wanted: no foreign involvement, spend the money at home, not on arms. Look what happened last time: won the war, yes, if you could call over seven hundred thousand British deaths, a million and a half wounded, *winning*. Ergo, the Germans aren't a threat. Or, if they are, let the Continent take care of them.

E's voice: "Why would the Germans go to all this trouble?"

"No trouble at all, old fellow. They give wireless sets to two or three drivers and set them loose around Germany, chatting up *Sturmweg* until they have us in a froth. Which is exactly the case."

There was a pause and rifling of papers. E was pretending to refer to his notes, though he had the situation memorized down to the last detail.

"There'll be hell to pay if your assessment is wrong," E murmured.

"Not a bit of it. Germany can't match our fleet. They're weak at sea, with the terms of the Armistice and our Naval Agreement—"

E interrupted. "—the Armistice! Really, Heath. You can't go along with that delusion. They're building secretly, all our intel points to it."

"Damn hard to hide a destroyer, wouldn't you say?" Millington's creamy voice.

Julian could imagine E sitting on the edge of his desk, handling his paperweight, restraining the impulse to see what kind of weapon it would make.

E's voice: "They've got Spain's blessing to build in their naval yards, and they are."

"Well. The military's on alert—good for the troop morale, give them something to do—and we're watching the coast. Anything crosses into our waters, we pound the daylights out of her."

The thought of the RAF being able to hit a moving target would have been funny if it hadn't been so sad. The military was constantly overestimating the damage of aerial bombings. Pleasant to think that war could be conducted by air alone. No need to have an army, after all.

"A good idea to pursue that Luckenwalde intel, I should think," E finally said. "We'd like to follow up on the *chorister* angle."

"Never heard such rubbish. You don't build up Talents like a mound of gunpowder. For example, take a group of *hypercognition* adepts," he said, lecturing the head of the intelligence service on his own bailiwick. "Each one is capable of an insight, but just putting them together, they can't pick a ten-to-one winner at the races."

"Quite. But suppose they *could?* Maybe a long shot, but we're prepared to go into Luckenwalde and see what the Germans have worked up. With the head start they've had in Talent research, they might have a secret weapon. Luckenwalde could confirm the whole picture: an invasion based on a new military Talent, one that could deliver us a disabling blow. We've got Harp ready to approach someone in Luckenwalde with anti-Hitler sympathies."

"I don't like it. Think of the cost, man. Blow Harp's cover, and next thing, the Gestapo has him. Rather a lot to risk on the chance of a Spanish-built German destroyer steaming up the Thames."

A long pause, during which Julian chewed on his cold pipe-stem and longed to weigh in. But Millington didn't know him as SIS and would never know.

"How sure is Harp of his man?" Millington.

"Woman. She's a secretary at Luckenwalde. And his lover."

A long, dark silence. Millington disliked women, thought them completely unreliable as sources of intelligence.

The sound of feet shuffling, muffling the next few words.

". . . with the CID at nine thirty. I can tell you plainly that the PM doesn't put much store in this *Sturmweg* dust-up. The Secretary is solidly behind him, if it matters to you."

Bloody hell, of course it mattered. Alistair Drake was the conduit for every piece of intelligence going before the Committee of Imperial Defence. Julian shifted in his chair, itching to handle Heath Millington himself, man to terrier.

A few garbled words as they moved away from the pickup microphone. ". . . lose Harp, it's on your shoulders. But if you decide to send your agent's girlfriend in, ask her to find out where the Jerries are going to land. Awfully helpful to know."

As the two men said their goodbyes, Julian slammed the headphones on the table, Millington's needling final remark feeling like a gauntlet thrown down.

Olivia ducked in, saw Julian's expression, and said, "He wants a word with you. I take it Millie didn't behave."

"No, he took exception to every bloody idea we had."

"So nice when people are consistent, though," she sniffed, and waved him toward E's office.

When Julian entered, E was sitting in his chair, having swiveled it around to stare out the window.

From the depths of the chair, Julian heard E say, "Tell Harp to proceed."

Put it all on the line, then. Julian suppressed a smile.

KENSINGTON HIGH STREET, LONDON

In the recesses of the department store, someone was playing the piano. Standing in the perfumery section of Derry & Toms, Kim kept watch on the escalator. So far, her contact had not appeared.

Pendant lights hung from the ceiling in the spacious ground floor, shedding an elegant glow on perfume bottles and glass counters. The department store dazzled within and without. When one was standing in Kensington High Street and viewing the imposing art deco building, trees of the new roof garden could just be seen peeking over the edge.

Kim's mother had loved Derry & Toms, and so had Kim as a child. Once, they'd had lunch in the fifth-story dining room with a string quartet playing behind a bamboo screen. Although she had been only nine, it was the one time in Kim's life when she had felt elegant. Now here she was, about to step into a nest of spies. Last night, she had been bolstered by a fatalistic determination. Perhaps it was patriotism, or the sense that one must stop what was happening to England. Not only the physical threat, but the slow creep of bigotry that was just as evil. Now, by the light of day, on the threshold of meeting von Ritter, her stomach had begun to shred. What was she doing?

The floor was crowded with people, many still wearing their dark winter coats, and a few in mufflers, those who had just come in from the street. Cold swept in with them. A few well-turned-out shoppers, women in tailored black coats trimmed in lamb's wool, men in derby hats and camel-hair coats, meandered among the wares or engaged the salesgirls, and even the less well-dressed felt permitted to trail hands over scarves and leather gloves, leaving them behind as though they did not suit.

Derry & Toms had not been her first stop in what was turning out to be a highly orchestrated approach to Erich von Ritter. Georgi had said that he would meet her at Charing Cross Station under the flag at eleven thirty in the morning. Georgi had predicted that von Ritter would be too busy and she was clearly irritated to be arranging the *assignation*, as she put it. Kim didn't know what Georgi made of her request to meet von Ritter, or if the woman had warned him of her investigation. It was a possible flaw in her plan. Which was why Kim had made clear to Georgi that she was suspected of collusion in her brother's conspiracy. If Georgi had any inclination to warn von Ritter, Kim felt that her fervent self-interest would prevent it. England might be half asleep, but it still hung traitors.

At the train station, she found her contact. Not von Ritter himself but someone who worked for him, a stunning brunette in a fox-trimmed suit. The woman, pretending to watch for her ride, had set down her suitcase next to Kim. As she peered left and right, she told Kim to go to Derry & Toms at one o'clock and take the escalator to the top floor. "Don't look at me," she had snapped when Kim turned to her. Kim stood silently beside the woman for a few uncomfortable minutes, feeling exceedingly shabby in her green plaid. But she could not at all approve the fox trim coat.

Soon, the woman hailed her ride and disappeared into a cream-colored sedan.

Kim arrived on the bus at Derry & Toms at 12:43. Her instructions were to wait, pretending to shop, until she saw a man approach the escalator, holding an umbrella and rolled newspaper.

She did not expect that the next German agent she saw would be late.

Nor was he. At precisely one o'clock, a man approached who fit the description she'd been given: thin and mustached, carrying a furled umbrella in one hand like a cane, with a rolled newspaper under his arm. Kim contrived to meet him at the foot of the escalator, where he waved for her to precede him, as a gentleman might.

She moved onto the first step. He was directly behind her as they ascended to the second floor.

"Go to the Tudor garden on the roof," he said. "Wait for the woman you saw at the train." This time, she knew better than to turn around. She made her way to the top floor, men's furnishings. Umbrella man had vanished, having debarked on floor two or three. Inquiring, she was directed to the staircase to the roof garden.

As she emerged into the open air, she found herself under a wide London sky. High white clouds paraded over the West End and Kensington Palace in the near distance. Passing in front of the Moorish-style gallery, she headed down the central walkway, at one point asking a woman with a perambulator directions to the Tudor garden. She continued past a clematis-covered gazebo until she saw the stone arches of the Tudor garden. Entering, she found herself amid its shaded archways and dark flagstone walks. She was alone in this corner of the roof.

At a turn, Kim saw the woman from the train station. She gave a slight nod, a signal to follow her onto a side path. It dead-ended in a pergola overhung with wisteria. There, fox woman gave her instructions for meeting Erich von Ritter.

"I hope that this time I will really meet him," Kim said, meaning to show she could not be led by the nose.

The woman, in her beautifully cut suit and perfect makeup, gave a small smile. "That will depend on how well you follow directions."

The directions suggested to Kim that once she followed them, no one would ever know where she had gone. She began to feel that she was walking slowly into a great fog, one that comprised a world of lies, illusion and pretense, a world inhabited by people of the fog, those who lived and breathed their false lives. Kim also now had a false life. But the problem was, she didn't know the rules of this murky world.

Fox woman left without a backward glance. Kim consulted her watch. 1:13. She must wait five minutes before leaving. She sat on a stone bench, trying to quiet her heart.

Her next stop would mean facing Erich von Ritter. At Summerhill, he had taken an unusual interest in her. Perhaps she had been singled out because the other women in the salon were ten years or more older than she. Winning her loyalty would be reinforced with sex, perhaps his usual method when recruiting women. She had been flattered, if not tempted. But now she saw the seduction—both political and romantic—for what it was. His habitual attempt to collect chess pieces on any board he faced.

She was gambling he'd still like to win.

Her stomach had begun to knot over the prospect of trying to deceive the man. She thought of Robert and how he had been faced with that awful charge at Ypres. The charge might fail. He might die. And he went on; of course he had. He was a soldier. Less was asked of a citizen, but that didn't mean one must do less.

She took the 2:14 bus to the Strand Palace Hotel, where she had a room. Feeling wrung out, she kicked off her shoes and flopped on the bed. She reached to the nightstand for her well-worn copy of the London and North Eastern Railway schedule, but the lovely columns and connections failed to engage her. Instead, it suggested that she might do well to find the next train home. She could be there in two hours and forty-two minutes.

WESTMINSTER BRIDGE, LONDON

By the time Kim got to Westminster Bridge, it was nine fifteen. As the quarter-past chimes sounded, she could not help but look at her Elgin to check that Big Ben was on time. It was. No one else sharing the pavement appeared to notice the bells playing the quarter hour, but to her it was a great comfort, that sound of England. A double-decker trolley bus trundled by, packed with people. In the Thames, city lights wavered as white gulls rode the chop. She watched for a car to slow down, almost hoping now that none would.

She had parted ways on the Victoria Embankment with the young woman who had joined her in her hotel room. That woman now wore her green plaid belted coat as well as her brown hat. Kim had last seen her striding away down the walkway—past Waterloo Bridge under repair and toward Blackfriars—while Kim had taken the opposite direction toward Parliament. Her decoy would lead away anyone who might be following her. And who *would* follow? England had its own spy organizations, but she thought it unlikely they would be following *her*.

Or if they were, it could be because she had gone to see Georgi Aberdare. It would be an excellent thing if they were following Hugh. But if it was Georgi they watched, then they likely knew no more than Kim and Owen, and that was little indeed. Yet she was determined to discover why she had almost been killed over the *spill* of *chorister*, and why Alice Ward had seen a chain of ice. All she needed were a few more pieces. Key pieces that would bring the picture together instead of lying in fragments.

A dark Mercedes-Benz pulled up beside her. The door opened, pushed from inside. "Miss Tavistock," someone said. She bent down to see umbrella man sitting in the back seat. "My name is Gordon. Herr von Ritter has sent me."

Kim looked at the cave-like interior of the car and climbed inside. The car moved on instantly, throwing her against the back seat.

A driver in a chauffeur's cap and uniform drove. Gordon said, "I'm terribly sorry to have to insist." His British accent was perfect, so whoever he was he was undoubtedly homegrown. He handed her something. "Please."

She looked at what now lay in her lap. A blindfold.

"Herr von Ritter asks that you forgive the discomfiture."

She removed her hat and donned the blindfold, fashioned with a piece of elastic in back so it could stretch to fit.

"It will be an hour's ride. Herr von Ritter has said that if you change your mind at any time, we will drop you where you can secure a cab. Are you comfortable?"

"Yes, it's fine." They rode for a few minutes, speeding up onto what she supposed was a main road. She was chagrined to find herself trembling.

"I don't suppose you have a cigarette."

After a few moments, she heard him strike a match. He put a cigarette into her right hand. He took her other hand, putting it on an ashtray that extended from the back of the seat.

The cigarette was heavenly, calming her. She felt she knew why spies in movies always smoked. They wished to generate their own fog. And it kept one from digesting one's stomach.

26

TUESDAY, APRIL 28. A thin, cross woman with wiry black hair put down a plate with a sandwich on the dining room table and left without a word. The lights dimmed for a moment as she did so, bringing the room into a brief gloom. Kim picked up the top piece of bread to peer at it.

"It is not poisoned," von Ritter said. "And even if it was . . ." He shrugged. *We could have killed you in the Benz, or in the garden out there.* He wore an expensive white shirt rolled up to mid-arm, and camel-hair trousers. His jacket was flung across the back of one of the fourteen chairs around the table.

She bit into the sandwich, suddenly starving, since she had not been able to eat her dinner earlier in the evening. It was fresh chicken with tomato.

Von Ritter watched her with some amusement as she wolfed it down. "Had I known it was to be dinner, Lena could have prepared her special herring in cream."

Kim shook her head, mouth full. "This . . . good."

Von Ritter gave a silent laugh at her enthusiasm.

The chauffeur leaned against the archway to what she presumed was a foyer. They had taken her in a back way, through what might have been a garden door and a large yard. Once inside, they had removed her blindfold and she had used a lavatory off the kitchen of a home that was both grand and empty. So far, she had counted four people there besides herself: von Ritter, Lena, the chauffeur and Gordon, who had picked her up.

"I have been seeing quite a bit of your England," von Ritter began as he leaned back against his chair, watching her eat. "The Cornwall coast, a bit of Sussex. It is quite beautiful. I can understand why you have adopted it."

"I thought you were going to be busy in London." She tapped her mouth with her napkin. "Pharmaceuticals." She said it ironically, letting him know she was going to play it straight. Or letting him think so.

He tipped his head to the side, granting the point. "It is no use to pretend I'm selling to chemists in London. No, my work is larger than that. It was necessary to refrain from saying so before." He took out his cigarette case and lit a cigarette, blowing out a stream of smoke and acting as though they were catching up on gossip. "Actually, I think Georgiana would have liked me better if she had known I was not in a trade." He shrugged disarmingly. *What can one do? One can't please everybody.*

He really was nothing short of dashingly handsome. It shouldn't matter to her, and of course, it didn't. What was rather worse was that he was also charming and smart: harder to ignore.

"You knew I had a larger purpose in being in your country. Or why would you be here now?"

"Well, I know that now. Now that I could not just meet with you straight out. You made sure I wasn't followed. All very cloak-and-dagger."

He paused, considering this. It was a danger that he would think she had special knowledge about him. She must appear to be acting alone.

Relaxed, he went on. "I would like to go back to your city of Dover. The headlands, the beach—quite dramatic. I sometimes think that a land cannot be truly great without a great river. England is small, but it has the Thames. Someday I would like to show you the Rhine."

She picked at a few crumbs.

"Another?" he said playfully.

"No, thank you."

He offered her a cigarette, which she declined. "I hope the ride here was not too disagreeable. The blindfold . . . My people are overcautious."

She looked up at the chauffeur still at his post. With a short wrestler's build and squarish face, he was, she realized, the same driver who had accompanied von Ritter at Summerhill. *Is this the man who tried to run me off the road?* She almost spoke the words, but it would get them off on the wrong foot.

"Why are they so cautious? I've been all over London trying to meet you."

"Because, regrettably, the authorities are trying to throw me out of your country."

She affected surprise at this, but it was not difficult.

"Yes," he said, savoring his cigarette. He was very graceful as he smoked. Men had a way of smoking which was quite casual and elegant.

He raised an eyebrow at the chauffeur, who came forward to

remove Kim's plate. He was met at the kitchen door by Lena who, snatching away the plate, seemed to cast a shadow from the doorway by virtue of her hostility. In fact, the room did darken, didn't it? Kim looked at the kitchen door, where Lena had been standing.

Von Ritter noticed her glance. "Ah. You have discerned Lena's *darkening*. We are very proud of her. She is a 9.4, very useful indeed."

Darkening. Kim had heard of this Talent. Rare. Lena had the Talent to alter ambient light.

Von Ritter turned to his driver. *"Oscar, bring uns bitte zwei Weinbrand."* The man placed a cut-glass snifter in front of each of them. "But! Let us not drink at the table like farmers." He stood up and took her glass. "The parlor, mademoiselle."

He gestured for her to lead the way to the living room, which, past decorative columns, opened upon a vast parlor with two fireplaces and furniture arranged around each of them.

In front of a hearth with a fire turning to embers, von Ritter handed her her drink and raised his glass.

"No toast," Kim said. "I'm not sure we understand each other, Herr von Ritter. And I don't want to be rude."

He narrowed his eyes. "But to England. Yes?"

She nodded and raised her glass. After taking a sip—it was brandy, she noted—she asked, "Why are you being asked to leave?"

"They do not like me. They think I am SD. *Sicherheitsdienst.* The intelligence arm of the SS. They believe that, in that capacity, I have come to influence the opinions of the King."

"And have you?"

"Yes. I hope you are not shocked."

"And you are with—this SD? A spy organization?"

"All countries have such things." He stood up and took a

poker to stir the fire. A small flame jumped to life and he knelt
before the grate, adding small split logs. He looked back at her.
"Cold, yes?"

The house in fact was quite cold, as though it had long been
unoccupied.

He talked as he worked the fire. "I've met the lovely Wallis
Simpson, but I do not expect a royal introduction. Still, your
secret agencies are very concerned with what people think, and
they do not like that Mrs. Simpson is a friend to Germany." He
rose, slapping his hands together.

As he stood with his back to the fire, Kim looked up at him.
"And you wish to stay, even if you need to hide?"

He looked at her for a moment. "I will tell you presently. It is
not fair for me to lay myself bare, and you remain . . . mysterious.
It is your turn."

"One more question," she said. He sat next to her on the
couch, radiating masculine attraction. "Why are you still here
if it has become dangerous for you? They could throw you in
prison on some pretense, couldn't they?"

"Oh yes, and how do you say, throw away a key?" He sipped
his brandy. When he grew serious, he was not quite so handsome as when he smiled. There was something harsh about his
dark good looks that, in the firelight, did not soften.

He went on. "There are people in England who wish to
assure my country of goodwill. That we can have room to pros-
per. If England wishes for peace, and if she gives us room for
peace, we can stop what is coming. I am here to influence these
outcomes." He shrugged. "I do not blame your government for
not liking it. But I will not go under questioning by your SIS.
If I come into their hands, my superiors will not trust me again,
not completely."

Kim stared at the brandy glass she clasped in both hands. "You have a very strong Talent, Herr von Ritter. Everyone in this house has. Am I wrong?"

"Ah, but first, I think it is time for you tell me about yourself."

She took a quick gulp of brandy, to look concerned about what she was about to reveal. "I am involved with a group that is turning Talents into weapons. It's called HARC, the Historical Archives and Records Centre. In North Yorkshire at a place called Monkton Hall. And I have just broken the law by telling you this." It did scare her. She had to trust that Owen was right, that the Germans had penetrated Monkton Hall.

"So, then, are you a Talent yourself?"

"The *spill*," she acknowledged. "I am a 6 on the scale."

He made a show of being surprised, but of course he wasn't. He would certainly have checked up on her after Summerhill.

"I came to them to help England. But I learned it was not just for defense, but for . . . weapons. They test things. On the moors."

"Such as?"

"I don't know. One isn't supposed to be about when they have maneuvers, or whatever they do. But I know the Talents are not just personal ones, some are physical."

"And so you are here," he said.

"I am." She turned her brandy glass in her hand. "I don't like these weapons. Distorting the *bloom* toward . . ." She pretended to search for words.

"Toward war?" She nodded. "I know this subject is close to your heart because of your brother's death."

"Tell me the truth," she said. "Have you the *spill* Talent? It was very personal, that story."

"Yes. So, we have this in common, do we not." He was always

keen to emphasize their similarities. "A *spill* did occur between you and me. I am sorry if telling me about your brother made you uncomfortable."

She paused. "At Summerhill, you asked me to help. So I want to know, Herr von Ritter, that peace is your intention. And don't lie to me, or perhaps my *spill* will expose you."

He smiled, holding up his hands, palms out, as though fending off an artless threat. "No, I will not lie. Your government is rearming, readying for war. It is as though you mean to bankrupt us by forcing us to match you. But there are people here who mean to stop this march to arms. This government must be turned out of office. And it will be."

"By democratic means."

"By whatever means. I do not play the pacifist with you. Revolutions have happened before. The people will speak, whether by vote or in the street."

She glanced at him, showing a moment's confusion. As though revolution were a troubling idea instead of a laughable one. Did he think Welsh coal miners would march to London? That a National Socialist Party could take seats in Parliament? English politics were fractious. But if there were a change in government, it would bring a more warlike stance, not less. It would bring Churchill.

She turned to him. "I would like to help you, Herr von Ritter." She had made her plea to join him, all the while carefully avoiding his *chorister* slip at Summerhill. He assumed she had missed its implication. And she almost had.

His smile dazzled, persuasive and confounding. "I had despaired of you," he murmured.

She stood up to break the spell. Walking to the hearth, she put her half-full snifter on the mantel and turned back to him.

"If the *bloom* came for a reason, then I believe it came to bring something better into our lives. Otherwise, it is pointless. Evil, even. I would like to believe that great men have been endowed with Talents that will be turned to peace. If that is so, then I will help you. If I can."

"You can. I believe you have great ability. I am attracted to that quality, as you have noticed."

"I'm not going to sleep with you."

His smile slipped away in mock disappointment. "Are you not? It will be a very cold night, then."

"I'm not spending the night. I'm going back to London. Herr von Ritter, please don't play with me. I'm doing this on principle. If I didn't believe that, if I thought I was doing it for *you*, I couldn't live with myself."

"Ah. The principle! That is excellent. One always knows where such people stand. I appreciate this quality." He cocked his head. "But it can't be about both?" He laughed, and waved off her indignant response. "No, no, please do not falter. I am now hopeless for you. It is delightful."

He stood up. "You will earn my trust by other means, then. An assignment, Miss Tavistock. A difficult one."

"I won't kill anybody."

He laughed. "No indeed, you shall not. But you understand, it must be at some cost for you."

She managed to look worried, she hoped. She *was* worried. "Cost?"

"Bring Rose Babbage to Prestwich Home. Present the maid to Doctor Angus Dunn."

"Pardon? You're talking about Rose? My maid?"

"For testing, yes?"

"But why?"

"Without questions. I wish to know that you will follow orders, even when you may not understand."

Playing for time, she said, "I don't *like* Dr. Dunn."

"This may be so, but you will take her to Prestwich Home for this evaluation they wish to conduct, then she is returned home."

"How did you even hear about Rose?"

"Perhaps I am watching you." He shrugged. "*Sicherheitsdienst*," he said as though that explained it. He held her gaze. When she remained silent, he went on. "Come, now. The maid does not experience this as an insult. You cannot feel for her what she does not herself feel. She has not the capacity. You see? It is unpleasant but should not give you pause."

"Well, she isn't *your* maid," Kim threw back.

His eyes turned hard. "To be precise, she is not yours, either. She is your kitchen girl, and the maid vocation came suddenly upon her. Yes? Is this not the truth, that she lacks the mental judgment to even carry a vase and present tea?"

With a very great effort, Kim lowered her eyes. "I will need time to convince her parents."

"You may have until Sunday—since you still have the journey home."

Five days. Kim dared not make more of this. It would have to be done. And it *would* cost her; he was right. "I wish you had asked me something different."

"I know. There are harder things. Much harder."

They looked at each other for a few moments, until she nodded her consent.

He turned to his driver, who stood at the entry to the dining room. *"Den Mantel der Dame bitte, Oskar."*

Von Ritter led her to the back door, where Oskar met her

with her coat and hat. Von Ritter walked out with them into the walled garden, through which presumably she had been led when she arrived. The night was clear, with moonlight silvering the branches of the large elms dominating the back yard.

Lena appeared from a side door, wrapped in a sweater and looking cross to be part of the farewell party.

Von Ritter took Kim by the arm and led her down a narrow path between clipped hedges. "Something I wish you to see." Oskar preceded them, and Lena brought up the rear. The elm blocked out the moon. The night garden seemed carved from ebony, and Kim could hardly see von Ritter at her side. An alarm grew within her. Was he going to kill her after all? Had she said something that had given her away, something he had forced out of her that had been spoken so easily she did not even know her mistake?

They stood in a small clearing. There were only the shadows of von Ritter, Oskar and Lena, barely visible.

"Ein bisschen weniger, Lena."

At this, the clearing lightened just enough that Kim saw another person.

It was Gordon. Umbrella man was tied to a sturdy tree, ropes binding his ankles and his chest.

Gordon's face was beaten and bloody, one of his eyes a pulp. In shock, Kim gulped a horrified breath. "Oh, God," she whispered.

Oskar handed von Ritter a gun, and he strode forward with it. Gordon raised his head, his face filled more with sorrow than fear.

The sound of the shot was muffled, like a package had been dropped on the terrace. The body slumped heavily against the ropes. Then von Ritter handed the gun back to Oskar.

Kim found that she had backed up and staggered against Lena, who, in a guttural accent, snapped, "Get ahold of yourself, *Fräulein.*" She held Kim by the shoulders as von Ritter approached.

"He failed me. A botched assignment, you see." His white shirt was riddled with black flecks. Making eye contact with Lena, he said, "The dark, again."

And then it was very dark, as though all light had fled the world. A man had been murdered in a garden in England, easily, with just a soft sound of something falling.

Von Ritter took Kim by the arm and led her toward the main path. Somehow, the four of them ended up at the gate. Kim found herself sobbing.

Beside her, Lena said something in German, in unmistakable contempt.

Von Ritter took Kim in his arms to comfort her. When she realized how ludicrous this was, she pulled away and dried her face on her coat sleeve. Oskar handed something to von Ritter. It was a blindfold. For a moment, Kim panicked. But then she noted that they stood in front of the garden gate. If he were going to kill her, he would have done it at the tree.

"I am sorry that you are subject to these sights." Von Ritter took out a handkerchief and gently wiped her face. Then he took the blindfold and put it over her eyes, securing the band in the back of her head.

"Am I going back?" she whispered. Her mind was blank. The garden seemed an unearthly place, full of cruelty and demons.

"Oh, yes," she heard him say. She felt his hands cup her face. He was standing very close to her. Then, tipping her head up, he kissed her, and took his time, and her mind was so dark and cold that she let him.

PALLADIUM THEATRE, LONDON

TUESDAY, APRIL 28. Julian lay in wait for E late that night. His news couldn't wait for the morning. Dense fog lurked on Argyll Street, cloaking the smartly dressed theater patrons as they exited the Palladium Theatre. Julian had taken a position just inside the theater doors, from time to time checking the foyer as though waiting for someone. On the street, an intricate dance of cabs and patrons played out.

At last, he saw E leaving the theater. "I beg your pardon," Julian said, stepping in front of him on the steps. He continued down the stairs without making eye contact.

E, wearing an elegant midnight blue coat and bowler hat, had emerged with Idina Mae Henslow, leading her to a sleek black car that had maneuvered to curbside. Where E's wife was rail-thin, Idina was ample without being large, a woman comfortable with her body and the pleasures of food. Once seated in back, she leaned out the window and touched E's hand resting on the frame, as though accidentally, but to Julian's practiced eye saying, *See you in a few minutes, my dear.*

E waved the driver on. He might have gotten in the car with her, but now he must spend a moment with Julian, and to that end, he walked down the street, his form easily distinguishable from others by his height and purposeful stride. Julian followed him away from the milling Palladium crowd and caught up with him at Oxford Street.

"What is it, then?" E asked as they walked. The street was dark, draped with mist laden with coal smoke. Above the blurred lines of the rooftops, lights from the city center burned in the foggy sky.

Julian spoke words that he was astonished—and chagrined— to be uttering to the head of SIS. "We may want to have my daughter picked up."

E cut a glance at him and continued walking.

"We followed her tonight near her hotel. Turns out another woman wore her coat and hat."

E quirked his mouth in some amusement. "Lots of women wearing a drab winter coat this spring."

"Hers was green plaid. She went into Derry & Toms this afternoon and used the escalator to shake off her tail. No doubt she met someone. We picked her up again on the way down. She's not in her hotel room, so she went out tonight while we were onto green plaid."

"She had help, then."

"I would say so, yes."

"Pick her up, you say?"

"We'll have Rory question her. I think she'll tell us every-thing if a mild threat is used."

"A bit heavy-handed, don't you think?"

"She may be rashly pursuing Georgi Aberdare based on some theory she's drummed up that the woman is a spy. Her work at Monkton Hall might have something to do with it. We'll pay a visit to her Talent caseworker to see if he can shed light on something she may have learned there. In any case, it's time to pick her up."

"For her sake or ours?"

A beat while Julian digested the implications of the question. "Her sake?"

"Look here, Julian, you know as well as I do that it doesn't do to mix family with our business. I don't wonder you want to protect her, but she's got the bit properly between her teeth now. Let's see where she leads us."

As they walked, a few cars tunneled past them through the fog, shrouded black cars carrying their passengers from an evening of light entertainment. In case they were carrying anyone else—anyone with a particular interest in questions of state—E turned toward the shop windows to hide his profile.

"You're not thinking of confronting her," E said.

Well, he had been, actually, even while knowing it was not going to happen. "No, chief."

"Put two men on her and don't let her make a fool of us again."

E put his hands in his pockets against the chill. "Nothing else, then? No word from Harp or Woodbird?"

"Not yet." Their agents in Germany reported in every night by wireless. They had leads and were pursuing them aggressively.

E paused at the intersection, turning to Julian. "She'll have to ride it out, now she's weighed in." He held his glance for a moment. "I'm sorry, Julian."

Julian nodded, and a silent commiseration passed between

them. Never mix family and the service, but both men knew that one's second life braided into their business, sometimes in ways that made for hard decisions. Neither E's family nor Julian's knew their real jobs, and having to spend the weekend at the behest of Whitehall had strained more than one marriage in the Secret Intelligence Service.

Julian watched E as he stepped into the street to cross and head back to the theater on the other side. Streetlights pointed his way down the street, the standards growing fainter until the lights became disembodied globes.

E was right. Shocking, but Julian had let his personal feelings influence him. He wondered that E hadn't taken him off the case. He had wanted to protect Kim, snatch her out from whatever game she was playing before it was too late. What *too late* meant was a question. He believed that she was merely involved in some amateur investigation. It would be like her to try for an exposé or to get up to some patriotic mission. Now that they were going to give her some rein to see where she led them, he'd hold off having her researcher up at Monkton Hall questioned. It might put her on guard if the man told her.

Kim's involvement in half-baked amateur sleuthing was the best-case scenario. And worst case? There was no worst case. He'd bet the family silver that she was loyal. She'd just picked the wrong week to play against the Office. *Bad timing, Kim, very bad timing.*

THE TRAIN TO UXLEY

WEDNESDAY, APRIL 29. It was 11:34 AM. As the train clattered north out of London, Kim clutched a bulging paisley valise in her arms, using it as a cushion for her head as, sitting up, she repeatedly fell asleep and woke up. She had a private compartment on the train, something she thought needful since she was in possession of a rather enormous amount of cash: Georgi's twenty thousand pounds.

Kim had set a meeting with Georgi at nine that morning at the south entrance to St. Paul's, on a walkway near the great columns of the church. She thought Georgi would come but half-expected to see von Ritter arrive instead, shadowed by Lena.

As she had waited, sporadic organ music had come to her ears, muffled by noble stone. It had been a practice session, as the organist had repeated over and over the opening of a classical piece. Given her wretched state, she had found the stuttering organ distressing, as though expressing doubt upon the doctrines of the Church.

Eight minutes late, Georgi had emerged from her maroon-and-black car and headed up the walkway as her driver waited. Kim stepped out from behind a pillar, feeling like a spy from some film she had seen in her old life. Georgi carried a small portmanteau. Inside was a great deal of money, Georgi said, part of Hugh's cash payoffs. His sister had clearly wanted to distance herself from any association with illicit money. Thrusting the paisley valise into Kim's hands, she said she had found the cash in Hugh's suite at her London house, and now Kim should hand it over to the authorities and make clear that she had nothing to do with her brother's schemes. Also inside, Georgi said, was an envelope with bank receipts for what she claimed were a half a million pounds now residing in bank accounts belonging to her brother. *The pathetic creature* was careless of money and paperwork, so his side income had been only thinly disguised.

Kim gazed out the train window in a dazed state as the train sped through Herefordshire, her own reflection riding beside her, clad in the green plaid coat and brown hat, her spy apparel, unless her real disguise had been the black wool from last night. Her green plaid coat and brown hat had been waiting for her in her hotel room when she had returned from seeing von Ritter. She left the black wool coat in the room, feeling sure the Germans would retrieve it, but how they managed these things—any of it—was baffling to her. *The people of the fog.* How disquieting to be among them and know so little.

The train made a stop in Leicester. People in spring hats and light-colored blazers moved past the club car windows, finding their seats. When could one wear pale blue if not in April? Spring was surely here, by the calendar at least. Vicar Hathaway had said it was neither winter nor summer, but he had been wrong. It was winter still, a dread assessment bolstered by what she knew of an ice-and-cold intrigue that could not possibly be related to lingering winter fogs. Unless it could.

The murdered man's face came into the coach window. Bloody, face broken, knowing he would die there in the garden. Von Ritter raising the gun . . . The memory came again and again. And then the kiss. His precise and ghastly timing. If she had turned from him, he would not have forced her. He wished to test that his personal lure held sway even after blowing a man's brains out against a tree. And she did not turn away, stunned and terrified as she was. The excuse sufficed but did her no credit, nor did those disorienting moments when, before the garden, she had actually found him tempting.

He was a master of seduction, his own brand of it. How fragile were people's tethers to their better selves, faced with a handsome man, a naked girl in the town square, a charismatic leader preaching blame and fear.

She turned from the window, pushing back these deeper thoughts, trying to focus on what to do. As she clutched the valise, it exhaled its pound-note fustiness. She had no idea what to do with this fortune except to hide it. Along with the receipts for the other deposits from Hugh's bank, it was the first hard evidence that Hugh was on the payroll of some agent of influence. She was getting closer. Despite her missteps, she was closer to uncovering the *chorister* scheme.

It was Wednesday. On Sunday, she must deliver Rose to Prestwich Home and somehow justify this to the Babbages. Von Ritter had chosen a perverse test, one that he knew would be morally repellent to her. How had he known this? The idea that German intelligence had a presence in Uxley and maybe even Prestwich Home was bizarre and troubling. Given the shocking events of last night, she was glad she'd had the presence of mind to protect Georgi.

Upon her return from von Ritter's, she had paid the doorman at the Strand five pounds to deliver a note to Georgi at home, disguising it in a large box tied with a ribbon that she had paid to secure from a desk clerk. The note had told Georgi not to contact Kim by phone or post unless absolutely necessary, and then only by using false names for any reference to Hugh ("my aunt") or von Ritter ("Vincent"). If von Ritter was working with Hugh, he could well have a watch on Georgi's house, and she didn't doubt he would kill Georgi to protect the conspiracy.

Lying down on the bench seat was a seductive idea for the two-and-a-half-hour ride to York, where she'd take the 1:46 spur line home. But she needed to eat, no matter the state of her stomach. She made her way to the dining car, paisley valise in hand, like an old woman who could not be parted with her pajamas and toothbrush and must have them at luncheon. The porter stared as she tucked it under the table by her feet.

"May I store that for you, madam?"

She gave a startled glance at the balding, middle-aged man in his ill-fitting uniform jacket. Indeed not.

One could never be sure.

Of anyone.

28

WRENFELL HOUSE,
EAST YORKSHIRE

THURSDAY, APRIL 30. Dust motes rode the shafts of sunlight from the dormer windows. From one of Wrenfell's third-story windows, Kim looked down on the main yard, where the Austin was parked and shining after its scrub. In her room, the Leica sat in its spot on the corner table, having braved its moment of peril yet deprived of an accompanying dramatic photo. The reporter in her could not fail to feel disappointed.

Beyond the yard, she could see a vast quilt of farms lying alternately green and fallow into the distance of the Holderness plain. Kim found comfort in this splendid patchwork and Wrenfell's place in it. As a child, she had often played up there in rainy weather, creating tents and tea parties, for as long as the light from the windows lasted. Electricity had never made it to the third floor.

That morning, she had waited until each of the Babbages

was engaged outside the house, and made her way up the old back stairs with Shadow and her twenty thousand pounds in tow. She must find a place to hide Hugh Aberdare's payoff money, and at Wrenfell, that would be the third floor.

Shadow sniffed at the boxes and trunks. This room had belonged to the housekeeper in the time of Kim's great grand-parents, Llewellyn and Jane Tavistock, with their household of seven children and domestics. Shadow nudged his cold nose against her hand for pats, and she absently stroked his silky border collie coat.

In this east-facing room, they kept Robert's things: his uni-versity books stored in trunks, and the gift-wrapped presents from 1914, the year they thought he might get leave to come home for Christmas. Now they had forgotten what was in them, and no one had the heart to open and bundle them off for the living. The wardrobe over there, that was the hardest thing. Lately, she had been on the verge of asking Mrs. Babbage to fold up the shirts and trousers and give them to All Saints for the charity drive, but of course it would be no easier for Mrs. Babbage to do it, and so it would have to be Kim.

Finding herself in front of the old mahogany armoire, she opened it.

She stood in mute surprise. It was empty.

Shadow put his paws on the lip of the wardrobe and peered in with her. It shocked her to see the empty hangers, the com-pletely bare wardrobe, redolent of cedar planking. So Julian had taken it upon himself, she thought bitterly. How long ago had he come up there and decided that Robert was never coming back?

She slammed the door shut, anger building against her father. Shadow had slunk to the door, watching her with a puzzled, cocked head.

But what was wrong with her? She put her hand to her forehead, trying to brush away her confusion. Of course he was not coming back. At what point had she begun to believe that he *was*?

She went over to the trunks. The books were gone. In the bottom of the second trunk were a few items even Julian could not part with: Robert's bedside clock, letters in a bundle, trophy rosettes from riding competitions. But it could all be kept in a rather small drawer. As the years passed, things would trickle away, and it must be so; she knew it must. Still, the sense of betrayal lingered.

Out the window, she caught a glimpse of Walter pushing a wheelbarrow toward the barn. Today wasn't about her father. It was about Rose. About Kim herself, and how she had turned into an ends-justify-the-means sort of person, one on the verge of sending an innocent girl to Prestwich Home and the clutches of Angus Dunn.

She picked up the paisley valise. She must get on with it.

Shadow bolted out the door, eager for further exploration. But she paused.

It was peculiar in the extreme, the whole situation. Von Ritter was putting her to the test by asking something difficult of her. He chose something that he knew would be emotionally wrenching. But had he done so as a test or just perverse and casual manipulation? If it was a test, then he did believe her capable of helping Germany. She thought he did. Because he knew about Robert and believed she could not bear the thought of another war.

Oh, yes. He believed it. He prided himself on psychological manipulation, making people do things, say things. He had learned this from his *spill* ability, and it had turned him cruel.

Had given him a taste for blood. Some people, experience had taught her, were made permanently uneasy by a Talent. Others lived for it.

Shadow appeared at the door. *Hurry up.* Paisley bag in hand, she made her way down the narrow and dark hall, preceded by Shadow. Here and there, the bare wood flooring was stained from roof leaks. Remnants of lumber lay piled against the walls where workmen had left them. Doors lay open to the servants' rooms, smelling as always of cold and ancient dust and the barley-hull mattresses still covering the bedsprings, awaiting a fresh change of sheets. Walking as far as the west-facing dormer at the end of the hall, she turned around, dissatisfied with her options.

She walked back to the housekeeper's old room. Entering, she opened the armoire and put the paisley valise inside. She just could not stand for it to be *empty*, and somehow the paisley bag with its evidence of German perfidy seemed to complete a circle of logic. She was still fighting Robert's war. Owen had awakened it in her, and she would not hold back for fear of her own death or a week's discomfort on Rose's part. It was all very harsh, but she had reason to believe that she must act swiftly to expose an almost unthinkable disaster.

Shadow barked once, very loudly, suggesting it was time to leave, as the day was fine and there were no mice to chase up there this time.

At the head of the staircase, at the door, he looked up at her. He would have pawed it open as he did the farm gates, but the brass doorknob defied him.

She put her hand on it, her story for the Babbages ready. Rose must go to Prestwich, but just for a quick evaluation. She could not possibly be deemed some kind of danger to society. *All settled, then?*

Shadow leapt down the stairs, flying faster than seemed possible even for a border collie.

"'Ere, now, Shadow, what're you doin'?"

Mrs. Babbage's voice.

Kim walked down to face her.

Walter frowned mightily. "Ye canna be serious!" The three of them sat in the parlor, the Babbages side by side on the divan, and Kim in her father's wingback.

"Those beggars up there meddlin' wi' people and dinna know owt aboot 'er!" He held his red-and-yellow plaid cap in his thick hands, wringing it like a piglet that must be put down.

Mrs. Babbage was shaking her head doubtfully, trying to grasp this new approach. Kim felt Walter's indignation like a cold and righteous judgment. But she had hardened herself against this confrontation and meant to see it through. "It's the quickest way to have it over with. A few locals are making a stink in the village, talking against her and complaining that my father pulled strings. We can have this over and done within a week if we let her go."

Walter folded his arms, showing the patches in his darned woolen cardigan. He saw that Kim had set her mind to it. "Can ye no leave it alone?"

"I wish I could. But the Order of Decency—"

"The bastards!"

"—will be back in the yard twice a week, making us cower in the buttery."

"By Gawd, I'll send 'em on their way, right enough." Walter punctuated her story with little nuggets of truth, like bullets striking home.

"They coom 'ere yesterday. . . ." Mrs. Babbage allowed, casting a worried look to Kim.

"You see? We'll never be left in peace. It's only an evaluation, and they write it up and then she comes home."

Walter gave another twist to the plaid hat. "That doctor won' let 'er go, an' yer the only one as dinna know it."

"He'll let her go. Because I'm going to drive up to Prestwich in a week and pull whatever bloody strings I have to in order to bring her home." She and Walter locked eyes, and neither one was willing to back away.

The door opened and Rose ducked into the parlor. "Mum?" She wore her beloved white ruffled apron.

"We can talk later," Kim said, rising from the chair. Mrs. Babbage met Rose at the door and they disappeared down the hallway, leaving Kim and Walter alone in the parlor for a moment.

He stood, slowly shaking his head. "What d'ye think yer playin' at?"

Kim could not answer. He held her gaze for another moment, then plopped his hat back on his head and left the house.

She could hear subdued voices from the kitchen. Mrs. Babbage and Rose. The back door slammed as Shadow let himself out. Chickens strutted across the yard beyond the back garden, their murmurous clucking drifting down the hall. She wandered into the foyer. Rose's best coat hung on a peg, a little puddle of water underneath it.

The scene with the Babbages in the parlor had not gone well, but she must keep trying. She would talk to Mrs. Babbage again. Kim thought she, at least, would eventually see the wisdom in having the Prestwich testing over with.

In the foyer, she eyed the telephone, planning how to update Owen on what she was doing with Rose. The bag of Hugh's money. What had happened with von Ritter. If only she could run up to Monkton Hall and finagle an appointment. But by now, von Ritter was likely to have discussed her with Fitz. As soon as she'd told him she was being tested at Monkton Hall, he would have checked on her. She had told him in order to establish her sincerity, but she hadn't taken Fitz into consideration. He might note any unscheduled visits with Owen, and she must at all costs avoid leading them to Owen.

There was the dead drop. A phone call. But now that von Ritter had his eye on her—figuratively or in reality—she must avoid any slips that could lead to discovery.

They needed to know the exact nature of the plot, and they must find it—she must find it—with von Ritter.

UXLEY, EAST YORKSHIRE

Alice Ward looked up from wrapping a package for Mrs. Pengelley, nodding at Kim as she entered the Dropped Stitch. There was no smile. Earlier Alice had rung up, asking if Kim would come by, and there hadn't been a smile in her voice, either. She must have spoken to Mrs. Babbage or Walter.

Mrs. Pengelley put the parcel in her string shopping bag and gave Kim an acerbic nod as she left. *The one who's harboring the nudist* had been telegraphed in that little nod. Kim was in no mood for it and ignored her.

When the two women were alone, Alice rounded on her. "Prestwich Home?" The words stood in for an entire courtroom transcript. As punctuation, she slammed the cash register shut. "How can you?"

"I know how it looks." Kim approached the counter, taking the tall stool where Alice's guests sat to gossip and complain of battering husbands.

"It looks like hell. You're letting Angus Dunn intimidate you. Or is it something else?"

"The Order of Decency is out every other day. We can get them off our backs so they'll stop terrorizing Rose."

"Rubbish! Rose isn't terrorized, she doesn't even know who they are." Alice stomped over to the window and turned out the CLOSED sign. She stood in the middle of the shop, arms crossed.

"It's not what you think."

"What is it, then?"

Kim longed to tell her. Instead, she murmured, "We'll get it over with. A week at the most."

"A week." Alice stared at her. "Well, here's what I think. You're giving in to the thugs, is what it looks like."

Kim's misery deepened. "I'm not. I'm trying to put an end to something."

"Harassment? How bad is it out there? Walter told me he chases them off."

"It's going to get worse." Kim wanted to defend herself, even though she had already decided that being blameless was not an option open to her.

The steam went out of Alice. She came round to the counter and went for the Dodd's, pouring for both of them. "I rather hoped you'd tell me it wasn't so."

"I know," Kim said in deep dejection. Alice at least could tell that *that* was true, and they drank in companionable silence. Kim's glance fell on the *Daily Telegraph* on Alice's counter. HOMICIDE IN HUYTON showed over the fold. Turning the paper over, she glanced at the article. To her shock, she found a name she knew: Samuel Reuben. Found murdered in his flat. The Oxford-educated former professor of biology.

She must have blanched. "What is it?" Alice asked, narrowing her eyes.

"I . . ." Kim lost her voice for a moment. "I knew him." She turned the paper around for Alice to read. In another minute, she was out the shop door.

The sun fell heavily on the cobbled square, making it hard to breathe, to think. Within a few paces, Kim had taken off her coat, carrying it as she walked dazedly to the car. They had killed Sam Reuben. Killed him. A familiar car was parked out in front of the Barley and Mow. That brown Talbot that kept showing up at Wrenfell. Kim had dismissed the Order of Decency as an annoyance, but couldn't the Nazis or their sympathizers be using that as a cover to watch her?

In her car, she threw her purse on the seat next to her and stared out the windshield. She tried to quiet her anxiety, but it was no good. Suddenly, it seemed that even Uxley might be riddled with spies. And would von Ritter's henchmen come after her and Owen next?

Across the street, sitting on a bench beside Mayfield's Sweet Shop, Elsa, who was beginning to feel terribly bored by the assignment Julian had given her to keep Kim under surveillance, watched as her target rested her head on the car's steering wheel.

She dug into her sack of jelly beans, popping one in her mouth. *My, oh my. Our girl is having another bad day.*

29

THURSDAY, APRIL 30. It had become a ritual. At 11:20 PM on designated transmission nights, Julian would—as he did now—fill his pipe and light it to wait for Harp's report to come in on the wireless. Their agents in Germany would transmit for only ten minutes, lest the Gestapo pinpoint the origin of the signal. Tonight, he awaited the transmission in both high excitement and uneasiness. Harp had approached his mole at Luckenwalde. Would she accept or, disastrously, turn him in?

Julian inhaled deeply and watched as Fin sat down at the wireless desk, adjusting the headset and readying his pencil and tablet. Like most crack Morse code operators, Fin could translate Morse code directly upon hearing it, but for encrypted reports, he would need to transcribe and then refer to the encryption code. Depending on the length of the message, that could take fifteen to twenty minutes.

They always feared that their agents had been discovered and replaced or turned by the Germans, but it was almost impossible to duplicate a practiced operator's hand on the keys, his "fist." Fin knew Harp's transmission style, his distinctive rhythm. As a further precaution, Harp embedded variations in his code that looked like mistakes but which were additional proof to SIS that it was indeed he.

11:25 PM. Fin adjusted the gain on the crystal set. The designated channel came through in whorls of static and whining of electromagnetic interferences.

Harp might have done nothing yet and have merely a routine report. But he had been told to proceed with highest priority, so if he judged it safe, he might have already approached his potential informant, dubbed "Buttercup" by Julian's team in honor of Harp's having buttered her up for the assignment.

Perhaps tonight they'd get lucky and receive the kind of intelligence that would convince Stanley Baldwin of the invasion threat. Harp had his go-ahead to approach Buttercup, who was to try to get information about the *chorister* Talent, and if not direct information, at least which people—with which sorts of Talents—had recently been transported out of Luckenwalde to Wesermarsch.

11:26. Fin leaned into the radio, as though moving closer to it gave him better reception. "The band is noisy," he murmured. "That big front up north . . ."

The gale north of Scotland. If it veered south down the coast of England, they'd have a bit of electromagnetic interference, but that wouldn't be until Saturday at the earliest, if at all.

Fin cupped the left earpiece closer to his ear, pencil in his right hand over his tablet.

Precisely at eleven thirty, Harp began transmitting and

Fin's pencil went to the page, transcribing the code. The urgent bleats from the wireless always put Julian's nerves on edge. He got up and paced from the shuttered windows to the front door and back again, propelled by the tones and clicks rattling out of the crystal set.

Elsa and Rory were tailing his daughter now. No pretense of her getting SIS protection. She was under surveillance.

A man must know his own daughter, he ruminated. A man does not sit down to hundreds of meals with his own kin and not grasp her essence. He couldn't claim to know her beaus and her secret hopes; he'd stayed removed from her, as he must to keep his cover intact around a very subtle and strong Talent of the *spill*. But he knew her spirit, and it was loyalty to England. She was, by God, *English*, even if her mother always claimed otherwise.

"Gone," came Fin's voice.

Julian moved to the wireless table. "Signed off already?"

"No, the signal's gone. There's nothing."

He didn't like the sound of that. "Keep listening." 11:37. Harp would transmit for ten minutes. And he would sign off.

"Right."

11:39. Fin turned the knob to help bring in the signal, his pencil still in his hand, ready to transcribe. Still as stone.

"No, it's gone."

"Poor signal conditions, then."

Fin, the headphones still perched hopefully on his head, said, "He hit the first character for *Mayday*." He made eye contact with Julian. "Could have been the start of another string."

They listened to the static for a few minutes as Julian's pipe went cold. Fin reached for the wireless switch.

"Leave it on," Julian said.

With the radio band whistling in the background, Fin

opened the code book and began to transcribe what they had of the encrypted message.

Julian looked over his shoulder as he wrote out the message on a fresh sheet of paper. It was both good and bad news. The approach to Buttercup was successful. She was committed to her new role—*thrilled* was Harp's word.

Her first report was a bombshell. Kurt Stelling had indeed been tested at Luckenwalde, and was in possession of a Talent that the Germans called *Eis. Ice.* Not only did she report that he had been designated as a major ability—at 6.5—but all other tested individuals with *ice* Talents above 4 had been assigned within the last two months to the Wesermarsch sub camp. Then the message had stopped abruptly.

It could have been the weather. But the storm front was still in the North Atlantic. It wasn't the weather.

Fin would listen in to the band for another hour and had orders to wake Julian at his flat if anything more came through from Harp.

Not that Julian would be able to sleep.

THE ROAD TO EBBERSTON

FRIDAY, MAY 1. The sun glared through the window, baking the side of Kim's face as she drove north, forcing her to crank down the window. The morning air rushed in, cold from its sleep in the deep pockets of the Wolds.

The note for the dead drop lay on the seat beside her. She watched her rearview mirror as much as the road ahead, checking for that brown Talbot motorcar of the Order's. Or any car that seemed suspicious.

The dead drop was a risk, but now that the conspirators had killed Sam Reuben, Kim desperately wanted to tell Owen the latest events so that he would have the full picture. Or as full a one as she possessed. More than ever, she was aware of the danger of exposing her true role; the risk of communicating with Owen was deepening. She didn't know if she was responding in a panic, had a need for the comfort of a collaborator, or was doing exactly the right thing.

She drove on.

From time to time, Kim looked down at her note, to be sure it said all it must:

> Sam Reuben has been murdered. The Daily Telegraph, Thursday, April 30. I think a big operation is underway. What IS it? And when? I was blindfolded when taken to VR's villa outside of London. He has accepted me, it appears. He admitted being with a German intelligence agency, SD? He murdered an English helper of his in front of me. To scare me. Successfully. I'm afraid, but how can we stop? The test he set me is to take my maid Rose to Prestwich Home to be evaluated as someone whom VR has heard (somehow) is a mental defective. It may be that they've been watching Wrenfell. As promised, Georgi has turned over £20,000 of Hugh's bribery money as well as deposit slips for other cash deposits. It's hidden in the wardrobe on the 3rd floor at home. I'm going to try to get Rose's parents, staff at Wrenfell, to agree to the testing at Prestwich. I think he wanted me to betray someone. It will show I'm serious. I've told Georgi to use code words if she contacts me, though whether she would help us further, I have no idea. Yes, I'm afraid. But it doesn't matter, you see? We still have nothing that would convince the police. Nothing! I go on.

The note entirely exposed her. They should have thought to develop some kind of code. Even so, the dead drop seemed to be her and Owen's best communication method right now.

She motored on, rushing north to the dead drop in the village of Ebberston, twenty minutes north. On this particular morning the Wolds, with their graceful dales and hills bursting with fertile green, failed to charm her. She must hurry to get the note in place before Owen checked the dead drop on his way to work at Monkton Hall. In the lowest dips of the valleys, the sun disappeared behind the scarps, bringing cold shadows followed by thrusts of the sun between the hills. One eye on the note, the other on the mirror, she hardly saw the road.

In the garden, von Ritter had meant to show her that she must not fail him. She took home the lesson not only that she must deliver Rose to Dunn, but also that she must—by whatever means—deliver von Ritter into custody. And the sooner she completed her test assignment, the sooner she could see her SD handler again. This time, with luck, or the blessing of the *spill*, she would learn how England would be brought down. Then Owen could go to the very door of Downing Street if he had to.

If there was time.

The road descended steeply into a vale where a river curved close before plunging down a fall. There was no one behind her, or hadn't been for some miles, as what little traffic there was had peeled off onto private roads.

Then something moved onto the road in front of her. A deer. She slammed on the brakes, coming to a stop a stone's throw from the animal. It bounded away, its white tail flashing. She looked to see if it had companions waiting on the verge, but all seemed quiet. As she got underway again, something else caught her attention.

In her rearview mirror, there was a glint from a car windshield.

A car that had stopped at the top of the hill, mostly out of sight around the curve. She could just make it out in the side mirror, although it was nearly masked by the trees. A black car.

Someone had stopped when she stopped. They were following her. She drove on, trying to quiet her thudding heartbeat. She was now extremely anxious to be out of the thick trees and onto a more open stretch of the road. Was it Oskar, under orders to watch her every movement? Or perhaps Lena, a woman who, she thought, would take pleasure in pulling her into the shadows of her *darkening* Talent and killing her?

Hands tightly gripping the wheel, she drove on, now watching for her pursuer, a small black car that sometimes let her get very far ahead, often appearing at the last moment as she went into a curve. Once, a truck moved between them, but when it veered off at a market town, the car was still following.

Kim came into the village of Ebberston at last. She parked the car on the high street, with its closely packed houses and shops, and entered the Nooks and Books. It had been her plan all along to pretend to shop in the hamlet. A little outing on a fine day. Now she followed through, her mind a jumble.

She bought a few books so that she could be seen leaving with parcels. Her plan with Owen for dead drops had been that she would leave a mark on a selected side street in Ebberston: two downward slashes on a wooden post to signal that a message waited at the drop. Today, she merely stopped for tea and scones at the tearoom up the street.

Her hand shook as she raised the teacup. The cup and saucer clattered as she lowered her tea without drinking it. The dead-drop problem was of her and Owen's own devising. When they'd set the dead drop to be under the large stone by the statue in the park, they had erred. It should be in a private place, of course.

God, such a foolish mistake. Feeling certain she had been followed, she was not going to use it.

In the lavatory at the tearoom, she shredded her note, flushing it down the toilet.

She sat on the stool, contemplating the tile floor in front of her, with wisps of toilet tissue sticking to wet spots. How humble espionage was, contrary to popular assumption. It was not the glamorous business people made it out to be. It was tawdry, morally wretched and liable to get one killed.

Leaving the tearoom, she walked down the street to a phone box. Not a good solution, if Fitz would find out that Owen received a call from her. But she had come to believe that keeping Owen abreast of matters was not just comforting, it was essential. He would be the one handing their evidence to the authorities. He had to know it all.

When she got through to Owen, she gave him the number and told him to call her back from a phone box.

It took him twenty minutes. She grabbed the telephone on the first ring.

"Owen, Sam Reuben . . ."

"Yes. I heard. You have to stop. You're in terrible danger."

He would say that. They were going to argue, she was sure. She explained her approach to von Ritter.

Hearing about the murder in the garden, Owen said, "Stop now, Kim. I should never have gotten you involved. It's too much for us."

She decided not to tell him she'd been followed. He had lost his nerve. "I'm close, so close to getting to the bottom of this."

"But how? You think von Ritter will just tell you the plan?"

The *spill*. The defining *spill*, that was how it would happen. But he had lost faith; she heard it in his voice. Worse, she began to feel that he might go over her head and talk to the authorities now. "If something happens to me, if I go missing, then you must go to the police and tell them everything. But not before, Owen. Not before. They'll round me up for questioning. My chance will be gone."

"Your chance. To play the heroine?"

If he thought that . . . it galled exceedingly.

He changed his tone. "They're closing ranks, killing off people more recklessly. You may not be fooling your target. He could kill you; he *will* kill you if he has doubts."

"Precisely why you aren't to tell anyone. Until you hear from me."

"Why did you call me, then? You aren't listening to a thing I say."

"Someone besides me has to know. And when the time comes, you'll be the one to go to the officials. They'll listen to you much more than to me."

"I'm the messenger," he said bitterly.

"Owen. I'm ringing off." She paused, desperate to convince him but running out of time, out of words. "Wait for me."

She left the phone box and looked around the street for any spies. *Make of that what you will,* she thought fiercely at whoever was watching. *I made a phone call. Go hang yourself.*

Her hands had stopped shaking, she noted with satisfaction.

WRENFELL HOUSE, EAST YORKSHIRE

She had barely got in the front door at Wrenfell when her father rang.

The smell of apple pie wafted up the hall from the kitchen,

suffusing the house with a lovely normalcy, marred only by the necessity of Kim having to argue on the phone with her father.

"What's this about bringing Rose up to Prestwich?"

Kim glanced down the hall, not wishing to alarm Rose with the discussion. She was nowhere in sight. "With all these visits—they were here again today, Mrs. Babbage says—I just want Rose to have a clean bill of health."

"The Order of Decency, you're talking about. I thought it would blow over."

"Well, it hasn't. We're at our wits' end." *If you'd stay home* . . . Her usual rebuff fell away from her. His absences might have a sinister cause. Her uncertainty about this was maddening, but it was her job to suspect everyone now.

To her surprise, she heard, "I'm sorry. I should have taken care of this. Is Rose upset?"

"We haven't told her yet. I'm not even sure the Babbages will go for it."

"I shouldn't think these Order chaps will keep at it. You can't just take the visits in your stride, then?"

"No."

A longish pause. A whistling sound hovered faintly in the lines.

Julian said again, "I'm sorry that you're going through this. It must be a strain."

"We'll soon put it right." She stepped out of her shoes, splaying her feet on the cool flagstone floor.

"Kim. Is everything all right with you?"

"Of course it is." She hoped he was not going to be nice. Every time he took a turn for the concerned father, she began to hope for a relationship. Then he became impervious again and seemed to barely tolerate her.

"Look. I'm starving, and Mrs. Babbage has tea ready."

"You were out on a drive?"

"Yes."

"Where to? Someplace with Alice?"

"The bookshop in Ebberston. Just to get out of the house."

Another pause. "You might have rung up when you were in London."

So Walter was reporting on her left and right. Did he really think she would have just dropped in on him? "Sorry. I should have."

"Well. I expect Mrs. Babbage oughtn't be kept waiting." A pause. "I'll try to get home in a few days."

Wonderful. That should set things to rights. In point of fact, she didn't want Julian countermanding her in the Prestwich business. "We're perfectly fine. Really." And then, because he seemed to want to help: "You can come up and fetch her back from Dr. Dunn's once he's written up his report. And I don't care what it takes."

"Count on it. At the very least, I can bribe him with good whisky."

She wanted to ask what he'd done with the contents of the wardrobe. But now was not the time.

Although one question did suggest itself rather pressingly: *What did you burn in the barn in the middle of the night last week?*

She took tea at the zinc counter in the kitchen. Mrs. Babbage served the apple pie steaming hot directly from the huge baking sheet onto Kim's plate. On cue, the backdoor screen clicked open and shut, and in the next moment Blaze, the gray hen, came in to claim a few pieces of piecrust that Mrs. Babbage had baked separately for her.

The silver hen always seemed to know when pie might be served and when Shadow was elsewhere on the property.

"'Ere now, Blaze," Mrs. Babbage said, laying down a few bits of piecrust on the hearth. Blaze clucked happily over her meal, as calm a chicken as Kim had ever seen. A cuddler, too, when pie was not on offer.

Mrs. Babbage straightened up, wiping her hands on her apron and regarding Kim with a cool gaze. The subject between them loomed large.

"It's for her own good," Kim began.

Another noise from the back-porch screen, and Walter came in with Flint in tow. Two slices of pie got served out then, one on the counter, one on the floor. Flint gobbled his up, loftily ignoring Blaze, who returned the snub. Walter took a seat at the counter, looking uncomfortable.

Mrs. Babbage smoothed her apron, looking at Walter and then at Kim. "She must go."

"Pardon?"

"Rose must go, as you say. To put an end to it." She nodded solemnly. "And then coom 'ome."

Walter stared at the counter, biting his lip.

Relief watched over Kim. She tried not to show it. "It's so hard, I know."

Walter looked up, his gaze making his point. "So long as she coom right back."

Kim nodded. "We'll make it work, I promise."

Mrs. Babbage got out another plate, cut herself a square of pie and sat down at the counter with them.

"Delicious," Kim said, her eyes filling with tears at the heavenly taste, the sheer kindness of it.

"Nowt but pie," Mrs. Babbage said, pleased.

30

SUNDAY, MAY 3. Kim straightened the drapes in the parlor, arranging the pleats for regularity. That done—and it had to be done every day because Rose would dust the window reveals and leave the curtains awry—she lined up the candlesticks on the mantle and, even more exacting, the tilt of the candles themselves. It was aggravating how they looked straight from one angle and askew from another, and how fixing one alignment would ruin the next. She pressed an errant candle more firmly into its holder.

She was a wreck. Small chores soothed her, but as her glance drifted to the untidy fringe on the Turkish carpet, she knew her nerves were quite gone.

Rose had not taken well to the notion of returning to Prestwich Home. Of course she could not have been expected to embrace the idea, but there had been tears and pleading and raised voices heard all the way from the Babbage cottage. Mrs. Babbage thought it best to wait a day to let Rose calm down, and on Saturday, Rose settled into a close-lipped mope that Kim dared not intrude on. By that evening, Rose was resigned, mollified by Kim's promise of a picnic on the way to Prestwich. It looked as though Kim had won through, but never was a victory less sweet. Self-loathing warred with her sense of urgency.

She had put off as long as possible the call to Prestwich Home to let them know she was coming, but it was time. She eyed the untidy fringe on the carpet. . . . No, she would not give in. It would never lie straight, not absolutely, and once allowing herself to stoop and give the strands a flick, she would be lost.

She stalked into the hallway and rang up Angus Dunn.

He came to the phone after a very long wait, as though he had walked the cavernous hallways from some unthinkably dark and distant room.

"Yes? Miss Tavistock?"

"Dr. Dunn, I'm ringing up to ask if you would be so kind as to complete your evaluation of Rose Babbage. We are anxious to put this episode behind us, and feel it cannot be done without going through the process you suggest."

"Ah, I see. I'm happy to provide assistance, of course. It's the purpose of the Prestwich institution. When were you thinking of bringing the patient?"

Kim took a deep breath at hearing *patient*. She must keep this casual and with the firm implication that the Prestwich visit was a formality.

"Rose and I will come up today, midafternoon, if that's suitable."

"Yes, that will work admirably. We'll have her room prepared. I'm sure it must have been very difficult for you to reconcile yourself to professional help, but believe me, it's in Rose Babbage's best interests and the community's."

"My father and I will read your evaluation with great interest, Dr. Dunn. It will give us all something on which to base a broader discussion."

"Yes. Well. I'm at your disposal. Shall we say three o'clock?"

Shall we say you are a pompous, condescending twit?

Concluding the phone call, Kim placed the receiver in its hook with tight self-control. Dunn's tone was just what she had imagined it would be: disingenuous empathy masking a high satisfaction in having won.

A noise down the hall. She turned to see Walter come through from the back yard with a valise. Behind him, Rose stood framed in the doorway, a dark silhouette against the bright day behind her.

SIS HEADQUARTERS, LONDON

Julian entered the Veterans' Benefit Office with his key. It was empty, this being Sunday. Still, he took precautions not to be seen entering the office upstairs.

E had agreed to meet him and would not be happy to hear what Julian had to report. Harp's radio nest had been raided. They had confirmation at five that morning in an emergency communication from Woodbird, their man in the *Abwehr*. Harp was at Plötzensee Prison, and Buttercup at a women's prison run by the Gestapo. It was disastrous news, endangering all of Harp's friends even if they knew nothing. If and when he talked, he would reveal to the Germans that Luckenwalde was a British espionage target.

The problem went deeper, too. Heath Millington had opposed the risky approach to Buttercup, and his boss Alistair Drake would be sure that the Foreign Office heard of the debacle, thus undermining E at a time when he needed all the authority he could muster.

Had Buttercup been clumsy or traitorous? Or had Harp's transmission station finally—and at a fateful moment—been pinpointed by the Gestapo?

One last gift from Harp: Fin had decoded the last message, and it gave some critical information about Commandant Stelling.

Despite all this, his daughter was not very far from his thoughts. Julian kept thinking about his telephone conversation with Kim. He had, of course, been unable to ask her the question foremost in his mind: *What are you involved with?* He had very much wished to. SIS was giving her enough rope to . . . well, it wasn't possible that she would be suspected of espionage. That just was not bloody well possible.

In the employee canteen of the veterans' office, there was a door leading to a backstairs fourth-floor landing outside of E's office. The unlocked door led to a staircase that dead-ended on a broad landing with several false offices, all of them empty except one. If someone climbed the stairs, they would find the premises guarded by a sergeant-major type in a blue uniform who would politely redirect them to wherever they were trying to go.

The guard nodded to Julian and unlocked the door to the SIS headquarters.

Julian entered and walked down the long hallway to "Empire Press." This door led to the anteroom of E's domain, commanded by Olivia Hennessey.

She was just emerging from E's office, having announced

that Julian was on his way. She was apparently on weekend duty as well as E.

"One of these days, I'm going to find you reading a paperback novel," Julian said. The joke always went flat, given the guard's advance signal to her desk, but she seemed to enjoy the teasing. Olivia was known to be frightfully busy at all times, and E had made clear that he could not do without her.

"He's free?"

"Waiting for you." She nodded at the door, the upswept wave on her crown teetering.

E put his papers aside. "Julian. Good to see you. Tea?"

"Thank you." E leaned into the intercom, asking Olivia to bring it. "Bad news, then?" E surmised, noting Julian's demeanor.

"Yes. Harp and Buttercup have been arrested."

E's face darkened. They'd been prepared for the worst after the cut-off transmission the day before yesterday, but this news was the worst possible.

"He's being held at Plötzensee Prison. Woodbird doesn't know if interrogations have begun yet."

"Good Christ."

Plötzensee was notorious for its treatment of political prisoners, with German traitors usually executed with an axe in the courtyard.

"We think the secretary was sincere, but she must have led the Gestapo to Harp in some way. She's in a women's prison, but all she knew was Harp and her assignment at Luckenwalde."

"Anyone else compromised in Harp's network?"

"No. A separate cell." Julian paused. "We made a mistake." Buttercup hadn't been ready for her role. But they'd been in desperate need of intel out of Luckenwalde.

"Think Harp will talk?"

"I would say that Harp will hold out, at least for a few days. Buttercup will tell everything she knows immediately."

"Christ God."

Whether E was swearing about Buttercup talking or Harp having to hold out under torture, Julian wasn't sure.

"He'll try to give us time," Julian said. "He wasn't told why we need to know and he won't give up what he knows easily."

"Is there anything to be done?"

"No, not without jeopardizing our *Abwehr* contact. We can't appear to know where he's imprisoned, or even that he's been taken."

"Poor bastard."

"But Harp's last message broke some things loose for us."

"Yes?" E waited for some good news.

"Before Harp's transmission was cut off last Thursday, we learned that Stelling had a very strong Talent for something Luckenwalde calls *ice.*"

"*Ice?*"

"Apparently. We don't know what the capabilities of an *ice* Talent may be, but Stelling has a rating of 6.5—the Germans have a more finely calibrated scale than we use. And there was more. All those tested for *ice* at Luckenwalde over the last two months have been taken to Wesermarsch."

"To Wesermarsch! What do you make of it, then?"

"All we can do is guess at this point, but I think their invasion plan uses temperature. The cold."

"Bits and pieces, Julian. We need more." E began pulling the papers on his desk into folders. "I'll let Drake know what's happened. It should give him great satisfaction that we were warned by Millie." He stood, buttoning his suit jacket.

And of course, Heath Millington *had* been against it. In the circumstance of an impending invasion of England, this turn of events might not rise to the notice of the Secretary for Imperial Defence. But that was the bloody problem: no one was taking the idea of an impending attack seriously.

Olivia entered with tea service on a tray. She left it on the sideboard, carving a glance at Julian, discerning that there was tension in the room. He met her eyes. By God, he would like to commiserate with her over a drink. Not going to happen.

She closed the door behind her.

E moved to the sideboard. "Well, have a spot, Julian."

Julian poured tea, and E brought out a decanter of whisky. Tipping a liberal portion into both cups, E raised a toast, face grim. "The King."

"The King," Julian returned with equal gravity.

ALBEMARLE STREET, LONDON

Five hours later, at two o'clock, Julian was at the newsstand near his flat, picking up an afternoon paper. He was not surprised to see Rabbit walking up to peruse the racks. In fact, it was why he'd come to pick up a paper at this regular meeting place. If an agent was not waiting for Julian on any particular day, he'd at least have a paper.

As a truck pulled up to the stand delivering more papers, Julian surveyed the newspaper headline: ARABS TORCH JEWISH HOMES IN PALESTINE. The newsagent helped to offload the stacks bound in twine, leaving Rory and Julian alone for a minute.

Examining a magazine, Rory said in a low voice, "Foxhound is being sent home. It's the Harp affair."

Julian couldn't quite digest what he was hearing. His mind

staggered around for a moment as he tried to grasp the devastating news. E had been relieved of his post.

"Sacked, absolutely?"

"There'll be an inquiry, but Foxhound is relieved of duty. Until then, Hatter is taking his place."

Heath Millington would replace E. The idea was so absurd that Julian could hardly believe it, but from the way things had been going, it was all too plausible. Drake had been waiting for a chance to sink E and put an end to his long tenure at SIS. But how could the loss of a German agent be the cause?

Still looking at the news rack, Julian said, "Why the bloody hell isn't Lowry stepping up?" E's deputy director should be the one to fill in.

Rory's disgust came through in a low growl. "They don't trust our assessments of late. Looks like they mean to clean house. Also, the Security Service is directly involved now."

The Security Service, SIS's sister organization, was responsible for operations within British territory. Sometimes, the jurisdictions overlapped. They overlapped as much as they could get by with.

Rory went on. "Apparently, the Security Service had Sparrow under surveillance. She was seen accepting a package from Sunflower at St. Paul's. And despite the fact that if we *had* picked her up, it would have made us seem like we were protecting her, alerting her, they're bloody well trying to make something of the fact that we *didn't* pick her up."

Kim? A package from Georgi? Was his daughter really entering this equation? He was reeling now. Astonishingly, Britain's internal spy service was following her when she met Georgi Aberdare. Their own services not even sharing. The situation was compounding fast, and not in a good direction.

"Am I relieved of duty too?"

Rory reached in his pocket to find a shilling for the paper. "No, not yet. Bastards can't sack all of us." He saw that the deliveryman had sprung back into the truck. "Foxhound will meet you at the bench at six forty-five tonight."

Julian paid for his paper and turned away from the newsstand. He strolled up Albemarle toward his flat, feeling his mission unwind, trailing long, strangling ropes. E sent home. Kim having come to the attention of the Security Service. The investigation into *Sturmweg* overseen by Heath Millington.

All the while, the Germans preparing to land on English beaches, a possibility no one of influence except E was willing to entertain.

Walking along the pavement to his flat, he passed a bobby, ample belly bulging over his uniform's leather belt, smiling at a few women pushing prams. As he passed, the policeman jauntily tipped his hat at Julian. Good God, England was still living in 1926.

They had no idea what was coming.

31

ON THE ROAD TO PRESTWICH HOME

SUNDAY, MAY 3. Kim poured out another glass of Mrs. Babbage's cider for Rose. The two of them sat on a south-facing slope of a hill gloriously full of daffodils. The spate of fine weather had passed, replaced by high clouds and a thin and slicing wind, but here on the lee slope of the moor-side hill, they were warm.

Mrs. Babbage's Yorkshire sausages and biscuits had calmed both their nerves, and now they enjoyed feeling pleasantly full. In the end, the leave-taking at Wrenfell had not been as bad as Kim feared. Rose's parents had elected not to go along, judging that Rose would enjoy having the mistress of the house all to herself, and Mrs. Babbage doubting she could be stalwart enough not to further agitate Rose. So they were alone and, despite her gnawing fears, Kim did feel a certain peace in the country hillside. She abandoned herself to the sharp scent of spring grasses and the muted symphony of birds and crickets.

The mission could wait a few hours. If von Ritter did not

reveal anything further, if she had no contact with him—for her next contact with him was not planned—she and Owen would be left with no alternative but to lay all before the authorities. But Kim thought that von Ritter would boast. He would tell her something; he would want her admiration. It was her desperate hope that this time her *spill* ability would bring the final proof of an attack on England.

"Oh." Rose turned to look at their car parked at the crest of the hill down which they'd walked to their picnic spot. She frowned. "Oh no."

She got to her feet, wiping her hands on her heavy sweater, as though patting herself down for something missing.

"What is it, Rose?"

Rose's face crumpled into confusion. "I dinna pack it. I got t' go back!"

Kim got up in alarm lest they have to go home and start the goodbyes all over again. "But what did you forget?"

"Me apron, tha's what." She nodded. "Me apron."

Kim inhaled deeply, trying for patience. The bright white apron with the ruffles. Rose loved it and never failed to wear it in the house. "It will be all right—you won't need it for a couple days."

Rose rounded on her with surprising force. "I do need it! I do!"

"But why, Rose? It will still be there when you get back. When you'll really need it for your house duties. But for now, you'll have a rest, you see?"

Rose stood next to the picnic basket, facing off with Kim, her shoulders pulled back in a granite pose. "It proves summat."

Kim's face must have shown her confusion.

"It proves I'm a maid. A real 'un."

"Oh, we all know you're the housemaid! Everyone is so proud of you. We couldn't do without our Rose."

"Nay. They dinna know." She looked northward in the direction of Prestwich Home, where it waited just beyond a few bends in the road, on the western edge of the moors. "They think I'm slow." She nodded slowly, her eyes gazing north but her sight all inward. Kim's heart fell a fathom down. By God, Rose knew.

"That there's summat wrong wi' me, and tha's why the big car coom with those people and my da, 'e runs 'em off." Rose looked back at Kim. "Tha's why I go to the big place up there. The place where they's nowt right i' the head and they think I'm like that too."

Kim was stricken. She had not paid enough attention to what Rose thought about what was going on, had assumed—like the people she despised—that Rose couldn't understand. But, oh, she did.

Rose knew what the people in the village thought of her, knew exactly what was going on with the Order of Decency and with Dr. Dunn and his crew. She could see well enough the effect it had had on the household, and all the secrecy and steering her into the buttery on flimsy excuses had been totally ineffective. Maybe she didn't know all the implications and the details, but she knew enough to conclude that people thought she wasn't *right* and should be shut away.

"I want me apron, miss."

"Well, now," Kim said, thinking fast. "I have an idea."

Rose narrowed her eyes.

"What if I bring it up to you tomorrow? That way, I can see you again and make sure you're getting on all right."

Rose stared at the ground, concentrating on this offer, while Kim checked her watch. It was 2:35, getting late.

"Suppose we have another biscuit and think about this some more?" Kim plunged her hand in the picnic basket, pulling out the biscuit tin and feeling like a complete ass, bribing her with cookies. But Rose must get there today. She must not *disappoint* von Ritter.

Panic filled her chest as she waited for Rose to take a proffered biscuit, to decide whether she could suffer a night in Prestwich Home without her apron.

A cold breeze slipped over the hummock behind them, sluicing down the hill and thrashing the heads of the daffodils. Their warm shelter was no more.

Rose pulled her sweaters around her, crossing her arms in front of her. "I dinna like the cold."

"No, I don't either. Let's go back to the car and be on our way."

Rose looked up at the sky. "Storm."

"Oh, the day's all right. Just a little breeze." She put the biscuits back in the hamper, along with the jug of cider and their cups. "Rose, you carry the blanket, would you?"

Rose tugged at the blanket as Kim struggled to throw the remains of the lunch inside the hamper before Rose, suddenly in a great hurry, upended everything. Then off they went, Rose leading the way, charging up the slope.

Kim thrashed behind her, holding the big picnic basket and thermos of tea as best she could.

"Got to 'urry!" Rose said, looking behind at Kim.

When Kim reached the car, Rose was already sitting in the passenger seat, looking terrified.

Kim got the picnic basket into the back seat and, spurred on by Rose's sudden urgency to be gone, started up the car. Jouncing off the verge onto the strip of track that led to the highway, they headed north on the road as Rose urged her to higher speed.

They sped along, the sky darkening by the moment. The wind carried bullets of rain. How quickly the weather had changed, but how like Yorkshire, sunny one moment and ghastly the next. At Kim's side, Rose had slouched down in her seat, now and then making startled glances out the window as though seeing something outside pacing them in the bracken. "Can you go no faster?"

"It's all right, Rose. A little rain is all. Shall we sing a song?"

She began on "It's a Long Way to Tipperary" but soon let the tune peter out as Rose, who normally liked a good sing, remained frozen in fear.

The rain became sleet, bulking up on the windshield wipers. The temperature had dropped twenty degrees, making Kim wish she'd taken time, in the mad escape from the picnic site, to put on her coat. In the next moment—how bizarre—it was actually snowing.

"The storm. Oh, the storm . . ." Rose moaned.

They sped down into a dale and back up a hill, with the road getting harder to make out, and the cleared space on the windshield only a small fan in front of her. Her surprise at the weather soon became a real fear of driving off into a ditch.

Kim calculated that they were only a few miles from Prestwich Home. If she could battle the elements a few minutes longer, they could find shelter. They would have to, as Rose had begun to sway back and forth on her seat, in a furious rocking motion that seemed to presage an outburst of terror.

"Hold on, Rose, we're close to the place now. Not far, I'm sure. It will be so nice to be somewhere warm, won't it?" She spoke with more confidence than she felt, for the snow was now in full rage, blowing sideways in a great swarm of white. It was absurd to have a snowstorm in May, even in Yorkshire. Since she could hardly see the road, she might have to pull off, but if she did, she expected Rose would begin screaming.

At the top of the hill, Kim recognized the distinctive rock formation that held pride of place just before the road plunged into a valley where Prestwich lay. But she could drive no farther in this surge of white. She pulled into a field.

"Nay! Drive on!" Rose shouted. "The storm!"

"We can't outrun it. And we're safe in the car, as long as we're off the road. Please don't fret, Rose. We're perfectly safe. I'm right here with you."

In the next moment, Rose had thrown open the door and jumped out of the car, lumbering into the storm.

"Rose!" Kim swore, and, grabbing her coat from the back seat, rushed after her. Kim was certain the snowstorm would quickly dissipate, but Rose could get lost if she ran headlong away.

"Rose!" Kim could no longer see her through the clotted air. She staggered among the heather and bracken, all covered with their hoods of snow, in a suddenly bizarre and transformed world.

Buttoning her coat to the neck, Kim rushed over the uneven ground, glad she had worn her sturdy shoes and slacks instead of heels and a skirt. She called to Rose, hearing nothing except the gusting of the wind. A deep uneasiness fell over her. Where was the girl? Might she fall and tumble down one of the sheer walls of limestone that broke up the landscape?

The wind softened, and in a moment, the air had brightened to a dazzling blue-white. She could see a few trees in the immediate area, and above, the sun was a furious white disk in the sky. Oh, it was all passing! Thank God.

In another moment, the storm swept by her completely, leaving the snow-covered shrubs with their bonnets of ice. "Rose," she called again, turning in place to peer into the distance lest she had unknowingly run by her.

Up ahead, the storm battered the moor in a most unusual pocket. Nor was it moving on, but lying stationary in a tight and angry white fist.

Rose was still in trouble. Kim charged forward. As she approached the wall of the storm—it looked rather like a wall— she saw Rose standing, back to her, just a few feet away. She was hunched over, her shoulders and head piled with a few inches of snow.

Kim cried out to her, but with the wind trapped inside the wall, calling was useless. The girl staggered away, deeper onto the moor. As Kim rushed forward to overtake her, she tripped over a rock and fell heavily on her right knee. The pain of it left her breathless for a moment. Struggling to her feet, she winced as she tried to put weight on the damaged leg. She hobbled on, but it was no use: she could not match Rose's pace.

This could not be happening. They had been fine in the car, and it all would have passed over, but Rose rushed out in a panic, and now she was far ahead and Kim with a bad knee. She prayed that the whole thing would not turn uglier yet. If Rose would just come to her senses and come back!

As the storm moved slowly away, Kim could see Rose now and again in the midst of the wintry cell, like a waif seen through a frost-glazed window.

The storm was following her.

It couldn't be, but as Rose moved left, the storm shifted its perimeter a little to the left and when Rose wandered in another direction, the cell kept her in its cage.

Mother of God, what was going on?

It must be her imagination that the cell was following Rose, but it was most peculiar. She watched as the little storm wandered nearby, like a foraging creature, meandering without a destination.

Kim sat on a sopping wet rock and waited. There was nothing more she could do. In exhaustion, she put her hands to her forehead, forming a tent over her eyes, pressing on her skull, trying to stay calm.

When she took her hands away, Rose was walking toward her. Little crusts of snow melted rapidly on her head and the front of her sweater.

"'Tis over now," Rose said evenly.

"Is it?" Kim asked, looking into the calm day, with the quince bushes and heather glistening icily in the sun. The storm had indeed vanished.

"Aye. Lil' storms dinna stay long." She walked on past, heading toward the car, brushing the snow from her arms.

Kim hobbled after her, thinking *little storms*. Rose had seen them before. No, she had—God in heaven—caused them.

Rose took off her sweaters and lay them methodically on the back seat of the car to dry.

Kim stood watching her. "Is that why you always wear your sweaters, Rose? Because the storms follow you?"

Rose looked away, evasive. "It gets awfu' cold." She got in the car and started using the picnic ground cloth to dry her hair.

She stared at Rose. She was a *cold cell* Talent.

Kim went around to the driver's side. As she did so, she saw movement down in the valley. She felt a pang of anxiety as she noted that two cars were just leaving the yard at Prestwich. They began winding up the hill.

"The little storms come to you, don't they?"

Rose frowned. She stared at the cloth in her hands, murmuring, "An' when we're all together, we make a storm road. All us at the big place."

With a shock, Kim guessed this was a *spill*. She didn't know whether to probe for more or let Rose divulge things on her own. But the cars had crested the hill and were approaching.

"You make a road," Kim said gently. The world narrowed down to just her car, just the two of them. "How do you know it's a road?"

"I seen it, when we was practicin', an' it was all of ice."

"A road of ice, Rose?" Kim was hardly breathing.

"Aye. All of ice, an' we seen a truck coom through, right enough."

"A truck?"

"An' I 'eard Dr. Dunn say, the road, it goes over the water. The big water."

Kim saw that the cars were getting close. They had seen the little storm from Prestwich and had piled in their cars to rush up before Kim could suspect it was not an ordinary storm.

"The doctor told you that?"

Rose's face crumpled. "I weren't supposed to be there. But I 'eard 'im, when 'e was talkin' to someone." She cut a glance at Kim. "My mum says it's wrong to listen where you got no business."

"Rose, are you saying that the people in the home down there can make a road if they work together?"

"Aye. Together. 'Tis 'ard work. But 'tis a pretty road, all ice an' sparklin'."

So, this was Alice's ice chain, and the source of the *trauma view* had been Rose, sitting in church. . . .

"I should not 'ave told you. Mum says you dinna tell what's none o' your business."

"Rose. You must not let Dr. Dunn know you said anything."

Dunn was here. He knocked on the window. He smiled in at them.

Kim had the urge to start up the car and stomp on the gas pedal. The door wasn't locked, but she still had a moment when she might ram the car past the welcoming party and race away to safety. She had to get Rose out of there. They were making her help with the road.

Dunn opened the car door at Kim's side. "Miss Tavistock. We worried about you when you were late. We saw that a little weather came through. Looks like you got a soaking."

There were no words. She had made a terrible, dreadful mistake. Bringing Rose here wasn't a test for Kim. Rose was *useful*. For an invasion. Kim looked up into Dunn's watery blue eyes. His red bow tie hugged his neck like a clot of blood.

"What a bad patch!" she croaked. "Well, the sun came back after all."

He looked searchingly at her.

"We got caught in it. Imagine snow this time of year!"

He nodded carefully. His men were right behind him. "Yorkshire weather," he said. *Anything can happen in Yorkshire.*

Apparently, this was true.

"We'll take Rose now," he said. "No need for you to come down to the house. Unless you'd like to?"

Kim looked down the valley toward the lowering old keep. If she walked in that door, she would not come out. She put on a bright face. "Oh, thank you so much. But I think Rose is feeling ill. Perhaps if we came back tomorrow?" She turned to Rose. "You aren't feeling well, are you, Rose?"

"I'm all right, miss, dinna you worry."

Dunn was watching her with a feral expression. She temporized. "She got caught in the squall and was shivering so hard. I think it's best if we give her a chance to rest at home."

He smiled reassuringly. "Rest is just what we had in mind. As Rose said, I don't think you need to worry." He nodded for a burly attendant to approach.

There was no getting Rose from Dunn now. Kim had to tell this information to someone. "Well then, if you think you can manage." The attendant came round the other side and helped Rose out of the car. Now she seemed docile, reconciled. She pulled away to gather her sweaters off the back seat.

Dunn said, "Oh, that's all right, Rose. We'll have fresh for you, just leave them."

Rose turned a surly face to him. "I'll 'ave me sweaters."

"She likes her own things," Kim said through a wobbly smile.

"Yes, yes. That's understandable. Of course she must have them."

One of the men put Rose's suitcase in the boot as another opened the car door for her.

Before they bundled her inside, Rose craned her neck to make eye contact with Kim. "Dinna forget me apron, miss!"

Kim turned on the ignition and listened to the engine sputter. Flooded. One of Dunn's cars stopped in its maneuver to turn around on the road. The driver waited, watching.

She was digesting her stomach. She waved cheerily at him and let the engine rest. Then, with a fierce jerk of the key, she gunned the engine. As it lurched into action, the car pounced onto the road and squealed away.

PART IV

BLOOD AND ICE

WRENFELL HOUSE,
EAST YORKSHIRE

SUNDAY, MAY 3. Mrs. Babbage came in with a tray on which she had laid a cold salmon dinner and a steaming pot of tea.

"I thought you might like a bit o' supper after all, miss." She put the tray on the nightstand.

Kim smiled to cover her bright panic. "Thank you, Mrs. Babbage, but I don't think—"

"Oh, but you must eat summat, you know. No matter 'ow 'ard the day, it'll do you good." She gave a firm nod at the tray and left.

Out the bedroom window, an orange sunset spread along the horizon like a brush fire. Kim sat on her bed, trying to read the LNER timetable but thinking about tight little snowstorms and Angus Dunn's cold blue eyes.

Shadow lay on the floor by the bed, head on paws, facing toward the open bedroom door in case anyone passing by needed herding into the right room. His presence was a comfort, though he could hardly protect her. Earlier that evening, she had found an old revolver in her father's room. But she left it there, for what good it would do to carry it? If it came to guns, her enemies used them better.

She laid down the LNER timetable. An attack was coming. *Over the big water,* if what Rose had heard was true. A strike at the coast of England, then.

Kim believed her, even as impossible as an ice road sounded. If you had reason to think that the Germans planned for something to *bring England down,* then you would be a fool to ignore all the evidence of ice combined with unholy Talents.

And what would come over this *pretty road, all ice an' sparklin'?* Tanks. Troops. If it could carry a truck, what could it not carry?

Rose had spent three days at Prestwich Home, been tested, and been inducted into their chain gang, the one Alice had glimpsed in her icy vision. Why had Rose never said anything about what had happened there? But then Kim considered how Rose had sometimes talked about *little storms,* and everyone always blithely ignored her. And for the most damning information, the creation of a road, she had eavesdropped and felt guilty.

Oh, Rose. Kim had delivered her into the hands of the Germans.

It was all clear now, or as clear as it needed to be. Prestwich Home was a nest of *cold cell* Talent.

Owen. It was time, at last, for Owen to go to the authorities. Kim needed to get to him. How to do this was a serious question.

Mrs. Babbage called from the bottom of the stairs, "Will there be owt else afore I finish up, miss?"

Kim went to the door. "No, Mrs. Babbage, thank you. Goodnight."

"Aye then, goodnight, miss."

Kim heard her leave through the back door. Out in the hallway, she looked about her, feeling the house's emptiness and what seemed a false cheeriness with, here and there, a few lights left on to keep her company. Wrenfell creaked and sighed like an old man. It always had, with its old stone walls settling and the porte cochere straining against the south side of the house.

She padded barefoot down the stairs to lock the back door. Then the front. Leaning against the door, Kim closed her eyes, trying to concentrate. She must alert Owen about what was coming. But how?

She went back upstairs, put the plate of salmon on the floor for Shadow, and began to pace the room. All along, at some level, she had known that Rose was at the center of something larger than herself. She had always been disturbed by the girl's treatment, and horrified by the village's abandonment of her at the first sign of trouble. Then Dr. Dunn's insistence that she was a mental defective and the feeling that a Nazi mentality was encroaching on England. Plus, Rose's wet coat hanging in the hallway, her offhand mention of little storms, and finally von Ritter's demand that Rose go back to Prestwich Home. All these things should have alerted her to the events swirling around Rose, touching directly on her mission. Had she only paid more attention. And now, Rose was in terrible jeopardy and had suffered a betrayal by Kim herself.

So. Right here on English soil, Germany was collecting people to work *in concert*, to link them together to increase their effect. Nor was Rose the only one at Prestwich, Rose had said. Kim remembered the heavy jackets in the basement. The cold-weather gear had been for practicing.

Rose called it a road. It must somehow be a road between Germany and England, across the North Sea.

The old man who'd run after them that day at Prestwich—
Harry Parslow. He had tried to warn her, shouting about *the
road to hell.* How very convenient to identify people with the *cold
cell* ability and then find reasons to confine them in a mental
hospital!

Kim had played right into von Ritter's hands, giving them
Rose. She was totally unsuited to this job. Her earnest conviction that she must do her bit for England now appeared absurd.

An attack was coming, and it was coming soon, or why
would von Ritter have instructed her to bring Rose by today?
He would have known that they couldn't keep her long at
Prestwich; the Tavistocks were too influential to allow Rose's
long confinement.

She felt a profound urge to call her father. Since he had
friends in high places, he might get a hearing. Whatever his
political views, could he stand by and allow an attack? But he
would never believe her, might even conclude that she was
unbalanced, filling in her long days with wild imaginings.

Needling up from deep below came the sickening doubt.
Could she trust him? Every time she considered her suspicion,
she felt ashamed, first of him, and then of herself for her dark
conclusion. A burned piece of paper in the barn. His claims to
always be in meetings for the whisky trade or at the hunts. He
was seldom home.

She had no one.

ST. JAMES'S PARK, LONDON

E had brought a small sack of salted peanuts and threw a handful of them onto the grass by St. James's Park Lake. He and

Julian watched as the ducks clambered forward to grab the peanuts, quacking and pushing the others aside.

"Never enough to go around," E mused. "It's just peanuts to us, but to them, it's life or death."

"Hard for a duck to starve at St. James," Julian observed.

"Yes, well. We can always find something to fight about."

"Is the Foreign Office going to just stand by and watch the CID meddle in administration?"

E smiled grimly. "You want me to complain to the Secretary."

"Loudly."

"But I'm not going to. You've got to play your chits carefully, Julian. Until we have solid intelligence, I'm not going to win, and I would only make your job harder when it *is* time to pull strings."

The sun was low in the sky, just winking out behind Buckingham Palace in the distance.

E noticed Julian gazing in that direction. "Are you thinking the same thing as I am? The sun setting on England as we know it?" He let out a long breath. "We could be wrong. There might be nothing to this *Sturmweg* except a lot of chicken feed that the Germans want us to believe. But now with this Colonel Stelling thing, the 6.5 rating for, what was it . . . an *ice* Talent. . . . I'm convinced they've got an operation planned against us. And it might be what Stelling claimed: an invasion."

"We haven't put together the *ice* Talent with the suspected operation. How will they use *ice*, and what if anything can this *chorister* do? What are the military uses of *ice*? If we had that piece, we'd have all we need."

E muttered, "Keep working it, Julian. We're close, I can feel it. And you're the only one left now who sees the threat."

What a dismal thought. No one was going to listen to an

old spy, much less a protégé of a man whom they'd just sacked. "They can't banish you for long," Julian said. "You have too many friends in Whitehall."

E nodded without enthusiasm. "And enemies. Alistair Drake and I never got on. Millington, of course, is his bulldog."

"What does Drake have against you? Something from the war, I think you said once." Since Julian had come to work for E, they had stopped seeing each other socially, but Julian remembered that once, long ago over a meal, E had said that he and Drake had had a falling-out during the war.

The ducks stalked the bench where Julian and E sat, keeping watch on the bag in E's hand. "It was about Lydia. She had two suitors for a while, and Drake was one. He thought he was the favorite. She chose me."

"He never married."

"No. And over time, he blamed me that she wasn't happy. But it isn't about Lydia anymore. It's about"—E threw another handful from the bag—"peanuts, I suppose. Power, honors. Never enough to go around."

Julian didn't like to see his old friend this philosophical. It seemed like giving up.

E went on. "She had many admirers back then. Quite a beauty." Ironic, given how she had deteriorated and how they barely spoke to each other these days.

He turned to Julian. "It's on you now, old boy. *Sturmweg.* They'll try to take you off it, but you've already got questionnaires out, and if you learn more, raise holy hell."

"To Heath Millington? He won't go for it."

"Don't underestimate him. He's survived through several governments. You don't stay on if you're not sharp."

"He's Cambridge, isn't he?"

"Yes. Started out as a solicitor. It made him a collector of facts, a nitpicker and a stickler for rules. Just the same, if the evidence piles up, he won't want to be on the wrong side of things. Don't challenge him openly. Win him over. You'll be better at that than I was."

"Is it past tense already"?

"No, quite right. I won't give up. A few days with me cooling off at home, and they'll have made their point. But, mind you, they may bring Kim in for questioning." He scowled at the water, where a group of swans glided by, parting the glassy waters with their white breasts. "It's probably for the best. On the surface of things . . . well, she must explain herself, Julian."

"She's innocent of collaboration, of that I'm sure."

"All the same, watch yourself. If your daughter is involved with something, you can't be blamed. Don't give them your resignation. Not that Kim is up to anything."

"Richard . . ." He let himself use E's name now that they were talking as friends. ". . . I have no idea what she *is* up to. She may be in a jam."

"The sooner we clear the air, the better, then."

Julian liked to hear him say *we*. But the truth was, E might be done for. With the capture of Harp and the debacle at Luckenwalde, the Foreign Office would be hard pressed to protect the head office, if they even cared to do so.

"What will you do?" Julian asked.

"Oh, spend a few weeks down at Litchfield, I expect." He glanced at Julian with a half smile. "Waiting by the telephone."

He stood up and emptied the rest of the bag out on the grass. He looked less like E and more like Richard Galbraith, squire of Litchfield. He was sixty-six years old. Perhaps he was thinking this would be his retirement.

A hell of a way to go.

"Julian. *Sturmweg*'s on you now. You can't work miracles, but you must try to bring Millie around. Use some of that charm you're wasting on Olivia."

"It doesn't seem to have much effect on her."

"No, but she's wedded to the Office."

Julian nodded. He could understand.

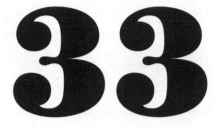

UXLEY, EAST YORKSHIRE

MONDAY, MAY 4. The next day, it took Kim until late afternoon, but she finally knew what she must do. She must go to the knitting shop.

Alice greeted her with a bright smile. Kim paused. With her nerves frayed, she felt an ugly pang of suspicion that Talents might be deployed against her. *Disguise* was one. The ability to look like someone else, to convince someone you did, at least. She would put nothing past them.

Alice stared at her as they faced off. "What? You look half-barmy."

But of course, this was Alice. She must get herself under control. Kim quickly thrust a note at her. *Please say NOTHING, but come into the lavatory with me. Important.*

A look of incredulity crossed Alice's face, and she arched an eyebrow, something which Kim had always thought was a great talent, if not a Talent, being able to raise only one eyebrow. Kim went toward the back of the shop and ducked into the loo. Alice was right behind her.

Alice closed the door and faced Kim. "What in the world?"

Kim turned on the faucet full blast and leaned against the sink.

"Have you gone daft?"

"I'm in trouble. *We're* in trouble. All of us."

"All right, then. But do we have to have the water thundering away?"

"Yes."

Alice looked to the sink, then to Kim, as the moment stretched longer. "Talk?"

Kim had planned to tell Alice everything. Now she was balking at her decision, afraid of what might happen if Alice believed her. And if she didn't.

"I don't know where to start. I'm in way over my head. They may be trying to kill me."

For once, Alice seemed incapable of responding. She stared at Kim.

With elaborate patience, as though speaking to a madwoman, Alice said, "If someone is trying to kill you, we'll go to the police."

Kim shook her head. "If it was that easy, I wouldn't be here."

"All right, I'm listening, but really, the tap . . ." She looked at the faucet.

"That's so if they've put a listening device in my best friend's shop, they won't hear us." Kim began to shake. But why tremble now, after all she'd been through?

Alice brushed by and turned off the tap. Turning to Kim, she put her hands on her shoulders. "I might not know what's going on, but no one has put a microphone in the loo." She looked

Kim fearlessly in the eyes and said, "Now tell me. Everything."

Kim swallowed, hard. "Monkton Hall," she began.

A half hour later, Alice was sitting on the bathtub edge, holding on as though the world were tipping out of balance, as perhaps it was. Kim paced in front of her in the tiny lavatory.

Alice had mostly been silent, except for a few clarifying questions. Then, when Kim seemed to be finished, she sighed. "So, the rotten Jerries are after us again."

Kim barked out a laugh.

"That's funny?"

"Yes. I mean, no. But you've got the essence of it, faster than anybody."

"It can't be a road or a bridge across the North Sea, though. That part . . . it just can't be. You can't have a bridge that long."

"I know." Kim had stopped shaking now that the story was out. "Maybe it's something that will help them unload tanks from ships, or who knows what. It's going to be bad for us, whatever it is. And Hugh Aberdare's caution to his sister about traveling anytime soon—that could mean an attack could come at any time." She looked at Alice sitting there, her hair so red against the porcelain it might have been on fire. "I need your help, Alice."

"What do you want me to do?"

"Go see Owen, tell him about Rose, Prestwich Home, and the road. He'll have to go to London now, today. Tonight. I can't go, because they're following me."

Alice scrunched up her mouth. "Now that we've been in the loo for an hour, maybe they'll follow me, too."

"I can't say it's not dangerous. In fact, it *is* dangerous."

Alice looked grim. "Maybe a telephone call?"

"I called Owen on Friday. I'm worried if I call him again, it'll throw suspicion on him. He's got to be the one who goes to the authorities, since he has more credibility than I do." She paused, looking at her friend. "I desperately need an ally."

Alice was considering it. By her expression, she was thinking hard. "And Rose . . . there's nothing we can do for her?"

"They've got her and it makes me ill. But right now, the best thing is for us to be sure they don't learn that she told me what's going on." Kim wasn't the only one who would pay. Rose, as well. She remembered what von Ritter did to people who failed him.

Alice shook her head, trying to process it all. "We need to settle down and do this methodically."

"We *are* being methodical. This is as straightforward as it gets. Everything else is hellishly confused."

Alice took a deep breath. "How would I get inside Monkton Hall?"

Kim handed her a piece of paper with a phone number on it. "Ring up this number when you get to a phone box. Speak only to Miss Drummond, the lead secretary. She's a bit of a friend to us, but I don't know how far she'll go to help. You'll need her cooperation to get past security. Tell her that you're calling for me. That Owen has a new *trauma view* recruit, one who has urgent information. And that you're it and you're coming in."

Alice's face fell. "My Talent. I'm to tell that part?"

She still didn't understand. Kim turned the cold water on in the basin and splashed her face with it, trying for calm. Drying off with a towel, she said, "Alice, if it's an invasion, nothing else matters, don't you see?"

The bathroom was deathly quiet as Alice considered this. Finally, she said, "I suppose I'm called on to do my part, if even an American can." Her eyes darted to Kim as she realized what she'd said. "Oh, me and my big mouth. You've been one of us from the moment you went to Monkton Hall, and no mistake."

Kim let it slide off her back. *Nothing else matters.* "So, you will help?"

"Why don't I just see Owen at his home?"

"I don't know where he lives." It was absurd, but she didn't know his address. She and Owen both made miserable spies.

"What if Drummond doesn't believe me?"

"Then you'll never get past her desk. If she won't give you access to Owen, the best outcome then is that she sends you packing—which she might do if she's feeling like helping a little. Worst case . . ." Kim paused.

Alice had begun to look a bit puckish. "They will do me in."

Incredibly, this was a possibility. "They did murder Sam."

"Or they could brave it out and just call the police. Accuse me of trying worm my way into Monkton Hall."

"If you're discovered, the very best place to be is in police hands or the government's. Tell them the truth. I doubt they'll believe anything you say, but it's all you have. Whatever you do, don't confess anything to Fitzroy Blum beyond our cover story. We think he can't be trusted."

"Maybe I'll see something in his presence. One of my visions."

"You won't. He has a Talent, if you've heard of it: *natural defender*. He's impervious to that kind of snooping."

"It's like a beastly chess game."

"Yes. Except there's blood on the board." Kim looked at her a long moment. "Are you really going to do this?"

"I may be daft, but I am." She snorted. "Bloody Jerries. And this time around, it's even worse. This time, they're Nazis."

Kim felt a smile stab at her face. "God, you're wonderful. I thought there were people who might help us, but everyone except you has come up short."

Now that Alice was going to Monkton Hall, Kim acutely felt the weight of what she had asked her to do. The real danger that Alice might die in the attempt to carry this information to Owen.

But Alice seemed unshakable. "Where *is* this place? Why is it even on the moors, of all places?"

"They use the moors to experiment with military uses of Talents." They went over the directions to Monkton Hall, and Alice wrote them down on the paper with the phone number.

That finished, Alice straightened. "It's now, then?"

"No. It's close to quitting time. But you must go first thing in the morning."

"I have my regular knitting class at one, though. Wouldn't it be best not to draw attention to my leaving? I could leave right after. Close up shop at two."

"If you could leave no later than that, then. After you're done, don't try to call me. I'll meet you at the Barley and Mow at five."

"One more thing," Alice said.

Reluctantly, Kim faced her. There was certainly a bit of unfinished business.

"You might have told me you had the *spill.*" In some ways, this was always going to be the hardest part of their conversation, and Kim had ducked it so far.

Alice went on, "I told *you,* and it was bloody hard."

"I know. I was afraid of losing you as a friend. Because you'd always think I was prying."

"So, freakish meets prying."

Kim took a long, ragged breath. She hadn't been proud of

herself for her duplicity, and her reasons didn't excuse things. All she could hope for is that they explained things. "All my life, I've been afraid of losing people because they wouldn't trust me. I'm so sorry, Alice. I've been a bit of a coward. And a bad friend."

Alice frowned in concern. "No, not that bad! But we have to start over. The thing is, people like us have got to stick together. Others don't get what it's like living with the *bloom*, even if they say they do. No more secrets. Agreed?"

It was a relief to say yes. And to mean it.

To make it seem that she'd been shopping, Kim chose a few skeins of blue, white and red worsted. She didn't knit, but the colors cheered her.

"What will you do while I'm gone?" Alice asked.

"It's best that you don't know."

After a pause, Alice nodded. "I do see. Of course."

"Good luck," Kim said cheerily, trying for bravado.

Alice threw back a confidant smile. "Righty-ho."

Kim walked out of the shop into a day turning gray with high clouds. "Thanks for the yarn!" she cried from the street, a little too loudly.

ST. JAMES'S CHURCH, PICCADILLY

Julian was glad of the church's calming aura. St. James's was very near his flat, and he'd been known to attend a service now and then, mostly to keep up appearances. He did find it uplifting to be in the place, even when he was using it to meet a contact.

Right on time, a few minutes past eleven, Fin entered St. James's and settled into the pew behind him.

"Peaceful place," Julian murmured.

Fin snorted. "Feels like a funeral in here." His sarcasm was clear even in a whisper. The entire team was shaken by E's removal.

"He's not dead yet," Julian said.

"Bundled off to Litchfield. Much the same."

He reached for a missal and pretended to read as Fin gave his report.

"Egret and Rabbit are still on Sparrow's tail. Sparrow drove to Prestwich Home with the maid. The maid got frightened in a patch of bad weather and went running out onto the moors. They couldn't see what happened, but Dunn drove up with his people and took her in hand. Sparrow drove back to Uxley after that."

"Safely home, then?"

"Egret practically tucks her in at night." An elderly couple entered and sat on the other side of the nave. Julian memorized their faces.

"We've got something new from Woodbird," Fin said. "An unscheduled transmission last night."

"*Sturmweg?*"

"Not specifically. It had to do with the *chorister* Talent. He doesn't know who the Germans have, but he does know this—and these might be old reports he's got ahold of—but an individual *chorister*, in order to operate as a *chorister*, has to have the same Talent as those he's aggregating. So, for instance, if the Germans wanted to cast a widespread dark pall over a battlefield, and they want to use a *chorister* to pull together lots of *darkening* Talents, they must find a *chorister* who also has the *darkening* Talent. So, that's at least one limit on the *chorister* Talent."

Julian mulled this over. "But then a *chorister* has two Talents. That in itself is new."

"Or it's an extension of a Talent. Making it more powerful."

"Whichever it is, we're facing military possibilities." Julian looked up to the altar with its elaborate carvings, its impression of power and authority. "Query Woodbird whether he can make a connection between the *chorister* and *ice*." If Woodbird could, then the invasion would use that, he felt sure.

"Already done."

"Good. Anything else?"

"No. We're all just wondering if we'll have jobs."

"I shouldn't worry."

"Maybe our jobs are the least of it."

"Good time for prayer, then," Julian said, half-wishing he'd said a good long one when he'd had the chance. As he left the pew, he glanced up at the crucifix at the altar. He wondered—he hoped it wasn't blasphemy—whether Jesus had been a *conceptor*.

At the very least.

The world didn't seem quite able to handle the Talents. It was why they'd been under wraps all these centuries, after all. And given what was going on at the moment, people weren't doing any better with them now.

34

TUESDAY, MAY 5. Alice walked across the flagstone walk, heading toward the front stairs of a redbrick Victorian mansion that looked more like the home of a maiden aunt than a secret arm of government.

She saw at once that a guard was on duty outside the door. Miss Drummond had said she would be watching for her to be sure she got past the guard. Her heart had begun to pound. *Do they haul you off in handcuffs or take you into a dingy back room and hit you with a sock full of sand?*

She took a deep breath as she climbed the stairs. The guard smiled at her. "Identity card?"

"Oh," Alice croaked. "Do I need one?"

An officious look clamped down on him. "This is government property. You'll need permission."

At that moment, the door swung open, and out came a thin

woman wearing a mauve jersey suit, her dark hair riddled with white strands.

"Oh, you'll be Alice Ward, then?" Drummond said. When Alice nodded, Drummond turned to the guard. "I'll take her in, Keith. We'll get her badge for next time."

"Yes, miss," he said, looking doubtful but unable to gainsay this woman who had the air of one who was not accustomed to back talk.

Drummond led her though the door, saying, "Very good of you to come on such short notice." Once inside, Miss Drummond scrutinized her, and when she was done, it did seem that Alice had not come off at all well. "When it's time for you to leave," she muttered, "have Mr. Cherwell buzz me. You will *not* appear again in this lobby until I say so, do you hear?"

"Yes. I'm to have Mr. Cherwell buzz your desk."

Drummond looked past her, where someone was just coming down the long hall that led to a wing of the building. He wore a white lab coat, and his hair stood out as though he'd had an electric shock. This, she gathered, was Owen Cherwell.

But Drummond's attention was suddenly taken by someone else approaching from a great curved staircase that swept into the foyer from above. The man, at least six-three and built like a rugby player, brightened seeing her. "Hallo, there." He turned to Miss Drummond. "New recruit?"

"For Mr. Cherwell," Drummond said.

"Oh. Did we have new people after all this week? Thought we didn't."

Drummond hesitated. "Well, it's a bit irregular, Mr. Blum." Her face had gone quite rigid.

Blum frowned. "Irregular? How's that?"

Drummond fixed Alice with a dark stare. "She says she was to have papers from the Talent Registration Office, but since they hadn't arrived, she thought she would come ahead and see what could be done."

"I hope it's all right," Alice said, trying to sound clueless and realizing with dismay quickly displaced by alarm that this was the German agent Kim had warned her of.

Blum probed his teeth with his tongue, perturbed. "It won't do at all, I'm afraid."

Cherwell and Drummond looked on stoically as things unraveled.

Blum peered at her with narrowed eyes. "Your name?

"Alice Ward."

"Well, Miss Ward, we must have a talk in my office." He looked up at the man in the lab coat. "Cherwell, I'm sure you're eager to get a new one, but this won't do, you know. We'll need to clear all this up." He turned to Drummond. "I trust you weren't writing her in an appointment."

"No, sir. She just arrived, and I was about to summon you."

Blum held her gaze for a moment. "Yes. Well, good."

He gestured for Alice to precede him, and she had a glimpse of Owen Cherwell's stricken expression. She and the director walked toward an imposing flight of stairs.

"Lovely old building," Alice remarked as they climbed.

"Not many people are privileged to see it."

"I imagine *not.*"

Her confidence vanished step by marble step. This was not shaping up to be an interview she could survive unscathed. Her story had been that she was dead set against registering, and now Drummond said that she claimed she had registered. Now, if she was truly exposed as a fraud, she would appear conniving instead of naive. She had no idea how to modify her story. Panic rose in her throat.

At the head of the stairs was a wide gallery looking down into the foyer. Fitzroy Blum led her into a spacious office with a broad and spotless cherrywood desk. Behind the desk was a bow window looking onto an overgrown garden gone gray under the heavy cloud cover.

After gesturing her to a chair, he perched on his desk like a bird of prey ready to swoop. "You've rather got yourself backward on things, Miss Ward." His voice was louder than it needed to be, and made him seem even more intimidating.

"Oh, I do apologize. I thought it would be all right."

"Didn't the registration office tell you to wait for credentials?"

"Oh yes, they did. But then, when the papers didn't come, Kim said it might be all right to come up and get the ball rolling." She shrugged. "Lost in the post? That's what we thought." She was making it up as she went.

"Kim who?"

"Kim Tavistock. She encouraged me to go down to the Talent Office in the first place, or I never would have."

"Ah. So that's how she knows that you registered. Because she talked you into it."

"Oh yes, she buys yarn at my shop."

He said with elaborate patience, "Because otherwise, you see, she oughtn't have known about you coming here at all. You did sign the Official Secrets Act?"

"Oh, that. Well, of course."

He looked at her very keenly, as though trying to bring her into better focus. "Where are you from, then?"

"Uxley. Same as Kim. Where my yarn shop is."

"Your Talent being what?"

"Well, am I supposed to say?"

Blum smiled. "I'm afraid you must say. I'm in charge here, so I do hope you'll be forthcoming."

"It's *trauma view*," she said. "I never wanted to be tested. If it hadn't been for Kim, I wouldn't have registered. I just worry that once things get into the public record—"

Blum held up a hand. "That's as may be, Miss Ward. We do appreciate those who are willing to come forward. But I'm sure you understand that we must confirm your story."

"My story?"

"That you're telling the truth. It does seem unlikely that one of our research subjects would have encouraged you to bypass—"

A knock at the door.

"Yes?" he boomed.

Miss Drummond entered. "Sir, I've checked with the registration office, and she's right, the papers were sent to her two weeks ago. They must have been lost. The office will reissue her identification work, and they've said for us to proceed in the meantime."

Alice tried to look completely neutral, but the relief that flooded over her made her almost weak.

Blum slapped his knee. "Excellent. That's done, then." He turned his hawkish gaze on Alice. "We shall count on you to follow procedure in future, once you're oriented here." To Drummond, he said, "We must have a chat with Miss Tavistock. This has been a bit loose. Can't have it, really."

"No, sir," Miss Drummond said primly. *Hang a medal on this woman*, Alice thought. Despite Kim's doubts, she was indeed a friend to the cause.

Blum waved her toward the door. "You're excused, Miss

Ward." She followed Drummond, trying not to wobble on her heels. She had almost reached the door when Blum's voice came: "Just one thing." He nodded at Drummond to wait outside.

Alice turned.

"What sort of things do you see?"

"See?"

He cocked his head a bit like a rooster. "Yes. Your *trauma view*. What have you seen? We don't get many like you."

The image of people chained together, dripping in ice, was never far from her thoughts. "Oh, you wouldn't believe the things I've seen!" She was trying to remember any of them. "It's all so . . . *common*, you know. Nothing dramatic. Nothing that would be useful in spying." She inwardly cringed. *Settle, Alice, for God's sake.*

"Spying? Why would you say that?"

Indeed. Why would she? "Well. Frankly? This place is under the Official Secrets Act, a secret military place, and I have been warned not to talk about it. This place isn't about potting geraniums."

He straightened, looking down at her with an appraising gaze. "And what do you see, then?"

"Domestic problems. Men who drink up the rent money; women who are in love with their parish vicar; men who take a hand after their wives. That sort of thing."

He was losing interest, his tongue probing his teeth again. "Well, Cherwell will get to the bottom of it."

"Cherwell?" she asked, mindful to sound new to it all.

"Your case worker. A bit dotty, but he's very good on the dynograph." He opened the door for her. "Well, carry on, then."

Indeed I shall, you bloody traitor.

She followed Miss Drummond down the stairs. Drummond murmured, "What did he want?"

"To bully me," Alice responded.

Drummond cast a sidelong glance.

"He got nothing."

"I should hope not."

This Drummond woman was stiff as a plank and with two expressions, sour and acid. But none of that could matter. Alice had been delayed but was now in a most desperate hurry to get to Owen Cherwell and tell him that the *ice* plot involved not only the German army but their own people. And that they must get to Prestwich Home and put a stop to the icy chain.

When they got to Drummond's desk, Owen Cherwell was waiting. Oddly, a small dog was lying in a basket by Drummond's feet.

"All put to rights, then?" Cherwell asked cheerfully, beads of sweat glistening at his hairline.

Miss Drummond sat at her desk and busied herself with writing something into a very large book. She waved them down the hall together.

"So you, Miss Ward, are the mysterious *trauma view* Talent," Owen said when they were alone in his lab.

"Alice, please. Did Kim tell you about me?" She hoped it was not the case.

"I never knew your name. But your vision . . . the icy chain. It was a key piece." He led her to a seat, removing a pile of papers piled there. "It's something big, isn't it. You've come with the last piece."

"I guess I have." She looked around the office, seeing the twisting electrical cords, the stacks of printouts of some kind, and a large machine with a leather cap resting on it.

"She was afraid to come herself, because they might be on to her." She took a shaky, steadying breath.

He brought her a glass of water from the lab sink. "You've been very brave. Just take your time."

She had been planning what to say all the way from Uxley, the order of things, but she could not now remember the plan.

"Kim says her maid Rose Babbage has a *cold cell* Talent and so do many at Prestwich Home up near Thirsk, where the chief doctor is making everyone practice to build a road out of ice." She looked at his astonished face. "For an invasion."

Owen stared at her for a moment, then dragged a chair over to sit facing her. "Slowly, then, Alice. From the beginning."

A half hour later, when Alice was finishing up with Owen, Miss Drummond came into Owen's office. She closed the door quietly and leaned against it.

"Miss Ward," she said, "you will go to the Talent Registration Office immediately upon leaving here. Take the train to London, and be there when they open in the morning."

"But mayn't I go home to collect my things?"

"I have saved you both"—here she glared at Owen Cherwell—"from some rather uncomfortable consequences, at great risk to myself. So, I don't care if it's convenient or not. Be there when they open, and get registered. Do you understand?"

Alice did, and nodded. She said to Owen, "We must call Kim. She's waiting to hear if I got through."

"All right, then, but not from here. A phone box."

He began throwing documents into a briefcase. "I'm feeling poorly. A fever, no doubt. I shall need a day or more of bed rest." He turned to Drummond. "Cancel my appointments."

"It's bad, then, I take it."

Owen stopped gathering papers and locked gazes with her. "It is. It is indeed." He snapped shut his briefcase. "I'll drive Alice to the station."

Drummond looked from one to the other of them. "Godspeed, then."

Alice murmured, "He'd bloody well better."

WAR OFFICE BUILDING, LONDON

Julian had heard somewhere that the baroque, white-stoned War Office Building had a thousand rooms. During the war, it had housed a vast bureaucracy but was now much reduced in population. Many of the career functionaries were staff to the Committee for Imperial Defence and its subcommittees.

He waited outside Millington's office as people passed in and out of his impressive teak door. They carried dossiers with, Julian imagined, the tally of ink pens and paper needed for the defense of the realm. Finally, Mr. Vickers, a chalky-faced secretary who seemed to carry a powdering of dust, said he could go in.

In Millington's tidy office, the acting head of SIS was busy writing something. At last, he looked up. "Ah, Tavisock."

"It is Tavistock, sir."

"What? Oh, quite. Tavistock. Have a seat."

Julian sat on one of the green leather chairs of which Whitehall seemed to have an endless supply.

"Thank you for making the trek over. I'm pleased to meet you, although I imagine you wish it were under different circumstances. Fond of Galbraith, were you?"

Galbraith was still "E" until he was sacked. Julian didn't like the implication that it was a done deal.

"I would say we have always got along."

"And so shall we, I trust." Millington pushed his spectacles farther up the bridge of his nose and regarded Julian for a few seconds. "It's always difficult to go through these things, especially where there are longstanding friendships. I understand. I hope I can count on your full support while discussions go on about Galbraith's future."

"Of course, sir." He was determined to be charming. So far, *sir* was as far as his charm could go. "I hope we can count on your support as well."

"*We?*"

"SIS. A tight group, all good people." He tried a disarming smile. "We're all keen on cooperating with you, of course."

Millington's forehead rippled in concern. "That's an odd way of putting it, don't you think? *Cooperating.* You are all working for me, at least temporarily." He picked up his pen, then put it down again. "Look here, Tavistock, I don't fancy myself at the helm of an intelligence organization. I'm used to the policy end, you see, and the operations are best handled by those who like the details. So, I have no long-term interest in the post, you may be sure. But for now, this is what you have. You are working for me. That rather sums it up, wouldn't you say?"

"Yes, sir. What will be the chain of command, if I may ask?"

"You may, and in your case, reports will be to me. I have a special interest in the *Sturmweg* matter, and I will be keeping CID appraised of any news."

"Shall I report here, at the War Office Building?"

"Yes. I'll be standing astride two jobs, and my main focus will be in assisting the Prime Minister's committee." A miniscule smile stabbed into his cheek. "If it's awkward for you undercover, we can give you a backdoor key."

The back side of the building was on Horse Guards Avenue, so it would hardly be more private than the front. "It might be best," he said gamely.

"Settled, then."

"As for news," Julian said, "we do have reports coming in by wireless every night. We're expecting new intel on whether the *chorister* Talent has any relation to the *ice* Talents being assembled at Wesermarsch."

"And these wireless reports come in from where?"

"We have five agents in Germany. Some of our most reliable intel comes from our *Abwehr* man, Woodbird."

Millington sat back in his chair. "So, this Woodbird . . . he's one of ours, pretending to work for the Germans but actually working for us?"

"Yes, sir."

"Which makes him disloyal. Hardly a man we can place confidence in."

"But he's—"

"He's a traitor to his government. These types are just a step away from being scoundrels, and a short one at that."

"It's war, sir, not a gentlemen's club."

Millington's face stiffened. "That's where you're wrong. This is not war. We were at peace the last time I looked. I fear the service is riddled with this kind of thinking, Tavistock, and I will not have it, you hear me? I will not have it."

"No, sir. It's just that I must defend a man who has risked his life for Britain under highly dangerous circumstances."

A beady stare showed that this had not smoothed it over. Millington leaned forward. "Well. Make your reports to me and we shall see what your *Abwehr* man can produce. I trust we will not have another agent ending up in Plötzensee Prison."

"Devoutly to be hoped, sir."

"Another thing. I'm afraid we're going to have to bring your daughter in for questioning. I cannot imagine why you did not pick her up immediately when she was seen passing information to Georgiana Aberdare, a known German agent."

"We felt she was more valuable to follow for leads."

"Meanwhile, your daughter may have done irreparable harm. Even blown your cover. It *is* possible."

"My daughter has no idea of my intelligence work." He didn't mind Kim being picked up. She must be warned off this project she was on, whatever it was. But Millie was starting to construct a damning view of the Office, and Julian could not let that go by.

"I have kept my role with the agency completely confidential at home, just as every other SIS agent has always done. It is *not* true that my daughter knows my involvement. And, to be frank, Georgiana Aberdare is not a known agent."

"No? The Security Service has other ideas."

"The Security Service has not followed the foreign threat as closely as SIS. They aren't in the picture."

"But they are to operate in British territory, which London is, the last I knew. I suggest you put them in the picture posthaste." He put up a hand to forestall argument. "The Security Service will pick her up. It's best we keep some separation between you and this business."

Julian had the urge to upend the desk onto Millington. But there was no recourse. The main thing now was to keep SIS in the picture and to establish rapport with his acting boss, lest things sink further into disaster. "Yes, sir, I understand."

Millington nodded with satisfaction. "Carry on, then. Remember, no adventuring, Tavistock. We're going to rein this situation in, and I will not have my people undermining me."

The idea was a bright spot in an otherwise dreadful hour. Adventuring. Undermining. "No, sir," Julian said.

As he left the War Office Building—through a side door—his thoughts were with Kim. She was at Wrenfell, Walter Babbage had said. They would come to the front door and allow her to collect her coat and purse.

He should be overseeing her debriefing, through Elsa or Rory. As it was, this was going to be highly unpleasant for her. He wanted to tell her how she must handle it, wanted to explain how these things worked. He wanted to protect her.

None of these things was going to happen.

UXLEY, EAST YORKSHIRE

TUESDAY, MAY 5. At the Barley and Mow, Kim had a table to herself and a barely touched pint of ale before her. Men, hunkered over their pints, gave her sidelong glances. Bad enough if she'd had a male companion, but unaccompanied, all the worse. It was five thirty, and Alice was late. Was she still at Monkton Hall, talking to Owen? Had she even gotten in?

She ordered food to justify taking the table. Not knowing if Alice had succeeded was unnerving. If only she knew how all this would end. If only she had the Talent of *precognition*. But *precognition* was only knowledge of possible futures, and she could already figure out a few of those: Alice's car going off a cliff. Miss Drummond calling the police. Owen leaving for London to raise bloody hell at Whitehall.

Mr. Sempill, the pub owner, brought her a plate from the kitchen and sat down with her. A huge man with a red and shining face, he was one of those in the village who, when she had first come home, had treated her as though she had never gone. "Ada's best meat pasty. And don't pay attention to the blokes in 'ere. Some of 'em bring their wives an' don't mind about sour looks then."

"Thank you," Kim said. "I was going to meet Alice. But I guess she's not coming." She took a bite of the pie. "Delicious."

"Oh, she's a right good cook, my Ada. You take your time with it, an' no one'll bother you." He wiped his brow with his bar towel. "Your mum an' Ada, they got on so well. We haven't forgotten 'er."

"And she mentions Ada in her letters, Mr. Sempill."

"Martin, Kim. Now that you're grown."

As she ate, he looked out the window onto the street, where a stray paper lifted in the breeze. "There's a bit o' a blow comin' in. A big storm, so I heard. We don't get 'em too often, not in May."

"Martin, I wonder, is there anyone here right now you don't usually see?"

"What?" He looked around. "Nay, they're all regulars. Know 'em all. Except that bloke on the stool, there."

"Don't look at him. But the one with the gray cap?"

"Aye, 'im. Come in a bit after you."

"I just wondered." She tried not to check out the newcomer too obviously.

Martin regarded her as she continued to eat. "No kind of trouble is it, now?"

"No, no difficulty. I just wondered. But please keep it to yourself, if you wouldn't mind."

Martin went back to his duties, leaving her to her supper, but presently he hailed her, pointing to the hallway. He made a gesture as though speaking on the telephone.

Alice, she thought. Alice was calling. She hurried out of the pub room to the telephone.

"I've got the yarn you asked for." Alice's voice.

"Oh! Oh, good." Relief made her feel light headed.

"But the shopkeeper thinks we should go to London together."

Kim puzzled it through. Alice was trying not to say much, but she must mean Owen.

"Are you using a phone box?" Kim hoped.

"Yes, don't worry. It's all fine and dandy."

Kim paused, then asked, "What color yarn did I buy at the shop last time?" Just in case Alice was speaking under duress.

"White, blue and red, of course."

"Oh, of course it was." Her voice trembled with emotion. "Good job, Alice. Well done."

She had reached Owen, and Owen was going to the authorities. With a story that could not fail to convince any reasonable person. Hanging up the receiver, Kim leaned against the wall for a moment. Something terrible, something of ice and hate was coming their way. But it would not come upon England unawares. The country was about to wake up.

Mrs. Babbage had retired to her cottage early, as she knew Kim would not be home for supper. But she had left a note on the hallway table. Kim read:

Lady Georgiana rung up and said as you might ring her anytime tonight.

Kim hastily dialed the number from her father's phone list. The butler picked up, and in another minute Georgi was on the line.

"I promised to tell you if anything happened," Georgi said. "And now it has."

"Has it?" Kim's voice came out high pitched, like a bird chirping.

"Yes, my brother has left town for a few days. It was this morning, when he said he was going down to our cousin's in Sussex."

Georgi had forgotten to use the code word to refer to Hugh. No help for it now. "Oh? His cousin's?"

"Yes, but he hasn't arrived. When I called, they were surprised to hear that Hugh might come down. And I doubt he'd drop in unannounced."

"I see."

"I don't keep track of him, of course, and he was staying at his club. But he came by this morning and we had a chat, rather excruciating, actually. He wanted to have some good words from me, as though he needed cheering up. I bolstered him as I always do, but he did seem agitated. I thought you should know. It may not signify a thing, but do remember that I have done my best." A pause while Kim did not answer, her mind whirling. "You will remember that I helped."

Kim sat abruptly on the chair next to the phone. "Oh. Yes. We'll remember that. Did he happen to repeat his request that you stay at home?"

"Well, he did, rather."

"What day?"

"Friday."

"*This* Friday?"

"Yes. Friday, May 8th."

And today is Tuesday, Kim noted, as a needle of panic moved through her.

Georgi sighed. "I suppose you'll try to make something of that. In any case, I promised the poor thing."

"Thank you. It's very good of you to have called."

"Try to leave us out of things if you possibly can. You will try?"

"Yes, of course. Have you heard from Vincent?"

Silence as Georgi realized that she had not followed directions about the made-up names, this one for von Ritter. "No, he's quite abandoned me. Gone home, most likely. He may have done. Perhaps that would be for the best."

Yes, it would, but it's not going to happen. "Call me if you hear anything. I know we can count on you."

Georgi sniffed. "One does one's best."

Kim would be happy never to hear that phrase again. She put the receiver in the cradle, feeling how warm it had gotten in her grip. She looked around her, thoughts racing. *Georgi, you great fool.* She had used Hugh's name. If they were listening to her phone calls, now they would know she was on to Hugh Aberdare.

She wandered into the parlor and closed all the drapes, then went back over them, spacing out the pleats along the rod.

She thought of Lena and Oskar, who might even now be coming for her. Lena with her *darkening*, and Oskar with who knew what Talent.

Walter knew how to use a gun. She might go out to the cottage and ask him to sit up with her. But she couldn't imagine how *that* conversation could be had.

Hugh had said goodbye to his sister. Not goodbye in so many words, but it *had* been a leavetaking. Georgi knew it. Kim knew it. God in heaven, it struck her anew: it was all going to break loose in three days.

The worry returned, of Alice risking her life, and Owen. And then an even worse worry than that: if the *cold cell* conspirators killed them, then their warning would not reach the government.

She had heard stories of battle situations where several couriers were sent to make sure one got through.

Sitting on the divan, she considered this new idea. Now that it was finally time to inform the authorities, it should not all depend on Owen and Alice getting to whatever government office was their destination.

That left her.

She checked her watch. She couldn't expect to catch a train and be in London before ten. Not tonight, then.

But if she went, who could she possibly talk to?

WEDNESDAY, MAY 6. In the morning, she dressed without bathing and had packed a small bag by 5:40. Through her ragged sleep last night, the words had kept circulating: *May 8th, May 8th, May 8th.* She was not sure that she had actually slept at all.

Now her plan was to drive to York to catch the train to London. She wouldn't take the spur line from Uxley, as people might see her on the train platform, and she must do whatever she could to cover her movements.

Last night, she had hit upon a possible contact in London. Her mother had a friend, a retired brigadier general of the army. He was the only person she knew with even a shred of authority. He might be willing to take her story to Whitehall and alert someone. The conversation she would have to have with him would be excruciating, but surely he would at least give her a hearing. And if not, as a last resort she would go to Scotland Yard. She was utterly without prospects otherwise. She did not trust her father, so all in all, she was scraping the bottom of the barrel for what to do. Henry Wollaston was the man's name. She thought of ringing him in advance, but it was too early to call.

Setting her suitcase in the hallway, she went up to the third floor and pinned a note to the paisley valise, saying where it had come from and how Georgi Aberdare had tried to be helpful by turning it over to someone she believed was investigating. Then she went downstairs to grab a piece of toast for the road. Mrs. Babbage, who had seen the lights on in the house, had come in to offer breakfast, which Kim declined.

"I'm going up to Prestwich Home to check on Rose," Kim told her. "There may be a reason to spend the night in Thirsk if I can't clear everything up today. I'll ring and let you know." It was a miserable lie, given Rose's grim situation, and she had so blithely delivered it.

"Oh, would you go? Thank you, miss, I'd feel so much better for it."

How she hated being a spy. Never again.

Looming over her, the specter of May 8th, the day after tomorrow. Georgi's pronouncement made her nearly frantic to be on her way. Shadow and Flint saw her off, with Mrs. Babbage bustling out to give her an umbrella, saying the weather was supposed to be turning, and if they had a bad blow, she should come home and not be on the roads.

WAR OFFICE BUILDING, LONDON

"How may I help you . . . Mr. Cherwell, is it?"

John Rennie sat opposite Owen in a small room with a single window overlooking Whitehall Place. To Owen's surprise, he had been seen within twenty minutes of arriving at the CID headquarters and asking to speak with someone. It put him on his guard, rather. It had been too easy.

Owen said, "I have a matter relating to national defense. It's of the utmost importance that I inform someone in authority."

"I am an administrative officer for the CID. You may tell me your business, Mr. Cherwell."

The Committee for Imperial Defence. But he must get through to a person of influence. "The CID, you say?"

"That's right." John Rennie was quite young. His hair was slicked back in a bit of a posh style, and he wore a very good suit, although as an administrative officer, he was on a low rung of the civil-service ladder. Owen scrutinized him, trying to decide whether he was in a position to help, and if he could grasp the delicate situation at Monkton Hall regarding Fitzroy Blum.

Owen had early on considered how he would proceed if it came to this. But he thought he could not mention his connection to Monkton Hall. Once HARC came into the discussion, it would quickly put the situation in Fitz's hands for investigation and a quick suppression. Earlier in the morning, after Owen had left Alice at the Talent Registration Office, he had walked down to the War Office Building, going over his approach. Would they listen to him? He knew that above all, he must not sound like a crank.

Owen tried to assume a judicial aspect. "I realize my presence here is highly unusual. But I have come into possession of very serious evidence of activities affecting the national welfare. I felt I had to alert authorities."

"Quite rightly. What is your line of work, Mr. Cherwell, if I may ask?"

"I work for a secret arm of the government."

"Oh, yes? Which one?"

"I'm afraid I can't tell you. It's protected by the Official Secrets Act." The atmosphere in the room became less conducive.

"I see. Go on."

"Mr. Rennie, I have evidence that the Germans have an operation underway against Britain. A military operation."

Rennie remained unmoved. He was a man who proceeded by degrees. "What evidence have you?"

"It's a very long story, but it involves an Englishman of some reputation who is working for the Germans. I am very eager to divulge this to the proper authorities, someone in position to understand the sensitivities. The implications."

"And you feel you cannot speak to me, is this correct?"

"I'm sorry, but I must see someone with a high level of clearance, ideally a member of the CID."

Rennie paused. "You realize that this is highly unlikely unless you can give me more information."

Owen took a deep breath. "It's a planned invasion targeted on the coast of England."

A blink. "An invasion."

"Yes. I have very strong evidence."

"Did you bring it with you?"

"It's not . . . not physical evidence, but it is a series of events about which I have knowledge, and which together make a very strong case that the Germans plan a military strike. And soon."

"So, these are things you have seen and heard, conversations, phone calls, that sort of thing?"

Owen tried not to let his annoyance show. "No, it's not that sort of thing at all. It has to do with Talents and substantial evidence given by the man's sister."

Rennie nodded, placing his hands on his thighs as though he had come to a conclusion. "Well, if you won't tell me what evidence you have, I suppose I must find someone with whom you *will* speak."

"Thank you. I don't mean to be difficult, but I must be very careful."

"Of course you must." Rennie stood. "Would you mind

waiting in the lobby? These things can take some time, as you no doubt understand."

It was very decent of Rennie to take this tone, very decent indeed. If it took a couple of hours to get the ear of the CID, Owen could wait.

He resumed his same chair in the lobby, watching people come and go through the grand marble foyer on their missions into the depths of the War Office Building. Not that there *was* a war, but they had not renamed the building on that account.

And it would soon be a name more apt.

36

WEDNESDAY, MAY 6. "If they want to be inconspicuous, the fancy blue car works against them," Elsa said. She pulled her wool coat close around her neck in the cool morning air.

She had put up the bonnet on her car, and Rory was pretending to tinker at the engine, his own car parked next to it on a side road near Wrenfell. The blue Vauxhall had arrived last night, and its occupants were watching the road, no doubt waiting for Kim Tavistock.

"Nice motorcar, the Vauxhall," Rory said. "I had a Kentish aunt who owned one. Said she paid five hundred pounds." He looked up from the perfectly fine engine. "Did you call in a report? That Sparrow has a tail?"

"Not yet. We weren't sure until we identified the woman in the car as a German agent." She looked down the road. "If they follow her, you're on the Vauxhall, and I'm on Sparrow."

"Right you are."

Rory hadn't gotten a good look at the driver of the Vauxhall, a man, but when the woman had stepped out to relieve herself this morning, Rory used his binoculars to get a glimpse of her. In her thirties, with dark hair in a bun at her neck and heavy eyebrows. Hauling the mug book out of the boot of his car, he had paged through until he found her. *Lena Mueller. 38 years old. Alias Helga Osterman, alias Ines Reinhardt. German national, known agent operating in Lisbon (1934–36) and Gibraltar (1933).*

"Here they come," Elsa said.

Kim's familiar Austin 10 sped down the road. A few moments later, the Vauxhall began moving slowly, checking out the two cars parked on the side road. Elsa clutched her straw bag and peered politely into the maw of the engine. Once the Vauxhall was well down the road, Rory and Elsa followed in their separate cars.

Elsa traded off the lead position to Rory behind the blue Vauxhall. She faded back a few miles, her watch over Kim Tavistock now feeling grimmer. SIS hadn't known that this woman, Lena Mueller, was in the country. The mug book had very little information about her except that she often posed as an art appraiser and had ties to the Gestapo.

Absently, she patted her handbag and the reassuring bulk of her revolver. She did wonder what on earth Julian's daughter had got herself involved with.

The girl looked to be heading to York. Following her car through the city center could be tricky. Elsa hoped she'd set out on foot, always easier to tail. By the outskirts of the city, though, it was clear she was heading to the train station. Elsa concluded that she didn't want people to see her catch the train in Uxley. She considered stopping to make a report by telephone, but she couldn't risk losing Kim.

At the station, Elsa noted the positions of Kim's car and the Vauxhall and parked close by. Reaching into her bag of supplies in the back seat, she chose a different hat and a pair of glasses. A bright green scarf completed her disguise. She grabbed her purse and moved quickly toward the depot as Kim disappeared around the corner of the ticket office. Rory, carrying a briefcase, was just ahead of Elsa, following Mueller and a man in a black bowler hat, presumably the Vauxhall driver.

The southbound train was waiting at the platform, venting steam with a loud hiss, and people were boarding. At the ticket window, Elsa got into line behind Mueller. She heard her say, "London, single." A one-way ticket. Elsa bought her own ticket right after Mueller, keeping Kim in view.

Kim stopped to look at her watch—she did that a lot—and then started walking toward the train.

As she did, Mueller charged toward her. Rory saw it and quickened his step. He collided with Mueller just in time, allowing his briefcase to clatter to the cement, spilling papers. Thrown off balance, Mueller swore at him—in English, marking her as a professional—and, collecting herself, staggered forward to follow Kim. As she did so, she turned to the man in the bowler hat, saying, "Catch up with me at Newark!"

Kim had noticed nothing.

Newark. Having failed to grab Kim here, Mueller meant to take her off the train in Newark. Forty-five minutes away.

Elsa rushed forward, managing to board at the last moment. As the train got underway, she saw that Rory could not catch up. She was on her own.

The carriages rolled forward out of the station, straining to pick up speed. The smells of scorched iron and coal smoke trailed after Kim as she found a compartment with room on a bench seat. She tucked her suitcase into the overhead rack and collapsed gratefully onto the seat. Opposite her sat a woman with two little girls about age seven or eight. An elderly man on the bench next to Kim did not look up at her, remaining engrossed in the *Times*. Normally, she loved trains, and of course she had the York schedules by heart, but she felt anxious about getting onto this one.

She had waited too long. All those days when she might have gone to the police or to her mother's friend, and she had not acted, waiting for more, teasing out more of the *cold cell* conspiracy. Eating up her time. And now she was in the most spectacular hurry.

It was seven fifty. Two hours to London. She consciously drew in a deep breath. The tiny second hand on her watch lurched forward in its way of doing two seconds at once. That jerking motion always made it seem as though time were passing rather more swiftly than it ought. But she loved her Helbros, a gift from her mother when she'd turned eighteen. Henry Wollaston had been a great admirer of her mother's during the England days. If only he could be found at home today.

It must all come out when she talked with him, beginning with why she had been at Summerhill. Owen Cherwell's suspicions of Fitz, and the *hypercognition* event that appeared to implicate Georgi Aberdare. The encounter with von Ritter and his *spill* of the *chorister*. And then, cascading down the chain of evidence, as circumstantial as it might be, to the attempt to run her off the cliff, to the damning *trauma view* of the people holding the icy chain. Sam Reuben's claim that *cold cell* research had been canceled by Fitz . . . the log entry for Hugh Aberdare and what looked like *10*. Cataloguing the great amount of evidence, she felt emboldened to carry out her London plan. Someone in authority would surely take very serious note.

The clatter of the wheels upon the rails kept her company. Across from her, the woman took her children to the lavatory. From time to time, people passed in the corridor outside the compartment. She looked out the window, willing the train to go faster.

In the corridor, Elsa rummaged in her bag, muttering to herself about her coin purse and where in the world it might be. Mueller had just looked into Kim's compartment and, having located Kim, moved on. The woman left the carriage by the forward door but might well be watching through the window. Elsa walked on, still digging in her purse, and turned into Kim's compartment, looking as though she hadn't noticed it was the wrong one.

"Oh, hallo," Elsa exclaimed to everyone when she entered. "Would you mind terribly if I joined you? There are some rowdy children back there, and I do so like some peace and quiet." She bustled to the empty bench.

Kim looked up, saying, "There's a woman with her children there, but she's just stepped out."

"Well, I shan't take up much room. You get smaller as you age. Food doesn't taste the same, you know."

Kim gazed out the window. The man next to her put down his paper and rested his head against the back of the bench seat, signaling that a conversation would not be welcome. The woman with children returned.

"I hope you don't mind?" Elsa said to the woman. "I switched compartments. Is there room for me, do you think?" She gave her best worried look. The woman smiled and settled her children into place. Dithering old women were always indulged, as though at any moment, should one frown at them, they might lose their fragile grasp on the world.

Now that Elsa had her target in full view—and two paces away—she felt herself in an advantageous position. If the girl stayed in place, watching over her would not be a difficulty.

Elsa checked her watch. Newark was seventeen minutes away.

Then, to Elsa's annoyance, Kim stood up and left the compartment. The lavatory. Blast.

Elsa tucked her green scarf into her coat pocket, along with her glasses, and hurried after her. Perhaps Mueller wouldn't recognize her immediately. Seconds mattered when you needed to catch someone off guard. Protecting Kim Tavistock would require that she take Mueller down; this had been clear since the train platform. She would aim to disable, not kill, but anything might happen.

As Kim approached the loo, Mueller entered the carriage and strode purposively down the corridor. She was coming at Kim with deadly intensity.

Elsa's purse was already open. Her hand went in, and she drew out the gun, but as she fired, the world went dark. To her consternation, she could barely see. Two seconds of disorientation were enough to bring Mueller to her side. A blow came down painfully on the side of Elsa's head. *"Gute Nacht, Fräulein,"* the woman said. Then an awful, sharp thrust into her chest. Something warm came up her throat. She coughed into the carpet runner on the floor where she appeared to be lying, the bristle hairs of the rug smashing into her cheek.

Kim heard a sharp *crack*, and the car went dark. They must have entered a tunnel. Standing in the doorway of the lavatory, she fumbled for the light switch. She clicked it on, but it didn't help much.

Then the light gained strength, and Kim closed the door, locking it. She used the toilet and the sink and, finding that the towels were missing, had to wipe her hands on her jacket. She looked into the mirror. Her face was quite pale and strained. She applied a little lipstick, then exited the lavatory.

From down the corridor, at the door to the compartment that connected one car to the other, someone called for help. A woman waved at her from the forward doorway, but she was turned away, struggling with something.

Kim went forward to see what was the matter. When she entered the small and very loud inter-carriage compartment, she saw a person slumped in the corner. The woman who had called her was bent over this person, but when the door closed behind Kim, the woman stood up and faced her. It was Lena.

Before Kim could react, Lena pricked her in the side of the neck with something. She tried to turn away and get through the door, but Lena pulled her back, and as she lost strength, she fell into Lena's arms. She felt herself lowered slowly to the floor. Her vision blurred, but she saw that Lena was pulling a body through the compartment door. With a supreme effort, Kim crawled after her, back into the carriage she had just left. The world was filled with the loud clacking of the train as the outer door was opened. To Kim's horror, she saw Lena shove the body out the door. A blast of cold air hit Kim.

The world was in slow motion. Lena stood over her. Kim felt herself hauled to her feet. She sagged against Lena, who had an arm tightly around her waist. They lurched down the corridor. It was becoming harder to think or grasp what was happening.

She heard, "My sister has had one of her spells. Can we sit

here a few minutes? I'm sure it will all be . . ." Kim was having
trouble paying attention. Sleep beckoned, but she was too sick to
sleep. Yes, she was dreadfully sick.

"No, she's fine . . . needs to rest . . . happens sometimes . . .
station at Newark."

Other people's concerned voices.

"Best if she doesn't lie down, we must keep upright . . . doctor
always advises."

"The station . . . her husband . . . so embarrassing, really."

Kim tried to speak, to ask for help, but all that came out was
a moan. After some time, she was helped to her feet and had a
person on each side of her, half-carrying her forward. Cool air
hit her as she was helped down the steps to the platform.

"Her husband will meet us. These spells of hers!"

"No, so kind, but no, thank you . . . over here to sit . . . he'll
be here soon."

Voices mixed up. Lena's German accent.

Then she was pulled up again from the bench on which she
had been sitting. Walking again, someone on each side of her.

"Darling, how do you feel?" A man in a bowler hat. She knew
him, somehow. "My darling, how are you?"

"Sick," Kim dutifully answered. Very sick. She was having a
great deal of difficulty thinking straight.

The door slammed. She was lying in the back seat of a car.

"*Verdammt noch mal,* get us out of here," barked the woman.
Oh yes, that was Lena.

Kim thought she might be in a great deal of trouble, but she
could not quite remember why.

37

WAR OFFICE BUILDING, LONDON

WEDNESDAY, MAY 6. It was an early dusk in London, with the dark bellies of the clouds shrouding the day. Whenever the front doors opened, a fist of wind came through and a few drops of rain. It was getting on to five o'clock. Owen watched as the building began to empty of secretaries and functionaries, buttoning up coats and securing hats firmly on their heads as they headed for the street.

At five fifteen, when he had almost given up on Rennie, the man came down the side corridor toward him. "Mr. Cherwell," he said. "I'm sorry to say that I could not get through to anyone on your behalf."

Owen nodded unhappily, seeing that his hopes were dashed.

Rennie paused. "May I sit down?"

Owen gestured to the bench beside him. "It's your territory; I should think you can."

Seating himself next to Owen, Rennie said, "You must

understand that we get many such . . . offers. I don't mean to
suggest that you're one of them, but frankly, we English are big
on conspiracies these days. It's the environment you've come
into here."

"I see. I suppose you did try." Owen picked up his hat and
gloves that he had laid on the seat beside him.

Rennie glanced at him. "If you could give me something
more, I might try again."

"Why would you? You don't believe me."

"Well, I don't, it's true. I don't *yet.*" Rennie lowered his
voice. "But I checked on you, Mr. Cherwell. You do happen to be
involved in affairs which are highly classified."

Owen waited to see if he knew about Monkton Hall.

Rennie gave a small smile. "That's all I know, and it was
rather a hard dig to get that much. But now I'm wondering if
someone at a higher level might possibly take an interest."

"But I thought you said you already tried."

"There are levels of trying. I didn't tackle the CID secretary
to the floor."

"But if I gave you some key details . . ."

"That's right." He stood. "Mr. Cherwell, I'm giving you a
chance to convince me. If you're willing to go a bit further than
you did at our first interview, we can go back to that room and
see what comes of it. I can't promise anything. And you'll have
to trust me, you see."

That went both ways. Owen followed Rennie back down the
hall. By the time they got to the interview room, Owen had
decided to tell everything. He would have to convince Rennie
and his superiors not to involve Fitzroy Blum. If alerted, Fitz
would bury the whole thing or at least delay it for the critical
hours the Germans needed to execute their operation.

"Mr. Rennie," Owen began. "I work for an organization at Monkton Hall in Yorkshire which studies Talents with an eye to their uses in the intelligence services and the military. It is called HARC, the Historical Archives and Record Centre. A year ago, HARC uncovered a new Talent."

From his suit pocket, Rennie drew out a small notebook and began to take notes.

Owen continued, "This new Talent was given the name *cold cell*. It is an ability to control or extrude frigid temperatures, a Talent that has turned out to have high military value. An individual of impeccable credentials in society was identified as having powerful abilities in this new Talent. His name is Hugh Aberdare, Earl of Daventry. Hugh Aberdare subsequently began working for the Germans, while the director of HARC, Fitzroy Blum, stopped the research on *cold cell* abilities and falsified all records of it."

Rennie put down his pen. "These are very grave accusations."

"Yes, I'm quite aware. Believe me." It was worrisome that Rennie had stopped taking notes. Owen plunged on: "Prior to his classification as a *cold cell* Talent, Hugh Aberdare was in profound financial difficulty that lifted when he began receiving German money. I have access to his financial records, given up by Hugh Aberdare's sister, which show that he has made very large lump-sum deposits in several bank accounts."

Rennie started writing again.

"Most alarming of all, Hugh Aberdare appears to have a Talent for coordinating others who have *cold cell* Talents. Directing them. In a way that certainly has military applications."

"In what way, exactly?"

Owen paused, and looked at John Rennie, trying to take his measure, trying to see if the man's imagination could grasp what came next. "With an ice road. Across the water." Owen plunged on. "And the date for the operation is likely to be soon. Perhaps very soon."

After another few minutes, Rennie left the room, asking Owen to wait.

Owen pulled in a deep breath of overheated, stuffy air. He had done what he could, but it would come to nothing if Rennie did not believe him and if someone at the highest level did not see fit to investigate. But the accusations of treachery, the disclosure of attack plans were out in the open now. They had been spoken. But heard?

Outside, a few drops of rain flattened in a gust against the window. At five forty-five, the day had turned dark with clouds. Owen tried not to see this as presaging defeat. There were surely some, even in this staid bureaucracy, who would believe a citizen who came to Whitehall with knowledge of a conspiracy.

Fifteen minutes later, Rennie came back.

He remained standing. "Here is our situation, Mr. Cherwell. Your story is quite incredible. I do not believe that we have a situation as dire as you have concluded. I'm very sorry, but I do not. However, I believe you are sincere, and certainly the facts you claim to have can be verified. So, you may be assured that I will bring this forward." He noted Owen's expression, which must have reflected his profound relief.

"I cannot say that you will be taken seriously, Mr. Cherwell. I cannot say so at all. You understand?"

"All I ask for is a hearing."

Rennie looked to the window as the wind rattled it in its frame. "The difficulty is that the proper individuals to bring in at this point have left for the day. Would you be willing to come back in the morning?"

"You understand that time is of the essence, that this operation may launch even in the next few days?"

Rennie pursed his lips. "Well, I shall certainly not interrupt my superior's dinner to announce the Germans are coming." He nodded at Owen and said with finality, "Eight o'clock, Mr. Cherwell. Be in the lobby. We shall try again."

ALBEMARLE STREET, LONDON

Julian was surprised at a knock at his door at half past eight. Putting down his book, he went to the door. It was Olivia Hennessey.

Looking onto the flat's landing, where there was no one else in sight, he gestured for her to enter.

As he closed the door, she put up a hand to forestall his rebuke. "I know. I oughtn't have come."

"Well, it's not exactly a breach of the rules. Has something happened?"

"No, it's nothing new. But with E gone, we're all at our wits' end. I thought that Heath Millington would be moving into E's office. But it's just—empty. I hoped you might know more about what's going on."

"I might, but it's not pretty. Now you're here, we might as well commiserate." He gestured to the divan. "I'll put tea on."

"That's a change," she said, "you, making tea."

He filled the kettle in the kitchen and called out, "Unless you want something stronger? I'm afraid I can't. I have work yet tonight."

"Oh, tea is fine. I could use something warm with this blow. Is this a bad time?"

He came back in. "No, I don't have to leave for a few hours. May I take your coat?"

"Please don't fuss." She unbuttoned her coat and shrugged out of it, laying it on the divan next to her. She left her hat on, tucked behind her forward swirl of hair. "Everyone wants to know what's going to happen. E called us all together on Monday and told us to wait it out, that it would blow over." She began removing her gloves, tugging on the fingers one by one. He thought it very sensual and was glad she didn't realize it. She set the gloves on top of her coat.

It had been a long time since he had entertained a woman in his flat. And he wasn't entertaining a woman now, either. This was Olivia Hennessey. It was about work.

"For starters, they'll be conducting an investigation," he said. "We're accused of being too aggressive. We lost Harp. God only knows if he's still alive. E's got the wrong politics at the moment. He might be done for."

Olivia looked contemptuous. "I thought you might cheer me up."

"I wish I could. I met with Millington yesterday, and he's dead set against us, talking about reining things in and getting reports from the Security Service on our operations."

"The Security Service! They've been half asleep since the war. Who pays any attention to them?"

"Heath Millington. He likes them because they're easier to control. Likes them a damn sight better than us."

Olivia colored. "It makes me quite sick. E is down at Litchfield. His office is vacant, which makes it seem like nobody's in charge. I might as well be on leave, too. The bloody fools. If they let E go, I'll go too, of course. I can't imagine working for anyone else."

"Yes, you can. What else is there for people like you and me?"

She looked at him ruefully as he went on. "Where would you find a job? I can't see you working for the Foreign Bible Society."

She snorted a laugh. "What about you?"

"So far, I'm working at charming Mr. Millington."

The teapot whistled, and Julian went into the kitchen, Olivia following. As he made the tea, she said, "Are you going to stay on?"

He shrugged. In fact, he'd considered leaving if they drummed E out, but the thought was depressing. "I don't know."

They sipped their tea, he leaning against the kitchen table, she against the hutch.

"It would be nice," she said, "to be able to tell one's friends what one does. Selling Bibles. That would at least be something to talk about. I suppose it's why I'm here."

"To sell me a Bible?"

She laughed. He thought she looked absolutely stunning in her fitted blue wool suit. And drinking tea . . . standing in his kitchen. It really did seem that the Office was far away.

"No," she responded. "To talk to the one person who's left."

"Not a very high recommendation. Your last resort." He sipped his tea, wondering what he was fishing for. She really should leave. It would be for the best. But of course, this was Olivia Hennessey, and she had never given him the slightest encouragement, as of course she should not, given that their being together was not in the best interests of their work. He would like to see that hair come down, though.

"I'm here," he said, inviting conversation.

"Yes, well. I oughtn't have come. If E returns, you won't tell?"

"Lips sealed."

She made no move to go. "I don't want to know what you're working on, of course. I just felt . . . well, it's too strong a word, but *bereft*."

"You might try *furious*. It gets me through those ghastly interviews with Millie."

"I'll give it a try." She put her cup down on the table. "Well. Thanks for the tea, Julian."

A longish pause. "Do you have to go?"

Her face had the most vulnerable expression. Sad, doubtful, ironic. "I don't know."

He stopped leaning against the table and stood up. "I don't know, either. You decide."

She shook her head in a helpless smile. "No, you."

Stepping forward, he pulled her gently toward him, kissing her briefly, softly. She allowed this, but he was still uncertain. "Shall I get your coat, then?"

Very slowly, her hands came up to her head, and she drew the hat pin out of her hat. "No," she whispered.

AN SIS WIRELESS STATION, LONDON

Fin looked up as Julian entered the small flat that served as their listening post. He arched an eyebrow. Julian had almost been late. It was eleven fifteen.

"Guv'nor," Fin said.

Julian nodded at him. "How's reception?"

"Static sounds like a bag of angry ferrets. The gale's been coming straight south at us but hovering now, just off the coast of Scotland. Playing havoc with transmissions."

Julian threw his coat onto a chair and took out his pipe. "What's the report from Elsa?" Julian asked.

"She's late."

"Rory?"

"Nothing. They must be on the move." Holding one earphone to his ear, Fin made small adjustments to the dial on the crystal set.

"It's not like her," Julian muttered. Elsa and Rory were watching Kim. It was likely the Security Service had come for her by now. He hoped they had; it was what he had wanted for days now. Get her off the street.

Now that they weren't trying to let Kim lead them to her contacts, Julian had sent two men up to Pickering to have a conversation with Owen Cherwell, in case he could be of assistance. But Mrs. Cherwell had told them that her husband was gone and she didn't know where he was. Troubling. Up until now, Julian doubted that the researcher could be mixed up in something foolish—much less sinister. His career would be on the line. Still, he'd been gone two days, and staff at Monkton Hall had no idea where he was. Well, the hunt was on for Cherwell. They'd find him.

Olivia would be gone when he got back to his flat. It was late and she had work in the morning, but he wanted to see her again. Again, tonight. Christ, what a fool he was. Olivia Hennessey.

He lit his pipe as Fin donned the headphones and picked up his pencil. It was 11:29. After a minute's wait, the distinctive clicks began. Woodbird was transmitting.

By midnight, Fin finished transcribing the code. He pulled the sheet off the notepad and handed it to Julian.

Julian read it. Then again.

Fin watched him. "So, then. The *chorister* individual can aggregate *ice* Talents. As we suspected. He doesn't say how far the Talent reaches, in the field sense."

"Do you believe the intel's accurate?"

Fin shrugged. "The *Abwehr* gets reports from Luckenwalde. Woodbird assigns this one high reliability."

Julian relit his pipe. "We know that individuals with the *ice* Talent have shipped out to Wesermarsch over the last weeks, and that *ice* is the Talent of the *chorister*. So, the attack might be using *ice*, but we don't know the mechanism, how they would use *ice* against us. Stelling said it was to be an invasion, but he withheld saying *how*."

"Because he wanted to bargain with that piece, the sod." Fin pushed back his chair, balancing it on the back legs. "What can you aggregate when it comes to *ice*?"

"The question is more what can a number of *ice* Talents do when their efforts are combined. Maybe you can freeze things. Especially water." Julian exchanged a rueful look with Fin. "A floating ice bridge."

"Bring the *Wehrmacht* over on a path of *ice*?"

"That's one way," Julian said. *Storm way*. It was a leap to think that *Sturmweg* was about *ice*. But Julian had a hunch, and over the years, he'd learned to trust his hunches: this one was about the coming storm. A storm of *ice*.

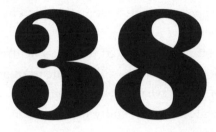

THURSDAY, MAY 7. "Your daughter has run, Tavistock. She's gone missing." Millington was leaning back in his chair, gazing darkly at Julian.

"Run? What do you mean, *run*?"

"Disappeared. She's not at home, nor is she at the place she told your housekeeper she was going. She deliberately threw us off the trail by lying about her whereabouts."

"The trail? She isn't a fugitive, and she didn't know you were going to pick her up."

Millington ignored this. "All this leads us to suspect that she may in fact be under enemy control. Consorting with Georgiana Aberdare. Passing secrets."

"What secrets?" Julian exploded. "We have her under surveillance to find out what she's doing. Because we do not know!"

"Lower your voice, Tavistock. I'll not have a shouting match."

Julian took a deep breath. "We have absolutely no reason to believe she's working for a foreign power. She's a journalist. She's probably investigating something but has no idea what she's dealing with."

"Well. You can't be expected to have a neutral view of this. It's why I took you off her case. That's the most generous interpretation I can put on what has happened."

A pause while Julian carefully marshaled his words. "What other interpretation is there?"

"I do not like to say. But on Tuesday, I told you that we were going to pick her up, and on Wednesday, she disappeared."

Julian stared at him. "If that *interpretation* is in play, then you must relieve me of my post."

"We're not at that point yet. But I warn you, I am watching."

Julian would have walked out right then. But he still needed Millington, needed him to accept the service's role in *Sturmweg*, and to listen to the latest evidence so that he would alert the defense committee. At the very least, they must prepare the coastal batteries and strengthen the home guard. They might have very little time.

The two men stared at each other in barely restrained anger. At last, Millington relented somewhat. "We'll keep up our search. Any ideas where she could have gone?"

"Where did she tell the housekeeper she was going?"

"Someplace called Presswick House on the moors."

"Prestwich. And you checked there?"

"I've just told you that we have. The director of the hospital said that she had come by on Sunday to bring her maid for an exam but that he hadn't seen her since."

A shadow of foreboding fell over Julian. *Missing.* He didn't like the word, didn't like it at all. And Elsa hadn't reported in.

Millington was cooling off, having made his displeasure clear. "Well, what is it you wanted to see me about?"

The abrupt turn of conversation was welcome. "A report came in last night from our *Abwehr* man. He's confirmed that the German asset, the one with the *chorister* Talent, is able to aggregate *ice* Talents. I think it's a very strong indicator that the Germans have a secret military use of the *ice* Talent, and I also believe it likely they will use this for the attack that Colonel Stelling warned of."

"An attack of *ice*? What does that mean?"

"We can't know, but I would venture it may provide them a landing advantage on our coast."

"I haven't the slightest idea what you're talking about."

"Yes, you do. It may very well be an *ice* bridge from Wesermarsch, from Norden. To England."

Heath rose from his chair. "That is preposterous."

He was about to bluster on, but Julian had had enough. He leaned over the desk. "Preposterous? I don't think so. We are living in new times. The era of the Talents. Our own HARC facility is investigating military uses of Talents. We know they exist, but we have the distinct disadvantage of having started our research a decade after Germany. They have developed new weapons in that time, powerful weapons. They will not be like the old weapons, and the new war will not be like the old. The truth is that we have very little idea of their capabilities. But when a highly placed German defector tells us that there will be an attack on England, and we have a great deal of evidence that Germany is concentrating Talents at Norden and that they have a *chorister* who can maximize the effect of Talents . . . when this is our situation, we must prepare for the worst. To stand by and do nothing invites disaster. And it is contemptible."

Millington gave a small smile. "You are an orator, sir." He paused. "And a great fool." He noted Julian's reaction and said, "Yes, a fool." He waved his hand toward the door. "Every day, people walk in off the street with tales of conspiracies. People are afraid. They hear all this talk of war, and it becomes part of their imaginations. It attracts crackpots of the highest order, I assure you. And it is hysteria. Assessments like yours are just the reason E lost his post and why you are on the verge of losing yours. My assistant John Rennie tells me that there's a man in the lobby right now who claims the Germans are coming. How does he know? He doesn't! He fears it, and he's spreading alarm. It undermines morale and should be against the law."

Julian's voice went soft. "You're going to ignore intelligence about a powerful new military Talent? That could be career suicide, Millington."

"You stand there and wish me to warn the CID that the Germans are constructing an *ice* bridge?"

Millington was not going to be persuaded. He no longer trusted Julian, had practically accused him of treason, and would not risk his reputation by sounding the alarm for an attack when his boss Alistair Drake and *his* boss, the Prime Minister, wished with all their hearts not to believe in a threat from Hitler.

Doggedly, Julian went on to finish what he had started. "That's not what I'm advocating. I've said we can't know the mechanism. But I'm warning you that they will use *ice* in an attack. A sensible countermeasure is to put the army on alert and call up the reservists."

Millington sat back down and gazed at Julian with pitying disdain. "Well," he sniffed. "I shall certainly take all this under advisement. Thank you for your report, Tavistock."

Julian held his gaze for another moment, then turned from the little man in wire-rimmed spectacles and narrow views, and left the room.

A SMALL ROOM WITH BARS

During the night, Kim awakened from bad dreams. She was nauseated and thick-headed, lying on a bed with her arms and legs in restraints. Even with a wool blanket, the room radiated a harsh cold. Her mouth was terribly dry. She fell back into a stupor.

When she next awakened, a gray light seeped through a barred window. She was in a small, institutional-looking room, and by the bedside sat Erich von Ritter.

"You are awake, yes?" He wore a brown leather jacket, and a heavy sweater and slacks.

"I think . . . so." Her tongue did not work as it should.

He stood. "These straps are uncomfortable. Of course we will not need them." He unbuckled her restraints. "Unless you will try to subdue me?"

"No promises."

He nodded agreeably. "I understand. I will trust you, but only so far." He reached for a cup. "Here, sit up. Would you like water?"

She pulled herself up to lean against the pillow and took the proffered cup of water.

"How do you feel?"

"Not good. Lena . . ." Well, what had Lena done to her? Drugs of some kind, she realized, and masking her activities with *darkening*.

"You would not have come willingly. I did not like the necessity."

"Where am I?"

"Prestwich Home. I doubt that you are surprised."

Prestwich. Oh, not good. A fortress. "Rose. Is . . . is she all right?"

"Yes. She is comfortable here. Do not concern yourself."

She closed her eyes, giving in to wave of dizziness. A whistling sound that she had been hearing through the night came again. She recognized it as wind. Gusts carried rain against the window like buckshot.

After the dizziness passed, she opened her eyes to find that von Ritter was standing by the window. "A beautiful storm. The one we have been looking for."

He turned to her, his expression kindly, as though concerned about some unfortunate choices she had been making. "Who do you work for, Kim?"

"Myself."

"This is true? I do not think so."

"But it *is* true."

As he took his seat again, he looked very relaxed. No gun. Maybe he wouldn't kill her.

She went on. "Because at the river, the gazebo. I knew you were . . ." She paused, trying to get her mind to function, to plan what to say. But there could be little point now in subterfuge.

"I was what?"

She wanted to say *bad.* "A spy. What you said about bringing England down."

"Yes, the *spill* of *chorister.* I am still shocked at my indiscretion." He paused. "So. We have been trading *spills,* as it were. You shared with me your brother's death in the war. I liked that we had that intimacy, although I almost killed you for it."

"When I rejected you."

He didn't bother to respond. Perhaps he did not care to be reminded that he had failed to recruit her. She liked having had some wins against him as she lay there helpless, subjected to his kindness, his menace.

"We have much in common," he said. "I still believe it. But why? You have betrayed me. But of course I let you, and so I can still pretend you are in my . . . *camp*, is it?"

Von Ritter was always difficult to talk to under the best of circumstances, with two or three things being discussed at once, but only one out loud. At the moment, her mind was not up to the game, so she just asked him directly: "Are you going to shoot me?"

"Give me no cause. I should not like to."

A knock at the door. Angus Dunn came into the room. He wore a heavy sweater vest over his shirt, adorned as usual by a maroon bow tie. They were all dressed for winter.

Dunn said, "I am sending a nurse to you, Miss Tavistock. She will help you with the necessities."

"How kind of you." Dunn, the conspirator. The defector.

"You'll be safe here until it's over."

"Until what's over?"

Dunn exchanged glances with von Ritter. "Well, you must rest now."

Kim stared at him. "You are a traitor. Isn't it strange how one can always tell the type?" She wondered if he'd wear that bow tie when they hung him.

"I sized you up as well, Miss Tavistock. I concluded you were naive, incompetent, and rash. You see the result of the contest."

"Where are you keeping Rose?" It was a hopeless question, and Dunn answered with an incredulous shake of his head.

"Is she all right? Can you at least tell me that?"

Dunn exchanged looks with von Ritter. When he glanced back at Kim, his face was filled with loathing. "Your useless scullery maid."

Useless? That was not what Kim expected to hear. They considered her a valuable tool, didn't they?

Von Ritter and Dunn left her alone then. She could hear them conferring outside the door when it clicked shut.

WAR OFFICE BUILDING, LONDON

Mr. Vickers looked up as Julian emerged from Millington's office. Julian walked past him, down the hallway. He passed the office of the Secretary of the CID, past the clerks, a teleprinter room, more functionaries. The office of the Joint Intelligence Committee. He left these precincts behind, heading for the back stairs.

Within the space of a few days, SIS had fallen far. The government no longer trusted its own intelligence agency. Facts were slaves to political persuasion, and the messengers of those facts subjected to intimations of treason.

E's words came back to him: *You're the only one left now. To do something about* Sturmweg.

The only one left.

Julian stopped in the hall, considering. Retracing his steps, he came to the broad staircase to the lobby. Just beyond was Millington's office. On the gallery that overlooked the ground floor, Julian looked down. A man sat on a bench by the front door. A woman sat opposite him, removing her galoshes.

Julian went down, sizing up the man as he went. About forty-five years old, high forehead, full, slightly frizzy hair. Dressed in an ill-fitting tweed jacket, with tie and sweater waistcoat. Academic-looking. Well, eccentrics came in all guises.

He approached the man. "I'm looking for someone. I wonder if you can help me."

"Yes?" The man looked up, wary.

"I wonder if you're the person who has come here with a warning. Something you've learned."

The man remained silent.

Julian said, "If you come outside, we can talk. But it can't be here." Then he turned and walked away, pushing through the front doors into a nasty, pelting rain.

In a few minutes, the man in the lobby came out onto the front steps and unfurled his umbrella. Then he joined Julian on the pavement, where the gutters streamed with water.

Julian said, "You came to tell these people something." He glanced at the War Office Building. "Am I right?"

"Maybe I did. But who are you?"

"My name is Claude Beven," Julian said, using one of his aliases. "I'm afraid I can't tell you more. Walk with me."

The man looked up uncertainly at the building behind them.

"You aren't going to be taken seriously," Julian said. He inclined his head to urge him to continue walking. "You can go back as soon as you like. But it will do no good."

"I see."

Julian gazed at this rather plain-looking man. What chance was there that he had anything but irrational theories about a German threat?

The man very kindly held out his umbrella so that Julian was out of the main downpour. They still hadn't moved away from the War Office Building, something Julian was keen to do. "What is your name, if I may ask?"

"Well, it's a secret."

"It would be a very good idea if you told me, however."

A long silence as the two men regarded each other. "Owen Cherwell."

"What? Come again?"

"Cherwell. Owen Cherwell."

By Christ. They'd been looking for him high and low, and he had been sitting in the War Office? "I see. Well, Mr. Cherwell. I am prepared to believe you."

"But I haven't told you anything!"

"You haven't. But it is really most urgent that you do. Will you come with me? A cab?"

"No cab."

He could pressure him to submit to questioning at an SIS safe flat, but Owen was ready to talk—he'd been trying to, for God's sake. He'd rather let the man be comfortable. "Three blocks, then. We can walk to a pub I know. What do you say?"

Cherwell's face turned stubborn. "You haven't told me why I should. Who you work for. And I have an appointment at the War Office."

"Mr. Cherwell. I have just come from the office of the Undersecretary of the Committee for Imperial Defence. You are considered a crackpot. Whatever you have told them, they do not believe it. Anyone who supports your story will be subject to ridicule or worse."

"Then why in the world should I trust you?"

A curtain of rain streamed down the sides of the umbrella,

creating a small cell of intimacy. It was all or nothing now.

"Because I am Kim Tavistock's father."

Cherwell said nothing for a moment. Then: "Does your daughter wear a watch?"

"A small silver Helbros. A gift of her mother's."

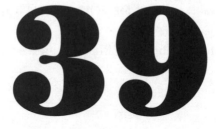

A LONDON PUB

THURSDAY, MAY 7, 10:05 AM. Sitting in a gratifyingly noisy pub on Cockspur Street, Cherwell told Julian his story of a grand conspiracy of Talents. Julian was still shaking his head over the irony of SIS hunting for Cherwell while the man was patiently waiting in the lobby of the War Office to tell them everything.

But before Cherwell would talk in the pub, it had been necessary for Julian to prove to him that he knew exactly what Monkton Hall was. It had set Cherwell more at ease.

"You're with the intelligence service, then?"

"Yes."

At that, Cherwell recounted the events that had led him to the War Office. Julian listened with near incredulity to the convoluted role his own daughter had played. His daughter, a spy. Working with Owen Cherwell, but virtually under her own auspices. He set aside his astonishment to hear the man's story beginning to end: The suspicion that Monkton Hall's Fitzroy Blum worked for the Germans, and Cherwell's recruitment of Kim to find proof of Blum's betrayal through his former lover Georgi Aberdare. Then the actual spy turning out to be her brother, Hugh Aberdare, who was in the center of a planned military operation against England. How Erich von Ritter had been at Summerhill—presumably as Hugh Aberdare's controller—and his *spill* to Kim of the term *chorister*. And at the moment, Julian thought grimly, Kim was personally dealing with von Ritter, who was not merely a spy but one directly involved with an invasion plot.

He now had no doubts why von Ritter had tried to have his daughter run over a cliff.

The story built ominously. The *chorister* that Hitler had at his disposal was not a German. He was an Englishman, a peer of the realm. Also possibly a traitor, Fitzroy Blum. If he was the mole that SIS suspected was in the highest circles of the intelligence service, then at least E would be cleared of suspicion.

Owen revealed that Hugh had said it was not safe to be on the streets at the present time. If the Germans launched their operation in the next few days, there might be little time to mobilize effective defenses. But they could at least call up what they had.

He had little reason to doubt Cherwell. Alice Ward would back him up—Alice Ward, by Christ—and Cherwell knew her hotel in London. What he didn't know was where Kim was.

Julian excused himself and used the phone in the corner of the pub, calling Fin. There was no answer.

Back at the table, Julian continued drawing out Cherwell's story. Their pints sat before them, untouched.

"And this Talent you've been tracking, that Blum suppressed. It's called *cold cell*?"

"Yes. I knew about it when we first began testing, but it was quickly dismissed as a dead end. Sam Reuben was in charge. Then he was murdered for it."

"Because you were sniffing around?"

"I think not. If they'd known that Kim and I visited Sam, they would have killed us, too. I believe he was killed because the operation was underway and they were taking no chances."

"And our housemaid, Rose Babbage . . ." He still could not quite imagine Rose creating storms.

"A *cold cell* Talent. Kim believes that they have other such individuals at Prestwich Home—perhaps in other locations as well."

"To work together to create a bridge." But a bridge could not be built in a day. It would make an excellent target for the Royal Navy.

"Well. Rose called it a *road*. Made of ice."

So far, they could only guess at what either a bridge or a road might mean. "As to timing, Hugh Aberdare gave no further indication of the date?"

"No. The phrase that Kim reported to me was that Georgiana Aberdare must stay close to home for a while." He smiled ruefully. "It could be days. Or weeks."

Or hours. Julian looked at this man who possessed the key to an attack on England. "How long has it been since you had something to eat?"

Cherwell shook his head.

"I'm going to make a phone call, Mr. Cherwell."

"Owen, please."

"I'll order you a plate of food." He stood up. "The beer

won't hurt you either." He paused. "We need to put you under
protection for a few days. You'll be looked after by one of ours
named Fin. And please remember: you will not reveal any of
what you know of me unless it is to a government agency. Not
to Alice Ward, not your wife. Not Kim. If you mention any
of us, you compromise people who are working under deep
cover."

"I understand."

Julian tried again to ring Fin. This time, he was home.

"Bloody hell, where are you?" Fin blurted.

"Nearby. But I need you here."

"Bad news, Julian. It's Elsa."

"Go on."

"She was found in a ditch south of York near the train route
to London. She's wounded and might not make it. She says she
was on the train with Kim."

"You mean someone has talked to her?"

"Damn right. The hospital called the number she gave
them, which was mine. When I couldn't reach you, I rushed
up to see her before the Security Service took control. I had
ten minutes with her before they tossed me out. Apparently,
yesterday Elsa and Rory followed Kim to the train station in
York. Kim was tailed by two German agents, including one
Lena Mueller. This Mueller tried to kidnap Kim at the train
station. Elsa and Rory intervened, but they tried to kill Elsa
when she attempted to protect Kim on the train. The woman
has a *darkening* Talent."

"They have Kim, then?"

"Yes."

"And Rory?"

"No sign of him."

"Get down here to the Lock as soon as you can." He used the code name for the pub. There's someone I need you to take under wing." Julian kept an eye on Owen across the room. The pub owner was serving him a plate.

"We're not going after Kim?"

"We will." Once they discovered where she was. "But I've found Owen Cherwell, and he's privy to Erich von Ritter's plans. It's just what we thought. And now we have proof."

"Sweet mother. Have you brought this to Millie?"

"No. And I'm not going to."

"Oh, Christ. Then we're on our own, is that it?"

"If you're with me."

"Of course I am."

"When can you be here?"

"Twenty minutes."

"Make it ten. Will Elsa pull through?"

"I don't know. The knife went in beneath her ribs, just missing her heart. And she's badly broken up from the plunge off the train."

Julian replaced the receiver in the cradle. Across the room, Owen was bent over his pub stew. The next ten minutes were the slowest he had ever experienced.

THURSDAY, MAY 7, 11:36 AM. Outside the office of the Secretary of CID, Julian told the assistant that he had an urgent and highly private message from E for Alistair Drake.

"Mr. Drake is not in," the man said.

"Then you must find him and tell him that E has a message for him of critical importance.

"And you are?"

"Special Agent Julian Tavistock." He showed his identification.

As the man hesitated, Julian said, "It would be a grave mistake to ignore me."

With great apprehension, the assistant murmured, "He is at his club."

"Interrupt him."

"I will have to inform Mr. Millington."

"You cannot do that, however." At the man's incredulous expression, Julian went on. "This is *about* Heath Millington. Among other things."

An hour and a half later, Julian and Alistair Drake sat on facing sofas before Drake's office fireplace. Drake looked every inch a veteran of the Great War. Military haircut still, a line of mustache, and the bearing of one who could have you shot.

Julian had told him what was coming, and how they knew, a story that at first elicited incredulity, then dark concentration, and finally apprehension.

"If you're wrong," Drake said at last, "this government will not survive."

"No. Perhaps the least of our worries."

Drake did not argue the point. "I want you to bring this Cherwell informant in."

"I need assurances."

"You do, do you?"

"Yes."

"How dare you negotiate with me, sir. I can have you jailed."

"But you see, I don't care. There are several people who know the whole story and who can get the ear of either the newspapers or someone in government. The word will come out. If it's after the attack, I'll have some company in prison."

Drake drew himself up. He was not accustomed to being

spoken to in this manner. "What assurances do you want?"

"A letter from you confirming that our best intelligence has confirmed an imminent attack on England. You will place it in a blank, stamped envelope, and I will leave to post it. When I return, I will bring Owen Cherwell."

"That is unnecessary. My word should be enough."

They gazed at each other, facing off over honor, pecking order and the fate of the country. Julian remembered all that E had told him about Alistair Drake. A man who didn't like to lose, who could love a woman for forty years. Who had agreed to see Julian when he had never met him.

"Your word, then," Julian said.

Drake nodded. "You have it. Provided that you produce a credible informant, I will alert the Prime Minister and use my powers of persuasion." For a man who had just learned that Britain would be attacked and who was about to inform the government, he was as rock-steady as the War Office Building itself.

Drake went on. "I am going to call Richard back to his post."

The phone call E was waiting for at Litchfield. Olivia would be ecstatic. The Office was back on its feet.

"I expect there'll be an emergency meeting of the CID this afternoon," Drake said. "I need you there. Heath will come. I suggest you avoid a confrontation. You must leave him to me."

The satisfying image came of Drake yanking rather hard on the leash attached to the Undersecretary's dog collar. "Yes, sir. But I would like to find my daughter as soon as possible."

"I expect you would. But we'll need you here for a few hours." Drake stood up, drawing the meeting to a close. "Time to bring in Mr. Cherwell, I should think."

Julian did. Owen Cherwell soon found himself speaking to the Secretary of the Committee for Imperial Defence. It was a surprisingly short meeting, where Drake, joined now by a Royal Navy admiral and chief of staff of the army, listened as Owen confirmed Julian's story and answered hurried questions with the calm of a Cambridge professor tutoring first-year students. His bearing and crisp recitation of the facts were entirely satisfactory. The man whom Heath Millington had pronounced a crank may not have convinced everyone in the room. But he had won Drake over.

Drake had obviously already put in a call to Stanley Baldwin, because the invitation to 10 Downing Street came during the Cherwell interview. Drake rose. "Gentlemen." He looked at the representatives from the army and navy. "Anyone care to accompany me?"

It was a risk. They could be right or they could be wrong. To be wrong was a career-killer. Drake went alone.

THURSDAY, MAY 7, 3:38 PM. Rain lashed the windows at the club where Julian ate a hasty supper. He had thought he wouldn't be able to eat, but he found he was ravenous, this being his first meal in twelve hours.

The CID had decided quickly that the army would move resources to the coastal defense. The Home Guard mobilized. The army assumed overall command, since the navy was hobbled by the storm.

Now came a lull. He had already sent Fin to Alice Ward's hotel to debrief her and bring in an agent to accompany her home. There was nothing more he could do. Kim was being held somewhere by German agents, likely those reporting to Erich von Ritter. The only thing he could think of to do was to get to

Elsa in Newark and see if she knew anything that might suggest
where they were hiding.

The army would send in a unit to raid Prestwich Home to
shut down its *cold cell* operations—whatever they were. He wondered, not for the first time, how people so far from the coast
could be expected to help secure a beachhead. But the task now
was to free the detained *cold cell* Talents and occupy the site. If
it was heavily fortified, as was quite likely, the operation was
dangerous and its outcome not assured.

The raid on Prestwich would likely come out of the Catterick
Garrison near Leeds, some two hours' drive from Prestwich, near
Thirsk. They were planning it now, but Julian was not confident
they could pull off an assault. First, because the garrison wasn't
prepared for wartime operations and lacked the training for an
assault. Second, because Prestwich had been built as a fortified
keep. Angus Dunn had bragged that over the centuries Prestwich
had never fallen to attacks from neighboring Lancashire.

The thought of Angus Dunn made him long to partake in
the assault. But he'd have no part in the military operation.

Rose was there. How had they all missed the fact that Rose
Babbage had a strong *ice* Talent? Owen had a report from Kim
that she had *seen* Rose controlling a snowstorm. Julian had
noticed nothing, believing that London was where his attentions
must be directed. He had been blind to so much.

Out in the street, a cold rain thundered onto the pavement.
There were to be high winds later in the day, but for now, the
rain fell like lead shot. At his flat, he'd grab dry clothes and take
the train to Elsa's hospital in Newark, first stopping for messages at Carlisle's.

Julian ducked into the tobacconist shop entryway, shaking off
his umbrella. The bottoms of his trousers were soaked, perhaps

the source of his profound chill, unless it was the thought of the German army on British soil.

As he entered, he welcomed the shop's warmth, saturated with the rich fragrances of exclusive, rich tobaccos. A few customers lingered over their choices, discussing them with Carlisle, the proprietor, forcing Julian to wait. He examined an antique tobacco jar in hues of deep blue and toffee.

When the last customer left, Carlisle came over to him. Julian's longtime tobacconist was thin and bald with a sergeant major–style mustache that was his trademark.

"A beauty," Carlisle said, looking at the tobacco jar Julian held. "1875. Scottish, Majolica glaze."

"Looks like a fault on the rim."

"Yes, manufacturing process. It's all original. No maker's mark, you noticed."

The preliminaries satisfied, Julian went to business. "Do you have anything else?"

Carlisle nodded. "Fin. Shortly after ten this morning. Said Egret's on vacation, and to meet him at the club."

Code for *Egret is hurt*. Old news.

"Earlier, Rabbit called. Sparrow is at Prestwich Home."

A stab of alarm. Kim at Prestwich? They had brought her *there?* Mind racing, he managed to ask, "Anything else?"

Carlisle handed over a piece of folded paper with the number Rory had left.

As Julian turned for the door, Carlisle said, "Sure you don't want the Majolica?"

"Have it sent. If I wait, it will be gone."

"Always the way. Thank you, Julian."

He managed not to hurry as he made his way to a phone box. To his relief, the connection went through.

"Rory?"

"Chief. Sparrow was taken off the train at Newark. German operatives."

"I got your message. She's at Prestwich Home, you're sure?"

"Yes. I missed the train at York when Egret got on. By the time I caught up with them again, Egret was no longer on their tail. I raced down to Newark, where one of the operatives was overheard to be meeting the woman agent. At the car park, I caught a glimpse of the two agents putting Sparrow in a car. She was staggering, maybe drugged. At Prestwich, I couldn't get close enough to confirm she went in. The area is surrounded by heavy security. I had to pull off the road early and make my way through the moor, but I saw their Vauxhall parked there. I couldn't risk getting back to my car, so I spent the night in the woods and this morning made my way to a nearby town."

Julian filled him in on Elsa's near-fatal push from the train.

"We've got Owen Cherwell now, and he's supplied key details on *Sturmweg*. CID has bought in on it, thank God. Millie is off the project, so they're going directly to the chief now. Swan is being briefed."

Rory whistled. Swan was always the Prime Minister's code name. "We're for it, then."

"At last. But if the Germans strike in the next few days, as is possible according to our intel, we'll be caught with our pants down."

"What do we do?"

"We did our job, but we're out of it now." He couldn't get his people involved in what he was going to do next.

He rang off.

His part of the job might be over. But he had his daughter

to think of. The daughter he wasn't supposed to consider in his clandestine work. He would bloody well like to consider her now, when her life might be in jeopardy. He began to think what might be done, now that he knew where she was being held. But one thing he wasn't going to do.

Ask permission.

40

THURSDAY, MAY 7, 5:49 PM. The contents of the meal tray lay scattered on the floor as Kim leaned over the toilet, throwing up. Exhausted, she slid back to the floor, resting her head against the tile wall.

She sat there for a time, listening to the storm throw itself against the stony sides of Prestwich Hall.

Von Ritter found her there. As he knelt by her, she looked up at him bitterly. "Poison?"

He wetted a towel, helping her to clean up. "Do not believe your country's propaganda against us. These are the effects of phencyclidine, the anesthetic." He helped her back to the bed and brought her a cup of water.

Very solicitous, he was. After she had betrayed him, she had expected anger. Perhaps that was to come. He must have known from tapping her phone that she had lied to him about her intention to help him, that she had just been tipped off by Georgi that an enemy action might be imminent. She couldn't understand why he had not already killed her.

She sat up on the bed. They had given her wool slacks and a sweater. Boots a size too large. "You never believed me, then."

"I feared that you were lying. But my instruction for you to give up your maid was an excellent test of your loyalty. And Rose might well have been useful to our operation."

Her stomach clenched with aftershocks. With her eyes closed against the spasms, she murmured, "I cannot help but wonder. How did you know she had a Talent?"

"We knew what to look for. We have had our people combing England for over a year."

"Even in Uxley?" Every time she closed her eyes, she hoped that she wasn't actually a prisoner at Prestwich. But when she opened her eyes again, von Ritter was still there, and the little window with bars.

"We are persistent, you see. The little storms are a sure sign of a very strong *ice* Talent. Strange how even the mentally defective can have their uses. Like a draft horse, she could have been very useful in a limited way."

Every now and then, his appalling ideas surfaced. "So, you didn't believe I was trying to help you." She had come so close to a bullet in the head, all the while believing she had fooled him.

"There were a few moments when I had a strong, irrational hope. I am not immune to such feelings. But no. I knew you were loyal to England. It was rather charming of you to be so earnest."

She put the cup down, still thirsty but feeling bilious. "Your Yorkshire girl," she said bitterly.

"Oh yes, that." The smile faded. "I would like to know who you are working for, however." He pulled out his cigarette case, opening it, then snapped it shut. "But no, I will not smoke. You are still sick." He slipped the case into his inside jacket pocket and waited for her to answer.

"I told you. I'm working for myself."

"Someone you met in Monkton Hall?"

"It was really Georgi who set it in motion," she said to deflect him. Owen was her only hope; she must protect him. "She found receipts for very large deposits in Hugh's accounts. She suspected it was German money. She did wonder what he'd done to earn it." Kim explained how she had stolen some time with the logbook and had found evidence of Hugh's Talent. As one who could direct Talents to synchronize them.

Von Ritter shook his head. "We should never have called him a *chorister*. It gave too much away." He was assuming that she had figured that particular Talent out. But it had been Alice's vision that led her and Owen to the truth.

"It is curious," von Ritter went on, "why Georgiana would discuss this with you."

She had a lie ready. "That weekend at Summerhill, Hugh *spilled* to me that he had an important job in Germany. I'm sure he wasn't aware of what he'd said. I went to Georgi and told her I worked for the police and that I was investigating Hugh. That she would be exonerated if she told what she knew."

Von Ritter nodded. "So that's why she called you yesterday to say that Hugh had disappeared."

"Yes. And you've also been following me for the past week and a half?"

"Actually, we have not. But your phone . . ." He shrugged. "Then I sent Lena and Oskar to pick you up. A British agent *was* following you, however. I was glad to hear this, because it meant you were not working for them."

Followed by a British agent? It was her first ray of hope.

He shook his head, as though he knew what she was think-ing. "No one will come for you, Kim. That agent bled to death in a ditch between York and London."

Kim wasn't sure if it was the drugs or the thought of people dying for her, but the nausea returned in force. As she waited for it to subside, she heard the window rattle heavily in the wind.

He went on. "You know the nature of our enterprise?"

"To bring England down. And with *cold cell*, Hugh Aberdare's Talent." She must not say it was Rose who had divulged the key piece, the road.

"Yes. It will be a path of ice, for the use of the *Wehrmacht*. It will be a glorious thing to witness." He regarded her. "I know that you hoped to prevent any plot against England, but do not reproach yourself. You have done very well. I wish that you worked for me, and as a matter of fact, I do not give up on that. Once we have taken control, we will have need of people of capacity. I know you do not think you could ever do so."

She wasn't sure she should deny this outright, and remained silent.

He went on. "I have made a consideration for you. A little peace offering, if you will. Your maid, whom you have affection for. We have come to the conclusion that she is not suitable for our operation—too easily upset." He glanced at her. "You know that Talents can be sensitive."

She frowned and he went on. "We must try to keep our workers calm. It is essential for effectiveness."

She had not realized that. Owen had not.

"They work better when they are not agitated. You under-stand. Perhaps it is the same with our *spill*, yes? If we are in distress, the secrets, they do not come."

Was that true? At the gazebo, during the storm, they had felt some warmth toward each other. She was charmed by his gallantry, his empathy. He had probably felt protective of her. It had always been clear to her that when she tried to create a *spill*, she seldom was able to. But she had never thought of the failure coming from agitation.

"Normally, she would be put down, but I have given her a reprieve. You may take her home when we are done. My gift to you."

They would live. He was telling her they both would live. She took a cold, deep breath. And yet, he would change his mind if the British army attacked.

He stood and walked to the window, looking out into the tempest. "You believe that you must be against me. A matter of principle. But it is soon going to be . . . moot, do you say?"

"Yes. Moot." Unless Owen could get to Whitehall. "But aren't the other Talents here also upset? Most of them can't be happy to be helping the enemy."

He shrugged. "Dr. Dunn told them they would be released if they cooperated. Otherwise, they would remain under detention. They are calm, willing to help."

He had turned toward her for a moment and now resumed his gaze out the window. "People are always quick to see their best interests. When Germany marches into England, we must have stability. Your fellow citizens will continue their lives. If you accept your conquerors, you can help us build. There comes a time—soon now—when we are no longer required to oppose each other."

There was a knock at the door. Oskar was there, beckoning to von Ritter, who left for a few minutes.

When von Ritter returned, he looked pleased. "This weather, it is perfect. Our people continue to report the most ideal conditions."

"How did you know there would be a storm on May eighth?" He knew that she knew the date. Georgi had mentioned it when she called.

"We did not know. We were poised to march at any time, and when the storm was well on its way, we had a few days' notice." He nodded in satisfaction. "We had hoped for a polar air mass creating a storm in the northeast. But even better, we have a very powerful storm from the Atlantic that moved around Scotland and has come down the coast. Over water, it is a devastating gale. Even on land, it will certainly ground your planes."

"I should have thought it would be a danger to your landing, too." One could hope.

"On the coast, you mean. But we are not landing on the coast."

"You aren't? But it is a road, I thought."

"A road? No. How remarkable that you would think so."

"But you said it was a path."

He shook his head. "Even you cannot imagine what *ice* can do. You naturally think of things you have seen before."

Kim gazed at him intently.

"It is a storm."

She glanced at the window.

"Oh, this gale," he said. "This is not under our control. We were required to wait for it so that natural weather would mask our own *sturm*. Ours will be of *ice* and cold. *Sturmweg.* To which many of your countrymen will contribute."

Von Ritter sat on the edge of the bed. "In concert, people here and in Germany will create a *way*, a path, of ice. But the path is not by ordinary means. I have told you, Kim, that everything will be different because of the *bloom*. Powers never seen before have come into our hands. Your people continue to think in the old ways, of roads and metal and guns. Let me tell you something."

He stood and began pacing. "When we first recruited Hugh Aberdare, we had only discovered a handful of people with what we call *ice* Talents. And we had no idea what a *chorister* was, what he could do. As a 10 for the *ice* Talent, we did hope that he might be useful on the battlefield. When we brought him to Germany— this was under cover of a holiday—we began to see the true possibilities. It was when we put him to work amid other *ice* Talents that there occurred an unexpected path connecting two locales hundreds of meters apart. It was a cell of *ice* that became a tunnel. With the right concentration, and directing the work of some ten or fifteen individuals, Hugh could sustain this tunnel before it evaporated. It bore the weight of trucks.

"In time, we learned that if individuals of the *ice* Talent grouped in two separate places, the tunnel thus created became strong as iron. Impregnable."

She tried to absorb this. A tunnel. A cell of *ice*. A heavy dread began to build. "You have German Talents working the other end."

"Hundreds. You have heard of our work camps."

"And in England? All over?"

"No." He looked around him. "Just here, at Prestwich. The great tunnel is coming here, to the moors."

CROYDON AERODROME, SOUTH LONDON

THURSDAY, MAY 7, 5:51 PM. At the airport, Julian saw planes moving into hangars, and passengers clambering for the few flights to the Continent that were still on schedule, hoping to get out before the worst of the gale tonight.

As was he. But not headed for the Continent. Prestwich. Rory had reported seeing her dragged into the place, a stroke of luck that he intended to take advantage of.

He was off the operation. But he would not stand by without getting Kim out of there before the army started an assault. The base at Catterick had at least a few old tanks and heavy artillery. The main response was, of course, going to the coast. But if Prestwich didn't stand down when called to, they could pound the place into rubble.

In the great hall of the terminal building, he took the stairs straight to Bert Doyle's office.

The director, rounder and redder than the last time Julian had asked for a favor, looked up from a desk with four telephones and a mountain of paper. "Julian. Don't tell me you're trying to get to Paris."

"I'm not."

"That's something, then."

"But I would like to get a lift to RAF Dishforth."

"Can't imagine why. Weather's worse up there than it is down here. I'll tell you what I've been telling everyone for short-haul flights: take a coach." He scowled. "And what makes you think Dishforth wants to see a civilian plane?"

"I've got a crate of very fine whisky. Major General Hart's orders."

Bert snorted. "I've got better things to worry about."

A harried secretary came in carrying more paper and with two pencils sticking out of her up-do.

Julian backed out of the office, saying, "But if I find a plane, I'll get clearance?"

"A plane?" Bert gestured out the window. "Take your pick. But no pilot's going north in this storm."

As it happened, that was not entirely true. For enough money, a pilot could be found who would fly into the teeth of a hurricane. Julian looked into the sky, roiling with black clouds, and hoped it wouldn't come to that.

His recruited pilot—paid cash in advance—was resourceful, commandeering a Handley Page H.P.42 four-engine biplane. With a wingspan of 130 feet, it held twenty-four passengers and required a crew of four.

In the hangar, Julian looked over the plane, with its canvas wings and impressive engines. *Four for safety* was the Handley Page motto. "How long will it take you to find a copilot?"

The man, wearing a well-worn leather flight jacket, ground his cigarette out on the hangar floor. "Give me ten minutes."

Julian watched as the pilot walked back through the rain into Croydon's neoclassical terminal building, where apparently, today in the aerodrome restaurant, pilots could be had.

LONDON—RAF DISHFORTH

THURSDAY, MAY 7, 6:28 PM. The H.P.42 wallowed heavily in the turbulence, making shuddering noises as though the wings were attempting to break free. They were flying into the wind, trying to make ninety miles per hour but going backward for all Julian could tell.

A murky light infused the cabin from a strip of floor lights, while the windows showed only a dense, black fog. The roar of the engines—*four for safety*—pounded in Julian's ears. At his feet, his rifle in its case. The empty seats all around seemed to reproach him for the waste of being the only passenger.

A crash came from the prow. The flight-deck door had

slammed open, revealing the pilot and copilot hunched over their controls. The lights from the bridge control panels held his attention, as the door continued to flap against the wall with each yaw of the plane.

This plane was his only chance of getting to Dunn's little nest of *ice* Talents before the contingent out of Catterick. Once their operation started, it would be impossible to gain entrance to Prestwich. The place would take a pounding if they didn't give themselves up. He well remembered the fortified look of the place, and Dunn saying it had never fallen to a siege. The army would likely bring a tank or howitzers to breach the place.

Landing at Dishforth, fifteen miles south of Prestwich, would give him a head start on the British raid. He hoped that Bert had alerted the RAF that a passenger plane was coming in. They wouldn't be happy about it, but Julian would settle for just not being shot down.

He thought of the mobilizations going on throughout the country, and the race to the coast. They still did not know the landfall point, and so would have to space out the defenses along the most likely beaches. It was not the response Britain might have mounted with a few more days to come up to strength. But the Germans would not land without meeting hot resistance. He fiercely hoped it would be enough.

He turned his thoughts to what he knew of the Prestwich layout from one visit. Where Kim might be in its long corridors. How he would find her. Rory had confirmed that Kim had been taken there, but he didn't know where in the manor she might be held.

By the whining of the engines, he discerned they were slowing for the landing. With a violent pitch forward, the H.P.42 made a shuddering bounce off the ground, then hit even harder, jolting Julian's teeth together. With a hard smack, the cockpit door slammed shut.

Julian braced his feet against the impact as the plane fishtailed wildly, yanking him against his seat belt in an effort to throw him into the aisle. At last, the plane came to rest and the engines rattled to a stop.

He could see nothing but rain outside the window.

Presently, the cockpit door opened, and Julian's pilot—rather tall—ducked out, smoothing his hair and grinning.

"A bit bumpy there at the end." He plopped his flight cap on. "RAF is rather steamed up. I'll let you smooth things over."

In the interview that followed, Julian wished he *had* brought whisky.

41

THURSDAY, MAY 7, 7:09 PM. "The attack is coming here. To the moors," von Ritter said. "It brings us into the heart of England." He had been gone for an hour or so. The manor was becoming noisy out in the corridor.

"You have an excellent motorway nearby, the great north road. It is convenient that it extends all the way to London, a perfect route for us to advance."

Kim had been pacing the room and straining to see out the window, which gave little indication of what was going on.

No one, not Owen, not anyone, suspected the invasion would come to the interior. In fact, Owen would alert them to the wrong place. The coast. She still had hopes that it would not work. How *did* it work, how could it? "What does the tunnel go *through?*"

"Ah. The very question. But we do not know. No more do

we know how you and I compel secrets with the *spill*, or Rose summons the *ice*. They are meta powers, if you will. They must, of course, be based in science, but it is a science we have not yet penetrated."

He went on. "This location on the southwest edge of the moors suits us very well. Our army will come through, and this remote location will provide time to amass our troops and equipment. Otherwise, we could have chosen London."

"The RAF will pick you off as you move south on the motorway."

"Ah. We had not thought of that." He laughed. "No, your air force is understrength and badly equipped. Those planes that survive the storm will fall to our anti-aircraft guns. You see, this is one reason we come now. Before you rearmed." He looked at her with an infuriating empathy. "I tell you this so that you will come to accept what is to happen." He shrugged. "It is up to you, of course."

A knock at the door. This time, someone in uniform. A German uniform, she noted with shock. They spoke in German at the door for a moment. Every hour she had spent there had been more dreadful than the previous one. And now, here was a German soldier. There would soon be more of them. How many days would they keep the tunnel open; how many thousands would have to come through to subdue England?

She thought he was preparing to leave. "I would like to see Rose." She saw his annoyance. "Just for a few minutes."

"You try my patience."

"Please. I want to tell her something. Something important."

A long moment while he gazed at her. "Well," he finally said, "I do not have pressing duties since my job is done." He opened the door and gestured her out.

In the hallway, German soldiers rushed on their errands to and from the recesses of Prestwich Home, where they must have commandeered the rooms for offices. Von Ritter held her firmly by the arm.

The corridor grew colder as they approached a cross hall-way that carried a frigid draft from somewhere, smelling of winter. The *cold cell* Talents, already at work?

They ascended a broad staircase to the next floor. The noises from below became muffled. Here, a lone desk where a soldier sat with a telephone and stacks of paperwork. When they stopped outside a room, von Ritter gestured for the soldier to open the door.

Inside, Rose sat on a cot with a sheet wrapped around her.

"Miss!" She jumped to her feet.

Von Ritter murmured to Kim, "You have five minutes." He waited with her.

A grimy window looked out on the rear of the manor. Rose had been looking outside, by the evidence of where she had swiped clean a small patch on the window.

Kim went to her and took her hands. "Rose. Are you all right? I've been so worried about you."

"Yes, miss. But I want to go 'ome. I want to something fierce."

Kim felt a heaviness pressing down on her. She wished to reassure Rose, but she wouldn't give her false comfort. Promises of going home from von Ritter that might not turn out to be true. She had been guilty of telling Rose half-truths and wouldn't do it again.

"I'm sorry, Rose," she said. "I've made so many mistakes. I wouldn't have brought you here if I'd known how it was going to be."

Rose looked at von Ritter. "Who is 'e, then?"

Kim took a deep breath and stepped away to give Rose a clear view of him. "This is Erich von Ritter."

Von Ritter clicked his heels and bowed. Mocking.

It was very cold in the room. To her consternation, it appeared to be snowing outside. She took off her sweater and handed it to Rose.

"No, miss, you'll be cold. It gets so cold, it 'urts."

Truly, Prestwich was a hellish place. Her time with Rose was brief, too brief to help her feel better. But she had come to apologize, and it had been necessary, for both of them. "Mr. von Ritter will give me another."

Rose looked up sharply at him, as though doubtful he had such gallantry in him.

Von Ritter said, "I will indeed, Rose. I will take good care of your mistress."

Rose didn't look convinced.

Kim wanted to tell her, *We'll be going home. You'll be all right.* But she wasn't sure at all, and she was not going to smooth things over as though Rose wouldn't notice.

Holding the sweater and her sheet, Rose seemed uncertain.

Kim gently took the sheet from her and tossed it on the bed. Then she held out the sweater for Rose to shrug herself into it.

"I hope to see you soon," Kim said as von Ritter led her to the door. "I'm sorry I never brought your apron. I couldn't, but I'm sorry because I did promise."

With that, von Ritter took her by the arm and steered her to the door.

The temperature in the corridors was dropping, the air brittle and smelling of winter. She and von Ritter walked silently back to her cell. Once she was inside, he put his hand on the doorknob, getting ready to leave. He turned back.

"I must tell you something. You will hear the commotion and you will be afraid. I am sorry to tell you, sorry for your sake, but it is not tomorrow, this strike on England." He gestured to the outside wall. "When the storm is at its highest strength, that is our ideal time for the operation."

Kim looked at him in alarm.

"So, it begins soon. Within the hour."

He left her then, as the door shut with a strong click.

So, it wasn't to be May 8. It was May 7. Today. Now. Her mind went white and empty.

At the window, through the bars, she could see a region of hillocks and banks and, moving over them, ragged gray clouds torn free from the mother storm above. Snow drifted down. Along the ridgeline were stunted oaks that a hundred years of strong moor winds had blown almost horizontal. This was country that had seen the worst that nature could hurl, and now it would see the worst that humans could do.

In her mind's eye, the stunted oaks looked like the forms of men. They were massing on the ridgeline, waiting for the signal to charge. Robert was there, riding his black. At Ypres, where the war ended for Robert. The horse stomped and breathed out in great cloudy exhalations. It was another village to take, or rather retake, as the fight traded goals between combatants. Why this village, and why now? Only the generals knew. There were thirty-eight men massing there, and by the end of the charge, how many? Every soldier must have wondered, *Will I live to nightfall?* And then they were advancing, and then charging across the mud-soaked earth, saturated by weeks of rain. They came on. . . .

Kim put her head on the deep sill of the window. It felt like a block of ice. She had seen this event so often in her mind, it no longer varied. She saw her brother's face, his fear and resolve. And Baron, his beloved horse, she saw him too, always the same, pawing the ground, impatient to do what he would have to do. And always, the pitiless rain.

When she turned around, Hugh Aberdare had come into the room.

"I'm sorry to disturb you," he said, incredibly. He was wearing a military-style leather jacket—German, she noted—with a thick sweater. Heavy wool trousers. He was thinner than she remembered, as though his role had worn him down. "It will soon begin out there. You knew?"

"Yes."

He glanced in the direction of where, presumably, the tunnel would touch down. "Georgi always thought I didn't live up to the Aberdare name. Now she'll know what I can do. She'll finally know." He paused, as though he hoped Kim would agree. But she said nothing. "I suppose you hate me now."

It was stunning that, at such a moment, he cared what she thought.

"It isn't that. I was just thinking about my brother, who died for England in Belgium. What was on his mind in the minutes before his unit was wiped out. The terror of it. And now we are just going to open a door and let them in." She went over to sit down on the bed, feeling utterly weary. "It doesn't seem bloody enough."

He had the grace to look down. "Try not to look at it like that. There was a bloody way to do this, and . . . this way. It's for the best, Kim. In a hundred years, who will even care? Who will remember? Lands change hands. It's all politics. And meanwhile, life goes on."

"Herr von Ritter said a similar thing. You two have been together a lot."

He cut a look at her, resentful. "Think of all the young men who died. It wasn't just your brother. You want that again?"

It stung, even from him. But she wouldn't argue.

"I have to go," he said. "I just wanted to say that I always liked you very much. I wish we could have been friends. Maybe we still can."

"I doubt that. But why don't you help me? Von Ritter is likely going to kill me. Just let me out and I'll walk onto the moors and lose myself."

Hugh frowned. "He won't kill you, of that I'm sure."

"Not your life to gamble with, though, is it?"

He hesitated. "Where would you go? There are soldiers everywhere."

She looked toward the window. "The moors." She saw that he was actually wavering. Climbing to her feet, she went to him, grasping his hand. "Let me go, Hugh. I'm by myself, and I have no weapon. Just don't latch the door. That's all you have to do."

He looked stricken. "They will shoot you if you're out there."

She shrugged. "They will shoot me anyway."

He gazed at her. Then he turned and left the room, shutting the door so gently that it did not latch.

THURSDAY, MAY 7, 7:30 PM. She could see some of the hallway through the slightly open door of her room. When by sight and sound she judged the corridor empty, she stepped outside.

Checking to her left, toward the back side of Prestwich

Hall, she saw a soldier with his back to her, looking out a line of windows at the action outside. From that direction she heard muffled shouts and the rumble of engines.

She must get a heavy jacket, or she would not last long enough in the storm to get to a village where she would raise an alarm. She knew where jackets were. In the basement.

Taking a right turn at Dunn's office, she faced the same corridor she had gone down once before in search of Rose. It was deserted. Her heart pounded against her breastbone. Lights burned everywhere, from the ancient chandeliers and the flickering wall sconces, transforming the great keep with a harsh radiance. In patches, the floor shone unnaturally, as though coated in a thin layer of ice.

A clatter of footfalls came from the staircase at the very end of the corridor. She veered off the hallway, rushing through a broad, arched doorway into a great room with furniture covered with sheets. She crouched behind a sofa as a group of German soldiers strode by in the hall, their boots clicking against the flagstone floor. As they passed the room where she hid, she saw that they carried rifles, and one, an officer, a pistol at his hip.

Their footfalls grew fainter. Kneeling on the carpeted floor, she felt the cold seeping up from below like a frigid miasma.

It was dangerous to go back into the hallway. She considered opening a window and trying to make her way across the grounds into the cover of the gorse and stunted oaks. At a large leaded glass window, she looked out. Snow gusted sideways in a strong wind. Faintly, through the curtain of white, she saw sentries walking on the edge of the car park. She opened the casement to get a view down the line of the building.

A churning noise that she had been hearing for the last minutes blasted into the room as a tank shouldered its way through the snow. It was heading straight down the side of the building toward her place at the window. Behind it, coming around from the back of the mansion, another one.

They were already coming through. The panic in her chest now felt like a small animal trying to claw its way out.

She fled the room and ran down the corridor for the stairs to the basement. With the stone floor covered in its icy rime, she lost her footing, falling heavily to the floor. Picking herself up, she lurched onward, barely aware of the sharp ache in her hip from the fall.

Down the narrow stairs she crept, peeking warily around the turn in the stairs to get a clear view of the lower corridor. She stared.

A white fog choked the passageway, with the floor a sheet of corrugated ice. A distant sound of martial music.

Soldiers stood at the far end, four or five of them, talking. She ducked into a service room designated LINENS. Inside, though it was dark, a little light came through the crack at the bottom of the door. Here in this basement was the heart of the cold, surely where the *ice* Talents had been sequestered. The music: to soothe them.

Around her, stacks of sheets, blankets, nurse uniforms and small, institutional pillows.

Her plan was not going to work. Prestwich was miles from the nearest village, and she did not know her way, except to follow the road, which would be carefully watched. Her escape had led her to a dead end in a closet next to the very machine of the invasion.

But that was not quite right. That room down the hall, the one where music blasted from a gramophone—Wagner, of course—was not the engine.

That would be Hugh Aberdare. He was the center of it all, the driving force that linked together every impulse to cold, winter cells, and tunnels of ice. And he must be kept calm.

Von Ritter had said *it is essential for effectiveness.* She was forcibly struck by the idea that, by God, von Ritter had erred again. He had given her a *spill*: Hugh Aberdare must be kept calm. A new plan instantly formed.

She began to strip. Throwing off her shirt and wool pants, she pawed through the nurse uniforms to find one that looked like it would fit a woman her size. She quickly buttoned it with hands already slowing from the cold. Next, an apron pinned to the bodice, with ties around the waist. She shoved her discarded clothes behind the shelf and took down two folded blankets.

With that, she opened the door and stepped into the corridor. Her goal was now to get to Hugh, and the best way to do that was to have the German army help her.

She closed the door rather harder than necessary and began walking toward the stairs, moving slowly.

"Halt!" came the shout. *"Bleiben Sie stehen!"*

Two soldiers ran forward, and one of them took her roughly by the arm.

She looked at him with what she hoped was indignity and not terror. "I've been told to bring these blankets to Lord Daventry."

The second soldier looked her over and strode back to the group he had come from. He spoke to someone else, and this individual came forward. He wore a leather trench coat buttoned high and a visored cap with insignia and silver piping.

"What are you doing here?" the officer asked in excellent English. He looked down at her feet. Unfortunately, she still wore the lace-up boots.

"Herr von Ritter told me to bring Lord Daventry these blankets." She tried to sound annoyed at the disruption of her duties. "And quickly."

The officer paused as her heart drummed hard in her chest. "I suggest you wear a coat, then, *Fräulein*. Yes?"

He jerked his head toward the shelving that lined the hallway, and one of the soldiers brought her a heavy gray-and-black plaid jacket, putting it around her shoulders.

In a dreamlike state, she heard the muffled but stirring choral music. Ice curdled along the exposed pipes in the ceiling. The Germans were smiling.

"*Bringt sie zum Choristen,*" the officer said to the solider.

"*Ja wohl, Herr Oberst.*"

She and her soldier escort climbed the narrow staircase. She retraced her steps down the cavernous hall, the lights glaring, their footfalls echoing. In another minute, they would be outside where the tanks came through, where Hugh was. She would only have a few moments. But she knew exactly what to say. It was what she should have said an hour before when he had come to her in her prison cell. Better late than never.

They turned at the junction of the two main hallways.

In a surreal walk, they proceeded toward the doors at the back of the building. Her fear had retreated to a small, hard kernel in her chest. Oddly, another emotion enveloped her in a warm embrace. Relief. She was finally doing what she should.

In front of the doors leading outside, she struggled into the wool coat while at the same time holding the blankets.

She and the soldier passed through the great rear doors of Prestwich Hall. Once outside, an icy wind scoured against her face and bare hands. The raw smell of gasoline assaulted her, along with the loud groaning of armored vehicles rumbling across the landscape. Heavy snow, blown sideways by the wind, blasted the scene. She squinted to see through the white veil, noting the lines of soldiers snaking through the convoys, their faces and uniforms plastered with snow.

Amid this polar scene, there reared up, as tall as Prestwich Hall, a brilliant hole like the entrance to a cave. A great knot of snow and wind twisted around and around, forming what she could now see was a tunnel. This was the tunnel that von Ritter had spoken of, and it was spilling its contents. As Kim watched, out of this hole appeared the enormous barrel of an artillery gun grinding forward, self-propelled. It emerged from the snowy maw and passed in front of her, moving toward a massive formation of trucks and equipment in the valley to the west of the manor.

This was the *way* that von Ritter had spoken of. Standing there in awe, in horror, she could not take her eyes off of it. The hole, the doorway through which now an armored vehicle on treads churned its way, was not a quiet thing. It produced a high whine, a zinging sound that Kim had sometimes heard from deep ice on a lake.

No one had guessed what Talents could do. What it would look like when the *bloom* went mad. Here was what it looked like.

She must go forward, to find Hugh. "Where is Lord Daventry?" she shouted at the soldier through the deafening sounds around her. Even though he did not speak English, he must have recognized the name, because he pointed to something she had not seen at first. A small, covered platform barely visible through the heavy veil of snow. Her escort pulled her into the controlled mayhem of the yard. Frigid winds slipped off of the churning tunnel and buffeted Kim as she and the soldier made their way forward. A tank crashed through the *way*, finding traction and clattering onward in a gout of black smoke into a slurry of mud and snow.

They crossed the yard, weaving among trucks mounted with guns and lumbering vehicles on treads.

Hugh's back was to them, and he was surrounded by men in uniform, all watching as the vehicles churned by the platform, coming from the white funnel. As Kim came around to the platform, she saw into the maelstrom.

Outside it was a maddened funnel, but inside, a still and icy presence, immaculate except for its issue, the engines of war, and soldiers riding them, marching with them.

Overhead, the sky flashed yellow-green. It lit up Hugh's face, giving it the cast of someone frozen to death. He sat on a bench, with his eyes closed. He was a man who had betrayed his country, who was willing to allow the slaughter of the English people, who could not identify the Nazi worldview as corrupt and horrific.

But he was also a man who depended on someone, cared for someone who felt nothing in return. His sister.

"I brought you a blanket," she called from the bottom of the stairs. The officers standing there converged on Kim and two of them restrained her.

He opened his eyes. "No. Let her come."

The soldiers released her and she went up the few stairs to his protected perch.

"You see?" he said, gesturing to the *way*. "Isn't it beautiful?" He looked at her with the pride of authorship, of creation.

She began to shake out the blankets, taking her time to smooth them over Hugh's lap. "I'm afraid there's something I didn't tell you. It's about Georgi."

That got his attention, as a flash of worry crossed his otherwise rigid face. "Is she all right?"

"Yes. But she betrayed you. She told us what you were up to. That you had taken German money and gone to Germany to practice making this tunnel. Thanks to her, I have your bank receipts to prove it. She was very disappointed in you. She said it was no more than she could expect from a pathetic creature like you."

"She wouldn't say that. Georgi wouldn't."

"But she did." Looking up, she saw von Ritter was rushing toward them from the manor.

"Georgi repeated it several times. *Pathetic creature.*"

"It's not true! It's not."

"I'm sorry, but it is. She told me that you could never do anything right, and now you were going to disgrace the Aberdare name. She knew that what you were doing was a hanging offense, but she turned you in."

He fixed a look on her, half-despairing, half-blameful. "Why would you say these things?"

She smoothed the last blanket over his knees. "Oh, Hugh. You know why. Because it's the truth. Georgi never cared about you. She despises you and always has."

He moaned, shaking his head.

Von Ritter rushed up the steps, his face a mask of fury.

She turned calmly to him. "I brought Hugh a blanket."

He struck her viciously on the side of the head, sending her crashing to the wood floor of the platform.

Hugh shook off the blankets and, rising, staggered back toward the steps. The sky began to darken. Crouching now, still unable to stand, Kim saw the bright glare of the *way* subside like a fast-approaching dusk. There was a pause in the winds. Nothing came forth from the tunnel.

Shouts in German greeted this faltering.

On the platform, their attentions were grabbed by something in the distance. The crackle of gunfire. From the crest of the hill to the west, people were shooting. Kim saw figures on the ridgeline. This time, it was not her imagination. Outlined against the milky sky, two tanks with their turrets pointed down the hill.

Tanks. British tanks.

Kim struggled to her feet as the first shells exploded deafeningly among the German transports and tanks. Massed together, they were caught without room to maneuver. But they could still return fire and now did so with ear-shattering effect.

Nearby, the spiral of ice was gone. Von Ritter stared in that direction as though willing it back to life. But that feat could only be accomplished by Hugh Aberdare, whose peace and calm lay shattered.

The German officers around them had scattered. Soldiers ran frantically to join their units, those that had managed to come through before the *way* failed.

Von Ritter grabbed Kim by the elbow, hauling her roughly to her feet. He pulled out his pistol. Oh God, he was going to kill her. Here on the platform, it was her last moment. She turned to face him, to meet his gaze, her terror colder than the snow that laced down from the sky.

Instead, von Ritter turned his gun on Hugh, who was looking toward the vanished tunnel, trying and failing to resume his command of ice.

"Do it," von Ritter commanded. "Bring it back." He had apparently forgotten that what Hugh needed was calm.

"I can't," Hugh moaned.

Von Ritter cocked the gun.

"You can't kill me. I'm a 10."

"Yes," von Ritter said, "but now you will belong to the British." He shoved the barrel of the gun against Hugh's head and fired. A red hole appeared in Lord Daventry's forehead. He fell, sprawling backward.

42

PRESTWICH HOME,
NORTH YORK MOORS

THURSDAY, MAY 7, 7:49 PM. From a third-story window of Prestwich, through the open casement window, Julian trained his rifle on the little hut set up in front of the bright hole from which, to his utter consternation, a stream of armored units was pouring. The Germans had directed their bridge there, to the far west side of the moors. To Prestwich Home. It was audacious and brilliant. How they could have done so was a question for another time, but the evidence that it was in fact what they were doing lay before him in the line of military equipment and personnel coming seemingly out of nowhere, to form up on the moors. And that meant that the marshaling of defenses on the coast was disastrously in the wrong place.

He aimed the rifle, waiting for his shot at Hugh Aberdare, who was moving back and forth, pacing. Julian would have only one or two shots before they converged on his position in the room overlooking the yard. He waited for Hugh to stop pacing.

The man did, but now there was someone in the way, an army officer.

Julian waited.

He had spent the last hour making his way through the perimeter and into Prestwich Hall, breaking a ground-level window. The snowstorm was excellent cover, as was the commotion coming from the back of the manor, which he now knew was the *Wehrmacht* coming through. Better yet would have been a full-scale assault by the army units out of Catterick, even as feeble as they might be, but he had beat them to the moors. Once inside Prestwich, he had found an intense scene of German soldiers, barked orders and hurried movement. He had moved with slow and nerve-wracking stealth, waiting for passages to clear as more attention became focused on what was occurring outside.

Now, at the window in his upper-story room, he glanced down at the floor, where Dunn was tied fast with strips of sheet from the room's hospital bed. Gagged and trussed, the man watched him with hatred. Julian had spent valuable minutes finding the man and getting him up to the third floor, minutes he feared he did not have to waste, but he had needed information. Dunn had suffered before giving up the information that Julian asked for, that Hugh Aberdare was the man on the platform. Julian had broken six of Dunn's fingers before getting all the information he needed. He had guessed it would only take two. *Never underestimate the enemy.*

He had Kim's room number and would grab her as soon as he had taken out Hugh Aberdare. He had made clear that if Dunn was lying about which room Kim was in, he would return to resume his interrogation.

"Where is Rose?" Julian asked as he knelt by the window.

When he looked at Dunn, the man winced. Dunn garbled something through the gag.

"One grunt for ground floor, two for first, three for second."

Dunn indicated it was the floor just below him.

All right, then—he had his next objective. He resumed his aim along the rifle barrel, waiting. Then he saw two people, one a soldier, approaching the platform. The other was his daughter. She wore a white dress that hung below a gray coat, and at this distance of some hundred yards, in the middle of a snowstorm, he could barely see her face. But it was she. A man knows his own daughter.

Kim. Somehow, they had brought her out. The snow came furiously as he strained to watch. Sheets of green lightning flickered, bruising the snow that covered everything. There were now several people on the platform. When he got a clear shot, he was ready to fire.

Then, with a startling suddenness, gunfire came from the ridge to the west. The hill lit up with a fierce volley, aimed into the midst of the massed German tanks. *By God*, Julian thought with elation, *the Catterick Garrison*. The army had gotten there at last. A British tank hove into view, cresting the hill. Catterick's tank corps. Still, it could not be as large as what the Germans already had amassed here.

Mortar fire erupted from the British tank, striking what must have been a fuel tank in the staging area. An angry ball of fire mushroomed up as German troops scrambled to bring artillery to bear upon the British position.

Julian's attention swung back to the platform. One part of his brain noted that the hole in the sky was gone, or appeared to be. The rest of his attention focused on a commotion on the platform. The German officers gathered there were gesturing wildly and milling, ruining his chance for a kill shot. He could no longer identify Hugh Aberdare among them. Nor Kim. Then he spotted her. Someone was running with her toward the side yard, away from the hilltop where the British forces had appeared. Losing sight of them along the line of the manor, he slipped out of the room, determined to follow.

In his immediate vicinity on this floor, all was still. From the lower floors he heard shouts and the pounding of boots. In the confusion of the British attack, no one stopped him as he rushed down the stairs. On the ground floor, pandemonium. He hurried, along with most of the others, toward the rear of Prestwich Home.

On the long back veranda, he emerged into the chaos of the German encampment scrambling to maneuver and return fire. A German armored personnel carrier lumbered by, rushing to battle as the hill lit up with artillery fire. From below, anti-tank guns stuttered.

He moved along the back of the manor, in the direction he'd seen Kim being dragged.

Around him raged the chaotic sounds of artillery fire and the roar of huge unmuffled engines. Julian ran into the yard, shoving his way through German soldiers rushing in the opposite direction. The brilliant blue-white of the sky had gone, but the storm still raged. A Panzer clambered slowly by with a loud clatter of rolling treads, its turret already rotating toward the crest of the ridge, bringing to bear its 50mm gun. Mud churned up from its track, splattering against Julian as he ran.

Then, up ahead, he spied Kim again. She had fallen and was struggling with a man in civilian dress. She resisted him, but at last he pulled her to her feet.

He followed them around the end of the building, where he

saw them getting into a black Mercedes. He was close enough now to see who her captor was. Erich von Ritter, the man he'd shadowed at the races at Newmarket, the operative who had eluded SIS for weeks. Julian took aim with his pistol as von Ritter paused, alone, on the driver's side. He fired. Von Ritter returned fire. Blood from Julian's hands and neck splattered against his jacket as he took stone shrapnel off the manor wall.

The Mercedes roared away down a side road. Unthinkably, he had missed taking down his target.

RIEVAULX ABBEY,

NORTH YORK MOORS

THURSDAY, MAY 7, 8:02 PM. Gray rain. The car had emerged suddenly from the swirling snow and ice-clad ground.

Von Ritter drove, one hand on the steering wheel, the other pointing a gun at Kim. The exchange of gunfire had been terrifying. It must have been English soldiers who fired at von Ritter, but why would they single him out?

They had left the German storm behind. What remained was a plain storm of heavy spring rain and a lowering sky. They climbed a steep road farther into the moors of moss green and dusky lavender.

Now he would kill her. She had used what she knew to crush Hugh's spirit. But she thought she would never forget the anguish on his face as he heard Georgi's summation of him. *Pathetic creature*. Watching him die gave her no satisfaction, but seeing the *way* evaporate, drained of its power and deprived of its *chorister*—that moment would remain with her forever.

Von Ritter stopped the car. It was then that she noticed the blood. It leaked from under his leather jacket onto the seat beside him.

"Get out of the car," he said. He noted her look of alarm and shook his head. "Not yet, my Kim."

Her mind leaden with fear, she opened the door and stepped out. He was right behind her.

"Now we get in the other side." They walked around to the right-hand side of the car, where he got in first, pulling her after him. "You must drive," he said.

She turned to him. "Give yourself up, Erich." She had avoided using his first name, but now . . . she thought he was dying. All this time, she had tried to remain aloof from him, and she had succeeded, barely. But in truth, their stories were now tightly wound together. Erich, then. "It's over now," she said gently.

"Drive onward, into the valley. It is just ahead."

"What is?"

He pointed out the windshield, and his eyes were black with determination. She drove on.

Presently, they came around the shoulder of a hill to face a prospect of a glen protected by low hills. Before them lay a ghostly scene: a ruined abbey seen through a curtain of rain lit silver by the westering sun. This was Rievaulx Abbey, the fabulous twelfth-century Gothic ruin. She had been there several times but had forgotten it was so close to Prestwich.

But why had they come there? Did he have a doorway hidden in this ancient church, or some Talent that he had not yet shown her? She would not have been surprised to learn anything that the German army could do, now that she had seen the *ice* way.

He gestured her to get out of the car. She thought of slamming the door at him as he followed her out that side of the car, but he followed too closely, giving her no chance.

"They will follow us. They saw us leave."

"Yes." He looked up to the magnificent ruined walls of Rievaulx. The rain began to ease, washing the stately ruins with a romantic blur. "Beautiful, is it not?"

A colonnade of pillars formed the long side of the abbey, each one peaked in Gothic style and marching toward the chancel, where the altar had been. The Cistercian monks had built the place far from human habitation, in the most serene valley they had ever seen. All these centuries, it was this remote location that had protected its stones from being carted away.

"Why are we here?"

Gun still drawn, he pushed her gently along the side of the abbey, past the tall, empty lancet windows pointing toward heaven. She saw that he was having difficulty. He must be in very great pain.

He directed her around the side of the church toward another part of the ruins. "There," he said. "The refectory."

It was the monks' dining hall, its arcading walls repeating the patterns of the church.

Her coat had become sodden in the rain, but because it was wool, she was not desperately cold. Von Ritter, however, had begun to shake.

"Sit over there," he said. As she did so, he knelt down with great difficulty next to a metal suitcase hidden behind a shard of fallen masonry. As he opened it up, she saw that it was full of wires and canisters. A trunk of explosives.

He had set his gun on the ground beside him, but it was within quick reach. He worked over the suitcase, breathing laboriously. "They will come for us soon, I believe. They will die."

An ache of fear sat on her chest. "So will you."

"Oh, yes." As he worked, he kept the lid of the chest tented at an angle over the contents. "It will be a very great explosion. A good way to die, I think." He looked up at her, with a stab of a smile. "One always has a plan to fall back to. And beyond that plan, yet another. The progress of war is never sure." He braced his hand on a carved stone buried in the grass as his voice fell to a whisper. "So. I came here and placed the trunk. In case of need."

He would wait for the soldiers to surround them and then he would set off the explosives. She looked at the suitcase with its bristling wires and did not think it a good way to die, blown apart in some unthinkable bloom of fire. Her heart thudded. They would be there any moment.

At last he finished, sitting on the ground facing her with his back to a fallen piece of carved stone. Out from the suitcase snaked a braid of wires leading to a small box with a toggle switch.

"Are you cold? Take my jacket." He unzipped the heavy leather jacket but was too weak to shrug it off.

She shook her head.

"Kim. Do not be afraid. I would not like for you to be afraid."

"But this is your revenge for what I did."

"What did you say to Hugh that broke his will?"

She told him.

"Ah." He closed his eyes against the pain. "Brilliant. You won over us all. I salute you."

The rain had stopped, and a quasi-dusk fell on the ruins, the last sunlight glistening on the stones.

His voice was only a murmur. "It is noble for you to die for your country. When you came to me in London . . . you understood that you would die. Did you not?"

She listened in dread for the sounds of cars on the road.

"And now," he said, "you can at last make it up to Robert."

It was startling to hear him say her brother's name. "Make up for what?"

"For living."

Cold tears sprang to her eyes. How did he know her so well?

"Come," he said. "Die with me, my Valkyrie." A brief, affectionate smile came to his lips. "Sit next to me for a last minute, yes?"

He held the little box in his hand. She might get the gun from him, but the merest flick of his hand and the trunk would explode. It was exceedingly strange, but she did not want to die huddled alone, facing her enemy, separated from any human feeling except terror.

She crawled over to him, taking off her coat. He moved the gun to the far side of his body. She sat next to him, placing the wool coat around their legs.

"Is it dusk?" he whispered. "I can't tell if it is the light or it is my eyes."

"Night is coming."

"It is so peaceful here," he said. "The monks chose well."

"They believed in it all. In God, in peace." But her thoughts weren't with the monks but with Robert. She wondered if she would see him again. She chose to believe it.

From beyond the abbey, she heard the cars approach. "Do it now," she whispered. "Before they get here. Just you and me. No need to include others."

He turned to her, but whether he could see her through his now cloudy eyes, she did not know.

"My Yorkshire heroine," he whispered. "But. If we do this, no one will know your story. It . . . deserves to be known."

Voices came from the church ruins.

"Kim." His eyes were closed, but he managed to say, "Go now. I think you have . . . tasted enough of this horror."

Her voice broke. "Go?"

"Quickly."

She could hear the soldiers searching the abbey.

Von Ritter stared into the ruins of the refectory. She wasn't sure he could see any longer. He was giving her this chance to leave. But she paused. The suitcase.

Crawling around to the other side of him, she put her hand on the box he held. He looked up at her.

"It is one of the great abbeys of England," she said. "This place."

He made a small smile and released his grip on the box.

Taking it, she tucked it and the attaching wires into the suitcase, clicking it shut.

"Goodbye, Erich," she said softly.

He found his pistol on the ground and placed it on his thigh, hand on the trigger.

Standing up, she found that she could carry the weight of the suitcase. She left Erich von Ritter sitting there on the ground, propped against a large stone, staring into the beautiful ruins.

Within a few steps, the soldiers saw her and ordered her to stop.

"Bomb," she said looking at a British soldier. "Stay back. This is a bomb."

The soldier backed off and she began walking to the east, away from the abbey, away from the refectory, toward the hill.

"Kim." It was her father. Where had he come from? He approached her. "Put the suitcase down."

She looked at him, trying to stir herself awake from the stunned dream she found herself in.

In the direction of the refectory, a gunshot split the silence. It was a sound that she feared would haunt her in the years to come, that sharp report of a gun, coming from the ruins. Night was falling rapidly now, as though once dusk had begun, it must gather velocity.

"Kim," Julian said again.

"I think it's a very large bomb," she finally said, standing with the suitcase, facing off with her father and about two dozen soldiers gathered by the transept of the church.

Gently, Julian took the suitcase from her. "Go back to the road."

"Where will you take it?"

"To the woods."

She was dressed only in a white nurse's uniform with ankle-high boots a size too large. When she walked into the shadow of the abbey's chancel walls, the cold hit her hard. She began to shake.

A soldier put a blanket around her shoulders. "It's a very large bomb," she repeated. When they absorbed this, they began to withdraw from the abbey.

After a few minutes, she saw Julian emerge from the stand of trees. He was met by several soldiers. They had set up some kind of large gun on a stand. Then they fired in the direction where Julian had taken the trunk of explosives. With a profound roar, a blast erupted that sent them all to the ground, even at a distance of two hundred yards. Trees flattened, and those that remained standing lit up like torches as black smoke drifted across the ruins.

She watched for him in the roiling smoke. It occurred to her that she did love her father and hoped it would not be too late to tell him.

At last, a few figures emerged from the cauldron of smoke. Soldiers. And Julian. He walked toward her. It was odd to see him here, in the abbey, among the soldiers. They embraced. He smelled of char and gunpowder. It was wonderful.

When they separated, he asked, very quietly, "How did you get the suitcase from him?"

"He was dying and decided to go alone."

Julian nodded. He seemed content to let the story wait.

"The Germans have tanks. . . ." she said, looking off in the direction of Prestwich Hall.

"Yes. There was actually a fight going on when I got there. But these army chaps tell me our forces have them in hand now. Odd that they managed to get tanks here, and that they thought a few would do much damage."

She looked at him blankly. Where to start? She was too tired to even begin.

"Let's get you home. There are people who will want to talk to you about what you know. But later." He took her by the elbow, but she held back, gazing at the natural ruins of Rievaulx.

"It's all right to live," she said.

"Yes," Julian said. "It is."

"The dead know that they will see us sometime soon."

Julian looked at her as though he understood. Then he put his arm around her and she let him walk her down to the road.

43

SIS HEADQUARTERS, LONDON

MONDAY, MAY 11. Julian and Kim didn't make it to Uxley that night. Julian recognized signs of concussion and took Kim to the hospital in York, where she was now recovering from an ugly dose of phencyclidine and a blow to the head that Erich von Ritter had given her on the *chorister* stand at Prestwich.

Julian was on leave, but with Kim in hospital, he spent a day in London, debriefing with E, who was now reinstated in his office.

The pieces had come together regarding the events at Prestwich on the moors, primarily from Kim's debriefing carried out over the first two days of her hospital stay. Art Lowry, the service's deputy director, had supervised the debriefing, aided by Elsa, who insisted on being there. She had been brought in a wheelchair. Lowry said she had not been in a good mood at all, both because of her injuries and also because of the fact that she had allowed Lena Mueller to throw an SIS agent from a train.

Julian was still trying to grasp the idea that his daughter, using her wits and cunning, had prevented Hugh Aberdare from directing the invasion. The invasion by *ice* bridge, which Kim clarified was really a tunnel.

His daughter. This would take awhile.

E sat behind his desk, looking as though he had aged. That was the thing about the intelligence service: when you lived for SIS and no longer had a place in it, you started to go downhill. That was why Elsa went to Kim's debriefing, just to remind the service that she wasn't an old lady with a broken leg and shoulder.

"We missed you, chief," Julian said.

"Apparently, you got on quite well without me." E was pleased with Julian, delighted with the downfall of Heath Millington, and chagrined to have missed the action. "You got nicked a bit with that shrapnel, though."

"A few scratches," he acknowledged. One on his neck had taken a few stitches. "The operation would have gone much easier if you hadn't been lounging about down at Litchfield." Julian smiled at his old friend. "And Olivia was fighting mad. We should have given her a pistol and sent her to the War Office. It might have saved some time."

Ah yes, Olivia. He'd have to find a way to broach that subject with E. And perhaps now was the time, with his reputation enjoying a temporary burnish.

"I'm afraid Olivia and I—"

E waved off his confession. "Yes. She told me. Offered her resignation if I wanted it. I told her I'd sooner have yours."

Julian nodded agreeably. "Please accept my resignation."

"Refused. But I warned her it's dangerous to be associated with you. You will be discreet, Julian."

"Yes, sir."

"And your maid. The intrepid Rose Babbage. She has recovered from her ordeal?"

"Very good of you to ask. I drove up to Prestwich that same night of the attack and brought her home. She seems to be handling it so far. I imagine it will take both her and Kim some time to recover."

E leaned back in his chair, turning the conversation to a new tack. "The CID met this morning. I thought you should hear the outcome of the discussion on the Prestwich Affair." That was how they were referring to *Sturmweg*.

Based on the fact that nothing truthful about *Sturmweg* had appeared in the papers since Friday, Julian had already guessed what Whitehall's approach would be.

"It will be treated as though it never happened," E said, barely disguising his contempt. "As far as the public is concerned, there was a freak ice storm on the moors. An ordnance explosion near Rievaulx. An accident."

"How is it possible to hide a dozen German tanks and hundreds of German soldiers?"

"War games. They use the moors for training all the time." E shrugged. "Repaint the tanks a nice British brown. I don't know. The army will do what they're told. The German soldiers . . ." He shrugged. "I suspect they have been quietly shipped home."

"And Hugh Aberdare's death? He happened to be out walking on the moors when a tank opened fire?"

"Georgiana has agreed to say that it was a traffic accident in York. She's as anxious as Whitehall is to keep this affair secret."

"What will they do with Angus Dunn?"

"I expect he will be hanged at Wandsworth after a very speedy review."

"It will leak out. Someone is bound to talk."

E shook his head. "They're mopping the whole thing up quite thoroughly. But if someone talks, it must not be us."

"It won't be. But the thing is, I would have thought that Stanley Baldwin would want credit for saving the country."

"It's not how they see it. They are more concerned that a peer of the realm betrayed England, and at the last minute, the army rushed to defend the coast while the real assault came on the North York Moors."

"This would have been our best moment to convince Parliament to rearm," Julian said, unwilling to leave it alone.

"Baldwin's afraid that rearmament will bankrupt the country. And the public won't stand for it. They believe if you build an army, you will use it. Use their boys for cannon fodder."

"So, when the Germans come at us again, we shall be just as unprepared."

E had picked up the paperweight on his desk and was examining it. "Not precisely." He glanced up with sly expression. "There's Monkton Hall. They'll have a rather large expansion of their budget. Their research will have top priority." He turned the paperweight over in his hand, letting the light from the window prism onto his desk. "The War of the Talents. We'll be fighting that one, at least. And Monkton Hall will be the jewel in the crown."

Julian nodded. There was great satisfaction in that. And he could see the logic: it was a damn sight cheaper than building up the armed forces. But: "What about Fitzroy Blum?"

"He's under the King's protection. There is no evidence that will stand up, but we have enough doubts about him that he's done for in the service. He'll be shipped off to an assignment where he can't do us damage."

He put the paperweight down and frowned. "Your daughter." E shook his head. "You'll keep your cover with her."

"Probably for the best." It was best for SIS, but if he could not tell her his job, he at least was done playing the fascist around her. He had two layers of deceit, the job and his political persuasion. Perhaps he could not have a close relationship with her, but at least it did not have to be an ugly one.

"You have your cover story for how you got up to Prestwich?"

"She thinks that I heard from the housekeeper that she was going up to Prestwich Home to check on Rose. As it happened, she did lie about where she was going when she went to York."

"She'll know that you saw the German units, saw them using the ice tunnel. What are you telling her you made of *that*?"

"I've told her that it appeared to be an unusual event, and that I'm betting it had to do with Talents, because what else could it have been? Some super Talent that the Germans used to move an advance force in. And that I've been interviewed and told not to discuss it."

"You think you can keep all the lies straight, then, if we invite her into the service?"

"Of course."

E shook his head. "All I have to do is tell Lydia I can't discuss it, and that's that."

Julian did wonder how much he told his mistress, though.

E went on. "Are you sure you want to go through with this?"

"I'm going to let her make up her own mind."

If Kim wanted to hunt out Nazi spies, she would be allowed to do so. She would be carefully groomed to continue her service, since it had already been spectacular. But she would be firmly under the control of the Office. Owen Cherwell had been thoroughly vetted, and though they weren't done, if he passed muster, he would run Kim and other operatives he might recruit out of Monkton Hall. And Julian would be his handler. Kim was never to come to SIS headquarters, a likely enough stricture since none of the field agents except Julian did.

"It's a dangerous profession," E said pointedly, still on the topic of his daughter.

Kim had almost died at Rievaulx. Harp, their agent at Luckenwalde, had been executed by the Gestapo. How did you decide whether to let someone risk their life? But you didn't decide for someone else. Not even when she was your daughter.

He had thought it through. She had been at loose ends up until now. He wouldn't take away from her this new passion, her mission to use her Talent. Some people searched very hard for meaning, and no one more than those who had lost sons and brothers in the Great War. He wouldn't deprive her of that.

E was not giving up. "She has a strong *spill* Talent. How will you, how *do* you keep from telling her your secrets?"

"We don't talk much." To change the subject, Julian asked, "What will Heath Millington do now?"

E kept his tone neutral. "I've heard he fancies being a gentleman farmer. Rye. Flax. Pigs. That sort of thing."

"Good to hear," Julian said, trying to picture it and failing.

WRENFELL HOUSE, EAST YORKSHIRE

THURSDAY, MAY 14. Kim rested on the couch in the parlor, her legs covered by a small blanket. There was so little to do that she had found that the LNER train timetable was not quite adequate. She still kept it on the coffee table, of course, but today she was well into a meaty little book, *Conversational German.* You never knew these days when it would be useful, perhaps even save one's life, to know a bit of German.

Walter came into the parlor without knocking. He was forever surprising one where he might show up. "Someone's coom to see you. Name of Cherwell, so 'e says."

She gave a start of surprise. "Oh, thank you, Walter! Do have him come in."

Walter paused in the doorway. They had made a peace of sorts. He was under the impression that she had gone to Prestwich Home to retrieve Rose, which of course had been a miserable lie, and now—especially given that she had been injured in the doing—she was redeemed in his eyes.

"You won't chase him off with a hoe?"

A twitch of his mouth. Not quite a smile, but the little joke was shared, she felt.

"No, I reckon not. An' Mr. Tavistock rung up sayin' 'e'll be 'ome this afternoon. Mrs. Babbage is doin' up a roast."

He swung back into the hall, and in another moment, Owen Cherwell entered.

She stood up to greet him, taking him by the hands. "You shouldn't have come," she admonished him.

"I was afraid that you wouldn't remember my visit to you in hospital."

"Of course I remember." She went to the door to close it.

They settled in, eager to talk but aware that even there, for security reasons, they could not say all they wished. Owen looked flushed and energetic. He relished the role that he had been asked to play, and it seemed to give him special pleasure that she would work with him.

"Are you sure about our new venture?" he asked.

"I believe we discussed this in hospital."

"I wasn't sure you'd remember."

"I remember everything, so please do stop saying that."

Yes, remembering everything was one reason she was still on the sofa in Wrenfell's parlor six days after Rievaulx. She had been retracing the events of the last three weeks in her mind, to remind herself how it had all wound up, and then how it had all unraveled. The things done well and those that had gone amiss. The events seemed a bit murky, as though they had happened a long time before, or just yesterday, seen through a curtain of snow. She thought about how they had unfairly dismissed Rose, and how she had been the one to give them the key piece. How Kim had taken the project in her own hands when Owen was afraid for her, how she had finally trusted Alice, how Miss Drummond had come through in the end, and how—she'd been told—old Harry Parslow, friend of her grandfather and inmate at Prestwich, had survived the battle on the moors—as Lena with her *darkening* had not. Most of all, she thought about Erich von Ritter and wondered what he would have been like if he had been English and had not come into prominence when a madman ruled his country. He had let her go at the end. Not that he had had any right to have her at gunpoint in the first place, but given what they had been through, including how she had ruined all his hopes, he had still let her go. It was a redemption of sorts. Perhaps the monks had worked their miracles.

"You went somewhere, just then," Owen said. With the window backlighting him, his hair stood out in a halo around his head.

"Oh, I did, didn't I."

"Miss Drummond sends her best wishes for your recovery." He nodded meaningfully. "She heard about your bad fall at Prestwich."

Meaning she knew everything. "That's very kind of her. Does she have a first name?"

Owen suppressed a smile. "Probably not. How is Rose getting on?"

"I'm not sure. She seems happy to be home. But I don't know what she makes of her experience at Prestwich. Or with the little storms. We do have to help her."

She explained to Owen her idea that if Rose could be tested, she could start to learn what Talents were, and that she needn't hide hers—from her parents, at least. Owen agreed to give it a try. "If you will be there too," he said.

He went on. "Alice will be tested."

"Yes, she told me. But isn't Fitz afraid that someone with *trauma view* would see his schemes?"

"He's a *natural defender*, though."

Oh, right, she thought.

"And I did tell you that Fitz has been assigned elsewhere where he can't do any damage."

Now she remembered. Fitz Blum wasn't in prison, but he was now a known German agent and would be removed from his post. Owen counted that as almost more important than thwarting the invasion of England.

"Take a few more days," Owen said. "No need to dash into the fray so soon."

"Is there a fray?" she asked with a little spike of hope.

He smiled. "All in good time, my dear. All in good time."

Damn, he was trying to control her again. But there was no hurry, she supposed. And *verdammt*, German was devilishly hard to learn. "Who will you report to at Whitehall?" She knew he was to work for the intelligence service, but she and Owen wouldn't refer to it except under complete security.

"You don't need to know. You *can't* know. It's how they make sure that the whole network doesn't fall down when one person is under . . ."

"Torture? Owen, stop coddling me. I've seen more people murdered than you have."

He blinked. "By George, that's true. Well. In any case, if you don't know names, you can't give them up."

"But I know *your* name."

"I'm sure you'd swallow poison before you'd give me up."

"I could be ready for a new assignment in a few days," she said.

"Except that the side of your face looks like a dairy cow put a hoof in it."

Kim put a hand to her temple, where she kept forgetting she had a bruise the size of a plate, from when von Ritter had struck her on the reviewing platform.

"I'll walk you to the door," she said. "I have that valise for you." Georgi Aberdare's paisley valise stuffed with money. She could hardly wait to get it out of the house. She had been expecting to be hauled in on charges and have to explain her role under harsh interrogation. In the end, they had believed everything, and rather easily, she thought, given how strange the whole episode had been.

She felt, oddly, as though both the authorities and she and Owen had been working for the same thing all along, with her story only confirming what they had already suspected.

And also, for some reason, she felt wonderfully *British*.

"Rose, can you stay a moment?"

Dressed in a flowered shift with her ruffled white apron, Rose had brought in a plate of scones. "Yes, miss."

Kim urged a scone on Rose, but it was too much for her to take in, sitting in the parlor and taking tea with Miss Tavistock.

"I wanted to say again that I'm sorry for what happened. I should have protected you from Prestwich Home, but I didn't know how. That's no excuse, but I feel very badly about it."

Rose twisted her hands in her lap.

"Sometimes people make mistakes," Kim went on.

At that, Rose looked up at her. "I know! Like when I took me clothes off tha' time."

"Yes, like that. But I need to say that I'm most dreadfully sorry. And I hope you will forgive me."

"Like the vicar says? Dinna cast stones?"

"Oh, yes, Rose! Like that." She pushed the plate of scones a bit closer, and this time, Rose took one.

"And I have an idea for something we can do together. It's about your Talent."

"Talent?"

"Yes, of the *cold cell*. The little storms."

Rose stopped eating.

"Because I have a Talent too."

"Like the storms?"

"No. Not like that. It's a different one. We can talk about it, Rose. Because we don't have to hide anymore. Not if you don't want to hide."

Rose nodded. "You dinna make storms like me?"

"No. My Talent's just small. While you eat your scone, I'll tell you all about it."

44

TUESDAY, MAY 19. The day came, and it was not too long after Owen Cherwell's visit, when Kim had had enough of books and timetables.

Setting out for a walk, she left by the back door, through the garden where the first climbing roses along the fence were surging into bloom.

Shadow and Flint found her and they raced ahead. If she was going south out of the yard, they knew where she was headed. Flint claimed precedent as the bigger dog, but Shadow did not give up on the idea that he needed herding in the right direction, and watching their game, Kim hadn't noticed that someone had come up behind her.

"Mind if I tag along?"

Julian was dressed in his hunting jacket and Wellingtons, having spent the morning with Walter currying briar and

AT THE TABLE OF WOLVES

discussing plans for the piggery, notions that took root every winter and, every summer, died away.

"No, I don't mind." She could not remember the last time she had taken a walk with her father. Or perhaps she knew exactly when it had been.

Julian looked at the porte cochere, with the building materials still waiting on their pallets. "From this angle, it does look like it might collapse."

"As I've been saying," she said, putting a smile into it.

"I hope you won't give up on the old place."

She glanced at him, wondering at his new tone, his sudden interest in the renovations. "I think the old place needs me."

"I'll take that for a yes."

They made their way past the Babbages' cottage and the vacant piggery and into the paddock. The valley had finally burst into full spring, its surrounding green heights hazy in the noon sun. Undulating across the flanks of the hills was the checkered pattern of cultivated fields.

As they walked, she asked, "Do you think you'll be seeing much of Georgi Aberdare?"

He quirked a look at her. "No, probably not. Why do you ask?"

"I don't know. She's really not your type."

He nodded in good humor. "Well, then. If you think not."

That set a companionable tone, and they continued on until they came to the edge of the wooded fell leading down to Abbey Pond. A thick carpet of pine needles gave up its honeyed scent as they descended.

Shadow and Flint crashed ahead of them, leaping down the slope. She wanted to tell them not to rush, not to cross out onto the ice; it might not hold them, and there might be wolves. But of course, there was no such thing. It was May, and even the patches of snow that had hidden under the trees so long this spring had vanished, feeding the crocus and mushrooms whose time it was.

She and Julian found the overgrown path around the lake and strolled along it. A gentle breeze scalloped the lake's surface, and when Flint jumped in at the edge, his plunge sent waves into the distance.

Uncharacteristically, her father had been home for a week, and they had fallen into a pattern of reading together in the parlor, where he refrained from smoking his pipe until she asked him to please stop treating her like an invalid. Yesterday, she had taken the liberty of reading to him some of her mother's letter, and he had smiled at the amusing parts.

But now, as they settled onto a fallen log to watch the pond, she risked spoiling the rapprochement.

"Why, really, did you bring me down here that day?" She had never asked him before, had never spoken of the animal shelter incident again after that cold winter morning when she had been brought to see the bodies on the ice.

He filled his pipe and tapped it down. "Because I wanted you to know the truth."

"I was eleven years old."

"The whole village knew," he said, as though that explained everything.

"You could have told me that the animals died." From the distance where they had stood on the hillside that day, she had seen the red stains, the scarlet shadows of what had once been pets. It was a memory she wished she could lose.

"It would have only been a story to you. I thought you should see it."

"But why?"

He ignited the tobacco with his lighter and drew on the pipe. He seemed less certain now, and he faced her, perhaps looking for forgiveness or, if not that, then understanding. Fathers raise daughters differently than mothers. This father did. "You learned there are wolves in the world. It's never too early to learn that."

She held his gaze. "Maybe that's something you should learn too."

"Perhaps I have."

Did he know that the world was growing darker, that Europe was under threat, that England was poised to enter another cataclysm? Looking at him then, she felt he could not be so unknowing, so comfortable with the surface of things that he could not see what was coming. And how the *bloom* had changed everything. She wanted to think the best of him.

They sat on the fallen log, looking out at the water. She rested her hand on his.

As he drew on his pipe, her father said, "This is a good place in the spring."

"It is," she agreed.

The peace of the moment was disrupted as Shadow and Flint raced down the path toward them, carrying the mysterious scent of the forest in their coats.

ACKNOWLEDGMENTS

First, my thanks to my husband and first reader, Tom Overcast, for sharing with me his love of history and particularly the period of this novel. In addition, for his story suggestions, unwavering support and, well, for everything. To my agent, Ethan Ellenberg, my gratitude for his encouragement of this story from the beginning and for working so hard on my behalf. I owe a debt of gratitude to the writers and readers who beta-read, sometimes in pieces, sometimes in full, and who advised me, cheered me on and helped me remember, once again, how important a community of writers is. Thank you to Jamie Howell, Pat Rutledge, Dan Gemeinhart, Ben Seims, Theresa Monsey, Louise Marley and Sharon Shinn. Thank you to my close friends Veronica and Steve Rood for joining Tom and me on research treks to the book's English locales, from one-lane roads in Yorkshire and getting lost in Wiltshire, to Rievaulx Abbey at sunset and high tea at Trafalgar Square. A special thank-you to Navah Wolfe, my amazing editor. Her belief in this story and her guidance in the nuances of plot and character helped me to understand—and, I hope, execute— the story I was trying so hard to tell. To all the friends and acquaintances who almost invariably said, when I told them my story concept, "Wow, I'd love to read that one": thank you. Such comments buoy spirits and help writers remember that it's for individual readers that we dream the stories and try to tell them well. I hope I have earned your confidence.

In creating a story that ties in to historical events, I have altered some names, people and places. It is a work of fiction, but one in which I strove to weave in an accurate political and social milieu. Any mistakes are entirely my own.